SOMETHING
RICH
and
STRANGE

ALSO BY RON RASH

FICTION

POETRY

ecco

An Imprint of HarperCollins*Publishers*

SOMETHING
RICH
and
STRANGE

Selected Stories

RON RASH

For Marly Rusoff

CONTENTS

SOMETHING
RICH
and
STRANGE

HARD TIMES

Jacob stood in the barn mouth and watched Edna leave the henhouse. Her lips were pressed tight, which meant more eggs had been taken. He looked up at the ridgetop and guessed eight o'clock. In Boone it'd be full morning now, but here light was still splotchy and dew damped his brogans. This cove's so damn dark a man about has to break light with a crowbar, his daddy used to say.

Edna nodded at the egg pail in her hand.

"Nothing under the bantam," Edna said. "That's four days in a row."

"Maybe that old rooster ain't sweet on her no more," Jacob said. He waited for her to smile. When they'd first started sparking years ago, Edna's smile had been what most entranced him. Her whole face would glow, as if the upward turn of her lips spread a wave of light from mouth to forehead.

"Go ahead and make a joke," she said, "but little cash money as we got it makes a difference. Maybe the difference of whether you have a nickel to waste on a newspaper."

"There's many folks worse off," Jacob said. "Just look up the cove and you'll see the truth of that."

"We can end up like Hartley yet," Edna replied. She looked past Jacob to where the road ended and the skid trail left by the logging company began. "It's probably his mangy hound that's stealing our eggs. That dog's got the look of a egg-sucker. It's always skulking around here."

"You don't know that. I still think a dog would leave some egg on the straw. I've never seen one that didn't."

"What else would take just a few eggs at a time? You said your ownself a fox or weasel would have killed the chickens."

"I'll go look," Jacob said, knowing Edna would fret over the lost eggs all day. He knew if every hen laid three eggs a night for the next month, it wouldn't matter. She'd still perceive a debit that would never be made up. Jacob tried to be generous, remembered that Edna hadn't always been this way. Not until the bank had taken the truck and most of the livestock. They hadn't lost everything the way others had, but they'd lost enough. Edna always seemed fearful when she heard a vehicle coming up the dirt road, as if the banker and sheriff were coming to take the rest.

Edna carried the eggs to the springhouse as Jacob crossed the yard and entered the concrete henhouse. The smell of manure thickened the air. Though the rooster was already outside, the hens clucked dimly in their nesting boxes. Jacob lifted the bantam and set it on the floor. The nesting box's straw had no shell crumbs, no albumen or yellow yoke slobber.

He knew it could be a two-legged varmint, but hard as times were Jacob had never known anyone in Goshen Cove to steal, especially Hartley, the poorest of them all. Besides, who would take only two or three eggs when there were two dozen more to be had. The bantam's eggs at that, which were smaller than the ones under the Rhode Island Reds and leghorns. From the barn, Jacob heard the Guernsey lowing insistently. He knew she already waited beside the milk stool.

As Jacob came out of the henhouse he saw the Hartleys coming down the skid trail. They made the four-mile trek to Boone twice a week, each, even the child, burdened down with galax leaves. Jacob watched as they stepped onto the road, puffs of gray dust rising around their bare feet. Hartley carried four burlap pokes stuffed with galax. His wife carried two and the child one. With their ragged clothes hanging loose on bony frames, they looked like scarecrows en route to another cornfield, their possessions in tow. The hound trailed them, gaunt as the people it followed. The galax leaves were the closest thing to a crop Hartley could muster, for his land was all rock and slant. You couldn't grow a toenail on Hartley's land, Bascombe Lindsey had once said. That hadn't been a problem as long as the sawmill was running, but when it shut down the Hartleys had only one old swaybacked milk cow to sustain them, that and the galax, which earned a few nickels of barter at Mast's General Store. Jacob knew from the Sunday newspapers he bought that times were rough everywhere. Rich folks in New York had lost all their money and jumped out of buildings. Men rode boxcars town to town begging for work. But it was hard to believe any of them had less than Hartley and his family.

When Hartley saw Jacob he nodded but did not slow his pace. They were neither friends nor enemies, neighbors only in the sense that Jacob and Edna were the closest folks down the cove, though closest meant a half mile. Hartley had come from Swain County eight years ago to work at the sawmill. The child had been a baby then, the wife seemingly decades younger than the cronish woman who walked beside the daughter. They would have passed without further acknowledgment except Edna came out on the porch.

"That hound of yours," she said to Hartley, "is it a egg-sucker?" Maybe she wasn't trying to be accusatory, but the words sounded so.

Hartley stopped in the road and turned toward the porch.

Another man would have set the pokes down, but Hartley did not. He held them as if calculating their heft.

"What's the why of you asking that?" he said. The words were spoken in a tone that was neither angry nor defensive. It struck Jacob that even the man's voice had been worn down to a bare-boned flatness.

"Something's got in our henhouse and stole some," Edna said. "Just the eggs, so it ain't a fox nor weasel."

"So you reckon my dog."

Edna did not speak, and Hartley set the pokes down. He pulled a barlow knife from his tattered overalls. He softly called the hound and it sidled up to him. Hartley got down on one knee, closed his left hand on the scruff of the dog's neck as he settled the blade against its throat. The daughter and wife stood perfectly still, their faces blank as bread dough.

"I don't think it's your dog that's stealing the eggs," Jacob said.

"But you don't know for sure. It could be," Hartley said, the hound raising its head as Hartley's index finger rubbed the base of its skull.

Before Jacob could reply the blade whisked across the hound's windpipe. The dog didn't cry out or snarl. It merely sagged in Hartley's grip. Blood darkened the road.

"You'll know for sure now," Hartley said as he stood up. He lifted the dog by the scruff of the neck, walked over to the other side of the road and laid it in the weeds. "I'll get it on the way back this evening," he said, and picked up the pokes. Hartley began walking and his wife and daughter followed.

"Why'd you have to say something to him," Jacob said when the family had disappeared down the road. He stared at the place in the weeds where flies and yellow jackets began to gather.

"How'd I know he'd do such a thing," Edna said.

"You know how proud a man he is."

Jacob let those words linger. In January when two feet of snow had shut nearly everyone in, Jacob had gone up the skid trail on horseback, a salted pork shoulder strapped to the saddle. "We could be needing that meat soon enough ourselves," Edna had said, but he'd gone anyway. When Jacob got to the cabin he'd found the family at the plank table eating. The wooden bowls before them held a thick liquid lumped with a few crumbs of fatback. The milk pail hanging over the fire was filled with the same gray-colored gruel. Jacob had set the pork shoulder on the table. The meat had a deep wood-smoke odor, and the woman and child swallowed every few seconds to conceal their salivating. "I ain't got no money to buy it," Hartley said. "So I'd appreciate you taking your meat and leaving." Jacob had left, but after closing the cabin door he'd laid the pork on the front stoop. The next morning Jacob had found the meat on his own doorstep.

Jacob gazed past Hartley's dog, across the road to the acre of corn where he'd work till suppertime. He hadn't hoed a single row yet but already felt tired all the way to his bones.

"I didn't want that dog killed," Edna said. "That wasn't my intending."

"Like it wasn't your intending for Joel and Mary to leave and never darken our door again," Jacob replied. "But it happened, didn't it."

He turned and walked to the woodshed to get his hoe.

The next morning the dog was gone from the roadside and more eggs were missing. It was Saturday, so Jacob rode the horse down to Boone, not just to get his newspaper but to talk to the older farmers who gathered at Mast's General Store. As he rode he remembered the morning six years ago when Joel dropped his bowl of oatmeal on the floor. Careless, but twelve-year-olds did careless things. It was part of being a child. Edna made the boy eat the oatmeal off the floor with his spoon. "Don't do it," Mary had told her younger brother, but he had, whimpering the whole time. Mary, who was sixteen, eloped two weeks later. "I'll never come back, not even to visit," a note left on the kitchen table said. Mary had been true to her word.

As Jacob rode into Boone, he saw the truck the savings and loan had repossessed from him parked by the courthouse. It was a vehicle made for hauling crops to town, bringing back salt blocks and fertilizer and barbed wire, but he'd figured no farmer could have afforded to buy it at auction. Maybe a store owner or county employee, he supposed, someone who still used a billfold instead of a change purse, like the one he now took a nickel from after tying his horse to the hitching post. Jacob entered the store. He nodded at the older men, then laid his coin on the counter. Erwin Mast handed him last Sunday's *Raleigh News*.

"Don't reckon there's any letters?" Jacob asked.

"No, nothing this week," Erwin said, though he could have added, "or the last month or last year." Joel was in the navy, stationed somewhere in the Pacific. Mary lived with her husband and her own child on a farm in Haywood County, sixty miles away but it could have been California for all the contact Jacob and Edna had with her.

Jacob lingered by the counter. When the old men paused in their conversation, he told them about the eggs.

"And you're sure it ain't a dog?" Sterling Watts asked.

"Yes. There wasn't a bit of splatter or shell on the straw."

"Rats will eat a egg," Erwin offered from behind the counter.

"There'd still be something left, though," Bascombe Lindsey said.

"They's but one thing it can be," Sterling Watts said with finality.

"What's that," Jacob asked.

"A big yaller rat snake. They'll swallow two or three eggs whole and leave not a dribble of egg."

"I've heard such myself," Bascombe agreed. "Never seen it but heard of it."

"Well, one got in my henhouse," Sterling said. "And it took me near a month to figure out how to catch the damn thing."

"How did you?" Jacob asked.

"Went fishing," Sterling said.

That evening Jacob hoed in his cornfield till dark. He ate his supper, then went to the woodshed and found a fishhook. He tied three yards of line to it and went to the henhouse. The bantam had one egg under her. Jacob took the egg and made as small a hole as possible with the barb. He slowly worked the whole hook into the egg, then tied the line to a nail head behind the nesting box. Three yards, Watts had said. That way the snake would swallow the whole egg before a tight line set the hook.

"I ain't about to go out there come morning and deal with no snake," Edna said when he told her what he'd done. She sat in the ladderback rocking chair, her legs draped by a quilt. He'd made the chair for her to sit in when she'd been pregnant with Joel. The wood was cherry, not the most practical for furniture, but he'd wanted it to be pretty.

"I'll deal with it," Jacob said.

For a few moments he watched her sew, the fine blue thread repairing the binding of the Bear's Claw quilt. Edna had worked since dawn, but she couldn't stop even now. Jacob sat down at the kitchen table and spread out the newspaper. On the front page Roosevelt said things were getting better, but the rest of the news argued otherwise. Strikers had been shot at a cotton mill. Men whose crime was hiding in boxcars to search for work had been beaten with clubs by lawmen and hired railroad goons.

"What you claimed this morning about me running off Joel and Mary," Edna said, her needle not pausing as she spoke, "that was a spiteful thing to say. Those kids never went hungry a day in their lives. Their clothes was patched and they had shoes and coats."

He knew he should let it go, but the image of Hartley's knife opening the hound's throat had snared in his mind.

"You could have been easier on them."

"The world's a hard place," Edna replied. "There was need for them to know that."

"They'd have learned soon enough on their own," Jacob said.

"They needed to be prepared, and I prepared them. They ain't in a hobo camp or barefoot like Hartley and his clan. If they can't be grateful for that, there's nothing I can do about it now."

"There's going to be better times," Jacob said. "This depression can't last forever, but the way you treated them will."

"It's lasted nine years," Edna said. "And I see no sign of it letting up. The price we're getting for corn and cabbage is the same. We're still living on half of what we did before."

She turned back to the quilt's worn binding and no other words were spoken between them. After a while Edna put down her sewing and went to bed. Jacob soon followed. Edna tensed as he settled his body beside hers.

"I don't want us to argue," Jacob said, and laid his hand on her shoulder. She flinched from his touch, moved farther away.

"You think I've got no feelings," Edna said, her face turned so she spoke at the wall. "Stingy and mean-hearted. But maybe if I hadn't been we'd not have anything left."

Despite his weariness, Jacob had trouble going to sleep. When he finally did, he dreamed of men hanging onto boxcars while other men beat them with sticks. Those beaten wore muddy brogans and overalls, and he knew they weren't laid-off mill workers or coal miners but farmers like himself.

Jacob woke in the dark. The window was open and before he could fall back asleep he heard something from inside the henhouse. He pulled on his overalls and boots, then went out on the porch and lit a lantern. The sky was thick with stars and a wet moon lightened the ground, but the windowless henhouse was pitch dark. It had crossed his mind that if a yellow rat snake could eat an egg a copperhead or satinback could as well, and he wanted to see where he stepped. He went to the woodshed and got a hoe for the killing.

Jacob crossed the foot log and stepped up to the entrance. He held the lantern out and checked the nesting box. The bantam was in it, but no eggs lay under her. It took him a few moments to find the fishing line, leading toward the back corner like a single strand of a spider's web. He readied the hoe in his hand and took a step inside. He held the lamp before him and saw Hartley's daughter huddled in the corner, the line disappearing into her closed mouth.

She did not try to speak as he kneeled before her. Jacob set the hoe and lantern down and took out his pocketknife, cut the line inches above where it disappeared between her lips. For a few moments he did nothing else.

"Let me see," he said, and though she did not open her mouth she did not resist as his fingers did so. He found the hook's barb sunk deep in her cheek and was relieved. He'd feared it would be in her tongue or, much worse, deep in her throat.

"We got to get that hook out," Jacob told her, but still she said nothing. Her eyes did not widen in fear and he wondered if maybe she was in shock. The barb was too deep to wiggle free. He'd have to push it the rest of the way through.

"This is going to hurt, but just for a second," he said, and let his index finger and thumb grip the hook where it began to curve. He worked deeper into the skin, his thumb and finger slickened by blood and saliva. The child whimpered. Finally the barb broke through. He wiggled the shank out, the line coming last like thread completing a stitch.

"It's out now," he told her.

For a few moments Jacob did not get up. He thought about what to do next. He could carry her back to Hartley's shack and explain what happened, but he remembered the dog. He looked at her cheek and there was no tear, only a tiny hole that bled little more than a briar scratch would. He studied the hook for signs of rust. There didn't seem to be, so at least he didn't have to worry about the girl getting lockjaw. But it could still get infected.

"Stay here," Jacob said and went to the woodshed. He found the bottle of turpentine and returned. He took his handkerchief and soaked it, then opened the child's mouth and dabbed the wound, did the same outside to the cheek.

"Okay," Jacob said. He reached out his hands and placed them under her armpits. She was so light it was like lifting a rag doll. The child stood before him now, and for the first time he saw that her right hand held something. He picked up the lantern and saw it was an egg and that it was unbroken. Jacob nodded at the egg.

"You don't ever take them home, do you," he said. "You eat them here, right?"

The child nodded.

"Go ahead and eat it then," Jacob said, "but you can't come back anymore. If you do, your daddy will know about it. You understand?"

"Yes," she whispered, the first word she'd spoken.

"Eat it, then."

The girl raised the egg to her lips. A thin line of blood trickled down her chin as she opened her mouth. The shell crackled as her teeth bit down.

"Go home now," he said when she'd swallowed the last bit of shell. "And don't come back. I'm going to put another hook in them eggs and this time there won't be no line on it. You'll swallow that hook and it'll tear your guts up."

Jacob watched her walk up the skid trail until the dark enveloped her, then sat on the stump that served as a chopping block. He blew out the lantern and waited, though for what he could not say. After a while the moon and stars faded. In the east, darkness lightened to the color of indigo glass. The first outlines of the corn stalks and their leaves were visible now, reaching up from the ground like shabbily dressed arms.

Jacob picked up the lantern and turpentine and went back to the house. Edna was getting dressed as he came into the bedroom. Her back was to him.

"It was a snake," he said.

Edna paused in her dressing and turned. Her hair was down and her face not yet hardened to face the day's demands and he glimpsed the younger, softer woman she'd been twenty years ago when they'd married.

"You kill it?" she asked.

"Yes."

"I hope you didn't just throw it out by the henhouse. I don't want to smell that thing rotting when I'm gathering eggs."

"I threw it across the road."

He got in the bed. Edna's form and warmth lingered on the feather mattress.

"I'll get up in a few minutes," he told her.

Jacob closed his eyes but did not sleep. Instead, he imagined towns where hungry men hung on boxcars looking for work that couldn't be found, shacks where families lived who didn't even have one swaybacked milk cow. He imagined cities where blood stained the sidewalks beneath buildings tall as ridges. He tried to imagine a place worse than where he was.

THREE A.M.
and the
STARS WERE OUT

Carson had gone to bed early, so when the cell phone rang he thought it might be his son or daughter calling to check on him, but as he turned to the night table the clock's green glow read 2:18, too late for a chat, or any kind of good news. He lifted the phone and heard Darnell Coe's voice. I got trouble with a calf that ain't of a mind to get born, Darnell told him.

Carson sat up on the mattress, settled his bare feet on the floor. Moments passed before he realized he was waiting for another body to do the same thing, leave the bed and fix him a thermos of coffee. Almost four months and it still happened, not just when he awoke but other times too. He'd read something and lower the newspaper, about to speak to an empty chair, or at the grocery store, reach into a shirt pocket for a neatly printed list that wasn't there.

He dressed and went out to the truck. All that would be needed lay in the pickup's lockbox or, just as likely, on Darnell's gun rack. At the edge of town, he stopped at Dobbins' Handy-Mart, the only store open. Music harsh as the fluorescent lights came from a counter radio. Carson filled the largest Styrofoam cup with coffee and

paid Lloyd Dobbin's grandson. The road to Flag Pond was twenty
miles of switchbacks and curves that ended just short of the Tennessee line. A voice on the radio said no rain until midday, so at
least he'd not be contending with a slick road.

Carson had closed his office two years ago, referred his clients to
Bobby Starnes, a new doc just out of vet school. Bobby had grown
up in Madison County, and that helped a lot, but the older farmers,
some Carson had known since childhood, kept calling him. Because
they know you won't expect them to pay up front, or at all, Doris
had claimed, which was true in some cases, but for others, like Darnell Coe, it wasn't. We've been hitched to the same wagon this long,
we'll pull it the rest of the way together, Darnell had said, reminding Carson that in the 1950s and half a world away they'd made a
vow to do so.

As the town's last streetlight slid off the rearview mirror, Carson
turned the radio off. It was something he often did on late-night
calls, making driving the good part, because what usually awaited
him in a barn or pasture would not be good, a cow dying of milk
fever or a horse with a gangrenous leg—things easily cured if a man
hadn't wagered a vet fee against a roll of barbed wire or a salt lick.
There had been times when Carson had told men to their faces they
were stupid to wait so long. But even a smart farmer did stupid
things when he'd been poor too long. He'd figure after a drought
had withered his cornstalks, or maybe a hailstorm had beaten the
life out of his tobacco allotment, that he was owed a bit of good
luck, so he'd skimp on a calcium shot or pour turpentine on an
infected limb. Waiting it out until he'd waited too late, then calling
Carson when a rifle was the only remedy.

So driving had to be the good part, and it was. Carson had always
been comfortable with solitude. As a boy, he'd loved to roam the
woods, loved how quiet the woods could be. If deep enough in them,

he wouldn't even hear the wind. But the best was afternoons in the barn. He'd climb up in the loft and lean back against a hay bale, then watch the sunlight begin to lean through the loft window, brightening the spilled straw. When the light was at its apex, the loft shimmered as though coated with a golden foil. Dust motes speckled the air like midges. The only sound would be underneath, a calf restless in a stall, a horse eating from a feed bag. Carson had always felt an aloneness in those moments, but never in a sad way.

Through the years, the same feeling had come back to him on late nights as he drove out of town. Doris would be back in bed and the children asleep as he left the house. Night would gather around him, the only light his truck's twin beams probing the road ahead. He would pass darkened farmhouses and barns as he made his way toward the glow of lamp or porch light. On the way back was the better time, though. He'd savor the solitude, knowing that later when he opened the children's doors, he could watch them a few moments as they slept, then lie down himself as Doris turned or shifted so that some part of their bodies touched.

The road forked and Carson went right, passing a long-abandoned gas station. The cell phone lay on the passenger seat. Sometimes a farmer called and told Carson he might as well turn around, but this far from town the phone didn't work. The road snaked upward, nothing on the sides now but drop-offs and trees, an occasional white cross and a vase of wilted flowers. Teenage boys for the most part, Carson knew, too young to think it could happen to them. It was that way in war as well, until you watched enough boys your own age being zipped up in body bags.

Carson had been drafted by the army three months after Darnell joined the marines. They had not seen each other until the Seventh Infantry supported the First Marine at Chosin Reservoir, crossing paths in a Red Cross soup line. It was late afternoon and the temperature already below zero. The Chinese, some men claimed a million of them, were pouring in over the Korean border, and no amount of casualties looked to stop them. Let's make a vow to God and them Chinese too that if they let us get back to North Carolina alive we'll stay put and grow old together, Darnell had said. He'd held out his hand and Carson had taken it.

The road curved a final time, and the battered mailbox labeled COE appeared. Carson turned off the blacktop and bumped up the drive, wheels crunching over the chert rock. The porch light was on, from the barn mouth a lantern's lesser glow. Carson parked next to the unlatched pasture gate, got the medicine bag and canvas tool kit from the truck box. He shouldered the gate open and pushed it back. This far from town the stars were brighter, the sky wider, deeper. As on other such nights, Carson paused to take it in. A small consolation.

The lantern hung just inside the barn mouth, offering a thin apron of light to help Carson make his way. He took slow careful steps so as not to trip on old milking traces. Inside, it took a few moments to adjust to the barn's starless dark. Near the back stall, the cow lay on the straw floor. Darnell knelt beside her, one hand stroking her flank. A stainless-steel bucket was close by, already filled with water, beside it rags and a frayed bedsheet. Darnell's shotgun, not his rifle, leaned across a stall door.

"How long?" Carson asked.

"Three hours."

Carson set the bags down and checked the cow's gums, then placed the stethoscope's silver bell against the flank before pulling on a shoulder glove.

"I think it's breeched," Darnell said.

Carson lubed the glove and slid his hand and forearm inside, felt a bent leg, then a shoulder, another leg, and, finally, the head. He slipped a finger inside the mouth and felt a suckle. Life stubbornly held on. Maybe he wouldn't have to pull the calf out one piece at a time. At least a chance.

"Not a full breech then," Darnell said when Carson pulled off the glove.

"Afraid it isn't."

Carson spread the tarp on the barn floor, set out what he'd need while Darnell retrieved the lantern and set it beside Carson. Inside the lantern's low light, the world shrank to a circle of straw, within it two old men, a cow, and, though curtained, a calf. Carson did a quick swab and pushed in the needle, waited for the lidocaine to ease the contractions. Darnell still stroked the cow's flank. As a young vet, Carson had quickly learned there were some men and women, good people otherwise, who'd let a lame calf linger days, not bothering to end its misery. They'd do the same with a sheep with blackleg. Never Darnell though. Because he'd witnessed enough suffering in Korea not to wish it on man or animal was what some folks would think, but Carson knew it to be as much Darnell's innate decency.

"Why the shotgun?" Carson asked.

"Coyotes. I've not heard any of late, but this is the sort of thing to draw them." Darnell nodded at the calf jack. "Figure you'll have to use it?"

"I'm going to try not to."

The cow's abdomen relaxed and the round eyes calmed. Somewhere in the loft a swallow stirred. Then the barn was silent and the lantern's light seemed to soften. The calf waited in its deeper darkness for Carson to birth it whole and alive or dead and in pieces. Carson's hands suddenly felt heavy, shackled. He looked down at them, the liver spots and stark blue veins, knuckles puffy with arthritis. He remembered another misaligned calf, not nearly as bad as this one.

He was just months into his practice and had torn the cow's uterine wall, killing both cow and calf. Doris had been pregnant with their first child, and when she'd asked Carson if the calf and cow were okay, Carson had lied.

Darnell touched his shoulder.

"You all right?"

"Yeah."

Carson lubed his hand, no glove now, and slid it inside, pushed the calf as far back as he could, making space. Sweat trickled down his forehead, his eyes closed now to better imagine the calf's body. He found the snout, tugged it forward a bit, then back, and then to one side, and then another. Carson's heart banged his panting chest like a quickening hammer. The muscles in his neck and shoulder burned. He stopped for a minute, his arm still inside as he caught his breath.

"What do you think?" Darnell asked.

"Maybe," Carson answered.

Half an hour passed before he got the head aligned. Darnell gave him a wet hand cloth and Carson wiped the sweat off his face and neck. He rested a while longer before nodding at the tarp.

"Okay, let's get that leg."

Darnell hooked the OB chain to the handle and gave the other end to Carson, who looped the chain around a front leg. Darnell gripped the handle, and dug his boot heels into the barn floor.

"Okay," Carson said, his hand on the calf's leg.

The chain slowly tightened. Carson bent the foreleg to ensure the hoof didn't rake the uterine wall. Darnell did the hard work now, grunting as his muscles strained. They spoke little, Carson nodding left or right when needed. Minutes passed as the leg gave and caught. Like cracking a safe, that's how Carson thought of it, finding the combination that made the last tumbler fall into place. It felt like that, the womb swinging open and the calf withdrawn. There were times he could almost hear the click.

"Home free," Darnell gasped when the leg finally aligned.

Come morning, liniment would grease their lower backs and shoulders. They would move gingerly, new twinges and aches added to others gained over eight decades.

"Lord help us if our kids knew what we were up to tonight," Darnell said as he rubbed a shoulder. "They'd likely fix you and me up with those electronic ankle bracelets, keep us under house arrest."

"Which would show they've got more sense than we have," Carson replied.

The second leg took less than a minute and the calf slipped into a wider world. Carson cleared mucus from the snout, placed a finger inside the mouth and felt a tug.

"Much as we've done this, you'd think it might get a tad bit easier," Darnell said, "but that's not the way of it."

"No," Carson said. "Most things just get harder."

The last thing was calcium and antibiotic shots, but Carson doubted his hand capable of holding the needle steady. It could wait a few minutes. The men sat on the barn floor, weary arms crossed on raised knees as they waited for the calf to gain its legs. Carson leaned his head on his forearms and closed his eyes. He listened as the calf's hooves scattered straw, the body lifting and falling back until it figured out the physics. Once it did, Carson raised his head and watched the calf's knees wobble but hold. The cow was soon up too. The calf nuzzled and found a teat, began to suckle.

"There's a wonder to it yet," Darnell said, and Carson didn't disagree.

They watched a few more moments, not speaking. The lantern's wick burned low now. Carson resettled his hands, let his fingertips shift straw and touch the firmer earth as he leaned back. Only when the flame was a sinking flicker inside the glass did Darnell raise himself to one knee.

"Now let's see if we can get up too," he said.

Darnell grunted and stood, knees popping as he did so. He reached a hand under Carson's upper arm and helped him up, Carson's hinges grinding as well. Darnell lifted the lantern, turned the brass screw until light filled the globe again. He set the lantern down and walked over to the barn mouth, only his silhouette visible until a match rasped and illuminated his face a moment.

"So you're smoking again," Carson said.

"Nobody around to argue against it," Darnell answered.

"Funny how you miss even the nagging."

"That's true," Carson said, and stepped over to the barn mouth and leaned against the opposite beam.

The stars sprawled yet overhead, though now Venus had tucked itself in among them. Though no more than a dozen feet apart, the men were mere shadows to each other. Carson watched the orange cigarette tip rise and hold a moment, then descend. A shifting came from the barn's depths, then a lapping sound as the cow's tongue washed the calf.

"Doris was a fine woman," Darnell said.

"Yes," Carson said, "she was."

"Four months now, ain't it?"

"Almost."

"It does ease up some, eventually," Darnell said.

He stubbed out his cigarette. Something between a sigh and a snicker crossed the dark between them.

"What's tickling your funny bone?" Carson asked.

"Just curious if the widows are showing up with their casseroles yet."

"No," Carson said. "I mean none since the funeral."

"Well, it won't be long and once it commences you'll think you're in the Pillsbury Bake-Off."

"I'm not looking for another wife," Carson said.

"I wasn't either but they came after me anyway. We're a rare commodity, partner. The one time I went down to that senior center, it was me and Ansel Turner and thirty blue-haired women. One of them decided we should have a dance. Soon as the music came on I got out of there and ain't been back, but poor old Ansel was in his wheelchair so couldn't get away. He was remarried in six months. They finally gave up on me but you're fresh game."

Darnell paused.

"I ain't making light of your loss."

"I know that," Carson said. "I've had plenty enough grieving words and hangdog faces. The sad part I don't need any help with."

He was rested enough now to give the shots, but waited. Except for speaking to his son and daughter on the phone, Carson hadn't much wanted to talk with people of late. But tonight, here in the dark with Darnell, there was a pleasure in it.

"The stars don't show out in town like they do here," Carson said.

"I'm not down there often of a night to know," Darnell answered, "but it's nice to look up and see something that never changes. When I was in Korea, I'd find the Big Dipper and the Huntress and the Archer. They hung in the sky different but I could make them out, same as if I was in North Carolina. There was a comfort in doing that, especially when the fighting got thick."

"I did that a couple of times too," Carson said.

Darnell lit another cigarette and stepped outside of the barn, listening until he was satisfied.

"They ain't yapping about it," Darnell said, "but they could still be out there."

Carson half stifled a yawn.

"I can put us on a pot of coffee."

"No," Carson answered. "I'll be on my way as soon as I give the shots."

"Back in Korea, we'd not have figured it to turn out this way, would we?" Darnell said. "I mean, we've gotten a lot more than we ever thought."

"Yes," Carson replied. "We have."

Carson went back inside, gave the shots, and packed up. Darnell lifted the lantern in one hand and the medicine bag in the other, led them back down to the pickup. Darnell opened his billfold and offered five ten-dollar bills that, as always, Carson refused. They shook hands and he got in the truck. As Carson bumped down the drive, he looked back and saw the lantern's glow moving toward the barn. Darnell would hang the lantern back on its nail, maybe smoke another cigarette as he stood at the barn mouth, attentive as any good sentry.

The ASCENT

Jared had never been this far before, over Sawmill Ridge and across a creek glazed with ice, then past the triangular metal sign that said SMOKY MOUNTAINS NATIONAL PARK. If it had still been snowing and his tracks were being covered up, he'd have turned back. People had gotten lost in this park. Children wandered off from family picnics, hikers strayed off trails. Sometimes it took days to find them. But today the sun was out, the sky deep and blue. No more snow would fall, so it would be easy to retrace his tracks. Jared heard a helicopter hovering somewhere to the west, which meant they still hadn't found the airplane. They'd been searching all the way from Bryson City to the Tennessee line, or so he'd heard at school.

The land slanted downward and the sound of the helicopter disappeared. In the steepest places, Jared leaned sideways and held on to trees to keep from slipping. As he made his way into the denser woods, he wasn't thinking of the lost airplane or if he would get the mountain bike he'd asked for as his Christmas present. Not thinking about his parents either, though they were the main reason he was spending his first day of Christmas vacation out here—better to be outside on a cold day than in the house where everything, the rickety chairs and sagging couch, the gaps where the TV and microwave had been, felt sad.

He thought instead of Lyndee Starnes, the girl who sat in front of him in fifth grade homeroom. Jared made believe that she was walking beside him and he was showing her the tracks in the snow, telling her which markings were squirrel and which rabbit and which deer. Imagining a bear track too, and telling Lyndee that he wasn't afraid of bears and Lyndee telling him she was so he'd have to protect her.

Jared stopped walking. He hadn't seen any human tracks, but he looked behind him to be sure no one was around. He took out the pocketknife and raised it, making believe that the pocketknife was a hunting knife and that Lyndee was beside him. If a bear comes, I'll take care of you, he said out loud. Jared imagined Lyndee reaching out and taking his free arm. He kept the knife out as he walked up another ridge, one whose name he didn't know. He imagined Lyndee still grasping his arm, and as they walked up the ridge Lyndee saying how sorry she was that at school she'd told him he and his clothes smelled bad.

At the ridgetop, Jared pretended a bear suddenly raised up, baring its teeth and growling. He slashed at the bear with the knife and the bear ran away. Jared held the knife before him as he descended the ridge. Sometimes they'll come back, he said aloud.

He was halfway down the ridge when the knife blade caught the midday sun and the steel flashed. Another flash came from below, as if it was answering. At first Jared saw only a glimmer of metal in the dull green of rhododendron, but as he came nearer he saw more, a crumpled silver propeller and white tailfin and part of a shattered wing.

For a few moments Jared thought about turning around, but then told himself that an eleven-year-old who'd just fought a bear shouldn't be afraid to get close to a crashed airplane. He made his way down the ridge, snapping rhododendron branches to clear a path. When he finally made it to the plane, he couldn't see much because snow and ice covered the windows. He turned the passenger side's outside handle, but the door didn't budge until Jared wedged in the pocketknife's blade. The door made a sucking sound as it opened.

A woman was in the passenger seat, her body bent forward like a horseshoe. Long brown hair fell over her face. The hair had frozen and looked as if it would snap off like icicles. She wore blue jeans and a yellow sweater. Her left arm was flung out before her and on one finger was a ring. The man across from her leaned toward the pilot window, his head cocked against the glass. Blood stains reddened the window and his face was not covered like the woman's. There was a seat in the back, empty. Jared placed the knife in his pocket and climbed into the backseat and closed the passenger door. Because it's so cold, that's why they don't smell much, he thought.

For a while he sat and listened to how quiet and still the world was. He couldn't hear the helicopter or even the chatter of a gray squirrel or caw of a crow. Here between the ridges not even the sound of the wind. Jared tried not to move or breathe hard to make it even quieter, quiet as the man and woman up front. The plane was snug and cozy. After a while he heard something, just the slightest sound, coming from the man's side. Jared listened harder, then knew what it was. He leaned forward between the front seats. The man's right forearm rested against a knee. Jared pulled back the man's shirt sleeve and saw the watch. He checked the time, almost four o'clock. He'd been sitting in the backseat two hours, though it seemed only a few minutes. The light that would let him follow the tracks back home would be gone soon.

As he got out of the backseat, Jared saw the woman's ring. Even in the cabin's muted light it shone. He took the ring off the woman's finger and placed it in his jean pocket. He closed the passenger door and followed his boot prints back the way he came. Jared tried to step into his earlier tracks, pretending that he needed to confuse a wolf following him.

It took longer than he'd thought, the sun almost down when he crossed the park boundary. As he came down the last ridge, Jared saw that the pickup was parked in the yard, the lights on in the front room. He remembered it was Saturday and his father had gotten his paycheck. When Jared opened the door, the small red glass pipe was on the coffee table, an empty baggie beside it. His father kneeled before the fireplace, meticulously arranging and rearranging kindling around an oak log. A dozen crushed beer cans lay amid the kindling, balanced on the log itself three red-and-white fishing bobbers. His mother sat on the couch, her eyes glazed as she told Jared's father how to arrange the cans. In her lap lay a roll of tinfoil she was cutting into foot-long strips.

"Look what we're making," she said, smiling at Jared. "It's going to be our Christmas tree."

When he didn't speak, his mother's smile quivered.

"Don't you like it, honey?"

His mother got up, strips of tinfoil in her left hand. She kneeled beside the hearth and carefully draped them on the oak log and kindling.

Jared walked into the kitchen and took the milk from the refrigerator. He washed a bowl and spoon left in the sink and poured some cereal. After he ate Jared went into his bedroom and closed the door. He sat on his bed and took the ring from his pocket and set it in his palm. He placed the ring under the lamp's bulb and swayed his hand slowly back and forth so the stone's different colors flashed and merged. He'd give it to Lyndee when they were on the playground, on the first sunny day after Christmas vacation so she could see how pretty the ring's colors were. Once he gave it to her, Lyndee would finally like him, and it would be for real.

Jared didn't hear his father until the door swung open.

"Your mother wants you to help light the tree."

The ring fell onto the wooden floor. Jared picked it up and closed his hand.

"What's that?" his father asked.

"Nothing," Jared said. "Just something I found in the woods."

"Let me see."

Jared opened his hand. His father stepped closer and took the ring. He pressed the ring with his thumb and finger.

"That's surely a fake diamond, but the ring looks to be real gold."

His father tapped it against the bedpost as if the sound could confirm its authenticity. His father called his mother and she came into the room.

"Look what Jared found," he said, and handed her the ring. "It's gold."

His mother set the ring in her palm, held it out before her so they all three could see it.

"Where'd you find it, honey?"

"In the woods," Jared said.

"I didn't know you could find rings in the woods," his mother said dreamily. "But isn't it wonderful that you can."

"That diamond can't be real, can it?" his father asked.

His mother stepped close to the lamp. She cupped her hand and slowly rocked it back and forth, watching the different colors flash inside the stone.

"It might be," his mother said.

"Can I have it back?" Jared asked.

"Not until we find out if it's real, son," his father said.

His father took the ring from his mother's palm and placed it in his pants pocket. Then he went into the other bedroom and got his coat.

"I'm going down to Bryson City and find out if it's real or not."

"But you're not going to sell it," Jared said.

"I'm just going to have a jeweler look at it," his father said, already putting on his coat. "We need to know what it's worth, don't we? We might have to insure it. You and your momma go ahead and light our Christmas tree. I'll be back in just a few minutes."

"It's not a Christmas tree," Jared said.

"Sure it is, son," his father replied. "It's just one that's chopped up, is all."

He wanted to stay awake until his father returned, so Jared helped his mother spread the last strips of tinfoil on the wood. His mother struck a match and told him it was time to light the tree. The kindling caught and the foil and cans withered and blackened, the fishing bobbers melting. His mother kept adding kindling to the fire, telling Jared if he watched closely he'd see angel wings folding and unfolding inside the flames. Angels come down the chimney sometimes, just like Santa Claus, she told him. Midnight came and his father still wasn't back. Jared went to his room. I'll lay down just for a few minutes, he told himself, but when he opened his eyes it was light outside.

He smelled the methamphetamine as soon as he opened his bedroom door, thicker than he could ever remember. His parents had not gone to bed. He could tell that as soon as he came into the front room. The fire was still going, kindling piled around the hearth. His mother sat where she'd been last night, wearing the same clothes. She was tearing pages out of a magazine one at a time, using scissors to make ragged stars she stuck on the walls with Scotch tape. His father sat beside her, watching intently.

The glass pipe lay on the coffee table, beside it four baggies, two with powder still in them. There'd never been more than one before.

His father grinned at him.

"I got you some of that cereal you like," he said, and pointed to a box with a green leprechaun on its front.

"Where's the ring?" Jared asked.

"The sheriff took it," his father said. "When I showed it to the jeweler, he said the sheriff had been in there just yesterday. A woman had reported it missing. I knew you'd be disappointed, that's why I bought you that cereal. Got something else for you too."

His father nodded toward the front door where a mountain bike was propped against the wall. Jared walked over to it. He could tell it wasn't new, some of the blue paint chipped away, one of the rubber handle grips missing, but the tires didn't sag and the handlebars were straight.

"It didn't seem right for you to have to wait till Christmas to have it," his father said. "Too bad there's snow on the ground, but it'll soon enough melt and you'll be able to ride it."

Jared's mother looked up.

"Wasn't that nice of your daddy," she said, her eyes bright and gleaming. "Go ahead and eat your cereal, son. A growing boy needs his breakfast."

"What about you and Daddy?" Jared asked.

"We'll eat later."

Jared ate as his parents sat in the front room, passing the pipe back and forth. He looked out the window and saw the sky held nothing but blue, not even a few white clouds. He thought about going back to the plane, but as soon as he laid his bowl in the sink his father announced that the three of them were going to go find a real Christmas tree.

"The best Christmas tree ever," his mother told Jared.

They put on their coats and walked up the ridge, his father carrying a rusty saw. Near the ridgetop, they found Fraser firs and white pines.

"Which one do you like best, son?" his father asked.

Jared looked over the trees, then picked a Fraser fir no taller than himself.

"You don't want a bigger one?" his father asked.

When Jared nodded no, his father kneeled before the tree. The saw's teeth were dull but his father finally broke the bark and worked the saw through. They dragged the tree down the ridge and propped it in the corner by the fireplace. His parents smoked the pipe again and then his father went out to the shed and got a hammer and nails and two boards. While his father built the makeshift tree stand, Jared's mother cut more stars from the newspaper.

"I think I'll go outside a while," Jared said.

"But you can't," his mother replied. "You've got to help me tape the stars to the tree."

By the time they'd finished, the sun was falling behind Sawmill Ridge. I'll go tomorrow, he told himself.

On Sunday morning the baggies were empty and his parents were sick. His mother sat on the couch wrapped in a quilt, shivering. She hadn't bathed since Friday and her hair was stringy and greasy. His father looked little better, his blue eyes receding deep into his skull, his lips chapped and bleeding.

"Your momma, she's sick," his father said, "and your old daddy ain't doing too well himself."

"The doctor can't help her, can he?" Jared asked.

"No," his father said. "I don't think he can."

Jared watched his mother all morning. She'd never been this bad before. After a while she lit the pipe and sucked deeply for what residue might remain. His father crossed his arms, rubbing his biceps as he looked around the room, as if expecting to see something he'd not seen moments earlier. The fire had gone out, the cold causing his mother to shake more violently.

"You got to go see Wesley," she told Jared's father.

"We got no money left," he answered.

Jared watched them, waiting for the sweep of his father's eyes to stop beside the front door where the mountain bike was. But his father's eyes went past it without the slightest pause. The kerosene heater in the kitchen was on, but its heat hardly radiated into the front room.

His mother looked up at Jared.

"Can you fix us a fire, honey?"

He went out to the back porch and gathered an armload of kindling, then placed a thick oak log on the andirons as well. Beneath it he wedged newspaper left over from the star cutting. He lit the newspaper and watched the fire slowly take hold, then watched the flames a while longer before turning to his parents.

"You can take the bike down to Bryson City and sell it," he said.

"No, son," his mother answered. "That's your Christmas present."

"We'll be all right," his father said. "Your momma and me just did too much partying yesterday is all."

But as the morning passed, they got no better. At noon Jared went to his room and got his coat.

"Where you going, honey?" his mother asked as he walked toward the door.

"To get more firewood."

Jared walked into the shed but did not gather wood. Instead, he took a length of dusty rope off the shed's back wall and wrapped it around his waist and then knotted it. He left the shed and followed his own tracks west into the park. The snow had become harder, and it crunched beneath his boots. The sky was gray, darker clouds farther west. More snow would soon come, maybe by afternoon. Jared made believe he was on a rescue mission. He was in Alaska, the rope tied around him dragging a sled filled with food and medicine. The footprints weren't his but those of the people he'd been sent to find.

When he got to the airplane, Jared pretended to unpack the supplies and give the man and woman something to eat and drink. He told them they were too hurt to walk back with him and he'd have to go and get more help. Jared took the watch off the man's wrist. He set it in his palm, face upward. I've got to take your compass, he told the man. A blizzard's coming, and I may need it.

Jared slipped the watch into his pocket. He got out of the plane and walked back up the ridge. The clouds were hard and granite-looking now, and the first flurries were falling. Jared pulled out the watch every few minutes, pointed the hour hand east as he followed his tracks back to the house.

The truck was still out front, and through the window Jared saw the mountain bike. He could see his parents as well, huddled together on the couch. For a few moments Jared simply stared through the window at them.

When he went inside, the fire was out and the room was cold enough to see his breath. His mother looked up anxiously from the couch.

"You shouldn't go off that long without telling us where you're going, honey."

Jared lifted the watch from his pocket.

"Here," he said, and gave it to his father.

His father studied it a few moments, then broke into a wide grin.

"This watch is a Rolex," his father said.

"Thank you, Jared," his mother said, looking as if she might cry. "You're the best son anybody could have, ain't he, Daddy?"

"The very best," his father said.

"How much can we get for it?" his mother asked.

"I bet a couple of hundred at least," his father answered.

His father clamped the watch onto his wrist and got up. Jared's mother rose as well.

"I'm going with you. I need something quick as I can get it." She turned to Jared. "You stay here, honey. We'll be back in just a little while. We'll bring you back a hamburger and a Co-Cola, some more of that cereal too."

Jared watched as they drove down the road. When the truck had vanished, he sat down on the couch and rested a few minutes. He hadn't taken his coat off. He checked to make sure the fire was out and then went to his room and emptied his backpack of schoolbooks. He went out to the shed and picked up a wrench and a hammer and placed them in the backpack. The flurries were thicker now, already beginning to fill in his tracks. He crossed over Sawmill Ridge, the tools clanking in his backpack. More weight to carry, he thought, but at least he wouldn't have to carry them back.

When he got to the plane, he didn't open the door, not at first. Instead, he took the tools from the backpack and laid them before him. He studied the plane's crushed nose and propeller, the broken right wing. The wrench was best to tighten the propeller, he decided. He'd straighten out the wing with the hammer.

As he switched tools and moved around the plane, the snow fell harder. Jared looked behind him and on up the ridge and saw his footprints were growing fainter. He chipped the snow and ice off the windshields with the hammer's claw. Finished, he said, and dropped the hammer on the ground. He opened the passenger door and got in.

"I fixed it so it'll fly now," he told the man.

He sat in the backseat and waited. The work and walk had

warmed him but he quickly grew cold. He watched the snow cover the plane's front window with a darkening whiteness. After a while he began to shiver but after a longer while he was no longer cold. Jared looked out the side window and saw the whiteness was not only in front of him but below. He knew then that they had taken off and risen so high that they were enveloped inside a cloud, but still he looked down, waiting for the clouds to clear so he might look for the pickup as it followed the winding road toward Bryson City.

NIGHT HAWKS

As she sat in the radio station's office, Ginny knew she could not have picked a better place to begin again. From midnight to six a.m., her main duty would be to slide disks into the beige CD player. Every fifteen minutes she would acknowledge requests, name artists and songs, and say pretty much anything to prove the music was not prerecorded.

"Research says almost ninety percent of people who listen from twelve to six are alone. It comforts them to know they're not the only person awake. Of course, that's what makes this job tough," Barry, the station manager, warned her at the interview. "The person you would replace claimed being alone here all night made him feel like the sole survivor of a nuclear holocaust. He was the third person I've hired in the last eighteen months. The solitude was harder on them than working nights." During most of the interview, Barry had looked slightly above and to the left of Ginny, but now his eyes met hers.

"Coming from a school, you're used to a classroom full of kids."

"I've had plenty of experience with solitude," Ginny said, turning her face so he could see the scar more clearly.

As she drove home from the interview, Ginny passed the middle school where she'd taught. She slowed and saw Andrew's jeep in the parking lot, its back filled with poster boards and paints and brushes. Andrew was the county's middle-school art teacher and, for a time, Ginny's boyfriend. During her hospital stay, she'd thought things might have turned out different if Andrew had been at her school the afternoon of the accident. But she no longer believed that. She checked the dashboard clock, then looked up at the second-floor classroom that had been hers. The sixth graders would be back from lunch now, seated in their desks. They would be sleepy, harder to motivate, the adrenaline rush of morning recess long gone. This had been the slowest part of her school day.

Ginny had been more conscientious than most of her colleagues. While others merely glanced at assignments, she wrote detailed notes in the margins, adorned the pages with bright-colored stars and smiley faces. Every week she e-mailed parents about each child's progress. Once a month, she spent a Saturday morning creating a new motif for the bulletin board. She'd had her failings as well. Dr. Jenkins, the principal, had noted on evaluations that some of her fellow teachers found her "aloof." Discipline had also been a problem. Two students whispering or a squabble at recess—each time Ginny felt her whole body tighten. Ginny usually could quell the misbehavior, but several times Dr. Jenkins had to come to restore order. But what had troubled Ginny the most, however, was the emotional distance between her and the students. She could not meet their obvious needs, even the boy with the purple birthmark splashed across his neck. She seemed unable to find the soothing words, know when to give the reassuring hug. Often she felt like an inmate pressing palm to glass and yet feeling no warmth from a hand less than an inch away.

No such distance had existed for Andrew on the Monday mornings she'd brought her class to the art room. His connection was evident as he moved from table to table, easel to easel, sometimes making suggestions but always finding something to praise. It was natural, instinctive. When he'd shown the class reproductions of famous paintings, his comments made each work seem created solely for the students.

Barry called the next morning and told her she had the job.

"When do I start?" she asked.

"I'm doing that shift myself now, so the sooner the better as far as I'm concerned. You can even start tonight if you want."

"What time should I be there?"

"Eleven. That'll give us an hour to go over what few bells and whistles we have, plus a chance for you to look over the CD library, get familiar with our board."

"Anything I need to do to prepare?"

"The best preparation is a lot of caffeine. Also, you'll need a moniker. There are kooks out there listening, especially late at night. Most are harmless, but not all. The less personal info you give the better."

"Anything else?" Ginny asked.

"The door will be locked when you get here. Knock loud so I can hear you."

Ginny found a notepad and pen. She'd written ten possible names before remembering the Edward Hopper painting Andrew had shown her students. On her way to the radio station that night, Ginny slowed again as she passed the middle school. When she saw there was no fund-raiser or PTA meeting, she parked the car and stepped onto the school grounds for the first time since the accident. The moon was almost full, and its pale light revealed the clearance where the oak tree had been. She zipped her jacket but still shivered as she stood below the north wing, the oldest part of the building.

That day she'd heard the storm approach, thunder coming closer like artillery finding the range. The windows were at the back of the classroom, so she saw the oak limbs begin to sway. One night a week earlier a limb had broken a pane.

The branches would be cut back soon, but until then Ginny was supposed to close the thick, plastic-backed drapes whenever a storm approached. But she had waited. David, her weakest student, was beside her desk, giving a report on Bolivia. Sheets of notebook paper quivered in his hands as he read with excruciating slowness. A student snickered when he read the same sentence twice. Other students, bored, quit paying attention. A balled-up piece of paper sailed across an aisle.

Stopping to close the drapes would only prolong the torment that was mercifully near its conclusion. But her concern was not just for David. If she stopped him now and went to the back of the room, she might lose complete control of the class. Spits of rain had begun to hit the glass. One of the oak tree's branches tapped a pane, demanding her attention. As David lost his place again, a student yawned loudly. The oak branch tapped the glass, more insistent this time.

"I'm sorry, David," Ginny said, standing up from her desk. "I must stop you so I can close the drapes."

Amy Campbell, who sat on the row closest to the windows, stood as well.

"I'll close them, Miss Atwell," she said, and turned to the window.

"No, that's my job," Ginny said, just as a branch shattered the glass.

Amy had not fallen, had not even moved as glass shards flew around and into her. She had not made a sound. It was as if Amy had been asleep and it took the other children's screams to wake her. She had turned slowly toward Ginny. A glass shard was imbedded an inch below her right eye like a spear point.

Amy had reached up and pulled the shard from her face. For a moment there was no blood. As Ginny came toward her, Amy held the glass shard out as she might gum or some other middle-school contraband. Ginny took the piece of glass and with her free hand pressed a handkerchief against the wound.

The teacher next door ran into the room, soon followed by Dr. Jenkins, who took one look at the saturated handkerchief and told the other teacher to call 911. He and Ginny laid Amy on the floor. The child's eyes remained open but unfocused.

"She's in shock," Dr. Jenkins said.

He placed his jacket over Amy, then took the handkerchief's last dry corner and delicately probed the wound.

"Why weren't the drapes closed?" Dr. Jenkins asked. Ginny said nothing and Dr. Jenkins turned his attention back to Amy. Another teacher herded the students out of the classroom and shut the door. For a few moments, all Ginny had heard was a siren wailing through rain loud as a waterfall.

Dr. Jenkins would later claim that Ginny also had been in shock, because that was the only way to explain what Ginny had done next. As she kneeled beside Amy, Ginny opened the hand that held the glass shard.

"Be careful. That can cut you too," Dr. Jenkins warned.

But the words were hardly out of his mouth before Ginny raised the glass and jabbed its sharpest edge into her cheekbone. She'd moved the shard down her cheek to her mouth as deliberately as a man shaving.

Ginny had been drugged when Andrew came to her hospital room, but even drugged she could see how hard it was for him to look at her.

"You'll be all right," Andrew had said, holding her hand. "Dr. Jenkins has placed you on medical leave for the rest of the year. As soon as I'm out, we'll get away from here awhile, maybe Europe. Wherever you want to go, Ginny."

When she hadn't replied, Andrew had squeezed her hand.

"Rest," he said. "We can talk more about this later. We have a future."

But as she'd lain in the hospital bed that evening she thought not of the future but of the past. It had been in the sixth grade when Ginny quit raising her hand in class and began pressing her lips together during photographs. Her permanent teeth had come in at angles that inspired nicknames and jokes. Former friends no longer asked her to sit with them at lunch. Ginny's father had been laid off at the mill, making braces unaffordable. One late night her father had awakened her, liquor on his breath as he told Ginny it was a shitty world when a man couldn't prevent his own daughter from being ashamed to smile. Only her teachers had made life bearable, especially Mrs. Ellison, her eighth-grade English teacher. She was the one who'd convinced Ginny to be the student announcer on the middle school's twice-weekly radio program. Once she was out of sight behind the principal's microphone, Ginny spoke without mumbling or covering her mouth. Mrs. Ellison praised how she never stumbled over words or rushed her sentences. She said Ginny was a natural. Late that spring Mrs. Ellison had cajoled an orthodontist into working on Ginny's teeth for free. By the end of ninth grade, she had no reason to turn her face from the world, but certain habits had become ingrained. All through high school, even into college, Ginny's hand gravitated to her upper lip as she spoke.

The habit of being alone was even harder to break, because solitude had its comforts. Most weekends she stayed in her room, reading and listening to music, filling out scholarship and financial-aid forms. When Chapel Hill offered Ginny a full academic scholarship, none of her teachers were surprised. Several of them had, however, questioned her decision to major in elementary education. As Ginny lay in the hospital bed, she knew they had been right. When Dr. Jenkins visited the next morning, she told him that she would not return in the fall. Dr. Jenkins looked relieved. He wished Ginny well in whatever future path she undertook. Ending her relationship with Andrew had been more difficult. I need to be alone, she had told him. He had responded that she couldn't let the accident change what they had together. He'd spoken of love and devotion, of her moving in with him, of marriage. When he'd pleaded to at least be allowed to see her occasionally, she'd told him no.

For several months he had tried anyway, calling nightly until she changed her cell number.

"This is the Night Hawk," Ginny said later that evening as the control booth clock ticked off the first seconds of the morning, "and I'll be with you till six. If you have a request, I'll do my best to play it for you. Just call 344-WMEK. Here's a song to get us started tonight."

Ginny hit the play button and the first notes of "After Midnight" filled the booth.

"Good choice," Barry said.

The next few hours went well. Barry helped her cue the advertisements and national news. He answered the phone for the occasional request. When she spoke into the microphone, she did little more than acknowledge a request or give the names of artists and songs she was about to play.

"I'm going home to get a few hours' sleep," Barry said after the three o'clock news.

"Tom Freeman will be in around five thirty. He's got a key." Barry pointed to a note card taped to the booth's one window.

"That's my home number. I'm only five minutes away. Call if you have a problem. But I don't think you'll need me. Except for getting comfortable enough to talk more, you've got this job down pat."

Ginny wasn't so sure, but after a few nights she did begin to talk more, though rarely about music. She brought in atlases and magazines, books that ranged from fat hardback tomes on western art to tattered paperback almanacs. Ginny quizzed her listeners twice an hour, rewarding those who answered correctly with WMEK T-shirts and ballcaps. Each night she picked a word from *The Highly Selective Thesaurus for the Highly Literate* and gave its definition. She read from a book titled *On This Day in History*. Some listeners called the station during business hours to complain about the new format, wanting less talk and more music. Several male listeners wanted some sports questions in Ginny's quizzes. But according to Barry, the calls and e-mails ran five to one in her favor, including several from immigrants who credited Ginny with teaching them about American history. Two months later the Arbitron ratings came out. WMEK's twelve-to-six slot had a two-point market share increase.

"As long as you get that kind of response, I don't care if you read the complete plays of William Shakespeare on air," Barry told her.

It was a Thursday in early February when Andrew called. Twelve inches of snow had fallen that day, and Barry, who owned a truck, had to drive Ginny to work. After reading cancellations for everything from schools to day-care centers to shifts at local mills, she offered a free ball cap to a listener naming the poem that began "Whose woods these are I think I know."

There were two wrong answers before Andrew's voice said, "Stopping by Woods on a Snowy Evening."

"You win a WMEK ball cap," Ginny said. "You can come by the station during business hours to pick up your prize."

For several seconds neither spoke. Ginny cut the volume in the control booth and heard the Norah Jones song she was playing. She wondered if it was the radio in Andrew's kitchen or the one in the back room where he painted.

"I knew you'd taken RTV classes, but I had no idea you were doing this," Andrew said. "How long have you had the job?"

"Almost three months."

"I just happened to have the radio on to find out about school cancellations."

"Well, it's a lucky night for you," Ginny said. "You've won a ball cap and no school tomorrow."

"The lucky thing is hearing your voice again," Andrew said. "I didn't realize how much I missed it until this last hour. Ten months haven't changed that. Don't you think it's time to let me back into your life?"

"I've got to go," Ginny said. "More cancellations to read."

Ginny hung up the phone. Only then did she realize her left hand was raised, her index finger touching her upper lip.

It was four hours later when she heard a banging on the door. Ginny cued another song and left the booth. She assumed it was Barry, but when she entered the foyer Andrew's face peered in through the glass. She kept the door latched.

"I've come to pick up my prize," he said, his breath whitened by the cold.

"The station doesn't open for business until eight thirty," Ginny said.

"You're here."

"I'm doing a program, a program I need to get back to."

"It's cold, Ginny. Let me come in."

She unlatched the door and he followed her to the control booth.

"You can sit over there," she said, pointing to a plastic chair in the corner.

Andrew watched and listened the next hour as she read cancellations, gave away another ball cap, and played several requests. Tom Freeman came in at 5:40 and Barry a few minutes later.

"This is the Night Hawk," Ginny said at 5:55, "and it's time to leave the airways to those birds that fly under the sun. So here's a song from those day-fliers The Eagles."

She turned up the volume as the intro to "Already Gone" filled the room.

"OK," she said to Andrew. "We can get your ball cap now."

Andrew followed her down the hall and into the station's reception room. Ginny opened a closet filled with ball caps and T-shirts.

"There," she said, handing him a cap. "Now you have what you came for."

"I wouldn't say that," Andrew said, fitting the cap on his head. "But it is a nice cap." He pulled the bill down slightly. "How does it look?"

"Perfect fit," Ginny said.

"I thought we might have breakfast together," Andrew said.

"Barry's supposed to take me home."

"I can take you home after we eat."

"I don't like to be around a bunch of strangers," Ginny said. "I get tired of the stares."

"We'll go where there aren't many people," Andrew answered. "That ought to be easy today. Everyone's hunkered down with their white bread and milk." When she hesitated, Andrew placed his hand on her forearm.

"Please," Andrew said, "just breakfast."

"Let me tell Barry I'm going with you," Ginny said.

Soon they were driving through the center of town in Andrew's jeep. Few tire tracks marked the snow the jeep passed over.

"This should fit the bill nicely," Andrew said, and turned into the Blue Ridge Diner's parking lot.

The snow had stopped but gray clouds smothered the dawn. The parking lot lights were still on, casting a buttery sheen over the snow. Inside, the waitress and cook stood across the counter from a middle-aged couple who sat in plastic swivel chairs. They were talking about the weather, their voices soft as if also muffled by the snow.

"Let's sit in a booth," Ginny said. The waitress turned from the others at the counter.

"You all want coffee?"

Andrew looked at Ginny and she shook her head.

"Just me," he said.

Andrew nodded toward the counter where the waitress continued to talk to the cook and the couple as she poured the coffee.

"A scene worthy of your moniker."

"No, not really," Ginny said. "Too much interaction."

Andrew turned his gaze back to her.

"In the painting the man and woman are a couple."

"I don't see that," Ginny said. "They aren't even looking at each other."

The waitress brought Andrew's coffee but no menus.

When she saw Ginny's face up close, her lips pursed to an O before she quickly turned to Andrew.

"There's not much choice as far as food," the waitress said. "Our deliveryman is running late, so it's pretty much waffles or toast."

"Waffles sound good," Andrew said.

Ginny nodded.

"Same for me."

Andrew stirred cream into his coffee. He held the cup but did not lift it to his lips. He leaned to blow across the coffee's surface, then raised his eyes.

"You're wrong about that couple in the painting."

"What do you mean?" Ginny asked.

"They are connected, the man and woman. Their faces may not show it but their arms and hands do."

"I don't remember that," Ginny said.

"Well, I'll show you then," Andrew said.

Coatless, he walked outside. Ginny watched through the window as he stepped into the lot, rummaged in the back of the jeep. The waitress brought their waffles as Andrew returned with a gray hard-back the width and thickness of a family bible. He pushed his plate and cup to the side and laid the book open on the table.

"There," he said when he found the painting. "Look at her left arm and hand."

Ginny leaned over her plate and studied the picture.

"I'm not convinced. Because of the perspective it could go either way, like whether the Mona Lisa is smiling or not."

"Maybe you just don't want to admit you're wrong," Andrew said, and paused. "Maybe you're wrong about several things, like not being able to teach again, like you and me."

Andrew reached out and laid his palm against the scar on Ginny's face. She jerked her head sideways as if slapped.

"OK," he said, slowly lowering his hand. "I made a mistake tonight. It won't happen again."

They finished their waffles in silence, and did not speak until Andrew slowed in front of her apartment.

"Don't pull into the drive," Ginny said. "You might get stuck if you do."

Andrew pulled up to the curb but did not cut the engine. Ginny got out and trudged across the yard, her black walking shoes disappearing in the white each time she took another step. She did not look back as she opened the front door. Inside, she took off her shoes and socks and brushed the snow off her pants. She looked out the window. Only one set of tracks crossed the yard. The jeep was gone.

Ginny slept as the sky cleared to a high, bright blue. By noon the temperature was in the forties. When her alarm clock went off at three, she lay in bed a few minutes listening to cars slosh through melting snow. She would not need a ride into work. She would drive herself across town, looking through safety glass as she passed the school where she had taught, then the hospital where her face had been stitched back together, the restaurant where she and Andrew had eaten breakfast.

At the radio station she would unlock the door, and soon enough Buddy Harper would end his broadcast and leave. She would say, This is the Night Hawk, and play "After Midnight."

Ginny would speak to people in bedrooms, to clerks drenched in the fluorescent light of convenience stores, to millworkers driving back roads home after graveyard shifts. She would speak to the drunk and sober, the godly and the godless. All the while high above where she sat, the station's red beacon would pulse like a heart, as if giving bearings to all those in the dark adrift and alone.

The TRUSTY

They had been moving up the road a week without seeing another farmhouse, and the nearest well, at least the nearest the owner would let Sinkler use, was half a mile back. What had been a trusty sluff job was now as onerous as swinging a Kaiser blade or shoveling out ditches. As soon as he'd hauled the buckets back to the cage truck it was time to go again. He asked Vickery if someone could spell him and the bull guard smiled and said that Sinkler could always strap on a pair of leg irons and grab a handle. "Bolick just killed a rattlesnake in them weeds yonder," the bull guard said. "I bet he'd square a trade with you." When Sinkler asked if come morning he could walk ahead to search for another well, Vickery's lips tightened, but he nodded.

The next day, Sinkler took the metal buckets and walked until he found a farmhouse. It was no closer than the other, even a bit farther, but worth padding the hoof a few extra steps. The well he'd been using belonged to a hunchbacked widow. The woman who appeared in this doorway wore her hair in a similar tight bun and draped herself in the same sort of flour-cloth dress, but she looked to be in her midtwenties, like Sinkler. Two weeks would pass before they got beyond this farmhouse, perhaps another two weeks before the next well. Plenty of time to quench a different kind of thirst. As he entered the yard, the woman looked past the barn to a field where a man and his draft horse were plowing. The woman gave a brisk whistle and the farmer paused and looked their way. Sinkler stopped beside the well but did not set the buckets down.

"What you want," the woman said, not so much a question as a demand.

"Water," Sinkler answered. "We've got a chain gang working on the road."

"I'd have reckoned you to bring water with you."

"Not enough for ten men all day."

The woman looked out at the field again. Her husband watched but did not unloop the rein from around his neck. The woman stepped onto the six nailed-together planks that looked more like a raft than a porch. Firewood was stacked on one side, and closer to the door an axe leaned between a shovel and a hoe. She let her eyes settle on the axe long enough to make sure he noticed it. Sinkler saw now that she was younger than he'd thought, maybe eighteen, at most twenty, more girl than woman.

"How come you not to have chains on you?"

"I'm a trusty," Sinkler said smiling. "A prisoner, but one that can be trusted."

"And all you want is water?"

Sinkler thought of several possible answers.

"That's what they sent me for."

"I don't reckon there to be any money in it for us?" the girl asked.

"No, just gratitude from a bunch of thirsty men, and especially me for not having to haul it so far."

"I'll have to ask my man," she said. "Stay here in the yard."

For a moment he thought she might take the axe with her. As she walked into the field, Sinkler studied the house, which was no bigger than a fishing shack. The dwelling appeared to have been built in the previous century. The door opened with a latch, not a knob, and no glass filled the window frames. Sinkler stepped closer to the entrance and saw two ladder-back chairs and a small table set on a puncheon floor. Sinkler wondered if these apple-knockers had heard they were supposed to be getting a new deal.

"You can use the well," the girl said when she returned, "but he said you need to forget one of them pails here next time you come asking for water."

Worth it, he figured, even if Vickery took the money out of Sinkler's own pocket, especially with no sign up ahead of another farmhouse. It would be a half-dollar at most, easily made up with one slick deal in a poker game. He nodded and went to the well, sent the rusty bucket down into the dark. The girl went up on the porch but didn't go inside.

"What you in prison for?"

"Thinking a bank manager wouldn't notice his teller slipping a few bills in his pocket."

"Whereabouts?"

"Raleigh."

"I ain't never been past Asheville," the girl said. "How long you in for?"

"Five years. I've done sixteen months."

Sinkler raised the bucket, water leaking from the bottom as he transferred its contents. The girl stayed on the porch, making sure that all he took was water.

"You lived here long?"

"Me and Chet been here a year," the girl said. "I grew up across the ridge yonder."

"You two live alone, do you?"

"We do," the girl said, "but there's a rifle just inside the door and I know how to bead it."

"I'm sure you do," Sinkler said. "You mind telling me your name, just so I'll know what to call you?"

"Lucy Sorrels."

He waited to see if she'd ask his.

"Mine's Sinkler," he said when she didn't.

He filled the second bucket but made no move to leave, instead looking around at the trees and mountains as if just noticing them. Then he smiled and gave a slight nod.

"Must get lonely being out so far from everything," Sinkler said. "At least, I would think so."

"And I'd think them men to be getting thirsty," Lucy Sorrels said.

"Probably," he agreed, surprised at her smarts in turning his words back on him. "But I'll return soon to brighten your day."

"When you planning to leave one of them pails?" she asked.

"Last trip before quitting time"

She nodded and went into the shack.

"The rope broke," he told Vickery as the prisoners piled into the truck at quitting time.

The guard looked not so much skeptical as aggrieved that Sinkler thought him fool enough to believe it. Vickery answered that if Sinkler thought he'd lightened his load he was mistaken. It'd be easy enough to find another bucket, maybe one that could hold an extra gallon. Sinkler shrugged and lifted himself into the cage truck, found a place on the metal bench among the sweating convicts. He'd won over the other guards with cigarettes and small loans, that and his mush talk, but not Vickery, who'd argued that making Sinkler a trusty would only give him a head start when he tried to escape.

The bull guard was right about that. Sinkler had more than fifty dollars in poker winnings now, plenty enough cash to get him across the Mississippi and finally shed himself of the whole damn region. He'd grown up in Montgomery, but when the law got too interested in his comings and goings he'd gone north to Knoxville and then west to Memphis before recrossing Tennessee on his way to Raleigh. Sinkler's talents had led him to establishments where his sleight of hand needed no deck of cards. With a decent suit, clean fingernails, and buffed shoes, he'd walk into a business and be greeted as a solid citizen. Tell a story about being in town because of an ailing mother and you were the cat's pajamas. They'd take the Help Wanted sign out of the window and pretty much replace it with Help Yourself. Sinkler remembered the afternoon in Memphis when he had stood by the river after grifting a clothing store of forty dollars in two months. Keep heading west or turn back east—that was the choice. He'd flipped a silver dollar to decide, a rare moment when he'd trusted his life purely to luck.

This time he'd cross the river, start in Kansas City or St. Louis. He'd work the stores and cafés and newsstands and anywhere else with a till or a cash register. Except for a bank. Crooked as bankers were, Sinkler should have realized how quickly they'd recognize him as one of their own. No, he'd not make that mistake again.

That night, when the stockade lights were snuffed, he lay in his bunk and thought about Lucy Sorrels. A year and a half had passed since he'd been with a woman. After that long, almost any female would make the sap rise. There was nothing about her face to hold a man's attention, but curves tightened the right parts of her dress. Nice legs too. Each trip to the well that day, he had tried to make small talk. She had given him the icy mitts, but he had weeks yet to warm her up. It was only on the last haul that the husband had come in from his field. He'd barely responded to Sinkler's "how do you dos" and "much obligeds." He looked to be around forty and Sinkler suspected that part of his terseness was due to a younger man being around his wife. After a few moments, the farmer had nodded at the pail in Sinkler's left hand. "You'll be leaving that, right?" When Sinkler said yes, the husband told Lucy to switch it with the leaky well bucket, then walked into the barn.

Two days passed before Lucy asked if he'd ever thought of trying to escape.

"Of course," Sinkler answered. "Have you?"

She looked at him in a way that he could not read.

"How come you ain't done it, then? They let you roam near anywhere you want, and you ain't got shackles."

"Maybe I enjoy the free room and board," Sinkler answered. He turned a thumb toward his stripes. "Nice duds too. They even let you change them out every Sunday."

"I don't think I could stand it," Lucy said. "Being locked up so long and knowing I still had nigh on three years."

He checked her lips for the slightest upward curve of a smile, but it wasn't there.

"Yeah," Sinkler said, taking a step closer. "You don't seem the sort to stand being locked up. I'd think a young gal pretty as you would want to see more of the world."

"How come you ain't done it?" she asked again, and brushed some loose wisps of hair behind her ear.

"Maybe the same reason as you," Sinkler said. "It's not like you can get whisked away from here. I haven't seen more than a couple of cars and trucks on this road, and those driving them know there's prisoners about. They wouldn't be fool enough to pick up a stranger. Haven't seen a lot of train tracks either."

"Anybody ever try?" Lucy asked.

"Yeah, two weeks ago. Fellow ran that morning and the bloodhounds had him grabbing sky by dark. All he got for his trouble was a bunch of tick bites and briar scratches. That and another year added to his sentence."

For the first time since she'd gone to fetch her husband, Lucy stepped off the porch and put some distance between her and the door. The rifle and axe too, which meant that she was starting to trust him at least a little. She stood in the yard and looked up at an eave, where black insects hovered around clots of dried mud.

"Them dirt daubers is a nuisance," Lucy said. "I knock their nests down and they build them back the next day."

"I'd guess them to be about the only thing that wants to stay around here, don't you think?"

"You've got a saucy way of talking," she said.

"You don't seem to mind it too much," Sinkler answered, and nodded toward the field. "An older fellow like that usually keeps a close eye on a pretty young wife, but he must be the trusting sort, or is it he just figures he's got you corralled in?"

He lifted the full buckets and stepped close enough to the barn not to be seen from the field. "You don't have to stand so far from me, Lucy Sorrels. I don't bite."

She didn't move toward him but she didn't go back to the porch, either.

"If you was to escape, where would you go?"

"Might depend on who was going with me," Sinkler answered. "What kind of place would you like to visit?"

"Like you'd just up and take me along. I'd likely that about as much as them daubers flying me out of here."

"No, I'd need to get to know my traveling partner better," Sinkler said. "Make sure she really cared about me. That way she wouldn't take a notion to turn me in."

"You mean for the reward money?"

Sinkler laughed.

"You've got to be a high cloud to have a reward put on you, darling. They'd not even bother to put my mug in a post office, which is fine by me. Buy my train ticket and I'd be across the Mississippi in two days. Matter of fact, I've got money enough saved to buy two tickets."

"Enough for two tickets?" she asked.

"I do indeed."

Lucy looked at her bare feet, placed one atop the other as a shy child might. She set both feet back on the ground and looked up.

"Why come you to think a person would turn you in if there ain't no reward?"

"Bad conscience—which is why I've got to be sure my companion doesn't have one." Sinkler smiled. "Like I said, you don't have to stand so far away. We could even step into the barn for a few minutes."

Lucy looked toward the field and let her gaze linger long enough that he thought she just might do it.

"I have chores to get done," she said and went into the shack.

Sinkler headed back down the road, thinking things out. By the time he set the sloshing buckets beside the prison truck, he'd figured a way to get Lucy Sorrels's dress raised with more than just sweet talk. He'd tell her there was an extra set of truck keys in a guard's front desk he could steal. Once the guards were distracted, he'd jump in the truck, pick her up, head straight to Asheville, and catch the first train out. It was a damn good story, one Sinkler himself might have believed if he didn't know that all the extra truck keys were locked inside a thousand-pound Mosler safe.

When he entered the yard the next morning, Lucy came to the well but stayed on the opposite side. Like a skittish dog, Sinkler thought, and imagined holding out a pack of gum or a candy bar to bring her the rest of the way. She wore the same dress as always, but her hair was unpinned and fell across her shoulders. It was blonder and curlier than he'd supposed. Set free for him, Sinkler knew. A cool, steady breeze gave the air an early-autumn feel and helped round the curves beneath the muslin.

"Your hair being down like that—it looks good," he said. "I bet that's the way you wear it in bed."

She didn't blush. Sinkler worked the crank and the well bucket descended into the earth. Once both his buckets were filled, he laid out his plan.

"You don't much cotton to my idea?" he asked when she didn't respond. "I bet you're thinking we'd have to get past them guards with shotguns but we won't. I'll wait until the chain gang's working up above here. Do it like that and we'll have clear sailing all the way down to Asheville."

"There's an easier way," Lucy said quietly, "one where you don't need the truck, nor even a road."

"I never figured you to be the know-all on prison escapes."

"There's a trail on the yon side of that ridge," Lucy said, nodding past the field. "You can follow it all the way to Asheville."

"Asheville's at least thirty miles from here."

"That's by the road. It's no more than eight if you cut through the gap. You just got to know the right trails."

"Which I don't."

"I do," she said. "I've done it in three hours easy."

For a few moments, Sinkler didn't say anything. It was as though the key he'd been imagining had suddenly appeared in his hand. He left the buckets where they were and stepped closer to the barn. When he gestured Lucy closer, she came. He settled an arm around her waist and felt her yield to him. Her lips opened to his and she did not resist when his free hand cupped a breast. To touch a woman after so long made him feather-legged. A bead of sweat trickled down his brow as she pressed her body closer and settled a hand on his thigh. Only when Sinkler tried to lead her into the barn did Lucy resist.

"He can't see us from down there."

"It ain't just that," Lucy said. "My bleed time's started."

Sinkler felt so rabbity that he told her he didn't care.

"There'd be a mess and he'd know the why of it."

He felt frustration simmer into anger. Sinkler tried to step away but Lucy pulled him back, pressed her face into his chest.

"If we was far away it wouldn't matter. I hate it here. He cusses me near every day and won't let me go nowhere. When he's drunk, he fetches his rifle and swears he's going to shoot me."

"It's all right," Sinkler said, and patted her shoulder.

She let go of him slowly. The only sound was a clucking chicken and the breeze tinking the well bucket against the narrow stone wellhead.

"All you and me have to do is get on that train in Asheville," Lucy said, "and not him nor the law can catch us. I know where he keeps his money. I'll get it if you ain't got enough."

He met her eyes, then looked past her. The sun was higher now, angled in over the mountaintops, and the new well bucket winked silver as it swayed. Sinkler lifted his gaze to the cloudless sky. It would be another hot, dry, miserable day and he'd be out in it. At quitting time, he'd go back and wash up with water dingy enough to clog a strainer, eat what would gag a hog, then at nine o'clock set his head on a grimy pillow. Three and a half more years. Sinkler studied the ridgeline, found the gap that would lead to Asheville.

"I've got money," he told Lucy. "It's the getting to where I can spend it that's been the problem."

That night as he lay in his bunk, Sinkler pondered the plan. An hour would pass before anyone started looking for him, and even then they'd search first along the road. As far out as the prisoners were working, it'd take at least four hours to get the bloodhounds on his trail, and by the time the dogs tracked him to Asheville he'd be on a train. It could be months, or never, until such a chance came again. But the suddenness of the opportunity unsettled him. He should take a couple of days, think it out. The grit in the gears would be Lucy. Giving her the slip in Asheville would be nigh impossible, so he'd be with her until the next stop, probably Knoxville or Raleigh. Which could be all for the better. A hotel room and a bottle of boot-leg whiskey and they'd have them a high old time. He could sneak out early morning while she slept. If she took what her husband had hidden, she'd have enough for a new start, and another reason not to drop a dime and phone the police.

Of course, many a convict would simply wait until trail's end, then let a good-sized rock take care of it, lift what money she had, and be on his way. Traveling with a girl that young was a risk. She might say or do something to make a bluecoat suspicious. Or, waking up to find him gone, put the law on him just for spite.

The next morning, the men loaded up and drove to where they'd quit the day before. They weren't far from the farmhouse now, only a few hundred yards. As he carried the buckets up the road, Sin-kler realized that if Lucy knew the trail, then the husband did too. The guards would see the farmer in the field and tell him who they were looking for. How long after that would he find out that she was gone? It might be just minutes before the husband went to check. But only if the guards were looking in that direction. When the time came, he'd tell Vickery this well was low and the farmer wouldn't let him use it anymore, so he had to go back down the road to the wid-ow's. He could walk in that direction and then cut into the woods and circle back.

Sinkler was already drawing water when Lucy came out. Primp-

ing for him, he knew, her hair unpinned and freshly combed, cur-
taining a necklace with a heart-shaped locket. She smelled good
too, a bright and clean smell like honeysuckle. In the distance, the
husband was strapped to his horse, the tandem trudging endlessly
across the field. From what Sinkler had seen, the man worked as
hard as the road crews and had about as much to show for it. Twenty
years older and too much of a gink to realize what Lucy understood
at eighteen. Sinkler stepped closer to the barn and she raised her
mouth to his, found his tongue with her tongue.

"I been thirsting for that all last night and this morning," Lucy
said when she broke off the kiss. "That's what it's like—a thirsting.
Chet ain't never been able to stanch it, but you can."

She laid her head against his chest and held him tight. Feeling
the desperation of her embrace, Sinkler knew that she'd risk her life
to help him get away, help them get away. But a girl her age could
turn quick as a weathervane. He set his hands on her shoulders and
gently but firmly pushed her back enough to meet her eyes.

"You ain't just playing some make-believe with me, because if you
are it's time to quit."

"I'll leave this second if you got need to," Lucy said. "I'll go get
his money right now. I counted it this morning when he left. It's near
seven dollars. That's enough, ain't it, at least to get us tickets?"

"You've never rode a train, have you?" Sinkler asked.

"No."

"It costs more than that."

"How much more?"

"Closer to five each," Sinkler said, "just to get to Knoxville or
Raleigh."

She touched the locket.

"This is a pass-me-down from my momma. It's pure silver and we
could sell it."

Sinkler slipped a hand under the locket, inspected it with the feigned attentiveness of a jeweler.

"And all this time I thought you had a heart of gold, Lucy Sorrels," Sinkler said and smiled as he let the locket slide off his palm. "No, darling. You keep it around your pretty neck. I got plenty for tickets, and maybe something extra for a shiny bracelet to go with that necklace."

"Then I want to go tomorrow," Lucy said, and moved closer to him. "My bleed time is near over."

Sinkler smelled the honeysuckle and desire swamped him. He tried to clear his mind and come up with reasons to delay but none came.

"We'll leave in the morning," Sinkler said.

"All right," she said, touching him a moment longer before removing her hand.

"We'll have to travel light."

"I don't mind that," Lucy said. "It ain't like I got piddling anyway."

"Can you get me one of his shirts and some pants?"

Lucy nodded.

"Don't pack any of it until tomorrow morning when he's in the field," Sinkler said.

"Where are we going?" she asked. "I mean, for good?"

"Where do you want to go?"

"I was notioning California. They say it's like paradise out there."

"That'll do me just fine," Sinkler said, then grinned. "That's just where an angel like you belongs."

The next morning, he told Vickery that the Sorrelses' well was going dry and he'd have to backtrack to the other one. "That'll be almost a mile jaunt for you," Vickery said, and shook his head in mock sympathy. Sinkler walked until he was out of sight. He found himself a marker, a big oak with a trunk cracked by lightning, then stepped over the ditch and entered the woods. He set the buckets by a rotting stump, close enough to the oak tree to be easily found if something went wrong. Because Sinkler knew that, when it came time to lay down or fold, Lucy might still think twice about trusting someone she'd hardly known two weeks, and a convict at that. Or the husband might notice a little thing like Lucy not gathering eggs or not putting a kettle on for supper, things Sinkler should have warned her to do.

Sinkler stayed close to the road, and soon heard the clink of leg chains and the rasp of shovels gathering dirt. Glimpses of black and white caught his eye as he made his way past. The sounds of the chain gang faded, and not long after that the trees thinned, the barn's gray planking filling the gaps. Sinkler did not enter the yard. Lucy stood just inside the farmhouse door. He studied the shack for any hint that the farmer had found out. But all was as it had been, clothing pinned on the wire between two trees, cracked corn spilled on the ground for the chickens, the axe still on the porch beside the hoe. He angled around the barn until he could see the field. The farmer was there, hitched to the horse and plow. Sinkler called her name and Lucy stepped out on the porch. She wore the same muslin dress and carried a knotted bedsheet in her hand. When she got to the woods, Lucy opened the bedsheet and removed a shirt and what was little more than two flaps of tied leather.

"Go over by the well and put these brogans on," Lucy said. "It's a way to fool them hounds."

"We need to get going," Sinkler said.

"It'll just take a minute."

He did what she asked, checking the field to make sure that the farmer wasn't looking in their direction.

"Keep your shoes in your hand," Lucy said, and walked toward Sinkler with the shirt.

When she was close, Lucy got on her knees and rubbed the shirt cloth over the ground, all the way to his feet. Smart of her, Sinkler had to admit, though it was an apple-knocker kind of smart.

"Walk over to the other side of the barn," she told him, scrubbing the ground as she followed.

She motioned him to stay put and retrieved the bedsheet.

"This way," she said, and led him down the slanted ground and into the woods.

"You expect me to wear these all the way to Asheville?" Sinkler said after the flapping leather almost tripped him.

"No, just up to the ridge."

They stayed in the woods and along the field's far edge and then climbed the ridge. At the top Sinkler took off the brogans and looked back through the trees and saw the square of plowed soil, now no bigger than a barn door. The farmer was still there.

Lucy untied the bedsheet and handed him the pants and shirt. He took off his stripes and hid them behind a tree. Briefly, Sinkler thought about taking a little longer before he dressed, suggesting to Lucy that the bedsheet might have another use. Just a few more hours, he reminded himself, you'll be safe for sure and rolling with her in a big soft bed. The chambray shirt wasn't a bad fit, but the denim pants hung loose on his hips. Every few steps, Sinkler had to hitch them back up. The bedsheet held nothing more and Lucy stuffed it in a rock crevice.

"You bring that money?" he asked.

"You claimed us not to need it," Lucy said, a harshness in her voice he'd not heard before. "You weren't trifling with me about having money for the train tickets, were you?"

"No, darling, and plenty enough to buy you that bracelet and a real dress instead of that flour sack you got on. Stick with me and you'll ride the cushions."

They moved down the ridge through a thicket of rhododendron, the ground so aslant that in a couple of places he'd have tumbled if he hadn't watched how Lucy did it, front foot sideways and leaning backward. At the bottom, the trail forked. Lucy nodded to the left. The land continued downhill, then curved and leveled out. After a while, the path snaked into the undergrowth and Sinkler knew that without Lucy he'd be completely lost. You're doing as much for her as she for you, he reminded himself, and thought again about what another convict might do, what he'd known all along he couldn't do. When others had brought a derringer or Arkansas toothpick to card games, Sinkler arrived empty-handed, because either one could take its owner straight to the morgue or to prison. He'd always made a show of slapping his pockets and opening his coat at such gatherings. "I'll not hurt anything but a fellow's wallet," he'd say. Men had been killed twice in his presence, but he'd never had a weapon aimed in his direction.

Near another ridge, they crossed a creek that was little more than a spring seep. They followed the ridge awhile and then the trail widened and they moved back downhill and up again. Each rise and fall of the land looked like what had come before. The mountain air was thin and if Sinkler hadn't been hauling water such distances he wouldn't have had the spunk to keep going. They went on, the trees shading them from the sun, but even so he grew thirsty and kept hoping they'd come to a stream he could drink from. Finally, they came to another spring seep.

"I've got to have some water," he said.

Sinkler kneeled beside the creek. The water was so shallow that he had to lean over and steady himself with one hand, cupping the other to get a dozen leaky palmfuls in his mouth. He stood and brushed the damp sand off his hand and his knees. The woods were completely silent, no murmur of wind, not a bird singing.

"You want any?" he asked, but Lucy shook her head.

The trees shut out much of the sky, but he could tell that the sun was starting to slip behind the mountains. Fewer dapples of light were on the forest floor, more shadows. Soon the prisoners would be heading back, one man fewer. Come suppertime, the ginks would be spooning beans off a tin plate while Sinkler sat in a dining car eating steak with silverware. By then, the warden would have chewed out Vickery's skinny ass but good, maybe even fired him. The other guards, the ones he'd duped even more, would be explaining why they'd recommended making Sinkler a trusty in the first place.

When the trail narrowed again, a branch snagged Lucy's sleeve and ripped the frayed muslin. She surprised him with her profanity as she examined the torn cloth.

"I'd not think a sweet little gal like you to know words like that."

She glared at him and Sinkler raised his hands, palms out.

"Just teasing you a bit, darling. You should have brought another dress. I know I told you to pack light, but light didn't mean bring nothing."

"Maybe I ain't got another dress," Lucy said.

"But you will, and soon, and like I said it'll be a spiffy one."

"If I do," Lucy said, "I'll use this piece of shit for nothing but scrub rags."

She let go of the cloth. The branch had scratched her neck and she touched it with her finger, confirmed that it wasn't bleeding. Had the locket been around her neck, the chain might have snapped, but it was in her pocket. Or so he assumed. If she'd forgotten it in the haste of packing, now didn't seem the time to bring it up.

As they continued their descent, Sinkler thought again about what would happen once they were safely free. He was starting to see a roughness about Lucy that her youth and country ways had masked. Perhaps he could take her with him beyond their first stop. He'd worked with a whore in Knoxville once, let her go in and distract a clerk while he took whatever they could fence. The whore hadn't been as young and innocent-seeming as Lucy. Even Lucy's plainness would be an advantage—harder to describe her to the law. Maybe tonight in the hotel room she'd show him more reason to let her tag along awhile.

The trail curved and then went uphill. Surely for the last time, he figured, and told himself he'd be damn glad to be back in a place where a man didn't have to be half goat to get somewhere. Sinkler searched through the branches and leaves for a brick smokestack, the glint of a train rail. They were both breathing harder now, and even Lucy looked tuckered.

Up ahead, another seep crossed the path and Sinkler paused.

"I'm going to sip me some more water."

"Ain't no need," Lucy said. "We're almost there."

He heard it then, the rasping plunge of metal into dirt. The rhododendron was too thick to see through. Whatever it was, it meant they were indeed near civilization.

"I guess we are," he said, but Lucy had already gone ahead.

As Sinkler hitched the sagging pants up yet again, he decided that the first thing he'd do after buying the tickets was find a clothing store or gooseberry a clothesline. He didn't want to look like a damn hobo. Even in town, they might have to walk a ways for water, so Sinkler kneeled. Someone whistled near the ridge and the rasping stopped. As he pressed his palm into the sand, he saw that a handprint was already there beside it, his handprint. Sinkler studied it awhile, then slowly rocked back until his buttocks touched his shoe heels. He stared at the two star-shaped indentations, water slowly filling the new one.

No one would hear the shot, he knew. And, in a few weeks, when autumn came and the trees started to shed, the upturned earth would be completely obscured. Leaves rustled as someone approached. The footsteps paused, and Sinkler heard the soft click of a rifle's safety being released. The leaves rustled again but he was too worn out to run. They would want the clothes as well as the money, he told himself, and there was no reason to prolong any of it. His trembling fingers clasped the shirt's top button, pushed it through the slit in the chambray.

BACK *of* BEYOND

When Parson drove to his pawnshop that morning, the sky was the color of lead. Flurries settled on the pickup's windshield, lingered a moment before expiring. A heavy snow tonight, the weatherman warned, and it looked to be certain, everything getting quiet and still, waiting. Even more snow in the higher mountains, enough to make many roads impassable. It would be a profitable day, because Parson knew they'd come to his pawnshop to barter before emptying every cold-remedy shelf in town. They would hit Wal-Mart first because it was cheapest, then the Rexall, and finally the town's three convenience stores, coming from every wayback cove and hollow in the county.

Parson pulled his jeep into the parking lot of the cinder-block building with PARSON'S BUY AND SELL hung over the door. One of the addicts had brought an electric portable sign last week, had it in his truck bed with a trash can filled with red plastic letters to stick on it. The man told Parson the sign would ensure that potential customers noticed the pawnshop. You found me easy enough, Parson had replied.

His watch said eight forty and the sign in the window said nine to six Tuesday through Saturday, but a gray decade-old Ford Escort had already nosed up to the building. The back windshield was damaged, cracks spreading outward like a spiderweb. The gas cap a stuffed rag. A woman sat in the driver's seat. She could have been waiting ten minutes or ten hours.

Parson got out of his truck, unlocked the door, and cut off the alarm. He turned on the lights and walked around the counter, placed the loaded Smith & Wesson revolver on the shelf below the register. The copper bell above the sill tinkled. The woman waited in the doorway, a wooden butter churn and dasher clutched in her arms. Parson had to hand it to them, they were getting more imaginative. Last week the electric sign and false teeth, the week before that four bicycle tires and a chiropractic table. Parson nodded for the woman to come on in. She set the churn and dasher on the table.

"It's a antique," the woman said. "I seen one like it on TV and the fellow said it was worth a hundred dollars."

When the woman spoke Parson glimpsed the stubbed brown ruin inside her mouth. He could see her face clearly now, sunken cheeks and eyes, skin pale and furrowed. He saw where the bones, impatient, poked at her cheeks and chin. The eyes glossy but alive, restless and needful.

"You better find that fellow then," Parson said. "A fool like that don't come around often."

"It was my great-grandma's," the woman said, nodding at the churn, "so it's near seventy-five years old." She paused. "I guess I could take fifty for it."

Parson looked the churn over, lifted the dasher and inspected it as well. An antiques dealer in Asheville might give him a hundred.

"Twenty dollars," Parson said.

"That man on TV said . . ."

"You told me," Parson interrupted. "Twenty dollars is what I'll pay."

The woman looked at the churn a few moments, then back at Parson.

"Okay," she said.

She took the cash and stuffed the bills in her jeans. She did not leave.

"What?" Parson asked.

The woman hesitated, then raised her hands and took off her high school ring. She handed it to him, and Parson inspected it. "Class of 2000," the ring said.

"Ten," he said, laying the ring on her side of the glass counter.

She didn't try to barter this time but instead slid the ring across the glass as if it were a piece in a board game. She held a finger on the ring a few moments before holding out her palm.

By noon he'd had twenty customers and almost all were meth addicts. Parson didn't need to look at them to know. The odor of it came in the door with them, in their hair, their clothes, a smell like cat piss. Snow fell steady now and his business began slacking off, even the manic needs of the addicted deferring to the weather. Parson was finishing his lunch in the back room when the bell sounded again. He came out and found Sheriff Hawkins waiting at the counter.

"So what they stole now, Doug?" Parson asked.

"Couldn't it be I just come by to see my old high school buddy?"

Parson placed his hands on the counter.

"It could be, but I got the feeling it isn't."

"No," Hawkins said, smiling wryly. "In these troubled times there's not much chance to visit with friends and kin."

"Troubled times," Parson said. "But good for business, not just my business but yours."

"I guess that's a way of looking at it, though for me it's been too good of late."

Hawkins took a quick inventory of the bicycles and lawn mowers and chain saws filling the room's corners. Then he looked the room over again, more purposeful this time, checking behind the counter as well. The sheriff's brown eyes settled on the floor, where a shotgun lay amid other items yet to be tagged.

"That .410 may be what I'm looking for," the sheriff said. "Who brought it in?"

"Danny."

Parson handed the gun to the lawman without saying anything else. Hawkins held the shotgun and studied the stock a moment.

"My eyes ain't what they used to be, Parson, but I'd say them initials carved in it are SJ, not DP."

"That gun Steve Jackson's?"

"Yes, sir," the sheriff replied, laying the shotgun on the counter. "Danny took it out of Steve's truck yesterday. At least that's what Steve believed."

"I didn't notice the initials," Parson said. "I figured it came off the farm."

Hawkins picked the shotgun off the counter and held it in one hand, studying it critically. He shifted it slightly, let his thumb rub the stock's varnished wood.

"I think I can talk Steve out of pressing charges."

"Don't do that as a favor to me," Parson said. "If his own daddy don't give a damn he's a thief, why should I?"

"How come you to think Ray doesn't care?" Hawkins asked.

"Because Danny's been bringing things to me from the farm for months. Ray knows where they're going. I called him three months ago and told him myself. He said he couldn't do anything about it."

"Doesn't look to be you're doing much about it either," the sheriff said. "I mean, you're buying from him, right?"

"If I don't he'll just drive down to Sylva and sell it there."

Parson looked out at the snow, the parking lot empty but for his and Hawkins's vehicles. He wondered if any customers had decided not to pull in because of the sheriff's car.

"You just as well go ahead and arrest him," Parson added. "You've seen enough of these meth addicts to know he'll steal something else soon enough."

"I didn't know he was on meth," Hawkins said.

"That's your job, isn't it," Parson replied, "to know such things?"

"There's too many of them to keep up with. This meth, it ain't like other drugs. Even cocaine and crack, at least those were expensive and hard to get. But this stuff, it's too easy." The sheriff looked out the window. "This snow's going to make for a long day, so I'd better get to it."

"So you're not going to arrest him?"

"No," Hawkins said. "He'll have to wait his turn. There's two dozen in line ahead of him. But you could do me a favor by giving him a call. Tell him this is his one chance, that next time I'll lock his ass up." Hawkins pressed his lips together a moment, pensive. "Hell, he might even believe it."

"I'll tell him," Parson said, "but I'll do it in person."

Parson went to the window and watched as the sheriff backed out onto the two-lane and drove toward the town's main drag. Snow stuck to the asphalt now, the jeep blanketed white. He'd watched Danny drive away the day before, the tailgate down and truck bed empty. Parson had known the truck bed would probably be empty when Danny headed out of town, no filled grocery bags or kerosene cans, because the boy lived in a world where food and warmth and clothing were no longer important. The essentials were the red-and-white packs of Sudafed in the passenger's seat as the truck disappeared back into the folds of the higher mountains, headed up into Chestnut Cove, what Parson's father had called the back of beyond, the place where Parson and Ray had grown up.

He placed the pistol in his coat pocket and changed the OPEN sign to CLOSED. Once on the road, Parson saw the snow was dry, powdery, which would make the drive easier. He headed west and did not turn on the radio.

Except for two years in the army, Ray had lived his whole life in Chestnut Cove. He'd used his army pay to buy a farm adjacent to the one he'd grown up on and had soon after married Martha. Parson had joined the army as well but afterward went to Tuckasegee to live. When their parents had gotten too old to mend fences and feed livestock, plant and harvest the tobacco, Ray and Martha did it. Ray had never asked Parson to help, never expected him to, since he was twenty miles away. For his part, Parson had not been bitter when the farm was willed to the firstborn. Ray and Martha had earned it. By then Parson owned the pawnshop outright from the bank, had money enough. Ray and Martha sold their home and moved into the farmhouse, raised Danny and his three older sisters there.

Parson slowed as the road began a long curve around Brushy Mountain. The road soon forked and he went left. Another left and he was on a county road, poorly maintained because no wealthy Floridians had second homes on it. No guardrails. He met no other vehicle, because only a few people lived in the cove.

Parson parked beside Ray's truck and got out, stood a few moments before the homestead. He hadn't been here in nearly a year and supposed he should feel more than the burn of anger directed at his nephew. Some kind of nostalgia. But Parson couldn't summon it, and if he had, then what for? Working his ass off in August tobacco fields, milking cows on mornings so cold his hands numbed—the very things that had driven him away in the first place. Except for a thin ribbon of smoke unfurling from the chimney, the farm appeared forsaken. No cattle huddled against the snow, no TV or radio playing in the front room or kitchen. Parson had never regretted leaving, and never more so than now as his gaze moved from the rusting tractor and bailer to the sagging fences that held nothing in, settled on the shambling farmhouse itself, then turned toward the land between the barn and house.

Danny's battered blue-and-white trailer squatted in the pasture. Parson's feet made a whispery sound as he went to deal with his nephew before talking to his brother and sister-in-law. No footprints marked the snow between house and trailer. Parson knocked on the flimsy aluminum door and when no one answered went in. No lights were on and Parson wasn't surprised when he flipped a switch and nothing happened. His eyes slowly adjusted to the room's darkness, and he saw the card table, on it cereal boxes, some open, some not, a half-gallon milk container, its contents frozen solid. The room's busted-out window helped explain why. Two bowls scabbed with dried cereal lay on the table as well. Two spoons. Parson made his way to the back room, seeing first the kerosene heater beside the bed, the wire wick's muted orange glow. Two closely lumped mounds rose under a pile of quilts. Like they're already laid out in their graves, Parson thought as he leaned over and poked the bigger form.

"Get up, boy," Parson said.

But it was Ray's face and torso that emerged, swaddled in an array of shirts and sweaters. Martha's face appeared as well. They seemed like timid animals disturbed in their dens. For a few moments Parson could only stare at them. After decades in the most cynical of professions, he was amazed that anything could still stun him.

"Why in the hell aren't you in the house?" Parson asked finally.

It was Martha who replied.

"Danny, he's in there, sometimes his friends too." She paused. "It's just better, easier, if we're out here."

Parson looked at his brother. Ray was sixty-five years old but he looked eighty, his mouth sunk in, skinny and feeble. His sister-in-law appeared a little better off, perhaps because she was a large, big-boned woman. But they both looked bad—hungry, weary, sickly. And scared. Parson couldn't remember his brother ever being scared, but he clearly was. Ray's right hand clutched a quilt end, and the hand was trembling. Parson and his wife, DeAnne, had divorced before they'd had children. A blessing, he now saw, because it prevented any possibility of ending up like this.

Martha had not been above lording her family over Parson in the past, enough to where he'd made his visits rare and short. You missed out not having any kids, she'd said to him more than once, words he'd recalled times when Danny pawned a chain saw or posthole digger or some other piece of the farm. It said much of how beaten down Martha appeared that Parson mustered no pleasure in recalling her words now.

He settled his eyes on the kerosene heater emitting its feeble warmth.

"Yeah, it looks to be easier out here all right," he said.

Ray licked his cracked lips and then spoke, his voice raspy.

"That stuff, whatever you call it, has done made my boy crazy. He don't know nothing but a craving."

"It ain't his fault, it's the craving," Martha added, sitting up enough to reveal that she too wore layers of clothing. "Maybe I done something wrong raising him, petted him too much since he was my only boy. The girls always claimed I favored him."

"The girls been up here?" Parson asked. "Seen you like this?"

Martha shook her head.

"They got their own families to look after," she said.

Ray's lower lip trembled.

"That ain't it. They're scared to come up here."

Parson looked at his brother. He had thought this was going to be so much easier, a matter of twenty dollars, that and relaying the sheriff's threat.

"How long you been out here, Ray?"

"I ain't sure," Ray replied.

Martha spoke.

"Not more than a week."

"How long has the electricity been off?"

"Since October," Ray said.

"Is all you've had to eat on that table?"

Ray and Martha didn't meet his eyes.

A family photograph hung on the wall. Parson wondered when it had been put up, before or after Danny moved out. Danny was sixteen, maybe seventeen in the photo. Cocksure but also petulant, the expression of a young man who'd been indulged all his life. His family's golden child. Parson suddenly realized something.

"He's cashing your Social Security checks, isn't he?"

"It ain't his fault," Martha said.

Parson still stood at the foot of the bed, Ray and Martha showing no indication of getting out. They looked like children waiting for him to turn out the light and leave so they could go to sleep. Pawnbrokers, like emergency room doctors and other small gods, had to abjure sympathy. That had never been a problem for Parson. As DeAnne had told him several times, he was a man incapable of understanding another person's heart. You can't feel love, Parson, she'd said. It's like you were given a shot years ago and inoculated.

"I'll get your electricity turned back on," Parson told his brother. "Can you still drive?"

"I can drive," Ray said. "Only thing is, Danny uses that truck for his doings."

"That's going to change," Parson said.

"It ain't Danny's fault," Martha said again.

"Enough of it is," Parson replied.

He went to the corner and lifted the kerosene can. Half full.

"What you taking our kerosene for?" Martha asked.

Parson didn't reply. He left the trailer and trudged back through the snow, the can heavy and awkward, his breath quick white heaves. Not so different from those mornings he'd carried a gallon pail of warm milk from barn to house. Even as a child he'd wanted to leave this place. Never loved it the way Ray had. Inoculated.

Parson set the can on the lowered tailgate and perched himself on the hitched metal as well. He took the lighter and cigarettes from his coat pocket and stared at the house while he smoked. Kindling and logs brought from the woodshed littered the porch. No attempt had been made to stack it.

It would be easy to do, Parson told himself. No one had stirred when he'd driven up and parked five yards from the front door. No one had even peeked out a window. He could step up on the porch and soak the logs and kindling with kerosene, then go around and pour the rest on the back door. Hawkins would put it down as just another meth explosion caused by some punk who couldn't pass high school chemistry. And if others were in there, they were people quite willing to scare two old folks out of their home. No worse than setting fire to a woodpile infested with copperheads.

Parson finished his cigarette and flicked it toward the house, a quick hiss as snow quenched the smoldering butt.

He eased off the tailgate and stepped onto the porch, tried the doorknob, and when it turned, stepped into the front room. A dying fire glowed in the hearth. The room had been stripped of anything that could be sold, the only furnishing left a couch pulled up by the fireplace. Even wallpaper had been torn off a wall. The odor of meth infiltrated everything, coated the walls and floor.

Danny and a girl Parson didn't know lay on the couch, a quilt thrown over them. Their clothes were worn and dirty and smelled as if lifted from a dumpster. As Parson moved toward the couch he stepped over rotting sandwich scraps in paper sacks, candy wrappers, spills from soft drinks. If human shit had been on the floor he would not have been surprised.

"Who is he?" the girl asked Danny.

"A man who's owed twenty dollars," Parson said.

Danny sat up slowly, the girl as well, black stringy hair, flesh whittled away by the meth. Parson looked for something that might set her apart from the dozen or so similar women he saw each week. It took a few moments but he found one thing, a blue four-leaf clover tattooed on her forearm. Parson looked into her dead eyes and saw no indication luck had found her.

"Got tired of stealing from your parents, did you?" Parson asked his nephew.

"What are you talking about?" Danny said.

His eyes were light blue, similar to the girl's eyes, bright but at the same time dead. A memory of elementary school came to Parson of colorful insects pinned and enclosed beneath glass.

"That shotgun you stole."

Danny smiled but kept his mouth closed. Some vanity still left in him, Parson mused, remembering how the boy had preened even as a child, a comb at the ready in his shirt pocket, nice clothes.

"I didn't figure him to miss it much," Danny said. "That gas station he owns does good enough business for him to buy another."

"You're damn lucky it's me telling you and not the sheriff, though he'll be up here soon as the roads are clear."

Danny looked at the dying fire as if he spoke to it, not Parson.

"So why did you show up? I know it's not to warn me Hawkins is coming."

"Because I want my twenty dollars," Parson said.

"I don't have twenty dollars," Danny said.

"Then you're going to pay me another way."

"And what's that?"

"By getting in the truck," Parson said. "I'm taking your sorry ass to the bus station. One-way ticket to Atlanta."

"What if I don't want to do that?" Danny said.

There had been a time the boy could have made that comment formidable, for he'd been broad-shouldered and stout, an all-county tight end, but he'd shucked off fifty pounds, the muscles melted away same as his teeth. Parson didn't even bother showing him the revolver.

"Well, you can wait here until the sheriff comes and hauls your worthless ass off to jail."

Danny stared at the fire. The girl reached out her hand, let it settle on Danny's forearm. The room was utterly quiet except for a few crackles and pops from the fire. No time ticked on the fireboard. Parson had bought the Franklin clock from Danny two months ago. He'd thought briefly of keeping it himself but had resold it to the antiques dealer in Asheville.

"If I get arrested then it's an embarrassment to you. Is that the reason?" Danny asked.

"The reason for what?" Parson replied.

"That you're acting like you give a damn about me."

Parson didn't answer, and for almost a full minute no one spoke. It was the girl who finally broke the silence.

"What about me?"

"I'll buy you a ticket or let you out in Asheville," Parson said. "But you're not staying here."

"We can't go nowhere without our drugs," the girl said.

"Get them then."

She went into the kitchen and came back with a brown paper bag, its top half folded over and crumpled.

"Hey," she said when Parson took it from her.

"I'll give it back when you're boarding the bus," he said.

Danny looked to be contemplating something and Parson wondered if he might have a knife on him, possibly a revolver of his own, but when Danny stood up, hands empty, no handle jutted from his pocket.

"Get your coats on," Parson said. "You'll be riding in the back."

"It's too cold," the girl said.

"No colder than that trailer," Parson said.

Danny paused as he put on a denim jacket.

"So you went there first."

"Yes," Parson said.

A few moments passed before Danny spoke.

"I didn't make them go out there. They got scared by some guys that were here last week." Danny sneered then, something Parson suspected the boy had probably practiced in front of mirror. "I check on them more than you do," he said.

"Let's go," Parson said. He dangled the paper bag in front of Danny and the girl, then took the revolver out of his pocket. "I've got both of these, just in case you think you might try something."

They went outside. The snow still fell hard, the way back down to the county road now only a white absence of trees. Danny and the girl stood by the truck's tailgate, but they didn't get in. Danny nodded at the paper bag in Parson's left hand.

"At least give us some so we can stand the cold."

Parson opened the bag, took out one of the baggies.

He had no idea if one was enough for the both of them or not. He threw the packet into the truck bed and watched Danny and the girl climb in after it. No different than you'd do for two hounds with a dog biscuit, Parson thought, shoving the kerosene can farther inside and hitching the tailgate.

He got in the truck and cranked the engine, drove slowly down the drive. Danny and the girl huddled against the back window, their heads and Parson's separated by a quarter inch of glass. Their proximity made the cab feel claustrophobic, especially when he heard the girl's muffled crying. Parson turned on the radio, the one station he could pick up promising a foot of snow by nightfall. Then a song he hadn't heard in thirty years, Ernest Tubb's "Walking the Floor Over You." Halfway down Brushy Mountain the road made a quick veer and plunge. Danny and the girl slid across the bed and banged against the tailgate. A few moments later, when the road leveled out, Danny pounded the window with his fist, but Parson didn't look back. He just turned up the radio.

At the bus station, Danny and the girl sat on a bench while Parson bought the tickets. The Atlanta bus wasn't due for an hour so Parson waited across the room from them. The girl had a busted lip, probably from sliding into the tailgate. She dabbed her mouth with a Kleenex, then stared a long time at the blood on the tissue. Danny was agitated, hands restless, constantly shifting on the bench as though unable to find a comfortable position. He finally got up and came over to where Parson sat, stood before him.

"You never liked me, did you?" Danny said.

Parson looked up at the boy, for though in his twenties Danny was still a boy, would die a boy, Parson believed.

"No, I guess not," Parson said.

"What's happened to me," Danny said. "It ain't all my fault."

"I keep hearing that."

"There's no good jobs in this county. You can't make a living farming no more. If there'd been something for me, a good job I mean."

"I hear there's lots of jobs in Atlanta," Parson said. "It's booming down there, so you're headed to the land of no excuses."

"I don't want to go down there." Danny paused. "I'll die there."

"What you're using will kill you here same as Atlanta. At least down there you won't take your momma and daddy with you."

"You've never cared much for them before, especially Momma," Danny sneered. "How come you to care now?"

Parson thought about the question, mulled over several possible answers.

"I guess because no one else does," he finally said.

When the bus came, Parson walked with them to the loading platform. He gave the girl the bag and the tickets, then watched the bus groan out from under the awning and head south. There would be several stops before Atlanta, but Danny and the girl would stay aboard because of a promised two hundred dollars sent via Western Union. A promise Parson would not keep.

The Winn-Dixie shelves were emptied of milk and bread but enough of all else remained to fill four grocery bags. Parson stopped at Steve Jackson's gas station and filled the kerosene can. Neither man mentioned the shotgun now reracked against the pickup's back window.

The trip back to Chestnut Cove was slower, more snow on the roads, the visibility less as what dim light the day had left drained into the high mountains to the west. Dark by five, he knew, and it was already past four. After the truck slid a second time, spun, and stopped precariously close to a drop-off, Parson stayed in first gear. A trip of thirty minutes in good weather took him an hour.

When he got to the farmhouse, Parson took a flashlight from the dash, carried the groceries into the kitchen. He brought the kerosene into the farmhouse as well, then walked down to the trailer and went inside.

The heater's metal wick still glowed orange. Parson cut it off so the metal would cool.

He shone the light on the bed. They were huddled together, Martha's head tucked under Ray's chin, his arms enclosing hers. They were asleep and seemed at peace. Parson felt regret in waking them and for a few minutes did not. He brought a chair from the front room and placed it by the foot of the bed. He waited. Martha woke first. The room was dark and shadowy but she sensed his presence, turned and looked at him. She shifted to see him better and Ray's eyes opened as well.

"You can go back to the house now," Parson said.

They only stared back at him.

"He's gone," Parson said. "And he won't come back. There will be no reason for his friends to come either."

Martha stirred now, sat up in the bed.

"What did you do to him?"

"I didn't do anything," Parson said. "He and his girlfriend wanted to go to Atlanta and I drove them to the bus station."

Martha didn't look like she believed him. She got slowly out of the bed and Ray did as well. They put on their shoes, then moved tentatively to the trailer's door, seemingly with little pleasure. They hesitated.

"Go on," Parson said. "I'll bring the heater."

Parson went and got the kerosene heater. He stooped and lifted it slowly, careful to use his legs instead of his back. Little fuel remained in it, so it wasn't heavy, just awkward. When he came into the front room, his brother and sister-in-law still stood inside the door.

"Hold the door open," he told Ray, "so I can get this thing outside."

Parson got the heater down the steps and carried it the rest of the way. Once inside the farmhouse he set it near the hearth, filled the tank, and turned it on. He and Ray gathered logs and kindling off the front porch and got a good flame going in the fireplace. The flue wasn't drawing as it should. By the time Parson had adjusted it a smoky odor filled the room, but that was a better smell than the meth. The three of them sat on the couch and unwrapped the sandwiches. They did not speak even when they'd finished, just stared at the hearth as flame shadows trembled on the walls. Parson thought what an old human feeling this must be, how ten thousand years ago people would have done the same thing on a cold night, would have eaten, then settled before the fire, looked into it and found peace, knowing they'd survived the day and now could rest.

Martha began snoring softly and Parson grew sleepy as well. He roused himself, looked over at his brother, whose eyes still watched the fire. Ray didn't look sleepy, just lost in thought.

Parson got up and stood before the hearth, let the heat soak into his clothes and skin before going out into the cold. He took the revolver from his pocket and gave it to Ray.

"In case any of Danny's friends give you any trouble," Parson said. "I'll get your power turned back on in the morning."

Martha awoke with a start. For a few moments she seemed not to know where she was.

"You ain't thinking of driving back to Tuckasegee tonight?" Ray asked. "The roads will be dangerous."

"I'll be all right. My jeep can handle them."

"I still wish you wouldn't go," Ray said. "You ain't slept under this roof for near forty years. That's too long."

"Not tonight," Parson said.

Ray shook his head.

"I never thought things could ever get like this," he said. "The world, I just don't understand it no more."

Martha spoke.

"Did Danny say where he'd be staying?"

"No," Parson said, and turned to leave.

"I'd rather be in that trailer tonight and knowing he was in this house. Knowing where he is, if he's alive or dead," she said as Parson reached for the doorknob. "You had no right."

Parson walked out to the jeep. It took a few tries but the engine turned over and he made his way down the drive. Only flurries glanced the windshield now. Parson drove slowly and several times had to stop and get out to find the road among the white blankness. Once out of Chestnut Cove, he made better time, but it was after midnight when he got back to Tuckasegee. His alarm clock was set for seven thirty. Parson reset it for eight thirty. If he was late opening, a few minutes or even an hour, it wouldn't matter. Whatever time he showed up, they'd still be there.

LINCOLNITES

Lily sat on the porch, the day's plowing done and her year-old child asleep in his crib. In her hands, the long steel needles clicked together and spread apart in a rhythmic sparring as yarn slowly unspooled from the deep pocket of her gingham dress, became part of the coverlet draped over her knees. Except for the occasional glance down the valley, Lily kept her eyes closed. She inhaled the aroma of fresh-turned earth and dogwood blossoms. She listened to the bees humming around their box. Like the fluttering she'd begun to feel in her stomach, all bespoke the return of life after a hard winter. Lily thought again of the Washington newspaper Ethan had brought with him when he'd come back from Tennessee on his Christmas furlough, how it said the war would be over by summer. Ethan had thought even sooner, claiming soon as the roads were passable Grant would take Richmond and it would be done. Good as over now, he'd told her, but Ethan had still slept in the root cellar every night of the furlough and stayed inside during the day, his haversack and rifle by the back door, because Confederates came up the valley from Boone looking for Lincolnites like Ethan.

She felt the afternoon light on her face, soothing as the hum of the bees. It was good to finally be sitting, only her hands working, the child she'd set in the shade as she'd plowed now nursed and asleep. After a few more minutes, Lily allowed her hands to rest as well, laying the foot-long needles lengthways on her lap. Reason enough to be tired, she figured, a day breaking ground with a bull-tongue plow and draft horse. Soon enough the young one would wake and she'd have to suckle him again, then fix herself something to eat as well. After that she'd need to feed the chickens and hide the horse in the woods above the spring. Lily felt the flutter again deep in her belly and knew it was another reason for her tiredness. She laid a hand on her stomach and felt the slight curve. She counted the months since Ethan's furlough and figured she'd be rounding the homespun of her dress in another month.

Lily looked down the valley to where the old Boone toll road followed Middlefork Creek. Her eyes closed once more as she mulled over names for the coming child, thinking about how her own birthday was also in September and that by then Ethan would be home for good and they'd be a family again, the both of them young enough not to be broken by the hardships of the last two years. Lily made a picture in her mind of her and Ethan and the young ones all together, the crops she'd planted ripe and proud in the field, the apple tree's branches sagging with fruit.

When she opened her eyes, the Confederate was in the yard. He must have figured she'd be watching the road because he'd come down Goshen Mountain instead, emerging from a thick stand of birch trees he'd followed down the creek. It was too late to hide the horse and gather the chickens into the root cellar, too late to go get the butcher knife and conceal it in her dress pocket, so Lily just watched him approach, a musket in his right hand and a tote sack in the left. He wore a threadbare butternut jacket and a cap. A strip of cowhide held up a pair of ragged wool trousers. Only the boots looked new. Lily knew the man those boots had belonged to, and she knew the hickory tree where they'd left the rest of him dangling, not only a rope around his neck but also a cedar shingle with the word Lincolnite burned into the wood.

The Confederate grinned as he stepped into the yard. He raised a finger and thumb to the cap, but his eyes were on the chickens scratching for worms behind the barn, the draft horse in the pasture. He looked to be about forty, though in these times people often looked older than they were, even children. The man wore his cap brim tilted high, his face tanned to the hue of cured tobacco. Not the way a farmer would wear a hat or cap. The gaunt face and loose-fitting trousers made clear what the tote sack was for. Lily hoped a couple of chickens were enough for him, but the boots did not reassure her of that.

"Afternoon," he said, letting his gaze settle on Lily briefly before looking westward toward Grandfather Mountain. "Looks to be some rain coming, maybe by full dark."

"Take what chickens you want," Lily said. "I'll help you catch them."

"I plan on that," he said.

The man raised his left forearm and wiped sweat off his brow, the tote sack briefly covering his face. As he lowered his arm, his grin had been replaced with a seeming sobriety.

"But it's also my sworn duty to requisition that draft horse for the cause."

"For the cause," Lily said, meeting his eyes, "like them boots you're wearing."

The Confederate set a boot onto the porch step as though to better examine it.

"These boots wasn't requisitioned. Traded my best piece of rope for them, but I'm of a mind you already know that." He raised his eyes and looked at Lily. "That neighbor of yours wasn't as careful on his furlough as your husband."

Lily studied the man's face, a familiarity behind the scraggly beard and the hard unflinching gaze. She thought back to the time a man or woman from up here could go into Boone. A time when disagreement over what politicians did down in Raleigh would be settled in this county with, at worst, clenched fists.

"You used to work at Old Man Mast's store, didn't you?" Lily said.

"I did," the Confederate said.

"My daddy used to trade with you. One time when I was with him you give me and my sister a peppermint."

The man's eyes didn't soften, but something in his face seemed to let go a little, just for a moment.

"Old Mast didn't like me doing that, but it was a small enough thing to do for the chaps."

For a few moments he didn't say anything else, maybe thinking back to that time, maybe not.

"Your name was Mr. Vaughn," Lily said. "I remember that now."

The Confederate nodded.

"It still is," he said, "my name being Vaughn, I mean." He paused. "But that don't change nothing in the here and now, though, does it?"

"No," Lily replied. "I guess it don't."

"So I'll be taking the horse," Vaughn said, "lest you got something to barter for it, maybe some of that Yankee money they pay your man with over in Tennessee? We might could make us a trade for some of that."

"There ain't no money here," Lily said, telling the truth because what money they had she'd sewn in Ethan's coat lining. Safer there than anywhere on the farm, she'd told Ethan before he left, but he'd agreed only after she'd also sewn his name and where to send his body on the coat's side pocket. Ethan's older brother had done the same, the two of them vowing to get the other's coat home if not the body.

"I guess I better get to it then," Vaughn said, "try to beat this rain back to Boone."

He turned from her, whistling "Dixie" as he walked toward the pasture, almost to the split-rail fence when Lily told him she had something to trade for the horse.

"What would that be?" Vaughn asked.

Lily lifted the ball of thread off her lap and placed it on the porch's puncheon floor, then set the half-finished coverlet on the floor as well. As she got up from the chair, her hands smoothed the gingham around her hips. Lily stepped to the porch edge and freed the braid so her blonde hair fell loose on her neck and shoulders.

"You know my meaning," she said.

Vaughn stepped onto the porch, not speaking as he did so. To look her over, Lily knew. She sucked in her stomach slightly to conceal her condition, though his knowing she was with child might make it better for him. A man could think that way in these times, she thought. Lily watched as Vaughn silently mulled over his choices, including the choice he'd surely come to by now that he could just as easily have her and the horse both.

"How old are you?" he asked.

"Nineteen."

"Nineteen," Vaughn said, though whether this was or wasn't in her favor she did not know. He looked west again toward Grandfather Mountain and studied the sky before glancing down the valley at the toll road.

"Okay," he finally said, and nodded toward the front door. "Let's you and me go inside."

"Not in the cabin," Lily answered. "My young one's in there."

For a moment she thought Vaughn would insist, but he didn't.

"Where then?"

"The root cellar. It's got a pallet we can lay on."

Vaughn's chin lifted, his eyes seeming to focus on something behind Lily and the chair.

"I reckon we'll know where to look for your man next time, won't we?" When Lily didn't respond, Vaughn offered a smile that looked almost friendly. "Lead on," he said.

Vaughn followed her around the cabin, past the bee box and chopping block and the old root cellar, the one they'd used before the war. They followed the faintest path through a thicket of rhododendron until it ended abruptly on a hillside. Lily cleared away the green-leaved rhododendron branches she replaced each week and unlatched a square wooden door. The hinges creaked as the entrance yawned open, the root cellar's damp earthy odor mingling with the smell of the dogwood blossoms. The afternoon sun revealed an earthen floor lined with crocks of vegetables and honey, at the center a pallet and quilt. There were no steps, just a three-foot drop.

"And you think me stupid enough to go in there first?" Vaughn said.

"I'll go in first," Lily answered, and sat down in the entrance, dangling one foot until it touched the packed earth. She held to the door frame and eased herself inside, crouching low, trying not to think how she might be stepping into her own grave. The corn shucks rasped beneath her as she settled on the pallet.

"We could do it as easy up here," Vaughn said, peering at her from the entrance. "It's good as some old spider hole."

"I ain't going to dirty myself rooting around on the ground," Lily said.

She thought he'd leave the musket outside, but instead Vaughn buckled his knees and leaned, set his left hand on a beam. As he shifted his body to enter, Lily took the metal needles from her dress pocket and laid them behind her.

Vaughn set his musket against the earthen wall and hunched to take off his coat and unknot the strip of cowhide around his pants. The sunlight made his face appear dark and featureless as if in silhouette. As he moved closer, Lily shifted to the right side of the mattress to make room for him. Lily smelled tobacco on his breath as he pulled his shirt up to his chest and lay down on his back, fingers already fumbling to free his trouser buttons. His sunken belly was so white compared to his face and drab clothing it seemed to glow in the strained light. Lily took one of the needles into her hand. She thought of the hog she'd slaughtered last January, remembering how the liver wrapped itself around the stomach, like a saddle. Not so much difference in a hog's guts and a man's, she'd heard one time.

"Shuck off that dress or raise it," Vaughn said, his fingers on the last button. "I ain't got time to dawdle."

"All right," Lily said, hiking up her hem before kneeling beside him. She reached and grasped the needle. When Vaughn placed his thumbs between cloth and hips to pull down his trousers, Lily raised her right arm and fell forward, her left palm set against the needle's rounded stem so the steel wouldn't slip through her fingers. She plunged the steel as deep as she could. When the needle stalled a moment on the backbone, Lily pushed harder and the needle point scraped past bone and went the rest of the way through. She felt the smooth skin of Vaughn's belly and flattened both palms over the needle's stem. Pin him to the floor if you can, she told herself, pushing out the air in Vaughn's stomach as the needle point pierced the root cellar's packed dirt.

Vaughn's hands stayed on his trousers a moment longer, as though not yet registering what had happened. Lily scrambled to the entrance while Vaughn shifted his forearms and slowly raised his head. He stared at the needle's rounded stem that pressed into his flesh like a misplaced button. His legs pulled inward toward his hips, but he seemed unable to move his midsection, as if the needle had indeed pinned him to the floor. Lily took the musket and set it outside, then pulled herself out of the hole as Vaughn loosed a long lowing moan.

She watched from above, waiting to see if she'd need to figure out how to use the musket. After almost a minute, Vaughn's mouth grimaced, the teeth locking together like a dog tearing meat. He pushed himself backward with his forearms until he was able to slump his head and shoulders against the dirt wall. Lily could hear his breaths and see the rise of his chest. His eyes moved, looking her way now. Lily did not know if Vaughn could actually see her. He raised his right hand a few inches off the root cellar's floor, palm upward as he stretched his arm toward the entrance, as if to catch what light leaked in from the world. Lily closed and latched the cellar door, covered the entrance with the rhododendron branches before walking back to the cabin.

The child was awake and fretting. Lily went to the crib but before taking up the boy she pulled back the bedding and removed the butcher knife, placed it in her dress pocket. She nursed the child and then fixed herself a supper of cornbread and beans. As Lily ate, she wondered if the Confederate had told anyone in Boone where he was headed. Maybe, but probably he wouldn't have said which particular farm, wouldn't have known himself which one until he found something to take. Ponder something else, she told herself, and thought again of names for the coming child. Girl names, because Granny Triplett had already rubbed Lily's belly and told her this one would be a girl. Lily said those she'd considered out loud and again settled on Mary, because it would be the one to match her boy's name.

After she'd cleared the table and changed the child's swaddlings,

Lily set him in the crib and went outside, scattering shell corn for the chickens before walking back through the rhododendron to the root cellar. There was less light now, and when she peered though the slats in the wood door she could see just enough to make out Vaughn's body slumped against the earthen wall. Lily watched several minutes for any sign of movement, listened for a moan, a sigh, the exhalation of a breath. Only then did she slowly unlatch the door. Lily opened it a few inches at a time until she could see clearly. Vaughn's chin rested on his chest, his legs splayed out before him. The needle was still in his stomach, every bit as deep as before. His face was white as his belly now, bleached looking. She quietly closed the door and latched it softly, as if a noise might startle Vaughn back to life. Lily gathered the rhododendron branches and concealed the entrance.

She sat on the porch with the child and watched the dark settle in the valley. A last barn swallow swept low across the pasture and into the barn as the first drops of rain began to fall, soft and hesitant at first, then less so. Lily went inside, taking the coverlet and yarn with her. She lit the lamp and nursed the child a last time and put him back in the crib. The supper fire still smoldered in the hearth, giving some warmth against the evening's chill. It was the time of evening when she'd usually knit some more, but since she couldn't do that tonight Lily took the newspaper from under the mattress and sat down at the table. She read the article again about the war being over by summer, stumbling over a few words that she didn't know. When she came to the word Abraham, she glanced over at the crib. Not too long before I can call him by his name to anyone, Lily told herself.

After a while longer, she hid the newspaper again and lay down in the bed. The rain was steady now on the cabin's cedar shingles. The young one breathed steadily in the crib beside the bed. Rain hard, she thought, thinking of what she'd be planting first when daylight came. Bad as it was that it had happened in the first place, there'd been some luck in it too. At least it wasn't winter when the ground was hard as granite. She could get it done by noon, especially after a soaking rain, then rest a while before scattering the potato seeds, maybe even have time to plant some tomato and squash before supper.

INTO *the* GORGE

His great-aunt had been born on this land, lived on it eight decades, and knew it as well as she knew her husband and children. That was what she'd always claimed, and could tell you to the week when the first dogwood blossom would brighten the ridge, the first blackberry darken and swell enough to harvest. Then her mind had wandered into a place she could not follow, taking with it all the people she knew, their names and connections, whether they still lived or whether they'd died. But her body lingered, shed of an inner being, empty as a cicada husk.

Knowledge of the land was the one memory that refused to dissolve. During her last year, Jesse would step off the school bus and see his great-aunt hoeing a field behind her farmhouse, breaking ground for a crop she never sowed, but the rows were always straight, right-depthed. Her nephew, Jesse's father, worked in an adjoining field. The first few times, he had taken the hoe from her hands and led her back to her house, but she'd soon be back in the field. After a while neighbors and kin just let her hoe. They brought meals and checked on her as often as they could. Jesse always walked rapidly past her field. His great-aunt never looked up, her gaze fixed on the hoe blade and the dark soil it churned, but he had always feared she'd raise her eyes and acknowledge him, though what she might want to convey Jesse could not say.

Then one March day she disappeared. The men in the community searched all afternoon and into evening as the temperature dropped, sleet crackled and hissed like static. The men rippled outward as they lit lanterns and moved into the gorge. Jesse watched from his family's pasture as the held flames grew smaller, soon disappearing and reappearing like foxfire, crossing the creek and then on past the ginseng patch Jesse helped his father harvest, going deeper into land that had been in the family almost two hundred years, toward the original homestead, the place she'd been born.

They found his great-aunt at dawn, her back against a tree as if waiting for the searchers to arrive. But that was not the strangest thing. She'd taken off her shoes, her dress, and her underclothes. Years later Jesse read in a magazine that people dying of hypothermia did such a thing believing heat, not cold, was killing them. Back then, the woods had been communal, NO TRESPASSING signs an affront, but after her death neighbors soon found places other than the gorge to hunt and fish, gather blackberries and galax. Her ghost was still down there, many believed, including Jesse's own father, who never returned to harvest the ginseng he'd planted. When the park service made an offer on the homestead, Jesse's father and aunts had sold. That was in 1959, and the government paid sixty dollars an acre. Now, five decades later, Jesse stood on his porch and looked east toward Sampson Ridge, where bulldozers razed woods and pastureland for another gated community. He wondered how much those sixty acres were worth today. Easily a million dollars.

Not that he needed that much money. His house and twenty acres were paid for, as was his truck. The tobacco allotment earned less each year but still enough for a widower with grown children. Enough as long as he didn't have to go to the hospital or his truck throw a rod. He needed some extra money put away for that. Not a million, but some.

So two autumns ago Jesse had gone into the gorge, following the creek to the old homestead, then up the ridge's shadowy north face where his father had seeded and harvested his ginseng patch. The crop was there, evidently untouched for half a century. Some of the plants rose above Jesse's kneecaps, and there was more ginseng than his father could have dreamed of, a hillside spangled with bright yellow leaves, enough roots to bulge Jesse's knapsack. Afterward, he'd carefully replanted the seeds, done it just as his father had done, then walked out of the gorge, past the iron gate that kept vehicles off the logging road. A yellow tin marker nailed to a nearby tree said U.S. Park Service.

Now another autumn had come. A wet autumn, which was good for the plants, as Jesse had verified three days ago when he'd checked them. Once again he gathered the knapsack and trowel from the woodshed. He also took the .32-20 Colt from his bedroom drawer. Late in the year for snakes, but after days of rain the afternoon was warm enough to bring a rattler or copperhead out to sun.

He followed the old logging road, the green knapsack slung over his shoulder and the pistol in the outside pouch. Jesse's arthritic knees ached as he made the descent. They would ache more that night, even after rubbing liniment on them. He wondered how many more autumns he'd be able to make this trip. Till I'm seventy, Jesse figured, giving himself two more years. The ground was slippery from all the rain and he walked slowly. A broken ankle or leg would be a serious thing this far from help, but it was more than that. He wanted to enter the gorge respectfully.

When he got in sight of the homestead, the land leveled out, but the ground grew soggier, especially where the creek ran close to the logging road. Jesse saw boot prints from three days earlier. Then he saw another set, coming up the logging road from the other direction. Boot prints as well, but smaller. Jesse looked down the logging road but saw no hiker or fisherman. He kneeled, his joints creaking.

The prints appeared at least a day old, maybe more. They stopped on the road when they met Jesse's, then also veered toward the homestead. Jesse got up and looked around again before walking through the withered broom sedge and joe-pye weed. He passed a cairn of stones that once had been a chimney, a dry well covered with a slab of tin so rusty it served as more warning than safeguard. The boot prints were no longer discernible but he knew where they'd end. Led the son of a bitch right to it, he told himself, and wondered how he could have been stupid enough to walk the road on a rainy morning. But when he got to the ridge, the plants were still there, the soil around them undisturbed. Probably just a hiker, or a bird watcher, Jesse figured, that or some punk kid looking to poach someone's marijuana, not knowing the ginseng was worth even more. Either way, he'd been damn lucky.

Jesse lifted the trowel from the knapsack and got on his knees. He smelled the rich dark earth that always reminded him of coffee. The plants had more color than three days ago, the berries a deeper red, the leaves bright as polished gold. It always amazed him that such radiance could grow in soil the sun rarely touched, like finding rubies and sapphires on the gloamy walls of a cave. He worked with care but also haste. The first time he'd returned here two years earlier he'd felt a sudden coolness, a slight lessening of light as if a cloud had passed over the sun. Imagination, he'd told himself then, but it had made him work faster, with no pauses to rest.

Jesse jabbed the trowel into the loamy soil, probing inward with care so as not to cut the root, slowly bringing it to light. The root was a big one, six inches long, tendrils sprouting from the core like clay renderings of human limbs. Jesse scraped away the dirt and placed the root in the knapsack, just as carefully buried the seeds to ensure another harvest. As he crawled a few feet left to unearth another plant, he felt the moist dirt seeping its way through the knees of his blue jeans. He liked being this close to the earth, smelling it, feeling it on his hands and under his nails, the same as when he planted tobacco sprigs in the spring. A song he'd heard on the radio drifted into his head, a woman wanting to burn down a whole town. He let the tune play in his head and tried to fill in the refrain as he pressed the trowel into the earth.

"You can lay that trowel down," a voice behind Jesse said. "Then raise your hands."

Jesse turned and saw a man in a gray shirt and green khakis, a silver name tag on his chest and U.S. Park Service patch on the shoulder. Short blond hair, dark eyes. A young man, probably not even thirty. A pistol was holstered on his right hip, the safety strap off.

"Don't get up," the younger man said again.

Jesse did as he was told. The park ranger came closer, picked up the knapsack, and stepped away. Jesse watched as he opened the compartment with the ginseng root, then the smaller pouch. The ranger took out the .32-20 and held it in his palm. The gun had belonged to Jesse's grandfather and father before being passed on to Jesse. The ranger inspected it as he might an arrowhead or spear point he'd found.

"That's just for the snakes," Jesse said.

"Possession of a firearm is illegal in the park," the ranger said. "You've broken two laws, federal laws. You'll be getting some jail time for this."

The younger man looked like he might say more, then seemed to decide against it.

"This ain't right," Jesse said. "My daddy planted the seeds for this patch. That ginseng wouldn't even be here if it wasn't for him. And that gun, if I was poaching I'd have a rifle or shotgun."

What was happening didn't seem quite real. The world, the very ground he stood on, felt like it was evaporating beneath him. Jesse almost expected somebody, though he couldn't say who, to come out of the woods laughing about the joke just played on him. The ranger placed the pistol in the knapsack. He unclipped the walkie-talkie from his belt, pressed a button, and spoke.

"He did come back and I've got him."

A staticky voice responded, the words indiscernible to Jesse.

"No, he's too old to be much trouble. We'll be waiting on the logging road."

The ranger pressed a button and placed the walkie-talkie back on his belt. Jesse read the name on the name tag. Barry Wilson.

"You any kin to the Wilsons over on Balsam Mountain?"

"No," the younger man said. "I grew up in Charlotte."

The walkie-talkie crackled and the ranger picked it up, said okay, and clipped it back on his belt.

"Call Sheriff Arrowood," Jesse said. "He'll tell you I've never been in any trouble before. Never, not even a speeding ticket."

"Let's go."

"Can't you just forget this?" Jesse said. "It ain't like I was growing marijuana. There's plenty that do in this park. I know that for a fact. That's worse than what I done."

The ranger smiled.

"We'll get them eventually, old fellow, but their bulbs burn brighter than yours. They're not big enough fools to leave us footprints to follow."

The ranger slung the knapsack over his shoulder.

"You've got no right to talk to me like that," Jesse said.

There was still plenty of distance between them, but the ranger looked like he contemplated another step back.

"If you're going to give me trouble, I'll just go ahead and cuff you now."

Jesse almost told the younger man to come on and try, but he made himself look at the ground, get himself under control before he spoke.

"No, I ain't going to give you any trouble," he finally said, raising his eyes.

The ranger nodded toward the logging road.

"After you, then."

Jesse moved past the ranger, stepping through the broom sedge and past the ruined chimney, the ranger to his right, two steps behind. Jesse veered slightly to his left, moving so he'd pass close to the old well. He paused and glanced back at the ranger.

"That trowel of mine, I ought to get it."

The ranger paused too and was about to reply when Jesse took a quick step and shoved the ranger with two hands toward the well. The ranger didn't fall until one foot went through the rotten tin, then the other. As he did, the knapsack dropped from his hand. He didn't go all the way through, just up to his arms, his fingernails scraping the tin for leverage, looking like a man caught in muddy ice. The ranger's hands found purchase, one on a hank of broom sedge, the other on the metal's firmer edging. He began pulling himself out, wincing as the rusty tin tore cloth and skin. He looked at Jesse, who stood above him.

"You've really screwed up now," the ranger gasped.

Jesse bent down and reached not for the younger man's hand but his shoulder. He pushed hard, the ranger's hands clutching only air as he fell through the rotten metal, a thump and simultaneous snap of bone as the ranger hit the well's dry floor. Seconds passed but no other sound rose from the darkness.

The knapsack lay at the edge and Jesse snatched it up. He ran, not toward his farmhouse but into the woods. He didn't look back again but bear-crawled through the ginseng patch and up the ridge, his breaths loud pants.

Trees thickened around him, oaks and poplars, some hemlocks. The soil was thin and moist, and he slipped several times. Halfway up the ridge he paused, his heart battering his chest. When it finally calmed, Jesse heard a vehicle coming up the logging road and saw a pale-green park service jeep. A man and a woman got out.

Jesse went on, passing through another patch of ginseng, probable descendants from his father's original seedlings. The sooner he got to the ridge crest, the sooner he could make his way across it toward the gorge head. His legs were leaden now and he couldn't catch his breath. The extra pounds he'd put on the last few years draped over his belt, gave him more to haul. His mind went dizzy and he slipped and skidded a few yards downhill. For a while he lay still, his body sprawled on the slanted earth, arms and legs flung outward. Jesse felt the leaves cushioning the back of his head, an acorn nudged against a shoulder blade. Above him, oak branches pierced a darkening sky. He remembered the fairy tale about a giant beanstalk and imagined how convenient it would be to simply climb off into the clouds.

Jesse shifted his body so his face turned downhill, one ear to the ground as if listening for the faintest footfall. It seemed so wrong to be sixty-eight years old and running from someone. Old age was supposed to give a person dignity, respect. He remembered the night the searchers brought his great-aunt out of the gorge. The men stripped off their heavy coats to cover her body and had taken turns carrying her. They had been silent and somber as they came into the yard. Even after the women had taken the corpse into the farmhouse to be washed and dressed, the men had stayed on his great-aunt's porch.

Some had smoked hand-rolled cigarettes, others had bulged their jaws with tobacco. Jesse had sat on the lowest porch step and listened, knowing the men quickly forgot he was there. They did not talk of how they'd found his great-aunt or the times she'd wandered from her house to the garden. Instead, the men spoke of a woman who could tell you tomorrow's weather by looking at the evening sky, a godly woman who'd taught Sunday school into her seventies. They told stories about her and every story was spoken in a reverent way, as if now that his great-aunt was dead she'd once more been transformed back to her true self.

Jesse rose slowly. He hadn't twisted an ankle or broken an arm and that seemed his first bit of luck since walking into the gorge. When Jesse reached the crest, his legs were so weak he clutched a maple sapling to ease himself to the ground. He looked down through the cascading trees. An orange and white rescue squad van had now arrived. Workers huddled around the well, and Jesse couldn't see much of what they were doing but before long a stretcher was carried to the van. He was too far away to tell the ranger's condition, even if the man was alive.

At the least a broken arm or leg, Jesse knew, and tried to think of an injury that would make things all right, like a concussion so that the ranger forgot what had happened, or the ranger hurting bad enough that shock made him forget. Jesse tried not to think about the snapped bone being in the back or neck.

The van's back doors closed from within, and the vehicle turned onto the logging road. The siren was off but the beacon drenched the woods red. The woman ranger scoured the hillside with binoculars, sweeping without pause over where Jesse was. Another green park service truck drove up, two more rangers spilling out. Then Sheriff Arrowood's car, silent as the ambulance.

The sun lay behind Balsam Mountain now, and Jesse knew waiting any longer would only make it harder. He moved in a stupor of exhaustion, feet stumbling over roots and rocks, swaying like a drunk. When he got far enough, he'd be able to come down the ridge, ascend the narrow gorge mouth. But Jesse was so tired he didn't know how he could go any farther without resting. His knees grated bone on bone, popping and crackling each time they bent or twisted. He panted and wheezed and imagined his lungs an accordion that never unfolded enough.

Old and a fool. That's what the ranger had said. An old man no doubt. His body told him so every morning when he awoke. The liniment he applied to his joints and muscles made him think of himself as a creaky rust-corroded machine that must be oiled and warmed up before it could sputter to life. Maybe he was a fool after all, he acknowledged, for who other than a fool could have gotten into such a fix.

Jesse found a felled oak and sat down, a mistake because he couldn't imagine summoning the energy to rise. He looked through the trees. Sheriff Arrowood's car was gone, but the truck and jeep were still there. He didn't see but one person and knew the others searched the woods for him. A crow cawed farther up the ridge. Then no other sound, not even the wind. Jesse took the knapsack and pitched it into the thick woods below, watched it tumble out of sight. A waste, but he couldn't risk their searching his house. He thought about tossing the pistol as well but the gun had belonged to his father, his father's father before that. Besides, if they found it in his house that was no proof it was the pistol the ranger had seen. They had no proof of anything really. Even his being in the gorge was just the ranger's word against his. If he could get back to the house.

Night fell fast now, darkness webbing the gaps between tree trunks and branches. Below, high-beam flashlights flickered on. Jesse remembered two weeks after his great-aunt's burial. Graham

Sutherland had come out of the gorge shaking and chalk-faced, not able to tell what had happened until Jesse's father gave him a draught of whiskey. Graham had been fishing near the old homestead and glimpsed something on the far bank, there for just a moment. Though a sunny spring afternoon, the weather in the gorge had suddenly turned cold and damp. Graham had seen her then, moving through the trees toward him, her arms outstretched. Beseeching me to come to her, Graham had told them. Not speaking, but letting that cold and damp touch my very bones so I'd feel what she felt. She didn't say it out loud, maybe couldn't, but she wanted me to stay down there with her. She didn't want to be alone.

Jesse walked on, not stopping until he found a place where he could make his descent. A flashlight moved below him, its holder merged with the dark. The light bobbed as if on a river's current, a river running uphill all the way to the iron gate that marked the end of park service land. Then the light swung around, made its swaying way back down the logging road. Someone shouted and the disparate lights gathered like sparks returning to their source. Headlights and engines came to life, and two sets of red taillights dimmed and soon disappeared.

Jesse made his way down the slope, his body slantways, one hand close to the ground in case he slipped. Low branches slapped his face. Once on level land he let minutes pass, listening for footsteps or a cough on the logging road, someone left behind to trick him into coming out. No moon shown but a few stars had settled overhead, enough light for him to make out a human form.

Jesse moved quietly up the logging road. Get back in the house and you'll be all right, he told himself. He came to the iron gate and slipped under. It struck him only then that someone might be waiting at his house. He went to the left and stopped where a barbed-wire fence marked the pasture edge. The house lights were still off, like he'd left them. Jesse's hand touched a strand of sagging barbed wire and he felt a vague reassurance in its being there, its familiarity. He was about to move closer when he heard a truck, soon saw its yellow beams crossing Sampson Ridge. As soon as the pickup pulled into the driveway, the porch light came on. Sheriff Arrowood was on the porch, one of Jesse's shirts in his hand. Two men got out of the pickup and opened the tailgate. Bloodhounds leaped and tumbled from the truck bed, whining as the men gathered their leashes. He had to get back into the gorge, and quick, but his legs were suddenly stiff and unyielding as iron stobs. It's just the fear, Jesse told himself. He clasped one of the fence's rusty barbs and squeezed until pain reconnected his mind and body.

Jesse followed the land's downward tilt, crossed back under the gate. The logging road leveled out and Jesse saw the outline of the homestead's ruined chimney. As he came closer, the chimney solidified, grew darker than the dark around it, as if an unlit passageway into some greater darkness.

Jesse took the .32-20 from his pocket and let the pistol's weight settle in his hand. If they caught him with it, that was just more trouble. Throw it so far they won't find it, he told himself, because there's prints on it. He turned toward the woods and heaved the pistol, almost falling with the effort. The gun went only a few feet before thunking solidly against a tree, landing close to the logging road if not on it. There was no time to find the pistol, though, because the hounds were at the gorge head now, flashlights dipping and rising behind them. He could tell by the hounds' cries that they were already on his trail.

Jesse stepped into the creek, hoping that doing so might cause the dogs to lose his scent. If it worked, he could circle back and find the gun. What sparse light the stars had offered was snuffed out as the creek left the road and entered the woods. Jesse bumped against the banks, stumbled into deeper pockets of water that drenched his pants as well as his boots and socks. He fell and something tore in his shoulder.

But it worked. There was soon a confusion of barks and howls, the flashlights no longer following him but instead sweeping the woods from one still point. Jesse stepped out of the creek and sat down. He was shivering, his mind off plumb, every thought tilting toward panic. As he poured water from the boots, Jesse remembered his prints led directly from his house to the ginseng patch. They had ways of matching boots and their prints, and not just a certain foot size and make. He'd seen on a TV show how they could even match the worn part of the sole to a print. Jesse stuffed the socks inside the boots and threw them at the dark. Like the pistol they didn't go far before hitting something solid.

It took him a long time to find the old logging road, and even when he was finally on it he was so disoriented that he wasn't sure which direction to go. Jesse walked a while and came to a park campground, which meant he'd guessed wrong. He turned around and walked the other way. It felt like years had passed before he finally made it back to the homestead. A campfire now glowed and sparked between the homestead and the iron gate, men hunting Jesse huddled around it. The pistol lay somewhere near the men, perhaps found already. Several of the hounds barked, impatient to get back onto the trail, but the searchers had evidently decided to wait till morning to continue. Though Jesse was too far away to hear them, he knew they talked to help pass the time. They probably had food with them, perhaps coffee as well. Jesse realized he was thirsty and thought about going back to the creek for some water, but he was too tired.

Dew wet his bare feet as he passed the far edge of the homestead and then to the woods' edge where the ginseng was. He sat down, and in a few minutes felt the night's chill envelop him. A frost warning, the radio had said. He thought of how his great-aunt had taken off her clothes and how, despite the scientific explanation, it seemed to Jesse a final abdication of everything she had once been.

He looked toward the eastern sky. It seemed he'd been running a week's worth of nights, but he saw the stars hadn't begun to pale. The first pink smudges on the far ridge line were a while away, perhaps hours. The night would linger long enough for what would or would not come. He waited.

RETURN

His eyes sweep the clearing cut through the woods that is all the evidence that a dirt road lies beneath the snow. It had been raining that morning in Charlotte. Only when the bus groaned and sputtered into the high mountains above Lenoir did the first snowflakes flutter against the windshield like moths, sticking for a moment, then swept away by the wipers.

He swings the duffel bag across his back, wincing when the helmet's hard curve bangs his shoulder blade. He steps off the two-lane hardtop that leads to Boone, walks across Middlefork Bridge, the pool below muddy, its edges iced, then onto the snow-hidden road that leads home. His right hand clasps the jacket lapels tight against his neck as he begins the two-mile walk up the mountain.

It is good to see snow, good to be cold again. He wonders how many times he's made this walk in his head the last two years. Six hundred, seven hundred? Those nights he had lain in his tent, his bare chest covered with sweat, listening to the loud insect whir, the chatter of sniper fire and the occasional mortar round not far enough away, on those nights the only way he'd been able to fall asleep was to imagine he was here at the foot of Dismal Mountain. He knew the ocean had streams the same way land did.

He'd imagine one drop of water that had made its way from his home in North Carolina to the green waters of the South Pacific. He would follow that drop of water to its source, back around the tip of South America to the Gulf of Mexico, then up the Mississippi to the Ohio, then east to the New River, then Middlefork, then here at the foot of Dismal Mountain where the creek that began on his family's land became part of a river. In his mind he would pass his uncle's farmhouse, crossing over the creek the road followed all the way up the mountain. Sometimes in those walking dreams he would step off the dirt road and fish, for on those long, tropical nights he always imagined it was summer and he sweated as he walked or fished up the mountain toward home. He never made it all the way back. Somewhere between what his grandfather called the Boone toll road and his family's farmhouse, he would fall asleep.

Snowflakes cling to his lashes. He shakes them free and clasps the jacket collar tighter around his throat. It is getting dark and he looks at his wrist, forgetting his watch is gone, lost somewhere between the Philippines and North Carolina. He passes the meadow where he and his Uncle Roy used to rabbit hunt, then his uncle's farmhouse, the tractor that has not been used since June rusting in the barn. No light comes from the windows, his aunt probably staying with her daughter until warm weather.

He steps onto the bridge, beneath him the slow, deep run that always held a trout. The snow muffles his footsteps. The wind is dying, not even a whisper now, and the world is as quiet as the moments after the Japanese sniper fired at him from the tree. He remembers the man he shot and killed, the man who would have killed him had he aimed six inches lower.

He had not heard the shot, only felt the blow as the bullet hit his helmet. He fell to the ground, his face looking up straight into the face in the tree. It was as if they were underwater, everything silent and in slow motion. He watched the Japanese soldier eject the spent shell, take a bullet from his ammo belt. Then he raised his own rifle, still dazed, the rifle wavering in his hand as he emptied his clip. The Japanese soldier let the rifle slide from his hands, then fell through the branches, the thud as he hit the ground the first sound he'd heard since the bullet hit his helmet. He turned the Japanese soldier over and saw a small, silver cross dangling from a chain. He was surprised. Peterson, the medic, who'd been to college, claimed the Japanese only worshipped their emperor. But he should have known better than believe Peterson, who didn't even believe in God.

The front of the uniform was soaked with blood but the Japanese soldier was still alive. He was talking, his words strange and rapid like bursts of machine gun fire, but he could tell the man was saying the same thing, over and over. Maybe the man was cursing him for taking his life. But he didn't think that was it. There was no tone of anger or defiance. Perhaps the Japanese soldier was forgiving him, maybe even asking forgiveness for trying to kill him.

By this time the rest of the squad was beside them. Peterson kneeled and jerked open the soldier's shirt and peered in.

"What's he saying?" he asked Peterson.

"Hell if I know," Peterson replied, standing up. "He probably wants water. Most dying men do."

"I'll go back to camp and get some," he said.

"Don't bother, Hampton," Peterson said. "He'll be dead by the time you get back."

And he was.

"Here," Peterson said, raising a palm toward him that held the cross. "Your kill. If you don't want it Vincetti does."

He opened his hand and let the silver slide into his palm.

"I didn't check his pockets or his teeth," Peterson said. "You can do that but I'd hurry up. He's already starting to stink."

Peterson and the rest of the squad walked across the clearing to where a canopy of palm trees offered more shade.

He stayed, kneeling beside the Japanese soldier, his back to the other men. The man's mouth was closed. He wedged his fingers between the teeth and pried the man's mouth open enough to slip the cross under the man's rigid tongue. He closed the mouth and joined the rest of the squad.

"Find anything?" Peterson had asked.

"No," he'd said.

It is snowing harder now. He stumbles in a drift and almost falls. He is following the road by memory, for he can see only a few yards ahead. Although the creek runs close to the road here, he cannot see or hear it, but as the road curves left and the incline steepens he knows Big Rock is just below him. That is the name he and his little brother had given the chunk of granite large as a tank, the deep pool itself. That had been eight years ago, the summer before Joel died, the summer Joel hauled a sixteen-inch speckled trout from where the big rock dammed the stream, the biggest speckled trout anyone could remember being caught in Watauga County.

As he passes above where the deep pool and rock are, he remembers the last hours Joel lived, the way his mother kept cold poultices on his brother's burning forehead, raising the pale, sweating face to drink cups of water while his father knelt in the corner, face to the wall as he wept and prayed. When it was over two aunts bathed and dressed Joel's body for the funeral. His mother couldn't bear to do it.

He is breathing hard now, unused to the thin mountain air that grows thinner with each step farther up Dismal. In the Philippines the air had been so humid that it felt like he'd been breathing water instead of oxygen. He looks behind him, his footprints vanishing almost as quickly as he makes them. The last light is fading behind Dismal Mountain, and the near dark makes the snow seem tinged with blue.

He wonders if it is snowing in Minnesota. That's where Peterson is, probably still limping from the shrapnel that got him out of the war six months early. They had been a half mile from their base camp, and the Japanese mortar rounds were hitting so close the ground shuddered under their feet. Sergeant Meyers had yelled for them to deploy, and they'd hurried back through the jungle. Meyers and Peterson had been together when a mortar round screamed out of the sky and found them.

After the mortars stopped, he and the rest of the squad had come back to find them. Meyers was dead, sprawled against a tree. Peterson's knee was torn up. He'd already cleaned the wound himself when they got there. He looked up at them and grinned. Peterson told them it was a bad enough wound to get him off this piece-of-shit island and back home. He told them he'd limp the rest of his life but didn't give a damn because he wasn't planning to do much walking anyway. He'd finish med school and then spend his time in an office with a good-looking nurse.

The road curves away from the creek and levels out. He can see the black spire through the snow and trees, then the wooden building itself. He steps into the church yard, goes around to the back. He leans on the barbed wire fence post and looks into the graveyard. He squints and makes out Joel's gravestone. He sees the new stone near Joel's and for a moment cannot shake the uneasy feeling that it is his own, that he's really still in the Philippines, dreaming this, maybe even dying or dead. But it's his uncle's name on the stone, not his.

He steps back onto the road, passes Lawson Triplett's place and then crosses a plank bridge, the creek running swiftly below his feet. A ghost couldn't do that, he tells himself.

He knows there are mountains in Japan, some so high snow never melts on their peaks. He wonders if the man he killed was from those mountains, a farmer like himself, just as unused to the loud, humid island nights as he'd been—a man used to nights when all you heard was the wind. He wonders if the Japanese soldier's last thoughts were of home.

He trudges past Tom Watson's pasture, a little farther the big beech tree he and Joel had dared each other up as kids. The snow is easing some, and he can see better. The creek runs close to the road here, hardly more than a trickle now.

The road curves a last time. On the righthand side is the barbed wire fence that marks his family's land. He passes above the bottomland where he and his father will plant corn and tobacco in a few months. He imagines the rich black dirt buried deep and silent under the snow, how it's there waiting for spring's plow and seed to fill it with life. Like the dead, he thinks, waiting to be resurrected.

He sees the candle in the front window but he will wait a few minutes longer before he steps onto the porch. He walks across the yard to the spring. He kneels beside it, unknots the duffel bag and removes the helmet. He fills the helmet and drinks.

WAITING *for the* END *of the* WORLD

So it's somewhere between Saturday night and Sunday morning clockwise, and I'm in a cinder-block roadhouse called The Last Chance, and I'm playing "Free Bird" for the fifth time tonight but I'm not thinking of Ronnie Van Zant but an artist dredged up from my former life, Willie Yeats, and his line "surely some revelation is at hand." But the only rough beast slouching toward me is my rhythm guitar player, Sammy Griffen, who is down on all fours, weaving through the crowd of tables between the bathroom and stage.

One of the great sins of the sixties was introducing drugs to the good-ole-boy element of Southern society. If you were some Harvard psychology professor like Timothy Leary, drugs might well expand your consciousness, but they worked just the opposite way for people like Sammy, shriveling the brain to a reptilian level of aggression and paranoia.

There is no telling what Sammy has snorted or swallowed in the bathroom, but his pupils have expanded to the size of dimes. He passes a table and sees a bare leg, a female leg, and grabs hold. He takes off an attached high heel and starts licking the foot. It takes about three seconds for a bigger foot with a steel-capped toe to swing into the back of Sammy's head like a football player kicking an extra point. Sammy curls up in a fetal position and blacks out among the peanut shells and cigarette butts.

So now it's just my bass player Bobo Lingafelt, Hal Deaton, my drummer, and me. I finish "Free Bird" so that means the next songs are my choice. They got to have "Free Bird" at least once an hour, Rodney said when he hired me, saying it like his clientele were diabetics needing insulin. The rest of the time you play what you want, he'd added.

I turn to Bobo and Hal and play the opening chords of Gary Stewart's "Roarin' " and they fall in. Stewart was one of this country's neglected geniuses, once dubbed honky-tonk's "white trash ambassador from hell" by one of the few critics who bothered listening to him. His music is two centuries' worth of pent-up Appalachian soul, too intense and pure for Nashville, though they tried their best to pith his brain with cocaine, put a cowboy hat on his head, and make him into another talentless music-city hack. Stewart spent some of his last years hunkered down in a North Florida trailer park: no phone, not answering the door, every window of the hulk of rusting tin he called home painted black. Surviving on what songwriting residuals dribbled in from Nashville.

Such a lifestyle has its appeals, especially tonight as I look out at the human wreckage filling The Last Chance. One guy has his head on a table, eyes closed, vomit drooling from his mouth. Another pulls out his false teeth and clamps them on the ear of a gal at the next table. An immense woman in a purple jumpsuit is crying while another woman screams at her. And what I'm thinking is maybe it's time to halt all human reproduction. Let God or evolution or whatever put us here in the first place start again from scratch, because this isn't working.

Like Stewart, I too live in a trailer, but I have to leave it more often than I wish because I am not a musical genius, just a forty-year-old ex-high-school English teacher who has to make money, more than I get from a part-time job proofing copy for the weekly newspaper. Which is why I'm here from seven to two four nights a week, getting it done in the name of Lynyrd Skynyrd, alimony, and keeping the repo man away from my truck.

I will not bore you with the details of lost teaching jobs, lost wife, and lost child. Mistakes were made, as the politicos say. The last principal I worked for made sure I can't get a teaching job anywhere north of the Amazon rain forest. My ex-wife and my kid are in California. All I am to them is an envelope with a check in it.

Beyond the tables of human wreckage I see Hubert McClain sitting at the bar, beer in one hand and Louisville Slugger in the other. Hubert is our bouncer, two hundred and fifty pounds of atavistic Celtic violence coiled and ready to happen. On the front of the ball cap covering his survivalist buzz cut, a leering skeleton waves a sickle in one hand and a black-and-white checkered victory flag in the other. The symbolism is unclear, except that anyone wearing such a cap, especially while gripping a thirty-six-ounce ball bat, is not someone you want to displease.

Sitting beside Hubert is his best friend, Joe Don Byers, formally Yusef Byers before he had his first name legally changed. While it seems every white male between fourteen and twenty-five is trying to look and act black, Joe Don is going the opposite way, a twenty-three-year-old black man trying to be a Skoal-dipping, country-music-listening good ole boy. But like the white kids with their ball caps turned sideways and pants hanging halfway down their asses, Joe Don can't quite pull it off. The hubcap-sized belt buckle and snakeskin boots pass muster, but he wears his Stetson low over his right eye, the brim's rakish tilt making him look more like a cross-dressing pimp than a cowboy. His truck is another giveaway, a Toyota two-wheel drive with four mud grips and a Dale Earnhardt sticker on the back windshield, unaware that any true Earnhardt fan would rather ride a lawn mower than drive anything other than a Chevy.

On the opposite side of the bar, Rodney is taking whatever people hand him—crumpled bills, handfuls of nickels and dimes, payroll checks, wedding rings, wristwatches. One time a guy offered a gold filling he'd dug out of his mouth with a pocketknife. Rodney didn't even blink.

Watching him operate, it's easy to believe Rodney's simply an updated version of Flem Snopes, the kind of guy whose first successful business venture is showing photos of his naked sister to his junior high peers. But that's not the case at all. Rodney graduated from the University of South Carolina with a degree in social work. He wanted to make the world better, but, according to Rodney, the world wasn't interested.

His career as a social worker ended the same week it began. Rodney had borrowed a church bus to take some of Columbia's disadvantaged youth to a Braves game.

Halfway to Atlanta the teenagers mutinied. They beat Rodney with a tire iron, took his money and clothes, and left him naked and bleeding in a ditch. A week later, the same day Rodney got out of the hospital, the bus was found half submerged in the Okefenokee Swamp. It took another month to round up the youths, several of whom had procured entry-level positions in a Miami drug cartel.

Rodney says running The Last Chance is a philosophical statement. Above the cash register he's plastered one of those Darwinian bumper stickers with the fish outline and four evolving legs. Rodney's drawn a speech bubble in front of the fish's mouth. Exterminate the brutes, the fish says.

Advice Rodney seems to have taken to heart. There's only one mixed drink in The Last Chance, what Rodney calls the Terminator. It's six ounces of Jack Daniel's and six ounces of Surrey County moonshine and six ounces of Sam's Choice tomato juice. Some customers claim a dash of lighter fluid is added for good measure. No one, not even Hubert, has ever drunk more than three of these and remained standing. It usually takes only two to put the drinkers onto the floor, tomato juice dribbling down their chins like they've been shot in the mouth.

When we finish "Roarin'" only three or four people clap. A lot of the crowd doesn't know the song or, for that matter, who Gary Stewart was. Radio and music television have anesthetized them to the degree that they can't recognize the real thing, even when it comes from their own gene pool.

And speaking of gene pools, I suddenly see Everette Evans, the man who, to my immense regret, is twenty-five percent of the genetic makeup of my son. He's standing in the doorway, a camcorder in his hands. Everette lingers on Hubert a few seconds, then the various casualties of the evening before finally honing in on me.

I lay down the guitar and make my way toward the entrance. Everette's still filming until I'm right up on him. He jerks the camera down to waist level and points it at me like it's an Uzi.

"What are you up to, Everette?" I say.

He grins at me, though it's one of those grins that is one part malice and one part nervous, like a politician being asked to explain a hundred thousand dollars in small bills he recently deposited in the bank.

"We're just getting some additional evidence as to your parental fitness."

"I don't see no we," I say. "Just one old meddling fool who, if he still had one, should have his ass kicked."

"Don't you be threatening me, Devon," Everette says. "I might just start this camcorder up again and get some more incriminating evidence."

"And I just might take that camcorder and perform a colonoscopy on you with it. Your daughter doesn't seem to have a problem spending the money I make here."

"What's the problem, Devon?" Hubert says, walking over from the bar.

"This man's working for National Geographic," I tell Hubert. "They're doing a show on primitive societies, claiming people like us are the missing link between apes and humans."

"That's a lie," Everette says, his eyes on Hubert's ball bat.

"And that's only part of what this footage is for," I say. "This asshole's selling what the Geographic doesn't want to the Moral Majority. They'll shut this place down like it's a toxic waste site."

"We don't allow no filming in here," Hubert says, taking the camcorder from Everette's hands.

Hubert jerks out the tape and douses it with the half-drunk Terminator he's been sipping. Hubert strikes a match and drops the tape on the floor. In five seconds the tape looks like black Jell-O.

Everette starts backing out the door.

"You ain't heard the last of this, Devon," he vows.

Rodney lifts a bullhorn from under the bar and announces it's one forty-five and anybody who wants a last drink had better get it now. There are few takers, most customers now lacking money or consciousness. I'm thinking to finish up with Steve Earle's "Graveyard Shift" and Dwight Yoakam's "A Thousand Miles from Nowhere," but the drunk who's been using a pool of vomit for a pillow the last hour lifts his head. He fumbles a lighter out of his pocket and flicks it on.

"Free Bird," he grunts, and lays his head back in the vomit.

And I'm thinking, why not. Ronnie Van Zant didn't have the talent of Gary Stewart or Steve Earle or Dwight Yoakam, but he did what he could with what he had. Skynyrd never pruned their Southern musical roots to give them "national appeal," and that gave their music, whatever else its failings, an honesty and an edge.

So I take out the slide from my jean pocket and start that long wailing solo for probably the millionth time in my life. I'm on automatic pilot, letting my fingers take care of business while my mind roams elsewhere.

Heads rise from tables and stare my way. Conversations stop. Couples arguing or groping each other pause as well. And this is the way it always is, as though Van Zant somehow found a conduit into the collective unconscious of his race. Whatever it is, they become serious and reflective. Maybe it's just the music's slow surging build. Or maybe something more—a yearning for the kind of freedom Van Zant's lyrics deal with, a recognition of the human need to lay their burdens down. And maybe, for a few moments, being connected to the music and lyrics enough to actually feel unshackled, free and in flight.

As I finish "Free Bird" Rodney cuts on every light in the building, including some high-beam John Deere tractor lights he's rigged on the ceiling. It's like the last scene in a vampire movie. People start wailing and whimpering. They cover their eyes, crawl under tables, and ultimately—and this is the goal—scurry toward the door and out into the dark, dragging the passed-out and knocked-out with them.

I'm off the clock now, but I don't take off my guitar and unplug the amp. Instead, I play the opening chords to Elvis Costello's "Waiting for the End of the World." Costello has tried to be the second coming of Perry Como of late, but his first two albums were pure rage and heartbreak. Those first nights after my wife and child left, I listened to Costello and it helped. Not much, but at least a little.

Hal is draped over his drum set, passed out, and Bobo is headed out the door with the big woman in the purple jumpsuit. Sammy's still on the floor so I'm flying solo.

I can't remember all the lyrics, so except for the refrain it's like I'm speaking in tongues, but it's two a.m. in western Carolina, and not much of anything makes sense. All you can do is pick up your guitar and play. Which is what I'm doing. I'm laying down some mean guitar licks, and though I'm not much of a singer I'm giving all I got, and although The Last Chance is almost completely empty now that's okay as well because I'm merging the primal and existential and I've cranked up the volume so loud empty beer bottles are vibrating off tables and the tractor beams are pulsing like strobe lights and whatever rough beast is asleep out there in the dark is getting its wake-up call and I'm ready and waiting for whatever it's got.

BURNING BRIGHT

After the third fire in two weeks, the talk on TV and radio was no longer about careless campers. Not three fires. Nothing short of a miracle that only a few acres had been burned, the park superintendent said, a miracle less likely to occur again with each additional rainless day.

Marcie listened to the noon weather forecast, then turned off the TV and went out on the porch. She looked at the sky and nothing belied the prediction of more hot dry weather. The worst drought in a decade, the weatherman had said, showing a ten-year chart of August rainfalls. As if Marcie needed a chart when all she had to do was look at her tomatoes shriveled on the vines, the corn shucks gray and papery as a hornets' nest. She stepped off the porch and dragged a length of hose into the garden, its rubber the sole bright green among the rows. Marcie turned on the water and watched it splatter against the dust. Hopeless, but she slowly walked the rows, grasping the hose just below the metal mouth, as if it were a snake that could bite her. She thought of Carl, wondering if he'd be late again. She thought about the cigarette lighter he carried in his front pocket, a wedding gift she'd bought him in Gatlinburg.

When her first husband, Arthur, had died two falls earlier of a heart attack, the men in the church had come the following week and felled a white oak on the ridge. They'd cut it into firewood and stacked it on her porch. Their doing so had been more an act of homage to Arthur than of concern for her, or so Marcie realized the following September when the men did not come, making it clear that the church and the community it represented believed others needed their help more than a woman whose husband had left behind fifty acres of land, a paid-off house, and money in the bank.

Carl showed up instead. Heard you might need some firewood cut, he told her, but she did not unlatch the screen door when he stepped onto the porch, even after he explained that Preacher Carter had suggested he come. He stepped back to the porch edge, his deep-blue eyes lowered so as not to meet hers. Trying to set her at ease, she was sure, appear less threatening to a woman living alone. It was something a lot of other men wouldn't have done, wouldn't even have thought to do. Marcie asked for a phone number and Carl gave her one. I'll call you tomorrow if I need you, she said, and watched him drive off in his battered black pickup, a chain saw and red five-gallon gas can rattling in the truck bed. She phoned Preacher Carter after Carl left.

"He's new in the area, from down near the coast," the minister told Marcie. "He came by the church one afternoon, claimed he'd do good work for fair wages."

"So you sent him up here not knowing hardly anything about him?" Marcie asked. "With me living alone."

"Ozell Harper wanted some trees cut and I sent him out there," Preacher Carter replied. "He also cut some trees for Andy West. They both said he did a crackerjack job." The minister paused. "I think the fact he came by the church to ask about work speaks in his favor. He's got a good demeanor about him too. Serious and soft-spoken, lets his work do his talking for him."

She'd called Carl that night and told him he was hired.

Marcie cut off the spigot and looked at the sky one last time. She went inside and made her shopping list. As she drove down the half-mile dirt road, red dust rose in the car's wake. She passed the two other houses on the road, both owned by Floridians who came every year in June and left in September. When they'd moved in, Marcie had come calling with a homemade pie. The newcomers had stood in their doorways. They accepted the welcoming gift with a seeming reluctance, and did not invite her in.

Marcie turned left onto the blacktop, the radio on the local station. She went by several fields of corn and tobacco every bit as singed as her own garden. Before long she passed Johnny Ramsey's farm and saw several of the cows that had been in her pasture until Arthur died. The road forked and as Marcie passed Holcombe Pruitt's place she saw a black snake draped over a barbed-wire fence, put there because the older farmers believed it would bring rain. Her father had called it a silly superstition when she was a child, but during a drought nearly as bad as this one, her father had killed a black snake himself and placed it on a fence, then fallen to his knees in his scorched cornfield, imploring whatever entity would listen to bring rain.

Marcie hadn't been listening to the radio, but now a psychology teacher from the community college was being interviewed on a call-in show. The man said the person setting the fires was, according to the statistics, a male and a loner. Sometimes there's a sexual gratification in the act, he explained, or an inability to communicate with others except in actions, in this case destructive actions, or just a love of watching fire itself, an almost aesthetic response. But arsonists are always obsessive, the teacher concluded, so he won't stop until he's caught or the rain comes.

The thought came to her then, like something held underwater that had finally slipped free and surfaced. The only reason you're thinking it could be him, Marcie told herself, is because people have made you believe you don't deserve him, don't deserve a little happiness. There's no reason to think such a thing. But just as quickly her mind grasped for one.

Marcie thought of the one-night honeymoon in Gatlinburg back in April. She and Carl had stayed in a hotel room so close to a stream that they could hear the water rushing past. The next morning they'd eaten at a pancake house and then walked around the town, looking in the shops, Marcie holding Carl's hand. Foolish, maybe, for a woman of almost sixty, but Carl hadn't seemed to mind. Marcie told him she wanted to buy him something, and when they came to a shop called Country Gents, she led him into its log-cabin interior. You pick, she told Carl, and he gazed into glass cases holding all manner of belt buckles and pocketknives and cuff links, but it was a tray of cigarette lighters where he lingered. He asked the clerk to see several, opening and closing their hinged lids, flicking the thumbwheel to summon the flame, finally settling on one whose metal bore the image of a cloisonné tiger.

At the grocery store, Marcie took out her list and an ink pen, moving down the rows. Monday afternoon was a good time to shop, most of the women she knew coming later in the week. Her shopping cart filled, Marcie came to the front. Only one line was open and it was Barbara Hardison's, a woman Marcie's age and the biggest gossip in Sylva.

"How are your girls?" Barbara asked as she scanned a can of

beans and placed it on the conveyor belt. Done slowly, Marcie knew, giving Barbara more time.

"Fine," Marcie said, though she'd spoken to neither in over a month.

"Must be hard to have them living so far away, not hardly see them or your grandkids. I'd not know what to do if I didn't see mine at least once a week."

"We talk every Saturday, so I keep up with them," Marcie lied.

Barbara scanned more cans and bottles, all the while talking about how she believed the person responsible for the fires was one of the Mexicans working at the poultry plant.

"No one who grew up around here would do such a thing," Barbara said.

Marcie nodded, barely listening as Barbara prattled on. Instead, her mind replayed what the psychology teacher had said. She thought about how there were days when Carl spoke no more than a handful of words to her, to anyone, as far as she knew, and how he'd sit alone on the porch until bedtime while she watched TV, and how, though he'd smoked his after-supper cigarette, she'd look out the front window and sometimes see a flicker of light rise out of his cupped hand, held before his face like a guiding candle.

The cart was almost empty when Barbara pressed a bottle of hair dye against the scanner.

"Must be worrisome sometimes to have a husband strong and strapping as Carl," Barbara said, loud enough so the bag boy heard. "My boy Ethan sees him over at Burrell's after work sometimes. Ethan says that girl who works the bar tries to flirt with Carl something awful. Of course Ethan says Carl never flirts back, just sits there by himself and drinks his one beer and leaves soon as his bottle's empty." Barbara finally set the hair dye on the conveyor. "Never pays that girl the least bit of mind," she added, and paused. "At least when Ethan's been in there."

Barbara rang up the total and placed Marcie's check in the register.

"You have a good afternoon," Barbara said.

On the way back home, Marcie remembered how after the wood had been cut and stacked she'd hired Carl to do other jobs—repairing the sagging porch, then building a small garage—things Arthur would have done if still alive. She'd peek out the window and watch him, admiring the way he worked with such a fixed attentiveness.

Carl never seemed bored or distracted. He didn't bring a radio to help pass the time and he smoked only after a meal, hand-rolling his cigarette with the same meticulous patience as when he measured a cut or stacked a cord of firewood. She'd envied how comfortable he was in his solitude.

Their courtship had begun with cups of coffee, then offers and acceptances of home-cooked meals. Carl didn't reveal much about himself, but as the days and then weeks passed Marcie learned he'd grown up in Whiteville, in the far east of the state. A carpenter who'd gotten laid off when the housing market went bad, he'd heard there was more work in the mountains so had come west, all he cared to bring with him in the back of his pickup. When Marcie asked if he had children, Carl told her he'd never been married.

"Never found a woman who would have me," he said. "Too quiet, I reckon."

"Not for me," she told him and smiled. "Too bad I'm nearly old enough to be your mother."

"You're not too old," he replied in a matter-of-fact way, his blue eyes looking at her as he spoke, not smiling.

She expected him to be a shy and awkward lover, but he wasn't. The same attentiveness he showed in his work was in his kisses and touches, in the way he matched the rhythms of his movements to hers. It was as though his long silences made him better able to communicate in other ways. Nothing like Arthur, who'd been brief and concerned mainly with satisfying himself. Carl had lived in a run-down motel outside Sylva that rented by the hour or the week, but they never went there. They always made love in Marcie's bed. Sometimes he'd stay the whole night. At the grocery store and church there were asides and stares. Preacher Carter, who'd sent Carl to her in the first place, spoke to Marcie of "proper appearances." By then her daughters had found out as well. From three states away they spoke to Marcie of being humiliated, insisting they'd be too embarrassed to visit, as if their coming home was a common occurrence. Marcie quit going to church and went into town as little as possible. Carl finished his work on the garage but his reputation as a handyman was such that he had all the work he wanted, including an offer to join a construction crew working out of Sylva. Carl told the crew boss he preferred to work alone.

What people said to Carl about his and Marcie's relationship, she didn't know, but the night she brought it up he told her they should get married. No formal proposal or candlelight dinner at a restaurant, just a flat statement. But good enough for her. When Marcie told her daughters, they were, predictably, outraged. The younger one cried. Why couldn't she act her age, her older daughter asked, her voice scalding as a hot iron.

A justice of the peace married them and then they drove over the mountains to Gatlinburg for the weekend. Carl moved in what little he had and they began a life together. She thought that the more comfortable they became around each other the more they would talk, but that didn't happen. Evenings Carl sat by himself on the porch or found some small chore to do, something best done alone. He didn't like to watch TV or rent movies. At supper he'd always say it was a good meal, and thank her for making it. She might tell him something about her day, and he'd listen politely, make a brief remark to show that though he said little at least he was listening. But at night as she readied herself for bed, he'd always come in. They'd lie down together and he'd turn to kiss her good night, always on the mouth. Three, four nights a week that kiss would linger and then quilts and sheets would be pulled back. Afterward, Marcie would not put her nightgown back on. Instead, she'd press her back into his chest and stomach, bend her knees and fold herself inside him, his arms holding her close, his body's heat enclosing her.

Once back home, Marcie put up the groceries and placed a chuck roast on the stove to simmer. She did a load of laundry and swept off the front porch, her eyes glancing down the road for Carl's pickup. At six o'clock she turned on the news. Another fire had been set, no more than thirty minutes earlier. Fortunately, a hiker was close by and saw the smoke, even glimpsed a pickup through the trees. No tag number or make. All the hiker knew for sure was that the pickup was black.

Carl did not get home until almost seven. Marcie heard the truck coming up the road and began setting the table. Carl took off his boots on the porch and came inside, his face grimy with sweat, bits of sawdust in his hair and on his clothes. He nodded at her and went into the bathroom. As he showered, Marcie went out to the pickup. In the truck bed was the chain saw, beside it plastic bottles of twenty-weight engine oil and the red five-gallon gasoline can. When she lifted the can, it was empty.

They ate in silence except for Carl's usual compliment on the meal. Marcie watched him, waiting for a sign of something different in his demeanor, some glimpse of anxiety or satisfaction.

"There was another fire today," she finally said.

"I know," Carl answered, not looking up from his plate.

She didn't ask how he knew, since the radio in his truck didn't work. But he could have heard it at Burrell's as well.

"They say whoever set it drove a black pickup."

Carl looked at her then, his blue eyes clear and depthless.

"I know that too," he said.

After supper Carl went out to the porch while Marcie switched on the TV. She kept turning away from the movie she watched to look through the window. Carl sat in the wooden deck chair, only the back of his head and shoulders visible, less so as the minutes passed and his body merged with the gathering dusk. He stared toward the high mountains of the Smokies, and Marcie had no idea what, if anything, he was thinking about. He'd already smoked his cigarette, but she waited to see if he would take the lighter from his pocket, flick it, and stare at the flame a few moments. But he didn't. Not this night. When she cut off the TV and went to the back room, the deck chair scraped as Carl pushed himself out of it. Then the click of metal as he locked the door.

When he settled into bed beside her, Marcie continued to lie with her back to him. He moved closer, placed his hand between her head and pillow, and slowly, gently, turned her head so he could kiss her. As soon as his lips brushed hers, she turned away, moved so his body didn't touch hers. Marcie fell asleep but woke a few hours later. Sometime in the night she had resettled in the bed's center, and Carl's arm now lay around her, his knees tucked behind her knees, his chest pressed against her back.

As she lay awake, Marcie remembered the day her younger daughter left for Cincinnati, joining her sister there. I guess it's just us now, Arthur had said glumly. She'd resented those words, as if Marcie were some grudgingly accepted consolation prize. She'd also resented how the words acknowledged that their daughters had always been closer to Arthur, even as children. In their teens, the girls had unleashed their rancor, the shouting and tears and grievances, on Marcie. The inevitable conflicts between mothers and daughters and Arthur being the only male in the house—that was surely part of it, but Marcie also believed there'd been some difference in temperament as innate as different blood types.

Arthur had hoped that one day the novelty of city life would pale and the girls would come back to North Carolina. But the girls stayed up north and married and began their own families. Their visits and phone calls became less and less frequent. Arthur was hurt by that, hurt deep, though never saying so. He aged more quickly, especially after he'd had a stent placed in an artery. After that Arthur did less around the farm, until finally he no longer grew tobacco or cabbage, just raised a few cattle. Then one day he didn't come back for lunch. She found him in the barn, slumped beside a stall, a hay hook in his hand.

The girls came home for the funeral and stayed three days. After they left, there was a month-long flurry of phone calls and visits and casseroles from people in the community and then days when the only vehicle that came was the mail truck. Marcie learned then what true loneliness was. Five miles from town on a dead-end dirt road, with not even the Floridians' houses in sight. She bought extra locks for the doors because at night she sometimes grew afraid, though what she feared was as much inside the house as outside it. Because she knew what was expected of her—to stay in this place, alone, waiting for the years, perhaps decades, to pass until she herself died.

It was mid-morning the following day when Sheriff Beasley came. Marcie met him on the porch. The sheriff had been a close friend of Arthur's, and as he got out of the patrol car he looked not at her but at the sagging barn and empty pasture, seeming to ignore the house's new garage and freshly shingled roof. He didn't take off his hat as he crossed the yard, or when he stepped onto the porch.

"I knew you'd sold some of Arthur's cows, but I didn't know it was all of them." The sheriff spoke as if it were intended only as an observation.

"Maybe I wouldn't have if there'd been some men to help me with them after Arthur died," Marcie said. "I couldn't do it by myself."

"I guess not," Sheriff Beasley replied, letting a few moments pass before he spoke again, his eyes on her now. "I need to speak to Carl. You know where he's working today?"

"Talk to him about what?" Marcie asked.

"Whoever's setting these fires drives a black pickup."

"There's lots of black pickups in this county."

"Yes there are," Sheriff Beasley said, "and I'm checking out everybody who drives one, checking out where they were yesterday around six o'clock as well. I figure that to narrow it some."

"You don't need to ask Carl," Marcie said. "He was here eating supper."

"At six o'clock?"

"Around six, but he was here by five thirty."

"How are you so sure of that?"

"The five-thirty news had just come on when he pulled up."

The sheriff said nothing.

"You need me to sign something I will," Marcie said.

"No, Marcie. That's not needed. I'm just checking off folks with black pickups. It's a long list."

"I bet you came here first, though, didn't you," Marcie said. "Because Carl's not from around here."

"I came here first, but I had cause," Sheriff Beasley said. "When you and Carl started getting involved, Preacher Carter asked me to check up on him, just to make sure he was on the up and up. I called the sheriff down there. Turns out that when Carl was fifteen he and another boy got arrested for burning some woods behind a ball field. They claimed it an accident, but the judge didn't buy that. They almost got sent to juvenile detention."

"There've been boys do that kind of thing around here."

"Yes, there have," the sheriff said. "And that was the only thing in Carl's file, not even a speeding ticket. Still, his being here last evening when it happened, that's a good thing for him."

Marcie waited for the sheriff to leave, but he lingered. He took out a soiled handkerchief and wiped his brow. Probably wanting a glass of iced tea, she suspected, but she wasn't going to offer him one. The sheriff put up his handkerchief and glanced at the sky.

"You'd think we'd at least get an afternoon thunderstorm."

"I've got things to do," she said, and reached for the screen door handle.

"Marcie," the sheriff said, his voice so soft that she turned. He lifted his right hand, palm open as if to offer her something, then let it fall. "You're right. We should have done more for you after Arthur died. I regret that."

Marcie opened the screen door and went inside.

When Carl got home she said nothing about the sheriff's visit, and that night in bed when Carl turned and kissed her, Marcie met his lips and raised her hand to his cheek. She pressed her free hand against the small of his back, guiding his body as it shifted, settled over her. Afterward, she lay awake, feeling Carl's breath on the back of her neck, his arm cinched around her ribs and stomach. She listened for a first far-off rumble, but there was only the dry raspy sound of insects striking the window screen. Marcie had not been to church in months, had not prayed for even longer than that. But she did now. She shut her eyes tighter, trying to open a space inside herself that might offer up all of what she feared and hoped for, brought forth with such fervor it could not help but be heard. She prayed for rain.

The WOMAN WHO BELIEVED *in* JAGUARS

On the drive home from her mother's funeral, Ruth Welborn thinks of jaguars. She saw one once in the Atlanta Zoo and admired the creature's movements—like muscled water—as it paced back and forth, turning inches from the iron bars but never acknowledging the cage's existence. She had not remembered then what she remembers now, a memory like something buried in river silt that finally works free and rises to the surface, a memory from the third grade. Mrs. Carter tells them to get out their *History of South Carolina* textbooks. Paper and books shuffle and shift. Some of the boys snicker, for on the book's first page is a drawing of an Indian woman suckling her child. Ruth opens the book and sees a black-and-white sketch of a jaguar, but for only a moment, because this is not a page they will study today or any other day this school year. She turns to the correct page and forgets what she's seen for fifty years.

But now as she drives west toward Columbia, Ruth again sees the jaguar and the palmetto trees it walks through. She wonders why in the intervening decades she has never read or heard anyone else mention that jaguars once roamed South Carolina. Windows up, radio off, Ruth travels in silence. The last few days were made more wearying because she's had to converse with so many people. She is an only child, her early lifelong silences filled with books and games that needed no other players. That had been the hardest adjustment in her marriage—the constant presence of Richard, though she'd come to love the cluttered intimacy of their shared life, the reassurance and promise of "I'm here" and "I'll be back." Now a whole day can pass without her speaking a word to another person.

In her apartment for the first time in three days, Ruth drops her mail on the bed, then hangs up the black dress, nudges the shoes back into the closet's far corner. She glances through the bills and advertisements, but stops, as she always does, when she sees the flyer of a missing child. She studies the boy's face, ignoring the gapped smile. If she were to see him, he would not be smiling. Her lips move slightly as she reads of a child four-feet tall and eighty pounds, a boy with blond hair and blue eyes last seen in Charlotte. Not so far away, she thinks, and places it in a pocketbook already holding a dozen similar flyers.

No pastel sympathy cards brighten her mail. A personal matter, Ruth had told her supervisor, and out of deference or indifference the supervisor hadn't asked her to explain further. Though Ruth's worked in the office sixteen years, her coworkers know nothing about her. They do not know she was once married, once had a child. At Christmas the people she works with draw names, and every year she receives a sampler of cheeses and meats. She imagines the giver buying one for her and one for some maiden aunt. There are days at the office when Ruth feels invisible. Coworkers look right through her as they pass her desk. She believes that if she actually did disappear and the police needed an artist's sketch, none of them could provide a distinguishing detail.

Ruth walks into the living room, kneels in front of the set of encyclopedias on the bottom bookshelf. When she was pregnant, her mother insisted on making a trip to Columbia to bring a shiny new stroller, huge discount bags of diapers, and the encyclopedias bought years ago for Ruth.

They're for your child now, her mother had said. That's why I saved them.

But Ruth's child lived only four hours. She was still hazy from the anesthesia when Richard had sat on the hospital bed, his face pale and haggard, and told her they had lost the baby. In her drugged mind she envisioned a child in the new stroller, wheeled into some rarely used hospital hallway and then forgotten.

Tell them they have to find him, she'd said, and tried to get up, propping herself on her elbows for a moment before they gave way and darkness closed around her.

Richard had wanted to try again. We've got to move on with our lives, he'd said. But she'd taken the stroller and bags of diapers to Goodwill. In the end only Richard moved on, taking a job in Atlanta. Soon they were seeing each other on fewer and fewer weekends, solitude returning to her life like a geographical place, a landscape neither hostile nor welcoming, just familiar.

That their marriage had come apart was not unusual. All the books and advice columnists said so. Their marriage had become a tangled exchange of sorrow. Ruth knew now that it had been she, not Richard, who too easily had acquiesced to the idea that it always would be so, that solitude was better because it allowed no mirror for one's grief. They could have had another child, could have tried to heal themselves. She'd been the unwilling one.

Ruth rubs her index finger over the encyclopedia spines, reading the time-darkened letters like braille. She pulls the J volume out, a cracking sound as she opens it. She finds the entry, a black-and-white photograph of a big cat resting in a tree. Range: South and Central

America. Once found in Texas, New Mexico, Arizona, but now only rare sightings near the U.S.-Mexico border.

There is no mention of South Carolina, not even Florida. Ruth wonders for the first time if perhaps she only imagined seeing the jaguar in the schoolbook. Perhaps it was a mountain lion or bobcat. She shelves the encyclopedia and turns on her computer, types *jaguar South Carolina extinct* into the search engine. After an hour, Ruth has found three references to Southeast United States and several more to Florida and Louisiana, but no reference to South Carolina. She walks into the kitchen and opens the phone book. She calls the state zoo's main number and asks to speak to the director.

"He's not here today," the switchboard operator answers, "but I can connect you to his assistant, Dr. Timrod."

The phone rings twice and a man's voice answers.

Ruth is unsure how to say what she wants, unsure of what it is that she wants, other than some kind of confirmation. She tells her name and that she's interested in jaguars.

"We have no jaguar," Dr. Timrod says brusquely. "The closest would be in Atlanta."

Ruth asks if they were ever in South Carolina.

"In a zoo?"

"No, in the wild."

"I've never heard that," Dr. Timrod says. "I associate jaguars with a more tropical environment, but I'm no expert on big cats." His voice is reflective now, more curious than impatient. "My field is ornithology. Most people think parakeets are tropical too, but once they were in South Carolina."

"So it's possible," Ruth says.

"Yes, I guess it's possible. I do know buffalo were here. Elk, pumas, wolves. Why not a jaguar."

"Could you help me find out?"

As Dr. Timrod pauses, she imagines his office—posters of animals on the walls, the floor concrete just like the big cats' cages. Maybe a file cabinet and bookshelves but little else. She suspects the room reeks of pipe smoke.

"Maybe," Dr. Timrod says. "I can ask Leslie Winters. She's our large animal expert, though elephants are her main interest. If she doesn't know, I'll try to do a little research on it myself."

"Can I come by the zoo tomorrow to see what you've found?"

Dr. Timrod laughs. "You're rather persistent."

"Not usually," Ruth says.

"I'll be in my office from ten to eleven. Come then."

Ruth calls her office and tells the secretary she will be out one more day.

The needs of the dead have exhausted her. Too tired to cook or go out, Ruth instead finishes unpacking and takes a long bath. As she lies in the warm, neck-deep water, she closes her eyes and summons the drawing of the jaguar. She tries to remember more. Was the jaguar drawn as if moving or standing still? Were its eyes looking toward her or toward the end of the page? Were there parakeets perched in the palmetto trees above? She cannot recall.

Ruth does not rest well that night. She has trouble falling asleep and when she finally does she dreams of rows of bleached tombstones with no names, no dates etched upon them. In the dream one of these tombstones marks the grave of her son, but she does not know which one.

Driving through rush-hour traffic the next morning, Ruth remembers how she made the nurse bring her son to her when the drugs had worn off enough that she understood what lost really meant.

She'd looked into her child's face so she might never forget it, stroking the wisps of hair blond and fine as corn silk. Her son's eyes were closed. After a few seconds the nurse had gently but firmly taken the child from her arms. The nurse had been kind, as had the doctor, but she knows they have forgotten her child by now, that his brief life has merged with hundreds of other children who lived and died under their watch. She knows that only two people remember that child and that now even she has trouble recalling what he looked like and the same must be true for Richard. She knows there is not a single soul on earth who could tell her the color of her son's eyes.

At the zoo, the woman in the admission booth gives Ruth a map, marking Dr. Timrod's office with an X.

"You'll have to go through part of the zoo, so here's a pass," the woman says, "just in case someone asks."

Ruth accepts the pass but opens her pocketbook. "I may stay a while."

"Don't worry about it," the woman says and waves her in.

Ruth follows the map past the black rhino and the elephants, past the lost-and-found booth where the Broad River flows only a few yards from the concrete path. She walks over a wooden bridge and finds the office, a brick building next to the aviary.

Ruth is twenty minutes early so sits down on a nearby bench, light-headed with fatigue though she hasn't walked more than a quarter mile, all of it downhill. On the other side of the walkway a wire-mesh cage looms large as her living room. THE ANDEAN CONDOR IS THE LARGEST FLYING BIRD IN THE WORLD. LIKE ITS AMERICAN RELATIVES, VULTUR GRYPHUS IS VOICELESS, the sign on the cage says.

The condor perches on a blunt-limbed tree, its head and neck thick with wrinkles. When the bird spreads its wings, Ruth wonders how the cage can contain it. She lowers her gaze, watches instead the people who pass in front of her. Her stomach clenches, and she realizes she hasn't eaten since lunchtime yesterday.

She is about to go find a refreshment stand when she sees the child. A woman dressed in jeans and a blue T-shirt drags him along as if a prisoner, their wrists connected by a cord of white plastic. As they pass between her and the condor, Ruth stares intently at the blue eyes and blond hair, the pale unsmiling face. She estimates his height and weight as she fumbles with her pocketbook snap, sifts through the flyers till she finds the one she's searching for. She looks and knows it is him. She snaps the pocketbook shut as the woman and child cross the wooden bridge.

Ruth rises to follow and the world suddenly blurs. The wire mesh of the condor's cage wavers as if about to give way. She grips the bench with her free hand. In a few moments she regains her balance, but the woman and child are out of sight.

Ruth walks rapidly, then is running, the pocketbook slapping against her side, the flyer gripped in her hand like a sprinter's baton. She crosses the wooden bridge and finally spots the woman and child in front of the black rhino's enclosure.

"Call the police," Ruth says to the teenager in the lost-and-found booth. "That child," she says, gasping for breath as she points to the boy, "that child has been kidnapped. Hurry, they're about to leave."

The teenager looks at her incredulously, but he picks up the phone and asks for security. Ruth walks past the woman and child, putting herself between them and the park's exit. She does not know what she will say or do, only that she will not let them pass by her.

But the woman and child do not try to leave, and soon Ruth sees the teenager with two gray-clad security guards, guns holstered on their hips, jogging toward her.

"There," Ruth shouts, pointing as she walks toward the child. As

Ruth and the security guards converge, the woman in the blue T-shirt and the child turn to face them.

"What is this?" the woman asks as the child clutches her leg.

"Look," Ruth says, thrusting the flyer into the hands of the older of the two men. The security guard looks at it, then at the child.

"What is this? What are you doing?" the woman asks, her voice frantic now.

The child is whimpering, still holding the woman's leg. The security guard looks up from the flyer.

"I don't see the resemblance," he says, looking at Ruth.

He hands the flyer to his partner.

"This child would be ten years old," the younger man says.

"It's him," Ruth says. "I know it is."

The older security guard looks at Ruth and then at the woman and child. He seems unsure what to do next.

"Ma'am," he finally says to the woman, "if you could show me some ID for you and your child we can clear this up real quick."

"You think this isn't my child?" the woman asks, looking not at the security guards but at Ruth. "Are you insane?"

The woman shakes as she opens her purse, hands the security guard her driver's license, photographs of her family, and two Social Security cards.

"Momma, don't let them take me away," the child says, clutching his mother's knee more tightly.

The mother places her hand on her son's head until the older security guard hands her back the cards and pictures.

"Thank you, ma'am," he says. "I apologize for this."

"You should apologize, all of you," the woman says, lifting the child into her arms.

"I'm so sorry," Ruth says, but the woman has already turned and is walking toward the exit.

The older security guard speaks into a walkie-talkie.

"I was so sure," she says to the younger man.

"Yes, ma'am," the security guard replies, not meeting her eyes.

Ruth debates whether to meet her appointment or go home. She finally starts walking toward Dr. Timrod's office, for no better reason than it is downhill, easier.

When she knocks on the door, the voice she heard on the phone tells her to come in. Dr. Timrod sits at a big wooden desk. Besides a computer and telephone, there's nothing on the desk except some papers and a coffee cup filled with pens and pencils. A bookshelf is behind him, the volumes on it thick, some leatherbound. The walls are bare except for a framed painting of long-tailed birds perched on a tree limb, their yellow heads and green bodies brightening the tree like Christmas ornaments, *Carolina Paroquet* emblazoned at the bottom.

Dr. Timrod's youth surprises her. Ruth had expected gray hair, bifocals, and a rumpled suit, not jeans and a flannel shirt, a face unlined as a teenager's. A styrofoam cup fills his right hand.

"Ms. Welborn, I presume."

"Yes," she says, surprised he remembers her name.

He motions for her to sit down.

"Our jaguar hunt cost me a good bit of sleep last night," he says.

"I didn't sleep much myself," Ruth says. "I'm sorry you didn't either."

"Don't be," he says, and smirks. "Among other things I found out jaguars tend to be nocturnal. To study a creature it's best to adapt to its habits."

Dr. Timrod sips from the cup. Ruth smells the coffee and again feels the emptiness in her stomach.

"I talked to Leslie Winters yesterday before I left. She'd never heard of jaguars being in South Carolina, but she reminded me that her main focus is elephants, not cats. I called a friend who's researched fieldwork on jaguars in Arizona. He told me there's as much chance of a jaguar having been in South Carolina as a polar bear."

"So they were never here," Ruth says, and she wonders if there is anything left inside her mind she can believe.

"I'd say that's still debatable. When I got home last night, I did some searching on the computer. A number of sources said their range once included the Southeast. Several mentioned Florida and Louisiana, a few Mississippi and Alabama."

Dr. Timrod pauses and lifts a piece of paper off his desk.

"Then I found this."

He stands up and hands the paper to Ruth. The words *Florida, Georgia,* and *South Carolina* are underlined.

"What's strange is the source was a book published in the early sixties," Dr. Timrod says. "Not a more contemporary source."

"So people just forgot they were here," Ruth says.

"Well, it's not like I did an exhaustive search," Dr. Timrod says. "And the book that page came from could be wrong. Like I said, it's not an updated source."

"I believe they were here," Ruth says.

Dr. Timrod smiles and sips from the styrofoam cup.

"Now you have some support for your belief."

Ruth folds the paper and places it in her purse.

"I wonder when they disappeared from South Carolina?"

"I have no idea," Dr. Timrod says.

"What about them?" Ruth asks, pointing at the parakeets.

"Later than you'd think. There were still huge flocks in the mid-1800s. Audubon said that when they foraged the fields looked like brilliantly colored carpets."

"What happened?"

"Farmers didn't want to share the crops and fruit trees. A farmer with a gun could kill a whole flock in one afternoon."

"How was that possible?" Ruth asks.

"That's the amazing thing. They wouldn't abandon one another."

Dr. Timrod turns to his bookshelf, takes off a volume, and sits back down. He thumbs through the pages until he finds what he's looking for.

"This was written in the 1800s by a man named Alexander Wilson," Dr. Timrod says, and begins to read. "'Having shot down a number, some of which were only wounded, the whole flock swept repeatedly around their prostrate companions, and again settled on a low tree, within twenty yards of the spot where I stood. At each successive discharge, though showers of them fell, yet the affection of the survivors seemed rather to increase; for after a few circuits around the place, they again alighted near me.'"

Dr. Timrod looks up from the book.

"'The affection of the survivors seemed rather to increase,'" he says softly. "That's a pretty heartbreaking passage."

"Yes," Ruth says. "It is."

Dr. Timrod lays the book on the desk. He looks at his watch.

"I've got a meeting," he says, standing up. He comes around the desk and offers his hand.

"Congratulations. You may be on the cutting edge of South Carolina jaguar studies."

Ruth takes his hand, a stronger, more calloused hand than she'd have expected. Dr. Timrod opens the door.

"After you," he says.

Ruth stands up slowly, both hands gripping the chair's arms. She walks out into the bright May morning.

"Thank you," she says. "Thank you for your help."

"Good luck with your search," Dr. Timrod says.

He turns from her and walks down the pathway. Ruth watches him until he rounds a curve and disappears.

She walks the other way. When she comes to where the river is closest to the walkway, Ruth stops and sits on the bench. She looks out at the river, the far bank where the Columbia skyline rises over the trees.

The buildings crumble like sand and blow away. Green-and-yellow birds spangle the sky. Below them wolves and buffalo lean their heads into the river's flow. From the far shore a tree limb rises toward her like an outstretched hand. On it rests a jaguar, blending so well with its habitat that Ruth cannot blink without the jaguar vanishing. Each time it is harder to bring it back, and the moment comes when Ruth knows if she closes her eyes again the jaguar will disappear forever. Her eyes blur but still she holds her gaze. Something comes unanchored inside her. She lies down on the bench, settles her head on her forearm. She closes her eyes and she sleeps.

WHERE THE MAP ENDS

They had been on the run for six days, traveling mainly at night, all the while listening for the baying of hounds. The man, if asked his age, would have said forty-eight, forty-nine, or fifty—he wasn't sure. His hair was close-cropped, like gray wool stitched above a face dark as mahogany. A lantern swayed by his side, the twine securing it chafing the bullwhip scar ridging his left shoulder. With his right hand he clutched a tote sack. His companion was seventeen and of a lighter complexion, the color of an oft-used gold coin. The youth's hair was longer, the curls tinged red. He carried the map.

As foothills became mountains, the journey was more arduous. What food they'd brought had been eaten days earlier. They filled the tote with corn and okra from fields, eggs from a henhouse, apples from orchards. The land steepened more and their lungs never seemed to fill. I heard that white folks up here don't have much, the youth huffed, but you'd think they'd at least have air. The map showed one more village, Blowing Rock, then a ways farther a stream and soon a plank bridge. An arrow pointed over the bridge. Beyond that, nothing but blank paper, as though no word or mark could convey what the fugitives sought but had never known.

They had crossed the bridge near dusk. At the first cabin they came to, a hound bayed as they approached. They went on. The youth wondered aloud how they were supposed to know which place, which family, to trust. The fugitives passed a two-story farmhouse, prosperous looking. The older man said walk on. As the day waned, a cabin and a barn appeared, light glowing from a front window. Their lantern remained unlit, though now neither of them could see where he stepped. They passed a small orchard and soon after the man tugged his companion's arm and led him off the road and into a pasture.

"Where we going, Viticus?" the youth asked.

"To roost in that barn till morning," the man answered. "No folks want strangers calling in the dark."

They entered the barn, let their hands find the ladder, and then climbed into the loft. Through a space between boards the fugitives could see the cabin window's glow.

"I'm hungry," the youth complained. "Gimme that lantern and I'll get us some apples."

"No," his companion said. "You think a man going to help them that stole from him."

"Ain't gonna miss a few apples."

The man ignored him. They settled their bodies into the straw and slept.

A cowbell woke them, the animal ambling into the barn, a man in frayed overalls following with a gallon pail. A scraggly gray beard covered much of his face, some streaks of brown in his lank hair. He was thin and tall, and his neck and back bowed forward as if from years of ducking. As the farmer set his stool beside the cow's flank, a gray cat appeared and positioned itself close by. Milk spurts hissed against the tin. The fugitives peered through the board gaps. The youth's stomach growled audibly. I ain't trying to, he whispered in response to his companion's nudge.

When the bucket was filled, the farmer aimed a teat at the cat. The creature's tongue lapped without pause as the milk splashed on its face. As the farmer lifted the pail and stood, the youth shifted to better see. Bits of straw slipped through a board gap and drifted down. The farmer did not look up but his shoulders tensed and his hand clenched the pail tighter. He quickly left the barn.

"You done it now," the man said.

"He gonna have to see us sometime," the youth replied.

"But now it'll be with a gun aimed our direction," Viticus hissed. "Get your sorry self down that ladder."

They climbed down and saw what they'd missed earlier. "Don't like the look of that none," the youth said, nodding at the rope dangling from a loft beam.

"Then get out front of this barn," his companion said. "I want that white man looking at empty hands."

Once outside, they could see the farm clearly. Crop rows were weed choked, the orchard unpruned, the cabin itself shabby and small, two rooms at most. They watched the farmer go inside.

"How you know he got a gun when he hardly got a roof over his head?" the youth asked. "The Colonel wouldn't put hogs in such as that."

"He got a gun," the man replied, and set the lantern on the ground with the burlap tote.

A crow cawed as it passed overhead, then settled in the cornfield.

"Don't seem mindful of his crop," the youth said.

"No, he don't," the man said, more to himself than his companion.

The youth went to the barn corner and peeked toward the cabin. The farmer came out of the cabin, a flintlock in his right hand.

"He do have a gun and it's already cocked," the youth said. "Hellfire, Viticus, we gotta light out of here."

"Light out where?" his companion answered. "We past where that map can take us."

"Shouldn't never have hightailed off," the youth fretted. "I known better but done it. We go back, I won't be tending that stable no more. No suh, the Colonel will send me out with the rest of you field hands."

"This white man's done nothing yet," the man said softly. "Just keep your hands out so he see the pink."

But the youth turned and ran into the cornfield. Shaking tassels marked his progress. He didn't stop until he was in the field's center. The older fugitive grimaced and stepped farther away from the barn mouth. The farmer entered the pasture, the flintlock crooked in his arm. Any indication of his humour lay hidden beneath the beard. The older fugitive did not raise his hands, but he turned his palms outward.

The white man approached from the west. The sunrise made his eyes squint.

"I ain't stole nothing, mister," the black man said when the farmer stopped a few yards in front of him.

"That's kindly of you," the farmer replied. The dawn's slanted brightness made the white man raise a hand to his brow. "Move back into that barn so I can feature you better."

The black man glanced at the rope.

"Pay that rope no mind," the farmer said. "It ain't me put it up. That was my wife's doing."

The fugitive kept stepping back until both of them stood inside the barn. The cat reappeared, sat on its haunches watching the two men.

"Where might you hail from?" the farmer asked.

The black man's face assumed a guarded blankness.

"I ain't sending you back yonder if that's your fearing," the farmer said. "I've never had any truck with them that would. That's why you're up here, ain't it, knowing that we don't?"

The black man nodded.

"So where you run off from?"

"Down in Wake County, Colonel Barkley's home place."

"Got himself a big house with fancy rugs and whatnot, I reckon," the farmer said, "and plenty more like you to keep it clean and pretty for him."

"Yes, suh."

The farmer appeared satisfied. He did not uncock the hammer but the barrel now pointed at the ground.

"You know the way over the line to Tennessee?"

"No, suh."

"It ain't a far way but you'll need a map, especially if you want to stay clear of outliers," the white man said. "You get here last night?"

"Yes, suh."

"Did you help yourself to some of them apples?"

The black man shook his head.

"You got food in your tote there?"

"No, suh."

"You must be hungry then," the farmer said. "Get what apples you want. There's a spring over there too what if your throat's dry. I'll go to the cabin and fix you a map." The white man paused. "Fetch some corn to take if you like, and tell that othern he don't have to hide in there lest he just favors it."

The farmer walked back toward the cabin.

"Come out, boy," Viticus said.

The tassels swayed and the youth reappeared.

"You hear what he say?"

"I heard it," the youth answered and began walking toward the orchard.

They ate two apples each before going to the spring.

"Never tasted water that cold and it full summer," the youth said when he'd drunk his fill. "The Colonel say it snows here anytime and when it do you won't see no road nor nothing. Marster Helm's house-boy run off last summer, the Colonel say they found him froze stiff as a poker."

"You believing that then you're a chucklehead," Viticus said.

"I just telling it," the youth answered.

"Uh-huh," his elder said, but his eyes were not on the youth but something in the far pasture. Two mounds lay side by side, marked with a single creek stone. Upturned earth sprouted a few weeds, but only a few. The youth turned from the spring and looked as well.

"Lord God," he said. "This place don't long allow a body to rest easy."

"Come on," Viticus said.

The fugitives stepped back through the orchard and waited in front of the barn. The farmer was on his way back, a bucket in one hand and the flintlock in the other.

"Why come him to still haul that gun?" the youth asked.

The older man's lips hardly moved as he spoke.

"Cause he ain't fool enough to trust two strangers, specially after you cut and run."

The farmer's eyes were on the youth as he crossed the pasture. He set the bucket before them and studied the youth's face a few more moments, then turned to the older fugitive.

"There's pone and sorghum in there," the farmer said, and nodded at the bucket. "My daughter brung it yesterday. She's nary the cook her momma was, but it'll stash your belly."

"Thank you, suh," the youth said.

"I brung it for him, not you," the farmer said. The older fugitive did not move.

"Go ahead," the farmer said to him. "Just fetch that pone out the bucket and strap that sorghum on it."

"Thank you, suh," the older fugitive said, but he still did not reach for the pail.

"What?" the white man asked.

"If I be of a mind to share . . ."

The white man grimaced.

"He don't deserve none but it's your stomach to miss it, not mine."

The older fugitive took out a piece of the pone and the cistern of sorghum. He swathed the bread in syrup and offered it to the youth, who took it without a word. Neither sat in the grass to eat but remained standing. When they'd finished, the older fugitive set the cistern carefully in the bucket. He stepped back and thanked the farmer again but the farmer seemed not to hear. His blue eyes were on the youth.

"You belonged to this Colonel Barkley feller too?"

"Yes, suh," the youth said.

"Been on his place all your life."

"Yes, suh."

"And your momma, she been at the Colonel's awhile before you was born."

"Yes, suh."

The farmer nodded and let his gaze drift toward the barn a moment before resettling on the youth.

"The Colonel got red hair, has he?"

"You know the Colonel?" the youth asked.

"Naw, just his sort," the farmer answered. "You call him Colonel. Is he off to the war?"

"Yes, suh."

"And he is a Colonel, I mean rank?"

"Yes, suh," the youth answered. "The Colonel got him up a whole regiment to take north with him."

"A whole regiment, you say."

"Yes, suh."

The white man spat and wiped a shirtsleeve across his mouth.

"I done my damnedest to keep my boy from it," he said.

"There's places up here conscripters would nary have found him, but he set out over to Tennessee anyway. You know the last thing I told him?" The fugitives waited. "I told him if he got in the thick of it, look for them what hid behind the lines with fancy uniforms and plumes in their hats. Them's the ones to shoot, I said, cause it's them sons of bitches started this thing. That boy could drop a squirrel at fifty yards. I hope he kilt a couple of them."

The older fugitive hesitated, then spoke.

"He fight for Mr. Lincoln, do he?"

"Not no more," the farmer said.

To the west, the land rose blue and jagged. The older fugitive let his eyes settle on the mountains before turning back to the farmer. The youth settled a boot toe into the grass, scuffed a small indentation. They waited as they had always waited for a white man, be it overseer, owner, now this farmer, to finish his say and dismiss them.

"The Colonel," the farmer asked, "he up in Virginia now?"

"Yes, suh," the older fugitive said, "least as I know."

"Up near Richmond," the youth added. "That's what the Miss's cook heard."

The farmer nodded.

"Black niggers to do his work and now white niggers to do his fighting," he said.

The sun was full overhead now. Sweat beads glistened on the

white man's brow but he did not raise a hand to wipe them away. The youth cleared his throat while staring at the scuff mark he'd made on the ground. The farmer looked only at the older fugitive now.

"I need you to understand something and there's nary a way to understand it without the telling," the farmer said to the other man. "Them days after we got the word, I'd wake of the night and Dorcie wouldn't be next to me. I'd find her sitting on the porch, just staring at the dark. Then one night I woke up and she wasn't on the porch. I found her here in this barn."

The farmer paused, as if to allow some comment, but none came.

"Me and Dorcie got three daughters alive and healthy and their young ones is too. You'd figure that would've been enough for her. You'd think it harder on a father to lose his onliest son, knowing there'd be never a one to carry on the family name after you ain't around no more. But he was the youngest, and womenfolk near always make a fuss over a come-late baby. That rope there in the barn," the farmer said, lifting a Barlow knife from his overall pocket. "I've left it dangling all these months 'cause I pondered it for my ownself, but every time I made ready to use it something stopped me."

The farmer nodded at a ball of twine by the stable door and tossed the knife to the older fugitive.

"Cut off a piece of that twine nigh long as your arm."

The fugitive freed the blade from the elk-bone casing. He stepped into the barn's deep shadow and cut the twine. The farmer motioned with the flintlock.

"Tie his hands behind his back."

The other man hesitated.

"If you want to get to Tennessee," the farmer said, "you got to do what I tell you."

"I don't like none of this," the youth muttered, but he did not resist as his companion wrapped the rope twice around his wrists and secured it with a knot.

"Toss me my Barlow," the farmer said.

The older fugitive did, and the farmer slipped the knife into his front pocket.

"All right then," the farmer said, and nodded at the tote.

"You got fire?"

"Got flint," the other man said.

The farmer nodded and removed a thin piece of paper from his pocket.

"Bible paper. It's all I had." The older fugitive took the proffered paper and unfolded it.

"That X is us here," the farmer said, and pointed at a mountain to the west. "Head cross this ridge and toward that mountain. You hit a trail just before it and head right. There comes a creek soon and you go up it till it peters out. Climb a bit more and you'll see a valley. You made it then."

"And him?" the man said of the youth.

"Ain't your concern."

"It kindly is," the man said.

"Go on now and you'll be in Tennessee come nightfall."

The youth's shoulders were shaking. He looked at his companion and then at the white man.

"You got no cause to tie me up," the youth said. "I ain't gonna be no trouble. You tell him, Viticus."

"He'd not be much bother to take with me," the older fugitive said. "I promised his momma I'd look after him."

"You make the same promise to his father?" the farmer said and let his eyes settle on the older fugitive's shoulder. "From the looks of that scar, I'd notion you to be glad I'm doing it. I'd think every time you looked at that red hair of his you'd want to kill him yourself."

The two men met each other's eyes but neither spoke.

"I didn't mean to hide from you," the youth said, his breathing short and fast now. "I just seen that gun and got rabbity."

"Go on now," the farmer told the older fugitive.

Two hours later he came to the creek. The burlap tote hung over one shoulder and the lantern hung from the other. He began the climb. The angled ground was slick and he grabbed rhododendron branches to keep from tumbling back down.

There was no shingle or handbill proclaiming he'd entered Tennessee, but when he crested the mountain and the valley lay before him, he saw a wooden building below, next to it a pole waving the flag of Lincoln. He stood there in the late-afternoon light, absorbing the valley's expansiveness after days in the mountains. The land rippled out and appeared to reach all the way to where the sun and earth merged. He shifted the twine so it didn't rub the ridge of scar. Something furrowed his brow a few moments. Then he moved on and did not look back.

THOSE WHO *are* DEAD
are ONLY NOW FORGIVEN

The Shackleford house was haunted. In the skittering of leaves across its rotting porch, locals heard the whispered misery of ghosts. Footsteps creaked on stair boards and sobs filtered through walls. An Atlanta developer had planned to raze the house and turn the thirty acres into a retirement village. Then the economy flatlined.

The house continued to fold in on itself and the meandering dirt drive became rough as a logging trail. So we'll be completely alone, Lauren had told Jody. When Jody mentioned the ghost stories, Lauren told him she'd take care of that. Leave us the hell alone, she said loudly each time they stepped inside. They'd let their eyes adjust to the house's gloaming, listening for something other than their own breathing, then spread the sleeping bag on the floor, sometimes in a bedroom but as often in the front room. He and Lauren would undress and slide into the sleeping bag and whatever chill the old house held was vanquished by the heat of their bodies.

Lauren had always spoken her mind. You're not afraid to show you are intelligent, most boys from out in the county are, Lauren had told him in their first class together. She'd asked what Jody wanted to major in at college and he said engineering. Education, she answered when asked the same question. Ninth grade was when students from upper Haywood were bused to Canton to attend the county's high school. Unlike the other boys he'd grown up with, Jody didn't fill a seat in the school's vocational wing. Instead, he entered classrooms where most of the students came from town. Their parents weren't necessarily wealthy, but they'd grown up in families where college was an expectation. As Lauren said, he'd not been afraid to show his intelligence, but first only when called on. Then he'd begun raising his hand, occasionally answering a question even Lauren couldn't answer. The teachers had encouraged him, and by spring he and Lauren both were being recommended for summer programs at Chapel Hill and Duke for low-income students.

The boys he rode the bus with no longer invited him on hunting and fishing trips. Soon they didn't bother to speak. During the long bus trip to and from school, Jody saw them staring at the books he withdrew from his backpack, not just ones for class but books Lauren passed on, tattered paperbacks of *The Catcher in the Rye* and *The Hitchhiker's Guide to the Galaxy*, books from the library on astronomy and religion. It was an act of betrayal to some. One morning near the school year's end Billy Rankin tripped Jody in the cafeteria, sent him and his tray sprawling to the floor. Billy outweighed him by fifty pounds and Jody would have done nothing if Lauren hadn't been with him. He went after Billy, driving him onto the linoleum, praying a teacher would break it up quick. But it was Lauren who got to them first. By the time a teacher intervened, Lauren had broken off two fingernails shredding Billy's left cheek.

As he left the blacktop, Jody found the dirt drive more traveled than a year ago. Less broom sedge sprouted in the packed dirt, and fresh tire prints braided the road. What's left of her is at the Shackleford place, Trey, Lauren's brother, had finally told Jody. The dirt road straightened and climbed upward. Oak trees purpled with wisteria lined both sides. Dogwoods huddled in the understory, a few last blossoms clinging to their branches. The drive curved and the trees fell away. Bedsprings appeared in a ditch, beside them a shattered porcelain toilet and a washing machine. The debris looked like a tornado's aftermath.

Each time they'd driven here their senior year, Lauren had leaned into Jody's shoulder, her hand on his thigh. Those moments had been as good as the actual lovemaking—hours alone yet awaiting them. Afterward, they stayed in the sleeping bag and made plans for what they'd do once Jody graduated from college. We'll live in a warm faraway place like Costa Rica, Lauren would say. When he said it was too bad they'd taken French, Lauren answered that learning another new language would only make it better.

More debris lay scattered on the drive and in the ditches—beer and soft drink cans, plastic garbage bags spilling contents like burst piñatas. One last curve and the Shackleford place rose before him. Next to the porch, a battered Ford Taurus appeared not so much parked as stalled in the wheel-high grass. The house's front door stood open as if he were expected.

Jody stepped onto the porch but lingered in the doorway. First he saw the TV set inside the fireplace. A rock band filled the screen but the sound was off. Shoved close to the fireplace was a bright-red couch, occupied, three faces materializing in the dusty light. The odor of meth singed the air as Jody stepped inside. Mixed and cooked by Lauren, he knew. In high school Billy and Katie Lynn hadn't attempted Chemistry I, much less the advanced courses he and Lauren passed with A's.

"Come to get the good feeling with us, Mr. College?" Billy asked.

"No," Jody said, standing beside Lauren now. Billy pointed to a felt-lined church collection plate on the floor, among its sparse coins and bills a glass pipe and baggie.

"Well, you can at least make an offering." Katie Lynn laughed, her voice dry and harsh.

"Come on, buddy, have a seat," Billy said, making room. "We can have us a regular high school reunion."

Jody stared at Lauren. Five months had passed since he'd last seen her. He was unsure which unsettled him more, how much beauty she'd lost or how much remained.

"I think he's still sweet on you, girl," Katie Lynn said. Lauren looked up, her eyes glassy.

"You still sweet on me, Jody?"

He studied the room's demented furnishings. A couch and TV but no tables or chairs, the floor awash with everything from candy wrappers to a tangle of multihued Christmas lights. In a corner were some of Lauren's books, *The World's Great Religions*, *Absalom, Absalom*, a poetry anthology. Her computer too, its screen cracked. An orange extension cord snaked around the couch and disappeared into the kitchen. A generator, Jody realized, now hearing the machine's hum.

"Get the fire going, Billy," Lauren said, "so it'll be cozier." He changed the disk in the DVD player and orange flames flickered on the screen. Billy's linebacker shoulders were bony now, his chest sunken.

"Want me to turn up the sound?" Billy asked.

Lauren nodded and the fireplace crackled and hissed.

"We got room for you," Katie Lynn said, patting a space between her and Lauren, but Jody remained standing.

"I want you to go with me," Jody said.

"Go where, baby?" Lauren asked.

"Back home."

"Haven't you heard?" Lauren said. "Bad girls don't get to go home. They don't even get prayed for, at least that's what Trey says."

"Then go with me to Raleigh. We'll get an apartment."

"He wants to save you from us trashy folks," Katie Lynn said, "but we ain't so bad. That collection plate, we didn't break into church and steal it. Billy bought it at the flea market."

"You ought to save us from Lauren," Billy said. "She does the cooking around here, and just look at us. We're shucking off weight like Frosty the Snowman."

"Save us, Jody," Katie Lynn said. "We're melting. We're melting."

"Come outside with me," Jody said.

Lauren followed him onto the porch. In the afternoon light he saw the yellow tinge and wondered if they were using needles too. Hepatitis was common from what he'd read on the internet. Lauren's jeans hung loose on her hips, her teeth nubbed and discolored.

"No one would tell me where you were," Jody said. "At least you could have."

"This is the land beyond the cell phone or internet," Lauren said. "Isn't it nice that there are a few places left where that's true?"

"You could have called from town," Jody said. "Didn't you think about what it was like for me, not knowing where you were, if you were okay?"

"Maybe I was thinking of you," Lauren said, averting her eyes. "But you've found me. Mission accomplished so now you can move on."

"Why are you doing this?" Jody asked.

The question sounded lame, like something out of a book or movie Lauren would mock.

"Oh, you know me," Lauren said. "I've never been much for delayed gratification. I find what feels good and dive right in."

"This feels good," Jody said, "living out here with those two?"

"It allows me what I need to feel good."

"What will you do when you can't get what you need?" Jody asked. "What happens then?"

"The Lord provides," Lauren said softly. "Isn't that what we learned in church? Has being around all those atheist professors caused you to lose your faith, Jody, like Reverend Wilkinson's wife warned us about in Sunday school?" Lauren moved closer, leaned her head lightly against his chest though her arms stayed at her sides. He smelled the meth-soured clothes, the unwashed skin and hair.

"Does being here bring back good memories?" Lauren asked.

When Jody didn't answer, she pulled her head away. Smiling, she raised her hand to his cheek. The hand was warm, blood pulsing through it yet.

"It does for me," Lauren said, and withdrew her hand. "You know I would have called or e-mailed, baby, but out here there's no signal."

"Come with me right now; don't even go back in there," Jody said. "You don't have to pack a thing. I've got money to buy you clothes, whatever else. We'll go straight to Raleigh right now."

"I can't leave, baby," Lauren said.

"Yes, you can," Jody said. "You're the one who showed me how to."

Katie Lynn came to the door.

"We need you to do some cooking, hon."

"Okay," Lauren said, and turned back to Jody. "I've got to go."

"I'll be back," he said.

Lauren paused in the doorway. "You probably shouldn't," she said, and went on inside.

Jody got back in the truck and drove toward town. If we make good enough grades, we can leave here, Lauren had told him. For the first three years of high school, he and Lauren made A's in the college-prep classes. They shared the academic awards, though Lauren could have won them all if she'd wanted to. Their junior year, she made the highest SAT score in the school. That summer Lauren cashiered at Wal-Mart while Jody worked with his sister and mother at the poultry plant. He used the money for a down payment on the pickup. They'd pile it with belongings when he and Lauren left Canton for college.

In the fall of their senior year, Lauren completed the financial-aid forms Ms. Trexler, the guidance counselor, gave them. Lauren and Jody continued to work afternoons and Saturdays, making money for what the scholarships wouldn't cover. Then one day in November Lauren told him she'd changed her mind. When neither he nor Ms. Trexler could sway her, Jody told her it was okay, that an engineer made good money, enough for them both. All Lauren had to do was wait four years and they could leave Canton forever, leave a life where checkbooks never quite balanced and repo men and pawn-brokers loomed one turn of bad luck away. Jody had watched other classmates, including many in college prep, enter such a life with an impatient fatalism. They got pregnant or arrested or simply dropped out. Some boys, more defiant, filled the junkyards with crushed metal. Crosses garlanded with flowers and keepsakes marked road-sides where they'd died. You could see it coming in the smirking yearbook photos they left behind.

Soon after he'd left for college, Lauren got fired for cursing a customer and took work at the poultry plant. Jody drove back to Canton once a month. Though phone calls and e-mails kept them connected, it seemed forever before Christmas break arrived. That first night back home, he'd picked Lauren up at her mother's house and they had gone to a party. Jody expected alcohol and marijuana, some pills. What surprised him was the meth, and how casually Lauren took the offered pipe. When Billy asked if Jody wanted to try it, he shook his head. Once back at school their e-mails and phone conversations became fewer, shorter. He'd seen Lauren only once, in late January.

She'd lost weight and also lost her job. At spring break, Trey told him Lauren was in Charlotte and could have no visitors. Then Jody had heard nothing. When Jody entered Winn-Dixie, Trey was help-ing a customer. He finished and came over to where Jody waited. Trey offered his hand after wiping it on his stained green apron.

"So you've finished your semester?"

"Yes," Jody answered.

"I bet you made good grades, didn't you?"

Jody nodded.

"Maybe you'll inspire some kids around here to have a bit of ambi-tion," Trey said. "What about this summer?"

"The school offered me a job in the library, but I think I'll live with Mom and slice up chickens."

"Why the hell do that?" Trey asked.

"Tuition's up again. Even with the scholarships, I'll have to get another loan. No rent and better pay if I stay here."

"They don't make it easy for a mountain boy, do they?" Trey said.

"No," Jody said.

"How's your sister?" Trey asked.

"Okay, I guess, considering."

"I heard they got Jeff for nonsupport," Trey said. "What a worth-less asshole, always was. When Karen started going with him, I told her she was setting her sights way too low. You and her both tended to do that."

Trey turned to see if a customer lingered in his area.

"I went up to the Shackleford place," Jody said, and Trey gri-maced.

"I knew I shouldn't have told you. I thought you had sense enough not to."

"I hadn't heard from her in over two months," Jody said.

"So now you've seen her and know not to go back," Trey said.

"Can't you do something?"

"Like what?" Trey said. "Talk to her? Pray for her? I did that.

I'm the one who went out there and got her in February, drove her to Charlotte. Three weeks, five thousand dollars. I paid half and Momma paid half."

"The law, they've got to know they're out there," Jody said. "I'd rather see her in jail than where she is."

"Six months, since they aren't dealing, Sheriff Hunnicut said, and that's with a so-called tough judge. Soon as she got out she'd be back out there."

"You can't know that," Jody said.

"Yes I can. She might have had a chance in February, but stay on that shit long as she has now and it ain't a choice. Your brain's been rewired. Besides, Hunnicut's got his hands full rounding up the ones so sorry they let their own babies breathe it, them and the ones selling to the high school kids."

"So you've given up on her, you and your momma both?" Jody asked.

"Sheriff Hunnicut told me he used to wonder why he never saw any rats inside a meth house. I mean, filth all over the place you'd expect them. Then he realized the rats were smart enough to stay clear. Think about that."

"What happened to your father at the power plant, the way it happened . . ."

Trey's face reddened.

"If she's using that as an excuse, then she's even sorrier than I thought. Momma and I had as hard a time with Daddy dying. We hold down jobs, act responsible."

"Lauren didn't say it," Jody answered. "I'm saying it."

"She had a daddy a lot longer than you did and you're doing good as anyone around here," Trey said. "That Trexler woman always put on about how smart Lauren was, such and such an IQ, such and such an SAT score. But I never saw much smarts in the decisions she made. I figured her to end up pregnant before finishing high school. Look, she'd have gotten where she is now a lot quicker if it hadn't been for you. You and me both, we've done more for her than she deserves." A customer called for Trey to weigh some produce. "Stay in Raleigh," Trey said. "This place is like a spider's web. You stay long enough you'll get stuck in it for good. You'll end up like her. Or me."

As he pulled out of the lot, Jody remembered the afternoon before he left for college, the last time he and Lauren went to the Shackleford house. After they'd made love, Lauren took his hand and led him upstairs, where they'd never been before. In a back bedroom were a bureau and mirror, a cardboard funeral-home fan, and a child's wooden rocking horse. Lauren had asked Jody if he knew why the house was supposedly haunted. He didn't, only that something had happened and it had been bad. As they went down the stairs, Lauren had turned to him. When I've dared them to show themselves, she had told him, I always hoped they would.

Supper was ready when Jody got back to his mother's house. Karen had come over with Jody's niece, Chrystal. His sister's hands were red and raw from deboning chicken carcasses and when she spoke to the child, there was harshness even when not chiding her.

"Have some corn, Jody," his mother said, lifting the bowl more with palms than fingers. When Jody was growing up, there'd been evenings after work when his mother could barely wring a washcloth. Her fingers froze up and pain radiated from her hands to her shoulders and neck. After she'd had to quit the poultry plant and became a waitress, the pain lessened, but the fingers still curled inward.

"Hard to believe it's already May," Jody's mother said. "Just three more years and you'll be a college graduate."

"And then gone from here for good," Karen said. "Little brother always knew what he wanted. I thought I did, but I confused a hard dick for love."

"Don't talk like that," their mother said, "especially in front of a child."

"Why not, Mom?" Karen answered. "You made the same mistake."

Their mother flinched.

"Too bad you didn't knock up Lauren in high school," Karen said to Jody. "You could have taken off like Daddy did. Kept up the tradition."

"I wouldn't have done that," Jody answered.

"No?" Karen said. "I guess we'll never know, will we, little brother."

"Please," their mother said softly. "Let's talk about something else."

"Lauren didn't last long at the plant," Karen said. "A good thing. High as she was half the time, she'd have cut a hand off. Still flaunting how smart she was though. At breaks she always sat with these two Mexican women, learning to speak their jabber, helping her 'madres' fill out forms."

Chrystal reached for another biscuit and Karen slapped the child's hand. Chrystal jerked her hand back, spilled her cup of milk, and began wailing.

"See what fun you've missed out on, little brother," Karen said.

Three more years, Jody thought as he lay in bed that night. More loans to pay back and, in such an uncertain economy, perhaps no job. He remembered the Friday afternoon Ms. Trexler sat in the house's front room and explained how coming from a single-parent family would be an asset. Your son deserves a chance at a better life, Ms. Trexler had told his mother, then explained the financial-aid forms she'd brought. The guidance counselor hadn't let her gaze linger on the shabby furniture, the cracked windowpane sealed by a square of blue tarp, but her meaning was clear enough. All the while his mother had tugged nervously at her dress, her Sunday dress, as she'd listened.

Sleep would not come, so Jody pulled on his jeans and a T-shirt, went outside and sat on the porch steps. The night was cool and silent, too early for the cicadas, no trucks or cars rattling the steel bridge beyond the pasture. A quarter moon held its place among the stars. Like a pale comma, Lauren once said, and spoke of phases of the moon. That Friday afternoon, after all the forms had been signed, Ms. Trexler asked Jody to walk outside. Lauren has let both of us down, Ms. Trexler had said as they'd stood by her car, but don't let that keep you from achieving what you want in life.

Jody went back inside and opened his laptop. His mother didn't have internet, but he'd downloaded before-and-after photos. He watched the faces wither like flowers in time-lapse photography. Each year appeared a decade. Deceased was slashed across several of the faces.

After his mother left for her shift at the diner, Jody packed a suitcase and backpack and headed into town. He went to an ATM and emptied his account, then drove on to the Shackleford house. He parked beside the Taurus and stepped up the rotting porch steps and opened the door. They were all on the couch.

"I want you to go to Raleigh with me," Jody said, and stepped closer to take Lauren's hand in his. "Please, I won't ask again."

As she looked up, something sparked deep in her pupils. Something, though it wasn't indecision.

"I can't, baby," Lauren said. "I just can't." Jody went back outside and returned with the suitcase and backpack. He set them in the center of the room and took the money from his pocket and placed it in the collection plate.

"Turn on the fire, Billy," Katie Lynn said as she filled the pipe. "This boy's been a long time out in the cold."

THEIR ANCIENT,
GLITTERING EYES

Because they were boys, no one believed them, including the old men who gathered each morning at the Riverside Gas and Grocery. These retirees huddled by the pot-bellied stove in rain and cold, on clear days sunning out front like reptiles. The store's middle-aged owner, Cedric Henson, endured the trio's presence with a resigned equanimity. When he'd bought the store five years earlier, Cedric assumed they were part of the purchase price, in that way no different from the leaky roof and the submerged basement whenever the Tuckaseegee overspilled its banks.

The two boys, who were brothers, had come clattering across the bridge, red-faced and already holding their arms apart as if carrying huge, invisible packages. They stood gasping a few moments, waiting for enough breath to tell what they'd seen.

"This big," the twelve-year-old said, his arms spread as wide apart as he could stretch them.

"No, even bigger," the younger boy said.

Cedric had been peering through the door screen but now stepped outside.

"What you boys talking about?" he asked.

"A fish," the older boy said, "in the pool below the bridge."

Rudisell, the oldest of the three at eighty-nine, expertly delivered a squirt of tobacco between himself and the boys. Creech and Campbell simply nodded at each other knowingly. Time had vanquished them to the role of spectators in the world's affairs, and from their perspective the world both near and far was now controlled by fools. The causes of this devolution dominated their daily conversations. The octogenarians Rudisell and Campbell blamed Franklin Roosevelt and fluoridated water. Creech, a mere seventy-six, leaned toward Elvis Presley and television.

"The biggest fish ever come out of the Tuckaseegee was a thirty-one-inch brown trout caught in nineteen and forty-eight," Rudisell announced to all present. "I seen it weighed in this very store. Fifteen pounds and two ounces."

The other men nodded in confirmation.

"This fish was twice bigger than that," the younger boy challenged.

The boy's impudence elicited another spray of tobacco juice from Rudisell.

"Must be a whale what swum up from the ocean," Creech said. "Though that's a long haul. It'd have to come up the Gulf Coast and the Mississippi, for the water this side of the mountain flows west."

"Could be one of them log fish," Campbell offered. "They get that big. Them rascals will grab your bait and then turn into a big chunk of wood afore you can set the hook."

"They's snakes all over that pool, even some copperheads," Rudisell warned. "You younguns best go somewhere else to make up your tall tales."

The smaller boy pooched out his lower lip as if about to cry.

"Come on," his brother said. "They ain't going to believe us." The boys walked back across the road to the bridge. The old men watched as the youths leaned over the railing, took a last look before climbing atop their bicycles and riding away.

"Fluoridated water," Rudisell wheezed. "Makes them see things."

On the following Saturday morning, Harley Wease scrambled up the same bank the boys had, carrying the remnants of his Zebco 202. Harley's hands trembled as he laid the shattered rod and reel on the ground before the old men. He pulled a soiled handkerchief from his jeans and wiped his bleeding index finger to reveal a deep slice between the first and second joints. The old men studied the finger and the rod and reel and awaited explanation. They were attentive, for Harley's deceased father had been a close friend of Rudisell's.

"Broke my rod like it was made of balsa wood," Harley said. "Then the gears on the reel got stripped. It got down to just me and the line pretty quick." Harley raised his index finger so the men could see it better. "I figured to use my finger for the drag. If the line hadn't broke, you'd be looking at a nub."

"You sure it was a fish?" Campbell asked. "Maybe you caught hold of a muskrat or snapping turtle."

"Not unless them critters has got to where they grow fins," Harley said.

"You saying it was a trout?" Creech asked.

"I only got a glimpse, but it didn't look like no trout. Looked like a alligator but for the fins."

"I never heard of no such fish in Jackson County," Campbell said, "but Rudy Nicholson's boys seen the same. It's pretty clear there's something in that pool."

The men turned to Rudisell for his opinion.

"I don't know what it is either," Rudisell said. "But I aim to find out."

He lifted the weathered ladderback chair, held it aloft shakily as he made his slow way across the road to the bridge. Harley went into the store to talk with Cedric, but the other two men followed Rudisell as if all were deposed kings taking their thrones into some new kingdom. They lined their chairs up at the railing. They waited.

Only Creech had undiminished vision, but in the coming days that was rectified. Campbell had not thought anything beyond five feet of himself worth viewing for years, but now a pair of thick, round-lensed spectacles adorned his head, giving him a look of owlish intelligence. Rudisell had a spyglass he claimed once belonged to a German U-boat captain. The bridge was now effectively one lane, but traffic tended to be light. While trucks and cars drove around them, the old men kept vigil morning to evening, retreating into the store only when rain came.

Vehicles sometimes paused on the bridge to ask for updates, because the lower half of Harley Wease's broken rod had become an object of great wonder since being mounted on Cedric's back wall. Men and boys frequently took it down to grip the hard plastic handle. They invariably pointed the jagged fiberglass in the direction of the bridge, held it out as if a divining rod that might yet give some measure or resonance of what creature now made the pool its lair.

Rudisell spotted the fish first. A week had passed with daily rains clouding the river, but two days of sun settled the silt, the shallow tailrace clear all the way to the bottom. This was where Rudisell aimed his spyglass, setting it on the rail to steady his aim. He made a slow sweep of the sandy floor every fifteen minutes. Many things came into focus as he adjusted the scope: a flurry of nymphs rising to become mayflies, glints of fool's gold, schools of minnows shifting like migrating birds, crayfish with pincers raised as if surrendering to the behemoth sharing the pool with them.

It wasn't there, not for hours, but then suddenly it was. At first Rudisell saw just a shadow over the white sand, slowly gaining depth and definition, and then the slow wave of the gills and pectoral fins, the shudder of the tail as the fish held its place in the current.

"I see it," Rudisell whispered, "in the tailrace."

Campbell took off his glasses and grabbed the spyglass, placed it against his best eye as Creech got up slowly, leaned over the rail.

"It's long as my leg," Creech said.

"I never thought to see such a thing," Campbell uttered.

The fish held its position a few more moments before slowly moving into deeper water.

"I never seen the like of a fish like that," Creech announced.

"It ain't a trout," Campbell said.

"Nor carp or bass," Rudisell added.

"Maybe it is a gator," Campbell said. "One of them snowbirds from Florida could of put it in there."

"No," Rudisell said. "I seen gators during my army training in Louisiana. A gator's like us, it's got to breathe air. This thing don't need air. Beside, it had a tail fin."

"Maybe it's a mermaid," Creech mused.

By late afternoon the bridge looked like an overloaded barge. Pickups, cars, and two tractors clotted both sides of the road and the store's parking lot. Men and boys squirmed and shifted to get a place against the railing. Harley Wease recounted his epic battle, but it was the ancients who were most deferred to as they made pronouncements about size and weight. Of species they could only speak by negation.

"My brother works down at that nuclear power plant near Walhalla," Marcus Price said. "Billy swears there's catfish below the dam near five foot long. Claims that radiation makes them bigger."

"This ain't no catfish," Rudisell said. "It didn't have no big jughead. More lean than that."

Bascombe Greene ventured the shape called to mind the pike-fish caught in weedy lakes up north. Stokes Hamilton thought it could be a hellbender salamander, for though he'd never seen one more than twelve inches long he'd heard tell they got to six feet in Japan. Leonard Coffey told a long, convoluted story about a goldfish set free in a pond. After two decades of being fed cornbread and fried okra, the fish had been caught and it weighed fifty-seven pounds.

"It ain't no pike nor spring lizard nor goldfish," Rudisell said emphatically.

"Well, there's but one way to know," Bascombe Greene said, "and that's to try and catch the damn thing." Bascombe nodded at Harley. "What bait was you fishing with?"

Harley looked sheepish.

"I'd lost my last spinner when I snagged a limb. All I had left in my tackle box was a rubber worm I use for bass, so I put it on."

"What size and color?" Bascombe asked. "We got to be scientific about this."

"Seven inch," Harley said. "It was purple with white dots."

"You got any more of them?" Leonard Coffey asked.

"No, but you can buy them at Sylva Hardware."

"Won't do you no good," Rudisell said.

"Why not?" Leonard asked.

"For a fish to live long enough to get that big it's got to be smart. It'll not forget that a rubber worm tricked it."

"It might not be near smart as you reckon," Bascombe said. "I don't mean no disrespect, but old folks tend to be forgetful. Maybe that old fish is the same way."

"I reckon we'll know the truth of that soon enough," Rudisell concluded, because fishermen already cast from the bridge and banks. Soon several lines had gotten tangled, and a fistfight broke out over who had claim to a choice spot near the pool's tailrace. More people arrived as the afternoon wore on, became early evening. Cedric, never one to miss a potential business opportunity, put a plastic fireman's hat on his head and a whistle in his mouth. He parked cars while his son Bobby crossed and recrossed the bridge selling cokes from a battered shopping cart.

Among the later arrivals was Charles Meekins, the county's game warden. He was thirty-eight years old and had grown up in Green Bay, Wisconsin. The general consensus was the warden was arrogant and a smart-ass, especially among the old men. Meekins stopped often at the store, and he invariably addressed them as Winken, Blinken, and Nod. He listened with undisguised condescension as the old men, Harley, and finally the two boys told of what they'd seen.

"It's a trout or carp," Meekins said, "carp" sounding like "cop." Despite four years in Jackson County, Meekins still spoke as if his vocal cords had been pulled from his throat and reinstalled in his sinus cavity. "There's no fish larger in these waters."

Harley handed his reel to the game warden.

"That fish stripped the gears on it."

Meekins inspected the reel as he might an obviously fraudulent fishing license.

"You probably didn't have the drag set right."

"It was bigger than any trout or carp," Campbell insisted.

"When you're looking into water you can't really judge the size of something," Meekins said. He looked at some of the younger men and winked, "especially if your vision isn't all that good to begin with."

A palmful of Red Mule chewing tobacco bulged the right side of Rudisell's jaw like a tumor, but his apoplexy was such that he swallowed a portion of his cud and began hacking violently. Campbell slapped him on the back and Rudisell spewed dark bits of tobacco onto the bridge's wooden flooring. Meekins had gotten back in his green fish and wildlife truck before Rudisell recovered enough to speak.

"If I hadn't near choked to death I'd have told that shitbritches youngun to bend over and we'd see if my sight was good enough to ram this spyglass up his ass."

In the next few days so many fishermen came to try their luck that Rudisell finally bought a wirebound notebook from Cedric and had anglers sign up for fifteen-minute slots. They cast almost every offering imaginable into the pool. A good half of the anglers succumbed to the theory that what had worked before could work again, so rubber worms were the single most popular choice. The rubber-worm devotees used an array of different sizes, hues, and even smells. Some went with seven-inch rubber worms while others favored five- or ten-inch. Some tried worms purple with white dots while others tried white with purple dots and still others tried pure white and pure black and every variation between including chartreuse, pink, turquoise, and fuchsia. Some used rubber worms with auger tails and others used flat tails. Some worms smelled like motor oil and some worms smelled like strawberries and some worms had no smell at all.

The others were divided by their devotion to live bait or artificial lures. Almost all the bait fisherman used nightcrawlers and redworms in the belief that if the fish had been fooled by an imitation, the actual live worm would work even better, but they also cast spring lizards, minnows, crickets, grubs, wasp larvae, crawfish, frogs, newts, toads, and even a live field mouse. The lure contingent favored spinners of the Panther Martin and Roostertail variety though they were not averse to Rapalas, Jitterbugs, Hula Poppers, Johnson Silver Minnows, Devilhorses and a dozen other hook-laden pieces of wood or plastic. Some lures sank and bounced along the bottom and some lures floated and still others gurgled and rattled and some made no sound at all and one lure even changed colors depending on depth and water temperature.

Jarvis Hampton cast a Rapala F 14 he'd once caught a tarpon with in Florida. A subgroup of fly fishermen cast Muddler Minnows, Wooly Boogers, Wooly Worms, Royal Coachmen, streamers and wet flies, nymphs, and dry flies, and some hurled nymphs and dry flies together that swung overhead like miniature bolas.

During the first two days five brown trout, one speckled trout, one ball cap, two smallmouth bass, ten knottyheads, a bluegill, and one old boot were caught. A gray squirrel was snagged by an errant cast into a tree. Neither the squirrel nor the various fish outweighed the boot, which weighed one pound and eight ounces after the water was poured out. On the third day Wesley McIntire's rod doubled and the drag whirred. A rainbow trout leaped in the pool's center, Wesley's ¼ ounce Panther Martin spinner imbedded in its upper jaw. He fought the trout for five minutes before his brother Robbie could net it. The rainbow was twenty-two inches long and weighed five and a half pounds, big enough that Wesley took it straight to the taxidermist to be mounted.

Charles Meekins came by an hour later. He didn't get out of the truck, just rolled down his window and nodded. His radio played loudly, and the atonal guitars and screeching voices made Rudisell glad he was mostly deaf because hearing only part of the racket made him feel like stinging wasps swarmed inside his head. Meekins didn't bother to turn the radio down, just shouted over the music.

"I told you it was a trout."

"That wasn't it," Rudisell shouted. "The fish I seen could of eaten that rainbow for breakfast."

Meekins smiled, showing a set of bright-white teeth that, unlike Rudisell's, did not have to be deposited in a glass jar every night.

"Then why didn't it? That rainbow has probably been in that pool for years." Meekins shook his head. "I wish you old boys would learn to admit when you're wrong about something."

Meekins rolled up his window as Rudisell pursed his lips and fired a stream of tobacco juice directly at Meekins' left eye. The tobacco hit the glass and dribbled a dark, phlegmy rivulet down the window.

"A fellow such as that ought not be allowed a guvment uniform," Creech said.

"Not unless it's got black and white stripes all up and down it," Campbell added.

After ten days no other fish of consequence had been caught and anglers began giving up. The notebook was discarded because appointments were no longer necessary. Meekins' belief gained credence, especially since in ten days none of the hundred or so men and boys who'd gathered there had seen the giant fish.

"I'd be hunkered down on the stream bottom too if such commotion was going on around me," Creech argued, but few remained to nod in agreement. Even Harley Wease began to have doubts.

"Maybe that rainbow was what I had on," he said heretically.

By the first week in May only the old men remained on the bridge. They kept their vigil but the occupants of cars and trucks and tractors no longer paused to ask about sightings. When the fish reappeared in the tailrace, the passing drivers ignored the old men's frantic waves to come see. They drove across the bridge with eyes fixed straight ahead, embarrassed by their elders' dementia.

"That's the best look we've gotten yet," Campbell said when the fish moved out of the shallows and into deeper water. "It's six feet long if it's a inch."

Rudisell set his spyglass on the bridge railing and turned to Creech, the one among them who still had a car and driver's license.

"You got to drive me over to Jarvis Hampton's house," Rudisell said.

"What for?" Creech asked.

"Because we're going to rent out that rod and reel he uses for them tarpon. Then we got to go by the library, because I want to know what this thing is when we catch it."

Creech kept the speedometer at a steady thirty-five as they followed the river south to Jarvis Hampton's farm. They found Jarvis in his tobacco field and quickly negotiated a ten-dollar-a-week rental for the rod and reel, four 2/0 vanadium-steel fish hooks, and four sinkers. Jarvis offered a net as well but Rudisell claimed it wasn't big enough for what they were after. "But I'll take a hay hook and a whetstone if you got it," Rudisell added, "and some bailing twine and a feed sack."

They packed the fishing equipment in the trunk and drove to the county library where they used Campbell's library card to check out an immense tome called *Freshwater Fish of North America*. The book was so heavy that only Creech had the strength to carry it, holding it before him with both hands as if the book were made of stone. He dropped it in the back seat and, still breathing heavily, got behind the wheel and cranked the engine.

"We got one more stop," Rudisell said, "that old mill pond on Spillcorn Creek."

"You wanting to practice with that rod and reel?" Campbell asked.

"No, to get our bait," Rudisell replied. "I been thinking about something. After that fish hit Harley's rubber worm they was throwing nightcrawlers right and left into the pool figuring that fish thought Harley's lure was a worm. But what if it thought that rubber worm was something else, something we ain't seen one time since we been watching the pool though it used to be thick with them?"

Campbell understood first.

"I get what you're saying, but this is one bait I'd rather not be gathering myself, or putting on a hook for that matter."

"Well, if you'll just hold the sack I'll do the rest."

"What about baiting the hook?"

"I'll do that too."

Since the day was warm and sunny, a number of reptiles had gathered on the stone slabs that had once been a dam. Most were blue-tailed skinks and fence lizards, but several mud-colored serpents coiled sullenly on the largest stones. Creech, who was deathly afraid of snakes, remained in the car. Campbell carried the burlap feed sack, reluctantly trailing Rudisell through broom sedge to the old dam.

"Them snakes ain't of the poisonous persuasion?" Campbell asked.

Rudisell turned and shook his head.

"Naw. Them's just your common water snake. Mean as the devil but they got no fangs."

As they got close the skinks and lizards darted for crevices in the rocks, but the snakes did not move until Rudisell's shadow fell over them. Three slithered away before Rudisell's creaky back could bend enough for him to grab hold, but the fourth did not move until Rudisell's liver-spotted hand closed around its neck. The snake thrashed violently, its mouth biting at the air. Campbell reluctantly moved closer, his fingers and thumbs holding the sack open, arms extended out from his body as if attempting to catch some object falling from the sky. As soon as Rudisell dropped the serpent in, Campbell gave the snake and sack to Rudisell, who knotted the burlap and put it in the trunk.

"You figure one to be enough?" Campbell asked.

"Yes," Rudisell replied. "We'll get but one chance."

The sun was beginning to settle over Balsam Mountain when the old men got back to the bridge. Rudisell led them down the path to the riverbank, the feed sack in his right hand, the hay hook and twine in his left. Campbell came next with the rod and reel and sinkers and hooks. Creech came last, the great book clutched to his chest. The trail became steep and narrow, the weave of leaf and limb overhead so thick it seemed they were entering a cave.

Once they got to the bank and caught their breath, they went to work. Creech used two of the last teeth left in his head to clamp three sinkers onto the line, then tied the hook to the monofilament with an expertly rendered hangman's knot. Campbell studied the book and found the section on fish living in southeastern rivers. He folded the page where the photographs of relevant species began and then marked the back section where corresponding printed information was located. Rudisell took out the whetstone and sharpened the metal with the same attentiveness as the long-ago warriors who'd once roamed these hills honed their weapons, those bronze men who'd flaked dull stone to make their flesh-piercing arrowheads. Soon the steel tip shone like silver.

"All right, I done my part," Creech said when he'd tested the drag. He eyed the writhing feed sack apprehensively. "I ain't about to be close by when you try to get that snake on a hook."

Creech moved over near the tailwaters as Campbell picked up the rod and reel. He settled the rod tip above Rudisell's head, the fish hook dangling inches from the older man's beaky nose. Rudisell unknotted the sack, then pinched the fishhook's eye between his left hand's index finger and thumb, used the right to slowly peel back the burlap. When the snake was exposed, Rudisell grabbed it by the neck, stuck the fish hook through the midsection, and quickly let go. The rod tip sagged with the snake's weight as Creech moved farther down the bank.

"What do I do now?" Campbell shouted, for the snake was swinging in an arc that brought the serpent ever closer to his body.

"Cast it," Rudisell replied.

Campbell made a frantic sideways, two-handed heave that looked more like someone throwing a tub of dishwater off a back porch than a cast. The snake landed three feet from the bank, but luck was with them for the snake began swimming underwater toward the pool's center. Creech came back to stand by Campbell, but his eyes watched the line, ready to flee up the bank if the snake took a mind to change direction. Rudisell gripped the hay hook's handle in his right hand. With his left he began wrapping bailing twine around metal and flesh. The wooden bridge floor rumbled like low thunder as a pickup crossed. A few seconds later another vehicle passed over the bridge. Rudisell continued wrapping the twine. He had no watch but suspected it was after five and men working in Sylva were starting to come home. When Rudisell had used up all the twine, he had Creech knot it.

"With that hay hook tied to you it looks like you're the bait," Creech joked.

"If I gaff that thing it's not going to get free of me," Rudisell vowed.

The snake was past the deepest part of the pool now, making steady progress toward the far bank. It struggled to the surface briefly, the weight of the sinkers pulling it back down. The line did not move for a few moments, then began a slow movement back toward the heart of the pool.

"Why you figure it to turn around?" Campbell asked as Creech took a first step farther up the bank.

"I don't know," Rudisell said. "Why don't you tighten your line a bit."

Campbell turned the handle twice and the monofilament grew taut and the rod tip bent. "Damn snake's got hung up."

"Give it a good jerk and it'll come free," Creech said. "Probably just tangled in some brush."

Campbell yanked upward, and the rod bowed. The line began

moving upstream, not fast but steady, the reel chattering as the monofilament stripped off.

"It's on," Campbell said softly, as if afraid to startle the fish.

The line did not pause until it was thirty yards upstream and in the shadow of the bridge.

"You got to turn it," Rudisell shouted, "or it'll wrap that line around one of them pillars."

"Turn it," Campbell replied. "I can't even slow it down."

But the fish turned of its own volition, headed back into the deeper water. For fifteen minutes the creature sulked on the pool's bottom. Campbell kept the rod bowed, breathing hard as he strained against the immense weight on the other end. Finally, the fish began moving again, over to the far bank and then upstream. Campbell's arms trembled violently.

"My arms is give out," he said and handed the rod to Creech.

Campbell sprawled out on the bank, his chest heaving rapidly, limbs shaking as if palsied. The fish swam back into the pool's heart and another ten minutes passed. Rudisell looked up at the bridge. Cars and trucks continued to rumble across. Several vehicles paused a few moments but no faces appeared at the railing.

Creech tightened the drag and the rod bent double.

"Easy," Rudisell said. "You don't want him breaking off."

"The way it's going, it'll kill us all before it gets tired," Creech gasped.

The additional pressure worked. The fish moved again, this time allowing the line in its mouth to lead it into the tailrace. For the first time they saw the fish.

"Lord amercy," Campbell exclaimed, for what they saw was over six feet long and enclosed in a brown suit of prehistoric armor, the immense tail curved like a scythe. When the fish saw the old men it surged away, the drag chattering again as the fish moved back into the deeper water.

Rudisell sat down beside the book and rapidly turned pages of color photos until he saw it.

"It's a sturgeon," he shouted, then turned to where the printed information was and began to call out bursts of information. "Can grow over seven feet long and three hundred pounds. That stuff that looks like armor is called scutes. They's even got a Latin name here. Says it was once in near every river, but now endangered. Can live a hundred and fifty years."

"I ain't going to live another hundred and fifty seconds if I don't get some relief," Creech said and handed the rod back to Campbell.

Campbell took over as Creech collapsed on the bank. The sturgeon began to give ground, the reel handle making slow, clockwise revolutions. Rudisell closed the book and stepped into the shallows of the pool's tailrace. A sandbar formed a few yards out and that was what he moved toward, the hay hook raised like a metal question mark. Once he'd secured himself on the sandbar, Rudisell turned to Campbell.

"Lead him over here. There's no way we can lift him up the bank."

"You gonna try to gill that thing?" Creech asked incredulously.

Rudisell shook his head.

"I ain't gonna gill it, I'm going to stab this hay hook in so deep it'll have to drag me back into that pool as well to get away."

The reel handle turned quicker now, and soon the sturgeon came out of the depths, emerging like a submarine. Campbell moved farther down the bank, only three or four yards from the sandbar. Creech got up and stood beside Campbell. The fish came straight toward them, face first as if led on a leash. They could see the head clearly now, the cone-shaped snout, barbels hanging beneath the snout like whiskers. As it came closer Rudisell creakily kneeled down on the sandbar's edge. As he swung the hay hook the sturgeon made a last surge toward deeper water. The bright metal raked across the scaly back but did not penetrate.

"Damn," Rudisell swore.

"You got to beach it," Creech shouted at Campbell, who began reeling again, not pausing until the immense head was half out of the water, snout touching the sandbar. The sturgeon's wide mouth opened, revealing an array of rusting hooks and lures that hung from the lips like medals.

"Gaff it now," Creech shouted.

"Hurry," Campbell huffed, the rod in his hands doubled like a bow. "I'm herniating myself."

But Rudisell appeared not to hear them. He stared intently at the fish, the hay hook held overhead as if it were a torch allowing him to see the sturgeon more clearly. Rudisell's blue eyes brightened for a moment, and an enigmatic smile creased his face. The hay hook's sharpened point flashed, aimed not at the fish but the monofilament. A loud twang like a broken guitar string sounded across the water. The rod whipped back and Campbell stumbled backwards but Creech caught him before he fell. The sturgeon was motionless for a few moments, then slowly curved back toward the pool's heart. As it disappeared, Rudisell remained kneeling on the sandbar, his eyes gazing into the pool. Campbell and Creech staggered over to the bank and sat down.

"They'll never believe us," Creech said, "not in a million years, especially that smart-ass game warden."

"We had it good as caught," Campbell muttered. "We had it caught."

None of them spoke further for a long while, each exhausted by the battle. But their silence had more to do with each man's self-reflection on what he had just witnessed than weariness. A yellow mayfly rose like a watery spark in the tailrace, hung in the air a few moments before it fell and was swept away by the current. As time passed crickets announced their presence on the bank, and downriver a whippoorwill called. More mayflies rose in the tailrace. The air became chilly as the sheltering trees closed more tightly around them, absorbed the waning sun's light, a preamble to another overdue darkness.

"It's OK," Campbell finally said.

Creech looked at Rudisell, who was still on the sandbar.

"You done the right thing. I didn't see that at first, but I see it now."

Rudisell finally stood up, wiped the wet sand from the knees of his pants. As he stepped into the shallows he saw something in the water. He picked it up and put it in his pocket.

"Find you a fleck of gold?" Campbell asked.

"Better than gold," Rudisell replied and joined his comrades on the bank.

They could hardly see their own feet as they walked up the path to the bridge. As they emerged they found the green fish and wildlife truck parked at the trail end. The passenger window was down and Meekins' smug face looked out at them.

"So you old boys haven't drowned after all. Folks saw the empty chairs and figured you'd fallen in."

Meekins nodded at the fishing equipment in Campbell's hands and smiled.

"Have any luck catching your monster?"

"Caught it and let it go," Campbell said.

"That's mighty convenient," Meekins said. "I don't suppose anyone else actually saw this giant fish, or that you have a photograph."

"No," Creech said serenely. "But it's way bigger than you are."

Meekins shook his head. He no longer smiled. "Must be nice to have nothing better to do than make up stories, but this is getting old real quick."

Rudisell stepped up to the truck's window, only inches away from Meekins' face when he raised his hand. A single diamond-shaped object was wedged between Rudisell's gnarled index finger and thumb. Though tinted brown, it appeared to be translucent. He held it eye-level in front of Meekins' face as if it were a silty monocle they both might peer through.

"*Acipenser fulvescens,*" Rudisell said, the Latin uttered slowly as if an incantation. He put the scute back in his pocket, and without further acknowledgement of Meekins stepped around the truck and onto the hardtop. Campbell followed with the fishing equipment and Creech came last with the book. It was a slow, dignified procession. They walked westward toward the store, the late-afternoon sun burnishing their cracked and wasted faces. Coming out of the shadows, they blinked their eyes as if dazzled, much in the manner of old-world saints who have witnessed the brilliance of the one true vision.

FALLING STAR

She don't understand what it's like for me when she walks out the door on Monday and Wednesday nights. She don't know how I sit in the dark watching the TV but all the while I'm listening for her car. Or understand I'm not ever certain till I hear the Chevy coming up the drive that she's coming home. How each time a little less of her comes back, because after she checks on Janie she spreads the books open on the kitchen table, and she may as well still be at that college for her mind is so far inside what she's studying. I rub the back of her neck. I say maybe we could go to bed a little early tonight. I tell her there's lots better things to do than study some old book. She knows my meaning.

"I've got to finish this chapter," Lynn says, "maybe after that."

But that "maybe" doesn't happen. I go to bed alone. Pouring concrete is a young man's job and I ain't so young anymore. I need what sleep I can get to keep up.

"You're getting long in the tooth, Bobby," a young buck told me one afternoon I huffed and puffed to keep up. "You best get you one of them sit-down jobs, maybe test rocking chairs."

They all got a good laugh out of that. Mr. Winchester, the boss man, laughed right along with them.

"Ole Bobby's still got some life in him yet, ain't you," Mr. Winchester said.

He smiled when he said it, but there was some serious in his words.

"Yes, sir," I said. "I ain't even got my second wind yet."

Mr. Winchester laughed again, but I knew he'd had his eye on me. It won't trouble him much to fire me when I can't pull my weight anymore.

The nights Lynn stays up I don't ever go right off to sleep, though I'm about nine ways whipped from work. I lay there in the dark and think about something she said a while back when she first took the notion to go back to school. You ought to be proud of me for wanting to make something of myself, she'd said. Maybe it ain't the way she means it to sound, but I can't help thinking she was also saying, "Bobby, just because you've never made anything of yourself don't mean I have to do the same."

I think about something else she once told me. It was Christmas our senior year in high school. Lynn's folks and brothers had finally gone to bed and me and her was on the couch. The lights was all off but for the tree lights glowing and flicking like little stars. I'd already unwrapped the box that had me a sweater in it. I took the ring out of my front pocket and gave it to her. I tried to act all casual but I could feel my hand trembling. We'd talked some about getting married but it had always been in the far-away, after I got a good job, after she'd got some more schooling. But I hadn't wanted to wait that long. She'd put the ring on and though it was just a quarter-carat she made no notice of that.

"It's so pretty," Lynn had said.

"So will you?" I'd asked.

"Of course," she'd told me. "It's what I've wanted, more than anything in the world."

So I lay in the bedroom nights remembering things and though I'm not more than ten feet away it's like there's a big glass door between me and the kitchen table, and it's locked on Lynn's side. We just as well might be living in different counties for all the closeness I feel. A diamond can cut through glass, I've heard, but I ain't so sure anymore.

One night I dream I'm falling. There are tree branches all around me but I can't grab hold of one. I just keep falling and falling for forever. I wake up all sweaty and gasping for breath. My heart pounds like it's some kind of animal trying to tear out my chest. Lynn's got her back to me, sleeping like she ain't got a care in the world. I look at the clock and see I have thirty minutes before the alarm goes off. I'll sleep no more anyway so I pull on my work clothes and stumble into the kitchen to make some coffee.

The books are on the kitchen table, big thick books. I open up the least one, a book called *Astronomy Today*. I read some and it makes no sense. Even the words I know seem to lead nowhere. They just as likely be ants scurrying around the page. But I know Lynn understands them. She has to since she makes all As on her tests.

I touch the cigarette lighter in my pocket and think a book is so easy a thing to burn. I think how in five minutes they'd be nothing but ashes, ashes nobody could read. I get up before I dwell on such a thing too long. I check on Janie and she's managed to kick the covers off the bed. It's been a month since she started second grade but it seems more like a month since we brought her home from the hospital. Things change faster than a person can sometimes stand, Daddy used to say, and I'm learning the truth of that. Each morning it's like Janie's sprouted another inch.

"I'm a big girl now," she tells her grandma and that always gets a good laugh. I took her the first day of school this year and it wasn't like first grade when she was tearing up when me and Lynn left her there. Janie was excited this time, wanting to see her friends. I held her hand when we walked into the classroom. There was other parents milling around, the kids searching for the desk that had their name on it. I looked the room over. A hornets' nest was stuck on a wall and a fish tank bubbled at the back, beside it a big blue globe like I'd had in my second-grade room. WELCOME BACK was written in big green letters on the door.

"You need to leave," Janie said, letting go of my hand.

It wasn't till then I noticed the rest of the parents already had, the kids but for Janie in their desks. That night in bed I'd told Lynn I thought we ought to have another kid.

"We barely can clothe and feed the one we got," she'd said, then turned her back to me and went to sleep.

It's not something I gnaw on a few weeks and then decide to do. I don't give myself time to figure out it's a bad idea. Instead, as soon as Lynn pulls out of the drive I round up Janie's gown and toothbrush.

"You're spending the night with Grandma," I tell her.

"What about school?" Janie says.

"I'll come by and get you come morning. I'll bring you some school clothes."

"Do I have to?" Janie says. "Grandma snores."

"We ain't arguing about this," I tell her. "Get you some shoes on and let's go."

I say it kind of cross, which is a sorry way to act since it ain't Janie that's got me so out of sorts.

When we get to Momma's I apologize for not calling first but she says there's no bother.

"There ain't no trouble between you and Lynn?" she asks.

"No ma'am," I say.

I drive the five miles to the community college. I find Lynn's car and park close by. I reckon the classes have all got started because there's not any students in the parking lot. There ain't a security guard around and it's looking to be an easy thing to get done. I take my barlow knife out of the dash and stick it in my pocket. I keep to the shadows and come close to the nearest building. There's big windows and five different classrooms.

It takes me a minute to find her, right up on the front row, writing down every word the teacher is saying. I'm next to a hedge so it keeps me mostly hid, which is a good thing for the moon and stars are out. The teacher ain't some old guy with glasses and a gray beard, like what I figured him to be. He's got no beard, probably can't even grow one.

He all of a sudden stops his talking and steps out the door and soon enough he's coming out of the building and I'm thinking he must have seen me. I hunker in the bushes and get ready to make a run for the truck. I'm thinking if I have to knock him down to get there I've got no problem with that.

But he don't come near the bushes where I am. He heads straight to a white Toyota parked between Lynn's Chevy and my truck. He roots around the backseat a minute before taking out some books and papers.

He comes back, close enough I can smell whatever it is he splashed on his face that morning. I wonder why he needs to smell so good, who he thinks might like a man who smells like flowers. Back in the classroom he passes the books around. Lynn turns the books' pages slow and careful, like they would break if she wasn't prissy with them.

I figure I best go ahead and do what I come to do. I walk across the asphalt to the Chevy. I kneel beside the back left tire, the barlow knife in my fist. I slash it deep and don't stop cutting till I hear a hiss. I stand up and look around.

Pretty sorry security, I'm thinking. I've done what I come for but I don't close the knife. I kneel beside the white Toyota. I start slashing the tire and for a second it's like I'm slashing that smooth young face of his. Soon enough that tire looks like it's been run through a combine.

I get in my truck and drive toward home. I'm shaking but don't know what I'm afraid of. I turn on the TV when I get back but it's just something to do while I wait for Lynn to call. Only she don't. Thirty minutes after her class let out, I still ain't heard a word. I get a picture in my mind of her out in that parking lot by herself but maybe not as by herself and safe as she thinks with the security guard snoring away in some office. I'm thinking Lynn might be in trouble, trouble I'd put her in. I get my truck keys and am halfway out the door when headlights freeze me.

Lynn don't wait for me to ask.

"I'm late because some asshole slashed my tire," she says.

"Why didn't you call me?" I say.

"The security guard said he'd put on the spare so I let him. That was easier than you driving five miles. Dr. Palmer had a tire slashed too."

"Who changed his tire?" I ask.

Lynn looks at me.

"He did."

"I wouldn't have reckoned him to have the common sense to."

"Well, he did," Lynn says. "Just because somebody's book-smart doesn't mean that person can't do anything else."

"Where's Janie?" Lynn asks when she sees the empty bed.

"She took a notion to spend the night with Momma," I say.

"How's she going to get to school come morning?" she asks.

"I'll get her there," I say. Lynn sets down her books. They're piled there in front of her like a big plate of food that's making her stronger and stronger.

"I don't reckon they got an idea of who done it?" I ask, trying to sound all casual.

Lynn gives a smile for the first time since she got out of the car.

"They'll soon enough have a real good idea. The dumb son of a bitch didn't even realize they have security cameras. They've got it all on tape, even his license. The cops will have that guy in twenty-four hours. At least that's what the security guard said."

It takes me about two heartbeats to take that in. I feel like somebody just sucker-punched me. I open my mouth, but it takes a while to push some words out.

"I need to tell you something," I say, whispery as an old sick man.

Lynn doesn't look up. She's already stuck herself deep in a book.

"I got three chapters to read, Bobby. Can't it wait?"

I look at her. I know I've lost her, known it for a while. Me getting caught for slashing those tires won't make it any worse, except maybe at the custody hearing.

"It can wait," I say.

I go out to the deck. I smell the honeysuckle down by the creek. It's a pretty kind of smell that any other time might ease my mind. A few bullfrogs grunt but the rest of the night is still as the bottom of a pond. So many stars are out that you can see how some seem strung together into shapes. Lynn knows what those shapes are, knows them by their names.

Make a wish if you see a falling star, Momma would always say, but though I haven't seen one fall I think about what I'd wish, and what comes is a memory of me and Lynn and Janie. Janie was a baby then and we'd gone out to the river for a picnic. It was April and the river was too high and cold to swim but that didn't matter. The sun was out and the dogwoods starting to whiten up their branches and you knew warm weather was coming.

After a while Janie got sleepy and Lynn put her in the stroller. She came back to the picnic table where I was and sat down beside me. She laid her head against my shoulder.

"I hope things are always like this," she said. "If there was a falling star that would be all I'd wish for."

Then she'd kissed me, a kiss that promised more that night after we put Janie to bed. But there wasn't any falling star that afternoon and there ain't one tonight. I suddenly wish Janie was here, because if she was I'd go inside and lay down beside her.

I'd stay there all night just listening to her breathe.

You best get used to it, a voice in my head says. There's coming lots of nights you'll not have her in the same place as you, maybe not even in the same town. I look up at the sky a last time but nothing falls. I close my eyes and smell the honeysuckle, make believe Janie's asleep a few feet away, that Lynn will put away her books in a minute and we'll go to bed. I'm making up a memory I'll soon enough need.

The MAGIC BUS

After changing out of her church clothes and helping cook noon dinner, after the table was cleared and the dishes washed and put away, Sabra went to the high pasture above the parkway to watch the cars pass. She had done it as long as she could remember. In past years her brother, Jeffrey, tagged along. They would choose any state except North Carolina and wait to see which car tag went by first. Jeffrey always picked Tennessee or Florida, so he most always won. Jeffrey had tired of the game years ago, so now Sabra went alone. A girl near sixteen is too old for such nonsense, her mother had said in June, but Sabra kept coming. Sunday afternoon was her only free time and she'd spend it however she liked.

She heard the truck's engine and looked down at the farmhouse. Her parents and Jeffrey were headed to Boone for an ice cream and then on to Valle Crucis to visit Aunt Corrie for news about Sabra's first cousin Jim, who was in Vietnam. They'd be back around six, but before then Sabra would need to start supper. Dust billowed behind the pickup until the county road dead-ended at a gray wooden sign that said BLUE RIDGE PARKWAY. The truck turned left, passed the pull-off and its picnic table, and disappeared. Sabra sat down and pulled her knees to her chest. Cars went by in a steady procession, which was no surprise, since it was two days before the Fourth.

One tag blurred into the next, but Sabra always knew the state. A few were tricky, especially North Carolina and Tennessee, which were white with black letters and numbers, but even then she could tell them apart. But Sabra hardly paid those any mind. It was the far places like New Mexico or California or Alaska, whose tags had blues and golds and reds in them, that she looked for.

Each time one passed she imagined what it would be like to live there instead of a gloomy farm where days dripped by slow as molasses and she did the same thing all week beginning at daylight milking a cow and ending at night putting up the supper dishes. Even Sundays, the best day, since her father didn't make her and Jeffrey do farm work, mornings were spent hearing about the world's wickedness, how everything from drive-in theaters to rock music was the devil's doing.

Once September came and school started back up, things wouldn't be much better. Sheila Blankenship, Sabra's best friend since third grade, had quit school in May to get married. There would still be afternoon and weekend chores, including, come fall, harvesting the tobacco, the hardest and nastiest job there was. Resin not even Lava soap got off would stain her hands and gum her hair, have to be cut out with scissors. Sabra had seen thirty-seven states when the minibus lurched into view. Flowers of different sizes and colors had been painted on the sides and top. On the back window, in large purple letters, were the words THE MAGIC BUS. The minibus made it to the pull-off and sputtered to a halt.

Two women got out. The taller one opened the hood and both women disappeared as steam billowed out. When the haze cleared, they and the minibus were still there. The radiator would need water, Sabra knew. She hesitated only a few moments before she stood and dusted off her blue jeans, walked down to the house, and took a milk pail from the porch.

As she came down the slope onto parkway land, Sabra saw that it wasn't two women but a woman and a man, both with long hair. The woman, who didn't look much older than Sabra, wore a loose-fitting brown dress made of soft leather. She wore no bra or makeup, but her neck was adorned with strands of beads. The man was older. He wore a red bandanna, ragged blue jeans, and a green army shirt with cutoff sleeves. A button pinned on the shirt's lapel said "Feed Your Head." He'd not used a razor for a while. Hippies, that's what they were called, though her father used worse names when he saw them on TV. Sabra stopped at the edge of the pull-off.

They were both barefoot but this hadn't stopped the woman from wandering into a blackberry patch, her fingers stained by berries she dropped in a paper cup. The woman hummed to herself as she moved to another bush. The man stood beside the minibus.

"You ain't supposed to pick them," Sabra said. The woman turned and smiled.

"Why not?" she asked softly.

"The park ranger says because it's federal land."

"That's all the more reason we should be able to pick them," the man said, looking at her now. "This land belongs to the people."

Like the woman's voice, his voice had a flatness about it, like the newsmen on TV. Sabra shifted the milk pail to her other hand.

"I'm just saying it so you'll know," she said. "That ranger comes by most every hour."

A station wagon passing the picnic area sign flicked on its turn signal, slowed, then sped up. Children's faces crowded the backseat's passenger window, their eyes wide.

"Better than seeing a bear, scarier too, at least for Mom and Pop," the man said, watching the station wagon disappear around a curve.

The woman came out of the blackberry patch and offered the cup to Sabra.

"Have some," she said.

"You can come closer, we're harmless," the man said, and walked over to stand beside the woman. "Like the song says, we're just groovin' on a Sunday afternoon."

"Okay," Sabra said, and stepped nearer.

The woman shook five berries into Sabra's free hand, did the same for the man. The berries were full ripe and their juice sweetened Sabra's mouth.

"My name is Wendy," the woman said when they'd eaten the berries, "and this is Thomas."

"I'm Sabra, Sabra Norris. I live across the ridge."

"Sabra, what a beautiful name," Wendy said.

"Very exotic sounding," the man said.

"Anyway," Sabra said. "I figured you to need this pail. There's a creek yonder side of the parkway."

"Where?" Thomas asked, taking the pail. Sabra pointed to a stand of birch trees.

"That's kind of you," Wendy said. "The best thing about being on the road is meeting so much love and goodness."

Thomas crossed the parkway and went into the woods. Wendy sat on the pull-off's curb, motioned for Sabra to join her.

"My cousin Jim is in the army," Sabra said. "Was Thomas?"

Wendy looked puzzled.

"Oh, you mean his shirt?"

"Yes," Sabra said.

"No, Thomas is into peace, not war."

"He must have got a high lottery number," Sabra said. "Jim's was thirty-two."

"Thomas is thirty years old," Wendy said, "so he was before the lottery. They still had a draft but he didn't get picked. Is your cousin in Vietnam?"

"Yes," Sabra said.

"Why wasn't he a conscientious objector?" Wendy asked.

"What's that?"

"It means you don't believe in hurting other people, especially in a war we shouldn't be in."

"I guess Jim figured it his duty," Sabra said, "same as when Uncle Jesse went to World War Two and my daddy went to Korea."

"Well, I hope we get out of Vietnam soon," Wendy said. "That way your cousin and all the rest can come home."

A car hauling a silver trailer went by, a line of cars behind it. Several drivers stared as they passed. Probably figure I'm with Wendy and the bus, Sabra thought. The notion pleased her, and she wished that she wasn't wearing a checked two-pocket cowgirl shirt.

"He must miss being away from this place," Wendy said. "It's so beautiful here."

"It's not always so pretty," Sabra answered. "Lots of times there's fog so thick it feels like you're being smothered, and the rain can last for days. Summer's the only time you get days like this."

"San Francisco's like that too," Wendy said, "but I love those gray days. It's like the world wraps a soft blanket around the city. It makes you feel cozy, safe and snug. On mornings like that Thomas and I will stay in bed half the day."

Sabra glanced at Wendy's left hand.

"Have you known Thomas a long time?"

"A year come this September," Wendy said.

"How did you meet?"

"My first semester of college I took a long walk one Sunday, just to see the city. It was obvious I didn't know my way around. Thomas came up to me and volunteered to be my guide."

"So you didn't grow up there?"

"Missouri."

"Do you still go to college?" Sabra asked.

"No," Wendy said. "I'm learning a lot more from being with Thomas."

"Like what?"

"How people need to do things instead of just talking about doing them. Like this trip. One day Thomas said we should do it and two hours later we were on the road."

Thomas came out of the woods, the pail in his right hand. As he crossed, water sloshed over the rim, darkened the parkway's gray asphalt.

"You need help, babe?" Wendy asked, shifting her hands to rise from the curb, but Thomas shook his head.

"I've never gone anywhere," Sabra said. "The only time I've even been out of North Carolina was a school trip to Knoxville."

"Your family never goes on vacations?" Wendy asked.

"Me and my brother, Jeffrey, have been begging to go to Florida long as I can remember," Sabra said, "but my parents say we don't have the money."

"You don't need money, not much at least," Wendy said. "Thomas and I had fifty dollars when we left San Francisco six weeks ago."

"But how do you eat, or buy gas?"

"You share things," Wendy said, and touched the beads on her neck. "I make some of these every day. People give me money for them, or food, even gas. Thomas, he has things to share too."

Sabra looked west toward Grandfather Mountain. The sun

had settled on the summit where, like a fishing bobber, it waited to be tugged under. Her parents and Jeffrey had probably already left Aunt Corrie's. Time to head back across the pasture, but Sabra didn't want to. She wished the bus had come earlier, right after her family left.

Thomas slammed the hood shut and walked over to the curb but did not sit down. He held the pail out to Sabra and she rose from the curb to take it. Wendy got up too and Thomas wrapped an arm around her waist, pulled her close, and kissed her on the brow.

"We're good to go, baby," he said.

"But it's so nice here," Wendy said. "Let's stay for the night."

"A nice place it is," Thomas answered, "but what about food, my lady?"

"We have enough bread and peanut butter left for a sandwich."

Thomas groaned.

"We've got eighteen dollars. I was thinking we could stop in Boone and get a real meal."

"I can get you a real meal," Sabra said, "and it won't cost you anything."

"What a kind thing for you to offer," Wendy said.

"What about your parents?" Thomas asked. "They might not like your doing that for strangers, especially ones who look like us."

"I won't let them know," Sabra said. "They go to bed soon as it gets dark. You can have chicken, green beans, and corn bread, and I'll make some potato salad. I can bring you fresh milk too."

"That's worth waiting a few hours for," Thomas said.

"But you'd have to bring it all here," Wendy said, "and in the dark."

"You could meet me in the barn," Sabra said. "I can show you where it is. Once it starts to get near dark, you can come there."

"How will we get back here?" Thomas said. "We don't have a flashlight."

"I'll get one you can use, or you can spend the night in the barn. Come morning, I'm the one that does the milking."

"We like being outside and seeing the stars," Thomas said, "but the food part, that sounds good."

"Are you sure it will be okay?" Wendy asked.

"I really want to," Sabra answered. "Like you said, it's good to share what you have."

Smiling, Wendy reached out and touched Sabra's cheek, let the hand stay a few moments. Sabra felt the warmth in the hand.

"You would love San Francisco, Sabra," Wendy said, "and it would love you."

There was only time to make the potato salad before Sabra's family returned. Jeffrey rushed in, grabbed his ball glove, and ran back outside as her parents entered the house.

"You go visiting and that boy gets like a coiled spring," Sabra's mother said.

"That's how a twelve-year-old boy should act," her father said. "I'd not want a son who acted different."

They could hear the ball thumping against the woodshed now.

"Dammit, that reminds me," her father said. "I need to fill the spray tanks for tomorrow."

He went back out the door. The ball stopped thumping for a few moments, then resumed. Her mother came into the kitchen and put on an apron.

"You look to have been dawdling, girl."

"I decided to make potato salad," Sabra said. "It took longer than I thought."

"Well, nothing to fret over," her mother said. "That ice cream will keep your daddy and brother from getting cranky."

While her mother floured and fried the chicken, Sabra put the beans on, mixed the corn bread, and placed it in the oven.

"How's Aunt Corrie?" Sabra asked.

"Fine except she's got this notion that Jim won't come home alive."

"Why does she think that?"

"Because of that second boy from Valle Crucis getting killed over there," her mother said. "Death always comes in threes, that's what she told your daddy and me."

Sabra grimaced.

"What is that look for?" her mother asked.

"It just seems everyone around here always expects the worst," Sabra said.

"I don't know that to be true," her mother said. "Anybody would have worries if their child was over there."

"Jim doesn't have to be there," Sabra said softly. "He could tell the army he's not wanting to fight anymore. He could be a conscientious objector."

Her mother stopped forking the fried chicken onto paper towels.

"Lord, girl, don't let your daddy hear you talk like that. You know how he gets just hearing about such things on the news. No need for his own daughter to rile him up more, especially when he's been extra sweet to you today."

"How?" Sabra asked.

"Your birthday present," her mother said. "I'm letting the cat out of the bag, but it's only five more days so I'll tell you. We went by Kmart and bought that record player you've been wanting."

"But you said it was too expensive," Sabra said.

"Your daddy argued we should figure in a couple of dollars for all the ice cream you've missed this summer. Anyway, it looks to be a good year for us. All that June rain will get us through this dry spell. We'll have that barn filled with hay and curing tobacco come fall."

Sabra's mother poured the last of the grease into an old coffee can, turned, and smiled.

"See, that's not expecting the worst, is it?"

"No, I guess not," Sabra said.

"Then put a smile on your face and call your daddy and brother in to eat, and don't let on you know about that record player. He wanted it to be a surprise."

Once all the farmhouse lights were out, Sabra took the flashlight from under her pillow. She took off her bra and put on an orange T-shirt with TENNESSEE on the front, quietly made her way to the kitchen, and filled a grocery bag. How she'd explain the missing food tomorrow, Sabra did not know. Probably won't need to explain it, she told herself, but I'm at least going to go see.

Sabra eased out the front door and headed to the barn, the porch's bare bulb, and habit, guiding her. She was almost to the barn mouth when she saw the small orange glow, thought it a lightning bug until she turned on the flashlight. Thomas sat on the barn floor, his back against a stable door. Wendy sat a few feet away. A bright-yellow backpack lay between them.

"Daddy don't allow lit cigarettes in the barn," Sabra said.

Thomas smiled.

"Well, it's not a cigarette, at least the kind he's thinking about."

The orange tip glowed as Thomas inhaled. After a few moments, he pursed his lips and let the smoke whisper out of his mouth. He passed what was in his hand to Wendy, who did the same thing.

"You ever smoked a joint?" Thomas asked.

Sabra shook her head and looked back toward the farmhouse. If the marijuana's odor lingered long enough, her father would smell it. It won't, Sabra told herself. You're just thinking the worst.

"You don't look like you much approve of it," Thomas said.

"I've heard what it does to you."

"Good things or bad?" Thomas asked, and took the joint from Wendy.

"Bad," Sabra said.

Thomas exhaled again, let the smoke haze the air between them.

"And who told you that?"

"My health teacher," Sabra said.

Thomas raised the joint and made a slow swirling motion as if writing something in the air.

"You think he's ever gotten stoned?"

Sabra tried to imagine gray-haired Mr. Borders, who was a church deacon and didn't even smoke cigarettes, inhaling and holding the marijuana smoke in his lungs, letting it out slow like Thomas and Wendy did.

"No," Sabra said.

"Then he doesn't know, does he?" Thomas said.

"I guess not," Sabra said, freeing a horse blanket from a nail.

The joint was just a stub now, hardly enough left to hold. Thomas brought it to his mouth a last time and laid what was left on his pants leg, rubbed it into the cloth with his palm.

"All gone," he said, raising the hand.

Sabra set down the grocery bag on the horse blanket, positioned the flashlight to cast the light before them. She took out two forks and two paper plates, then the Tupperware bowl and quart jar of milk.

"I'm sorry I couldn't heat it up for you," Sabra said, "and I didn't bring cups."

Thomas placed corn bread and chicken on his plate, forked out some potato salad. He took a big bite out of the chicken.

"Damn, that's good," he said, and pointed his fork at Wendy. "You had better dig in now or there will be nothing left."

"What about you, Sabra?" Wendy asked.

"I ate plenty at supper," Sabra said. "I didn't have room for cups, but I figured you'd not mind about that."

Though some milk remained in the jar, the Tupperware bowl was soon empty except for a few bones.

"The radiator boiling over was the best thing that could have happened," he said.

"It was," Wendy agreed. "We'd have passed right by and never known a new friend was just over the hill."

"Maybe it was meant to be," Thomas said, meeting Sabra's eyes. "Things happen for a reason. What's that quote you like so much, Wendy, the one about destiny?"

"We don't find our destiny, it finds us," Wendy answered.

"I believe that," Thomas said, still looking at Sabra. "Don't you?"

"I guess so," Sabra said.

Thomas settled his head against the stall door, his eyes half closed. Wendy opened the backpack and brought out a strand of beads like the ones she wore and gave it to Sabra.

"I made these for you while we waited."

"They're as pretty as anything I've ever seen, even a rainbow," Sabra said. "Thank you so much."

She held the beads in both hands, slowly stretched the elastic, and let them tighten around her neck.

"Do they look good on me?" Sabra asked.

"They look divine, but two strands would look even better," Wendy said. "You want to make one yourself? It's easy."

"Okay."

Sabra moved closer, crossed her legs the same way Wendy did. Wendy set a spool of elastic and a plastic bag of beads between them. Sabra picked up a piece of string, watched Wendy tie a double-knot an inch from one end and did the same. She began sifting beads from the plastic bag, trying to find one of each color.

"You can do it that way," Wendy said, "but it's better if you let the colors surprise you, like this."

Wendy reached into the plastic bag and pulled out a single green bead. She placed it on the string and, again without looking, brought up an orange one. Sabra did the same thing.

"They do look prettier this way," Sabra said when she'd finished. "I guess people do this all the time in San Francisco, make things I mean."

Wendy smiled.

"They do."

"What else do they do there?" Sabra asked.

"Sing and dance, look after each other, love each other."

"Get stoned," Thomas said, his eyes fully open now. He laid a hand on Wendy's thigh, caressed it a moment, and removed his hand. "Make love, not war."

"And everybody's young," Wendy said. "You have to go there to believe it."

"I want to go there someday," Sabra said.

"Then one day you will," Wendy said, "and once you get there, you will never want to leave."

"Well, when I do," Sabra said, "the first people I'll look for are you all."

"Of course," Wendy said. "You can stay with us until you find a pad of your own, can't she, Thomas?"

"Sure," Thomas said, "but why wait when you can hitch a ride on the magic bus."

At first Sabra thought Thomas was joking, but he wasn't grinning or even cracking a smile. Wendy wasn't grinning either. Sabra thought about what it would be like once Thomas and Wendy left. She'd see no one near her age until Sunday. But even then it would be the same people and they'd be talking about the same things and in the same way.

"You mean go with you?" Sabra asked. "Tomorrow, I mean?"

"Tomorrow or even tonight," Thomas said.

"I would like to go with you," Sabra said softly, wanting to pretend a bit longer that she actually might.

"You would be welcome," Wendy said, "but it might be better if you waited awhile. I mean, how old are you?"

"Seventeen."

Thomas looked at Wendy.

"Hell, you were just a year older when I found you. A lot of girls out there are as young or younger. This is what it's all about, babe, being free while you're young enough to realize what freedom is."

"I guess so," Wendy said.

Thomas nodded at the strand of beads coiled in Sabra's palm.

"Why don't you try them on," he said.

Sabra slipped the beads over her head, tugged at them so they settled next to the other strand. She thought about what her father would say if he saw them on her. Or her mother, she'd not like them either. Thomas sifted more marijuana onto the smoking papers, twisted the ends.

"What's it really like then?" Sabra asked. "The marijuana, I mean?"

"Like dreaming, except you're awake," Thomas said.

"But only good dreams," Wendy added, "the kind you want to have."

"But it doesn't hurt you?" Sabra asked, looking at Wendy.

"No," Wendy said. "It helps heal you, makes the bad things go away."

Thomas lit the joint and held it out to Sabra.

"You can try it if you like, or I've got some serious mind candy."

He reached into his pocket and pulled out an aspirin bottle, the label half torn away. Inside were round pink tablets mixed with blue and red capsules the shape of .22 shorts. Sabra took the joint.

"Breathe in and hold it in your lungs as long as you can," Thomas said.

"Not too long at first," Wendy cautioned, "because it will make you cough."

Sabra did what they said, stifled a cough, and handed the joint back to Thomas, who took two quick draws, exhaled.

They'd passed the joint around twice more before Thomas reached out his free hand, twined a portion of Wendy's hair around a finger. He pulled his finger back slowly, hair tugging the scalp a moment before he let the hair slip free.

"Come here, baby."

Thomas inhaled and Wendy moved closer, let the smoke funnel into her mouth.

"Now you," Thomas said.

When Sabra didn't move, he slid over to her.

"Open your mouth," Thomas said.

She shut her eyes, did what he asked, felt his warm smoky breath in her throat and lungs. As Thomas's breath expired, his lips brushed hers. Thomas pushed himself back against the stall door, took a long final draw, and rubbed the residue into his jeans. Wendy covered her face with both hands. She giggled, then lifted her hands to reveal a wide grin.

"I am soo stoned."

"I told you it was good shit," Thomas said.

"It is good," Sabra agreed, though she felt no difference except a dryness in the throat.

"If we had brought the transistor we could dance," Wendy said.

"I doubt they play much Quicksilver or Dead around here, baby," Thomas said. "Motown either."

Sabra thought of the record player, but even if she'd had some 45s there'd be no place to plug it in.

Wendy's face brightened.

"I can hum songs, though. That will be almost as good. I'll be like a jukebox and play anything we want."

Wendy moved the flashlight so that it shone toward the barn's center. She stood and placed a hand around Thomas's upper arm.

"Come on," she said.

Thomas got up and Wendy pressed her head against his chest.

"What song do you want, babe?"

" 'White Rabbit,' " Thomas said.

Wendy began to hum and she and Thomas swayed side to side, their feet barely moving. Sabra wished she had some water for her parched throat. She was reaching for the milk when it happened. Thomas and Wendy, the barn, the night itself slid back a ways and then returned, except everything felt off plumb. For a few moments all Sabra felt was panic.

She closed her eyes and tried to block out everything except Wendy's humming. Soon the humming seemed as much inside of her as outside. Sabra felt it even in her fingertips, a pleasant tingling. When she opened her eyes, it did feel like a dream, a warm good dream. She watched Thomas and Wendy dance, holding each other so close together. They were in love and not afraid to show it. Never had anything so beautiful, so wondrous, ever happened on this farm. Never. Wendy stopped humming but still pressed her head against Thomas's chest.

"What song now?" Wendy asked.

"I don't care," Thomas said, "but Sabra should get a dance too."

"Yes," Wendy agreed.

"I don't think I can," Sabra said. "I'm dizzy."

Thomas went over and helped Sabra to her feet, steadied her a moment, and led her to the barn's center.

"What song do you want, Sabra?" Wendy asked.

"I don't know," she answered. "You pick one."

"I'll do 'Both Sides Now,' " Wendy said. "It's a pretty song."

Wendy sat by the stall door and began to hum. Thomas put his arm around Sabra's waist and pulled her close. She let her head lie against his chest like Wendy had. A few times she and Sheila had pretended to dance, copying couples on television who glided across ballrooms, but this was easier. You just leaned into each other and moved your feet a little. A part of her seemed to watch from somewhere else as she and Thomas danced, close yet far away at the same time. She could smell Thomas, musky but not so bad. He leaned his face closer to hers.

"Someone as lovely as you has to have a boyfriend."

"No," Sabra said, not adding that her parents wouldn't allow her to date yet.

"I find that hard to believe," Thomas said, "just as hard to believe that you're really seventeen. How old are you, really?"

"Sixteen."

"Sweet sixteen," Thomas said. "That's old enough."

He placed his free hand against her back, brought Sabra even closer, her breasts flattening against his chest. The hand on her waist resettled where spine and hip met, all of her pressed into him now. She could feel him through the denim. Their feet no longer moved and only their hips swayed. Sabra looked over at Wendy, whose eyes were closed as she hummed the last few notes.

"What song do you two want next?" Wendy asked.

Sabra slipped free of Thomas's embrace. The barn wobbled a few moments and she had to stare at her sneakers, the straw and dirt under them, to keep her balance. When the barn resettled it had shrunk, especially the barn mouth.

"It's your turn, Wendy," Sabra said.

Wendy opened her eyes.

"I've had him all day, so you get him now."

Thomas settled a hand on Sabra's upper arm.

"Wendy doesn't mind sharing," he said.

"I'm dizzy," Sabra said, "too dizzy to dance anymore."

Thomas nodded, let his hand slide down her inner arm, his fingers brushing over her palm.

"That's fine," Thomas said. "The first time you do things, it's always a bit scary. It was the same for Wendy."

"So another dance with me, baby?" Wendy asked. "Or is it time to unplug the jukebox?"

"Time to unplug the jukebox," Thomas said. "Time to get back on the road."

"I thought you were staying until morning," Sabra said.

"This bus has no set schedule," Thomas said. "When it comes by, you either get on board or you're left behind."

Wendy put the elastic and beads in the backpack and tightened the straps. She stood up, a bit unsteadily, and walked over to the barn mouth.

"So," Thomas said, staring at Sabra, "ready to get on the bus?"

"I want to go, it's just . . . " Sabra paused. "I mean, I was thinking maybe you could give me your address, or a phone number. That way I can find you."

"But you're coming," Thomas said, locking his eyes on hers. "It's just that you're not sure you should leave tonight."

"Yes," Sabra said. "That's what I mean."

"The moon has turned sideways and is making a smiley face," Wendy said, "really and truly."

Thomas picked up the flashlight and leaned against a stall. He let the beam shine on the floor between him and Sabra. She could barely make out his face.

"Sometimes if you're chained," Thomas said, "other people have to set you free."

"I'm not chained," Sabra said.

"If that were true, you'd leave right now," Thomas said. "I can teach every part of you how to be free, your mind and your body."

"I've got to go," Sabra said. A match flared. Thomas slowly lowered the match into the stall. His hand came back up empty.

"Like I said, sometimes it takes someone else to set you free."

"That's not funny," Sabra said. "I think you need to leave too."

"Come see the smiley face," Wendy said.

Sabra heard the fire first, a crackling inside the stall, but she didn't believe it until she smelled smoke. Flames began licking through the slats. Sabra snatched the horse blanket from the barn floor, was about to the open the stall door when Thomas's arm stopped her.

"Come on," he said. "We've got to leave."

"No," Sabra shouted, and tore herself free.

She opened the stall door and swatted at the flames, but they had already leaped into the next stall. The blanket caught fire and she couldn't put it out. The fire climbed into the loft and soon Sabra could barely see through the smoke.

She stumbled out of the barn. Smoke wadded like cotton in her lungs and she coughed all the way to the spring trough. The farmhouse lights were on and her father was running toward the barn, Jeffrey and her mother trailing behind. In the high pasture she saw a beam of light pause where the fence was, then move onto parkway land and disappear.

Sabra didn't know if she had slept or not, but she was awake when the dark in the east began to lighten. Her mother came into her room a few minutes later and told Sabra that barn or no barn, the cow would need to be milked. Sabra got dressed. When she passed through the front room, her father was asleep on the couch, still in his overalls. Soot grimed his face and hands and he smelled of smoke. The black patch where the barn had been yet smoldered, the milk pail nearby, lying on its side. The cow was drinking at the spring trough and looked up as Sabra walked by. She went on past the charred ground and into the high pasture and slipped through the fence.

The bus wasn't there, but the flashlight was in the grass by the curb. She switched it off and made her way back up the slope and into the high pasture. Below, the cow had left the spring trough and stood by the barn's ashes, waiting to be milked, not knowing where else to go.

SOMETHING RICH

and

STRANGE

She follows the river's edge downstream, leaving behind her parents and younger brother who still eat their picnic lunch. It is Easter break and her father has taken time off from his job. They have followed the Appalachian Mountains south, stopping first in Gatlinburg, then the Smokies, and finally this river. She finds a place above a falls where the water looks shallow and slow. The river is a boundary between Georgia and South Carolina, and she wants to wade into the middle and place one foot in Georgia and one in South Carolina so she can tell her friends back in Nebraska she has been in two states at the same time.

She kicks off her sandals and enters, the water so much colder than she imagined, and quickly deeper, up to her kneecaps, the current surging under the smooth surface.

She shivers. On the far shore a granite cliff casts this section of river into shadow. She glances back to where her parents and brother sit on the blanket. It is warm there, the sun full upon them. She thinks about going back but is almost halfway now.

She takes a step and the water rises higher on her knees. Four more steps, she tells herself. Just four more and I'll turn back. She takes another step and the bottom is no longer there and she is being shoved downstream and she does not panic because she has passed the Red Cross courses.

The water shallows and her face breaks the surface and she breathes deep. She tries to turn her body so she won't hit her head on a rock and for the first time she's afraid and she's suddenly back underwater and hears the rush of water against her ears. She tries to hold her breath but her knee smashes against a boulder and she gasps in pain and water pours into her mouth. Then for a few moments the water pools and slows. She rises coughing up water, gasping air, her feet dragging the bottom like an anchor trying to snag waterlogged wood or rock jut and as the current quickens again she sees her family running along the shore and she knows they are shouting her name though she cannot hear them and as the current turns her she hears the falls and knows there is nothing that will keep her from it as the current quickens and quickens and another rock smashes against her knee but she hardly feels it as she snatches another breath and she feels the river fall and she falls with it as water whitens around her and she falls deep into the whiteness and as she rises her head scrapes against a rock ceiling and the water holds her there and she tells herself don't breathe but the need rises inside her beginning in the upper stomach then up through her chest and throat and as that need reaches her mouth her mouth and nose open and the lungs explode in pain and then the pain is gone as bright colors shatter around her like glass shards, and she remembers her sixth-grade science class, the gurgle of the aquarium at the back of the room, the smell of chalk dust that morning the teacher held a prism out the window so it might fill with color, and she has a final, beautiful thought—that she is now inside that prism and knows something even the teacher does not know, that the prism's colors are voices, voices that swirl around her head like a crown, and at that moment her arms and legs she did not even know were flailing cease and she becomes part of the river.

The search and rescue squad and the sheriff arrived at the falls late that afternoon. Two of the squad members were brothers, one in his early twenties, the other thirty. They had a carpentry business, building patios and decks for lawyers and doctors from Greenville and Columbia who owned second homes in the mountains. The third man, the diver, was in his early forties and taught biology at the county high school. The sheriff looked at his watch and figured they had two hours at most before the gorge darkened.

Even so the diver did not hurry to put on his wet suit and air tanks. He smoked a cigarette and between puffs talked to the sheriff about the high school's baseball team. They had worked together before and knew death punched no time clock.

When the diver was ready, a length of nylon rope was clasped tight under his arms. The older, stronger brother held the other end. The diver waded into the river, the rope trailing behind him like a leash. He dipped his mask in the water, put it on, and leaned forward. The three men onshore watched as the black fins propelled the diver into the hydraulic's ceaseless blizzard of whitewater. The men on the bank sat on rocks and waited. With his free hand, the older brother pointed upstream to a bend where he'd caught a five-pound trout last fall. The sheriff asked what he'd used for bait but didn't hear the answer because the mask bobbed up in the headwater's foam.

The brother tightened the slack and pulled but nothing gave until the others grabbed hold as well. They pulled the diver into the shallows and helped him onto shore. Between watery coughs he told them he'd found her in the undercut behind the hydraulic. She had been upright, her head and back and legs pressed against a rock slab. Only her hair moved, its long strands streaming upward. As the diver had drifted closer, he saw that her eyes were open. Their faces were inches apart when he slipped an arm around her waist. Then the hydraulic ripped free the mask and mouthpiece, grabbed the dive light, spiraling it toward the darkness.

The diver told the men kneeling beside him that the girl's blue eyes had life in them. He could feel her heart beating against his chest and hear her whispering. Before or after your mask was torn off, the sheriff asked. The diver did not know, but swore that he'd never enter the river again.

The younger brother scoffed, while the older spoke of narcosis though the pool was no more than twenty feet deep. But the sheriff did not dismiss what the diver said. He too had seen strange and inexplicable things involving the dead but had never mentioned them to others and did not choose to now. We'll find another way, he said, but that river has to lower some before I allow anyone else in there.

The diver had trouble sleeping afterward. Every night when he closed his eyes, he saw the girl's wide blue eyes, the flowing golden hair. His wife slept beside him, her body curled into his chest. They had no children and now he was glad for that. He had seen a picture of the parents in the local paper. They had been on the shore, within thirty feet of the undercut that held their daughter, the expressions on their faces beyond grief.

On the third night, the diver fell into a deeper sleep and the girl came with him. They were in the undercut again but now the river was tepid and he could breathe. As he embraced her, she whispered that this world was better than the one above and she should never have been afraid.

He emerged in his wife's embrace. It's just a bad dream, she kept saying until he quit gasping. His wife closed her eyes and was quickly asleep, but he could not so went into the kitchen and graded lab tests until dawn.

The girl remained in the river. Volunteers cast grappling hooks from the banks and worked them like lures through the pool or stood in shallows or on rocks and jabbed with long metal poles. Some of the old-timers suggested dynamite but the girl's parents would not hear of it. The sheriff said what they needed was a week without rain.

The diver slept little the next few nights. In class he placed the students in small groups and had them discuss assigned chapters among themselves. He knew they talked about the prom instead of pupae and chrysalides, but he didn't care. On the third afternoon, he skipped the teacher's meeting and sat alone in his classroom. The school, emptied of students, was quiet, the only sound the gurgle of the aquarium. He would never speak to anyone, not even his wife, about what happened in the classroom's stillness, but that evening he told the sheriff he'd dive for the girl again.

Days passed. Rain came often, long rains that made every fold of ridge land a tributary and merged earth and water into a deep orange-yellow rush. Banks disappeared as the river reached out and dragged them under. But that was only surface. In the undercut all remained quiet and still, the girl's transformation unrushed, gentle. Crayfish and minnows unknitted flesh from bone, attentive to loosed threads.

Then the rains stopped and the river ran clear again. Boulders vanished for weeks reappeared. Sandbars and stick jams regathered in new configurations. The water warmed and caddis flies broke through the river's skin to make their brief flights before falling back into their element.

The sheriff called the diver and told him the river was low enough to try again. The next day they walked the half mile down the path to the falls. There were five of them this time, the sheriff, his deputy, the two brothers, and the diver.

The sheriff insisted on two ropes, making sure they stayed taut. The water was clearer than last time and offered less resistance. The diver entered the abeyance as though parting a curtain, the river suddenly muted.

She was less of what she had been, the blue rubbed from her eyes, flesh freed from the chandelier of bone. He touched what once had been a hand. The river whispered to him that it would not be long now.

When he returned to shore, he told them her body was gone, not even a scrap of clothing or bone. He told them the last hard rain must have swept her downstream. The younger brother said the diver should go back and search the left and right sides of the falls. He argued the body could still be there. The deputy suggested they lower an underwater camera into the pool.

The sheriff shook his head and said to let her be. The men walked up the trail, back toward their vehicles, their lives. The midday sun leaned close and dazzling. Dogwoods bloomed small white stars. The diver knew in the coming days the petals would find their way into the river, drifting onto sandbars and gilding the backs of pools, and the diver knew some would drift through the rapids and over the falls into the hydraulic. They would furl amid the last bones and like the last bones they would finally slip free.

The DOWRY

After Mrs. Newell took away his plate and coffee cup, Pastor
Boone lingered at the table and watched the thick flakes fall.
The garden angel's wings were submerged, the redbud's dark
branches damasked white. Be grateful it's not stinging sleet, Parson
Boone told himself as Mrs. Newell returned to the rectory's dining
room.

"You'll catch the ague if you go out in such weather," the housekeeper said, and nodded at his bible. "Instead of hearing yourself read
the Good Book, you'll be hearing it read over your coffin."

"Hear it, Mrs. Newell?" Pastor Boone smiled. "Do you dispute
church doctrine that the dead remain so until Christ's return?"

"Pshaw," the housekeeper said. "You know my meaning."

Parson Boone nodded.

"Yes, we could wish for a better day, but I promised I would come."

"Another week won't matter," the housekeeper said. "Youthful
folk have all the time in the world."

"It's been eight months, Mrs. Newell," he reminded her, "and, alas, they are not so youthful, especially Ethan. Two years of war took much of his youth from him, perhaps all."

"I still say they can wait another week," the housekeeper said. "Maybe by then the colonel will die of spite and cap a snuffer on all this fuss."

"I worry more that in a week Ethan will be the one harmed," Pastor Boone replied, "and by his own volition."

The housekeeper let out an exasperated sigh.

"Let me fetch Mr. Newell to hitch the horse and drive you out there."

"No, it's Sunday," Pastor Boone said. "If he'll ready the buggy, that's enough. The solitude will allow me to reflect on next week's sermon."

The snow showed no signs of letting up as he released the brake handle, but the buggy's canvas roof kept him dry, and the overcoat's thick wool provided enough warmth. The wheels shushed through the town's trodden snow. There were no other sounds, the storefronts shuttered and yards and porches empty. The only signs of habitation were windows lambent with hearth light. He passed Noah Andrews's house. The physician would scold him for being out in such inhospitable weather, but Noah, also in his seventies, would do the same if summoned. Above, a low sky dulled to the color of lead. An appropriateness in that, Pastor Boone thought.

When the war had begun five years ago, he had watched as families who'd lived as good neighbors, many kin somewhere in their lineage, became implacable enemies. Fistfights occurred and men carried rifles to church services, though at least, unlike in other parts of the county, no killing had occurred within the community. Instead, local men died at Cold Harbor and Stones River and Shiloh, which in Hebrew, he'd told Noah Andrews, meant "place of peace." The majority of the church's congregants sided with the

Union, those men riding west to join Lincoln's army in Tennessee, but some, including the Davidsons, joined the Secessionists. Pastor Boone's sympathies were with the Union as well, though no one other than Noah Andrews knew so. To hold together what frayed benevolence remained in the church, a pastor need appear neutral, he'd told himself. Yet there were times he suspected his silence had been mere cowardice.

Now Ethan Burke, who fought for the Union, wanted to marry Colonel Davidson's daughter, Helen. The couple had come to him before last week's service, once again pleading for his help. They had known each other all their lives, been baptized in the French Broad by Pastor Boone on the same spring Sunday. When Ethan and Helen were twelve, they'd asked if he'd marry them when they came of age. The adults had been amused. Since the war's end last spring, Pastor Boone had watched them talking together before and after church, seen their quick touches. But when Ethan called on Helen at the Davidsons' farm, the Colonel met him at the door, a Colt pistol in his remaining hand. You'll not step on this porch again and live, he'd vowed. Ethan and Helen had taken Colonel Davidson at his word. Every Sunday afternoon for eight months Ethan, whose family owned only a swaybacked mule, walked three miles to the Davidson farm and did the chores most vexing for a one-handed man. While Helen watched from the porch, Ethan replaced the barn's warped boards and rotting shingles, cleaned out the well, and stacked hay bales in the loft. Afterward, he stood on the steps and talked to Helen until darkness began settling over the valley. Then he'd walk back to the farmhouse where his widowed mother and younger siblings awaited him.

The congregants who'd fought Union seemed ready to leave the war behind them, even Reece Triplett, who'd lost two brothers at Cold Harbor, but not Colonel Davidson, nor his nephew and cousin, who'd served under the Colonel in the North Carolina Fifty-Fifth. Easier for the victors than the vanquished to forgive, Pastor Boone knew. Colonel Davidson sat stone-faced through the sermons, and unlike Ethan and the other veterans, including his own kinsmen, the colonel wore his butternut field coat to every service. When Pastor Boone suggested that it was time to put the uniform away, Colonel Davidson nodded at the empty sleeve. Some things don't let you forget, Pastor, he had replied brusquely. Give me back a hand and I'll be ready to forgive, as your bible says.

Ethan had been there that Sunday, and knew, just as Pastor Boone knew, that the man was serious. Even before the war, Colonel Davidson had been a hard man, quick to take offense at the least slight. Once a peddler quipped that Davidson's stallion looked better suited for plowing and it took the sheriff and two other man to keep him from thrashing the fellow. A hard man made harder by four years of watching men die all around him, and, of course, the hand cleaved by grapeshot. But others had suffered too. Pastor Boone had seen it in the faces of old and young alike. He had witnessed families grieving, sometimes brought news of the death himself. Those who didn't have men in the war endured their share of fear and deprivation as well. Hardships he himself had been spared. Even in the war's brutal last winter, he had never lacked firewood and food, and, childless, no son to fear for.

The horse's nostrils exhaled white plumes, its hooves gaining cautious purchase on the slopes. A breeze came up and the snow slanted. Cold slipped under the pastor's collar, between buttons. Faint boot prints appeared in the snow. As the prints deepened, Pastor Boone made out where hobnails secured a heel, newspaper replaced worn-out leather. The youth had endured this trek while Davidson sat inside his warm farmhouse. Pastor Boone reconsidered next Sunday's sermon. Instead of a chapter from Acts on mercy, he pondered the opening verse in Obadiah, *The pride of thine own heart hath deceived thee.*

The boot prints continued to deepen, and the horse followed them toward a smudge of chimney smoke. As the buggy crossed a creek, ice crackled beneath the wheels. An elopement to Texas would have been what many other couples would do, but Ethan, whose father had died of smallpox in the war's final year, would not countenance being so far from his mother and siblings. The land bottomed out and the woods fell away. Parson Boone passed corn and hay fields drowsing under the snow.

Ethan was leaving the woodshed with an armload of kindling. He came to the porch edge, set the kindling beside three thick hearth logs, and returned to the shed. Helen stood on the porch, bundled in a woolen cloak and scarf. When she saw the buggy, Helen called out toward the shed. Ethan emerged, an axe gripped in his right hand. As the buggy halted in the yard, Colonel Davidson's stern visage appeared at the window, withdrew. Ethan leaned the axe against the shed and tethered the horse to a fence post. He helped Pastor Boone down from the seat, then fetched water for the horse as Pastor Boone went up on the porch. Helen took his free hand with one equally cold.

"We didn't know if you would come," she said, "what with the weather so bad."

The door opened and Mrs. Davidson appeared with a cup of coffee.

"Welcome, Pastor," Mrs. Davidson said, and turned to Helen. "Give this to Ethan, Daughter."

Helen took the cup and handed it to Ethan, who waited on the steps.

"Come in, Pastor Boone," Mrs. Davidson said, "and you, Daughter, you should come in as well, at least a few minutes."

"Unless Ethan comes, I'm staying on the porch," Helen replied, "but we *will* hear what is said."

As Pastor Boone stepped inside, Helen's firm hand on the jamb ensured the door remained ajar. Mrs. Davidson took his overcoat and disappeared into a back room. Dim as the afternoon was outside, the parlor was gloamier. What light the fireplace offered slowly unshrouded the room—a painting of a hunter and his dog, a burgundy rug, a settee and bookshelf, last, in the far corner, a Windsor armchair occupied by the Colonel. The patriarch gave the slightest acknowledgment and remained seated. Brown yet lingered in the gray swept-back hair. Though Davidson was a decade younger, Pastor Boone never felt older in his presence.

Mrs. Davidson returned from the back room with a cup of coffee. "Here, Pastor."

Pastor Boone took it gratefully because the cold sliced through the half-open door, tamped what heat the fire offered. He raised the cup to his mouth, blew slowly so the moist warmth glazed his cheeks and brow. He sipped and nodded approvingly.

"It's ever a blessing to drink real coffee again," Mrs. Davidson said. "We were long enough without it."

The Colonel shifted in his chair, his gaze locking on Pastor Boone's bible.

"Am I to assume your visit is in an official capacity?"

"I come at the request of your daughter and Ethan," Pastor Boone replied, "but I also come as a friend to everyone here, including you."

"That door needs to be shut," Colonel Davidson told his wife.

"Don't do it, Mother," Helen said from the porch. "We'll hear what is said."

Pastor Boone allowed himself a slight smile. He was tempted to speak of Helen being much her father's child, decided it prudent not to. Mrs. Davidson stared at the floor.

"Very well," Colonel Davidson said. "The chill can hasten us past civilities. Have your say, Pastor."

"It is time for all of us to heal, Leland," Pastor Boone said.

"Heal," Colonel Davidson answered, and lifted his left arm. "As your friend Doctor Andrews can inform you, there are things that cannot be healed."

"Not by man perhaps," Pastor Boone said, raising the bible, "but by God, by his grace. Colossians says *Forgive as the Lord forgave you.*"

"So you have come to bandy verses," the Colonel said, tugging back the sleeve so firelight reddened the stubbed wrist. "*Life shall go for life, eye for eye, tooth for tooth,* thus hand for a hand."

"Luke says *love your enemies, do good to them.*"

"Leviticus says to chase our enemies," Colonel Davidson countered, "*and they shall fall before you by the sword.*"

"You quote overly from the Old Testament," Pastor Boone said. "Therein lies more retribution than forgiveness."

"Yet they are cleaved together as one book," Colonel Davidson answered. "Thus we choose which verses to live by."

"Ethan has suffered as well," Pastor Boone said. "You have lost a hand, he has lost his youth. What you saw on the battlefield, he saw. What anger, what hatred you felt toward the enemy, he felt also."

"I accept his hatred now no less than then."

"But he doesn't hate you," Pastor Boone replied. "Moreover, he loves that which is part of you, and Helen loves him. You have seen his devotion to your daughter, to your whole family. He has put his uniform away. Ethan will burn it to appease you, he has told me so, and promised never to speak of the war in your presence. What more can you ask?"

The Colonel nodded at the missing hand.

"I've answered that," he said, "nothing more or less."

"Yes, you have, and in your family's presence," Pastor Boone said, allowing a terseness in his tone as well. "What about their wishes?"

"It was my hand taken and therefore my grievance, not theirs."

For a few moments the only sound was the fire's hiss and crackle.

"They could have married without your blessing," Pastor Boone said. "They can yet."

"Yes, and should they, let us be clear," the Colonel replied. "Helen will never step inside this house again, and if I see Ethan Burke on this land, or in town, or in church, I will kill him."

"You would need kill me too then, Father," Helen shouted from the porch.

Mrs. Davidson raised her hands to her ears.

"I will not listen to one word more," she said, her voice rising. "I will not. I will not."

When she turned to Pastor Boone, something seemed not so much to break inside her as wither. Mrs. Davidson's hands fell to her sides and her head drooped. For four years she had maintained the farm with her husband gone, no one to help but a daughter. Twice, outliers had come and stolen livestock, threatened to burn the house and barn down. Pastor Boone remembered how when the word came of Lee's surrender, no Confederate soldier's wife, including the woman before him, had mourned the lost cause. What tears had been shed were of relief it was finally over.

"There is no good in speaking of further violence," Pastor Boone said. "Haven't we all suffered enough these last years?"

"We, Pastor?" Colonel Davidson asked, his face reddening. "You dare speak to me of *your* suffering during the war."

"Fetch Pastor Boone's overcoat," the Colonel told his wife, and this time Mrs. Davidson did as she was told.

When Pastor Boone came outside, Ethan stood on the front step, Helen on the porch, their clasped hands bridging the boundary. They were arguing. Helen turned to Pastor Boone, tears in her eyes.

"Don't let Ethan do it."

"We shouldn't have bothered having you come," Ethan said. He freed his hands and gestured toward the axe. "It's the only thing to satisfy him. By God, I'll do it right now. I will."

Pastor Boone stepped close and took the youth by the elbow.

"You'll bleed to death or get gangrene. What good will come of that?"

"I've seen many a man live who lost a hand," Ethan said, shaking free Pastor Boone's hand. "He in there survived it, didn't he?"

"Ride back with me," Pastor Boone said. "I promise we'll find a way, a way that won't risk your life."

"Listen to him, Ethan," Helen said. "Please."

"We've waited long enough," Ethan said, tears in his eyes as well now. "I've done all of everything else and it's still not enough."

"Just one more week," Pastor Boone said. "Allow me one week."

"Please, Ethan," Helen said, sobbing.

Ethan dried his eyes with a swipe of his forearm. He nodded and addressed the house.

"One week," the youth said loudly. "One week and I will do it, Colonel Davidson, I swear I will."

"I have always taken you for a wise man, William, despite your primitive beliefs," Doctor Andrews said the following morning. "But what you purpose is unworthy of a rational mind."

The two men sat in the house's back portion that served as office and examining room. Sickness, his or a congregant's, had brought Pastor Boone to this room many times, but more often it served as a salon for the best-educated men in Marshall to discuss everything from literature and politics to science and religion. The room had changed little in three decades. The Franklin clock ticked on the top bookshelf, beside it jars holding powders and tinctures. On the middle shelf was a solemn row of leather-spined medical books, below that *Man's Place in Nature* and *On the Origin of Species* wedged between volumes by Shakespeare, Scott, and Thackeray. The examining table pressed against the opposite wall; in the room's center sat a mahogany desk, one side bedecked with pill cutter, ledger, mortar and pestle, the other a silver scale and balance aged to a dulled lustre. An oil lamp sat on the desk, its flame alive. Because of the closed curtains, a lacquered darkness gave the office the aura of a confessional booth, which, like the room's seeming immutability, no doubt made it easier to speak of fears too often confirmed.

"There is no other way," Pastor Boone said. "Elopement is not possible and the Colonel's own wife and daughter cannot dissuade him. The youth has done all he can. For eight months, he's performed all manner of chores. Even in this weather, he was out there cutting and stacking wood. He offered to burn his uniform, and him on the winning side."

"The Colonel sounds rather like Prospero," Doctor Andrews said.

"Prospero forgave his enemies," Pastor Boone answered. "It was Ethan's notion to do the labors, and he's shown himself worthy of any man's daughter."

Doctor Andrews removed a briar pipe and tobacco box from a drawer, as was his habit when anticipating a vigorous exchange. He tamped the tobacco and lit the pipe, doused the match with a sweep of the hand.

"I see that your new pipe has arrived."

"Yes," Doctor Andrews said, holding the briar pipe before them. "I only wish ideas could cross the ocean as quickly."

"So will you help us?"

"You have forgotten my oath, Parson, *primum non nocere*."

"You will be healing, Noah, and not just two families but a whole community."

"But at such cost, William," Doctor Andrews replied. "They are young folks, both likable and attractive. If this union is not made, they will find others to betroth. With time, even accept that it was wise to do so."

"Ethan is resolute," Pastor Boone said. "What you will not do, he will do with an axe."

"You truly believe so?" Doctor Andrews asked. "My experience avers that, once the axe is in hand, such brash valor abates. At Bowman-Gray I saw my fellows swoon cutting cadavers. The same in this office. Men you would think fearless get the vapors seeing a few drops of blood."

"He saw blood and wounds in the war, no doubt amputations," Pastor Boone said. "If it's not done by someone else, he'll do it. He would have done so yesterday with the Colonel's own axe if I had not intervened. As for Leland Davidson, you know the man. Do you believe he'd break a vow, any vow?"

"I do not," Doctor Andrews replied. "It would be an admission that he could be wrong."

The clock chimed on the half hour. Doctor Andrews set the pipe on the desk's spark-pocked wood.

"I must look in on Leah Blackburn. She has run a fever three days."

"You have proffered no answer," Pastor Boone said, but did not pause for one. "We are old men, Noah. Unlike the Colonel and this youth, we were spared the war's violence and suffering. Perhaps it's time for us to render what is our duty, even if we would wish it otherwise."

Doctor Andrews stood and Pastor Boone rose as well.

"Old men, William? Yes, I suppose we are," Doctor Andrews mused, rubbing his back. "I've watched others become gray and decrepit yet somehow presumed it was not happening to me. Is it so with you?"

"Sometimes," Pastor Boone answered.

"Perhaps it's because we are always looking for imperfections in others, and not ourselves," Doctor Andrews suggested.

"I've had cause to find plenty within myself," Pastor Boone said.

"If you mean your neutrality during the war, you protest too much, William. You did what you thought best, as did I."

"Best for the church or for myself?"

"Prudence was necessary," Doctor Andrews said. "I made no show of Unionist sympathies once the war began."

"But you did before. I did not even do that," Pastor Boone said. "Perhaps if I had, and done so forcefully, Leland Davidson would not have joined the Confederacy."

Doctor Andrews smiled.

"This present business should allay you of that vanity. Davidson is a man who values only his own opinion."

"But even now I don't understand his motivation to do so," Pastor Boone said. "He had no slaves to fight for."

Doctor Andrews set his pipe down.

"Perhaps I should not say this, William, but since you've broached the complexities of human motivation, might your involvement in this affair be of benefit to yourself as much as these young lovers?"

"In some ways, yes. I will admit that," Pastor Boone said, "but, as will be obvious, not in all."

"And you are certain he will sever his hand if I don't assent?" Doctor Andrews asked. "Absolutely certain?"

"Yes."

Doctor Andrews pressed his forehead with an open hand, as if to deflect some thought from breaking through.

"When would you have me do this?"

"Today," Pastor Boone replied. "Ethan said he'd wait a week, but I fear he won't wait that long."

"This afternoon at five o'clock then," Doctor Andrews said. "I visit my last patient at four, and I'll need to fetch Emma Triplett to assist me. But know I shall yet attempt to stop this folly. I will tell Ethan your motives are not solely in his interest, and point out that what seems brave and chivalrous today may not seem so when he has to support a family with one hand."

"No, not his hand," Pastor Boone said. "You have misconstrued my meaning."

The following afternoon the air still whitened each breath, but Pastor Boone and Ethan set out beneath a clear sky. The buggy passed slowly through town. Icicles dripped on posts and awnings, the thoroughfare a lather of mud and snow. Despite the cold, customers and storekeepers lined the boardwalks. Evelyn Norris, whose nephew had died in a Georgia prison camp, shook her head in dismay, but others tipped hats and nodded at Pastor Boone and Ethan. Several held out hands in the manner of a blessing. The bible and package lay on the buggy seat between them, the rings set deep in Ethan's right pocket.

As they rode out of town, the slashes left by other wheels vanished. By the time they entered the woods, the only indentions were those of squirrels and rabbits. They passed over snapped limbs shackled with ice. A cardinal swung low and settled on a post oak branch.

"It always comes down to guilt, does it not, that and somebody's blood," Noah had said when he'd taken the ether from his cabinet. "Your religion, I mean."

Pastor Boone had been sitting on the operating table, shirt off, his eyes on the pieces of steel Emma Triplett had boiled and then set on a white towel. The woman had left the room and they were alone.

"I suppose, though I would add that hope is also a factor."

Doctor Andrews had grimaced.

"I can't believe I've allowed you to talk me into this barbarism, and for no other reason than some bundles of papyrus written thousands of years ago. We may as well be living in mud huts, grinding rocks to make fire. Huxley and his X Club will soon end such nonsense in England, but in this country we still believe the recidivists, not the innovators bring advancement in human endeavors."

"I would say our country's military believe so," Pastor Boone answered as Emma Triplett came back in the room, "as evidenced by the number of deaths in this last conflict."

Emma Triplett handed a kerchief to the doctor, who nodded for Pastor Boone to lie down.

"Since a man of your advanced years may not rouse from this, I'll allow you the last word," Doctor Andrews said as he poured ether on the cloth, "although if you do pass on, and your metaphysics are correct, you shall quickly settle our debate once and for all."

Pastor Boone was about to speak of Mrs. Newell's similar doctrinal view, but the kerchief settled over his nose and mouth and the world wobbled a moment and then went black.

The woods thinned and the valley sprawled out before them. The Davidson farmhouse appeared and Ethan shook the reins to quicken the horse's pace. Pastor Boone's wrist throbbed, a vaguer ache where the hand had once been. The bottle of laudanum and a spoon were in his coat pocket, but if he took a dose, it would be just before the return to town. As the buggy jostled over the creek, Pastor Boone gasped.

"Sorry, Pastor," Ethan said. "I should have slowed the horse more."

"As long as you've waited," Pastor Boone replied, "a bit of haste is understandable."

A hound came off the porch, barked until it recognized Ethan. The buggy halted in front of the farmhouse and Ethan wrapped the check reins around the brake and jumped off. He helped Parson Boone from the buggy's seat, being careful not to bump the bandaged wrist. The front door opened and Helen came out on the porch. Pastor Boone took the bible off the seat.

"Bring the package," Pastor Boone said to Ethan, and stepped onto the porch.

"What happened, Pastor?" she asked, but then her face paled.

Ethan brought the package and Pastor Boone used his elbow and side to secure it.

"Stand behind me," he told them. "I'll call you when it's time to come inside."

Pastor Boone entered the parlor's muted light, set the bible and package on the lamp stand. Mrs. Davidson offered to take the overcoat and he told her she'd have to help him. She held the overcoat in her hand, did not move to hang it up. Pastor Boone opened the bible with his hand and found what he searched for. He left the bible open and slipped two fingers between the pasteboard and the knot of twine. He lifted the package with the fingers in the manner of measuring its weight. He crossed the room to where the Colonel sat.

"I take you as a man of your word, Leland," Pastor Boone said, and placed the package beside the Windsor chair. "Open it if you wish."

Pastor Boone went to the door and motioned Ethan and Helen inside. He took up the bible and balanced it in his hand, positioned himself between the two young people.

"Mark 10, verse nine" Pastor Boone said. "*What therefore God hath joined together.*"

A SORT *of* MIRACLE

Baroque wished he and Marlboro were back at the house watching medical shows with their sister, Susie. Instead, they were in a truck with Denton, their brother-in-law. Baroque wasn't used to Denton being this close. Denton was an accountant, and Monday through Friday he was at work all day. When he came home, he usually disappeared into the back bedroom after dinner. Of course Saturdays and Sundays Denton was around more, and often in the front of the house, and it was starting to take just a little thing like opening the refrigerator door for their brother-in-law to give Baroque and Marlboro a look, a real unfriendly look. One night Denton had called him and Marlboro lard-asses and claimed they lacked ambition and would never amount to anything if that didn't change.

He'd said it just the one time, but Baroque could tell Denton had thought it more than one time. He and Marlboro had even sat on the porch for a few minutes yesterday, just to get somewhere Denton wasn't.

But they were with him now and they sure couldn't get away from him in a truck cab, and the three of them were riding up a bumpy dirt road in the Great Smoky Mountains National Park, doing something that Baroque was pretty sure wasn't just a little illegal, like smoking pot or running a stop sign, but a lot illegal, like getting sent to prison, regardless of Denton saying it was a public service. When Baroque asked why they had to go bear hunting this particular day, Denton said this cold spell would soon send the bears into hibernation. Marlboro had asked what hibernation was and Denton had answered that it was when dumb, lazy creatures laid around for months doing nothing.

The dirt road came to a dead end. Cinder blocks marked the parking lot, and there was a trail on the other side. Denton told them again everything they were supposed to do and handed Baroque the cell phone, then left with the pistol and knife strapped around his waist. Once up the trail a few yards, Denton was suddenly gone, like the woods had just swallowed him up. It made Baroque feel spooky, but everything about this bear business had been spooky. Like the way two weeks ago Denton had brought a big carton home after work and pulled out a steel trap, a pistol, a yellow box of bullets, and then a knife. A big knife, the kind Baroque had seen only in movies where maniacs hacked people to death, maniacs who always had some mask or hood covering everything except their eyes, which made it worse, because it could be anybody who was the maniac, even the person in the movie who seemed most normal. Like Marlboro, Baroque wore only a regular shirt and a sweatshirt. The warmth from the heater seemed to have whooshed right out the moment Denton opened the truck door. Baroque and Marlboro hadn't been with Denton when he set the bear trap, but Baroque wished now that Denton had made them come then instead of now, because it had to have been a lot warmer that day. His breath clouded the windshield and Baroque felt his body start to shiver. He looked at the trail, then cranked the engine and put the heater on high.

"Denton said we shouldn't do that unless we got real cold," Marlboro said.

"Well, I am real cold," Baroque said, "aren't you?"

Marlboro nodded and clapped his hands together and rubbed them.

"How cold do you think it is?"

"Eighteen degrees," Baroque said. "That was the number on the bank sign."

"I don't think we've ever been in weather like this," Marlboro said.

"No," Baroque agreed. "It's probably never been this cold in Florida, except maybe during the Ice Age."

"I wish Susie could have come down to Florida to help us get a job there instead of up here."

"That would have been better," Baroque said, "but there's nothing we can do about that."

"I guess this is our first job," Marlboro said, "being here, I mean."

"Yes, I guess it is."

"You think we'll lose our nose and fingers, like that guy on the medical show?"

"No," Baroque said. "That guy was stuck on a mountaintop three days. We won't be here that long."

"I sure hope not," Marlboro replied. "I don't think I could eat if I couldn't breathe through my nose."

"You'd learn to get used to it," Baroque said. They listened to the heater hiss against the cold.

"You think he's really going to kill a bear?"

"That's what he said," Baroque answered.

As the cab warmed, the breath fogging the windshield evaporated, but all Baroque could see were woods, woods where someone or something could be watching him and Marlboro right now.

"It's sort of spooky when there aren't any streets or houses around," Marlboro said, evidently feeling the same way.

"It wouldn't hurt to lock our doors," Baroque said, "just to be on the safe side."

They pressed down the locks and for a few minutes didn't speak. It was Marlboro who broke the silence.

"He wouldn't just leave us out here, would he? I mean, he's not acted very friendly lately."

"No," Baroque said. "He'd have made us get out of the truck and driven off if he was going to do that."

Denton felt better as soon as he left the truck. Being that close to his brothers-in-law made him feel like a fungus was starting to grow on him. They both had a moldy sort of smell, like mushrooms. Which was no surprise, since Baroque and Marlboro moved about as much as mushrooms. They never left the house, and got up from the couch only to eat or go to the bathroom. Hell, mushrooms probably did more than that. They actually grew. They were finding nutrients, some kind of work was going on down there in the soil.

Baroque and Marlboro had been with him and Susie two months, up from Florida to find jobs, they claimed. Evidently they expected the jobs to haul themselves up to Denton's front porch and wait for Marlboro and Baroque to step out the door and be whisked away. Denton blamed a lot of it on their being from Florida. He'd never met anyone from the place who didn't get on his nerves, like all the Florida retirees who drove ten miles an hour on any road that wasn't straight and wide as an airport runway. Admittedly, Denton hadn't been around many younger Floridians, but his brothers-in-law were indictment enough.

Baroque, whose name sounded a lot like "a roach" to Denton, was the older of the two by eleven months. Their father was a self-

proclaimed "free spirit" who'd drifted like a spore—that's the way
Denton always envisioned it, anyway—into Colorado and attached
himself long enough to find Susie's mother and have a baby with her.
Then the three of them drifted on down to Florida, where Baroque
and Marlboro were born. It was the father who'd named the two boys.

Susie didn't know how the name Baroque had come about, but
Marlboro had been named after the Marlboro Man, the cigarette
cowboy. Susie said it was meant as a comment on society. Thank God
that Susie, at thirty the oldest by six years, had been named by the
mother. Susie wasn't a Floridian, in Denton's view. She'd been born
in Colorado and had gotten out of Florida quick as she could, earning
a scholarship to Gulf Coast College, in Alabama. She met her first
husband there, a fifty-year-old admissions counselor.

As soon as Susie graduated, they married and moved to North
Carolina, so mountains could blot out some sun. The first husband
had problems with psoriasis. But he had at least gotten her to North
Carolina, where she and Denton met.

Susie's first marriage hadn't worked out any better than Denton's. Her first husband had made Susie wear his dead aunt's Sunday
church hat every time they had sex. An awful thing, but Denton's first
wife had been even worse. The admissions counselor's aunt might've
been dead but at least the man hadn't lain there like he was dead.
Denton's first wife was so frigid that each time they had sex she might
as well have been embalmed. Eventually, every time they did it he'd
hear organ music inside his head, the same kind that oozed out of
funeral home walls. It was a wonder he and Susie could ever touch
another naked person after the two partners they'd had.

The two of them had overcome a lot, no doubt about that, but
now they had a nice marriage and a fine house and Denton had a
good job as an accountant and Susie was the head nurse at the county
clinic. Which was why she'd let Baroque and Marlboro come up from

Florida in the first place. She'd wanted to help her brothers improve themselves, and Denton couldn't blame her for that. After all, hard as it was to believe, they were her brothers. She was even trying to get them, or at least Baroque, interested in medicine. Baroque was sort of smart, Susie claimed, and if Baroque got a job as a med tech maybe Marlboro could be an orderly or something. She'd taken them to the clinic with her for a day, and now she had them watching the medical shows. It might inspire them, she claimed, though Denton was of a mind that a good kick in their lardy asses would inspire them more.

Susie watched the medical shows as much as she could. She might need to know this sometime, she always said when Denton complained. He understood it could be helpful to someone in the medical field, but Susie didn't watch the shows about a heart transplant or a knee operation or a woman having a baby. Susie watched shows with names like *Medical Mysteries* or *I Survived*, shows about hundred-pound tumors or people who'd lost all their toes to frostbite or who internally combusted, and it all gave Denton the willies.

He would go in the back room and watch the fourteen-inch TV on the bureau, catch the news on CNN and then maybe one of the business shows, or get on the computer, where he'd been doing the bear research. Anything was better than the medical shows. The worst thing to Denton was how they always ended. There'd be upbeat music and the announcer would talk about miracles, and the person who'd had the hundred-pound tumor or the man whose leg had been snapped off by a shark always acted like it was a good thing this had happened. Now Susie had Baroque and Marlboro watching them every night, probably even a few about bear attacks.

They did at least watch them. Whenever Denton ventured into the front room, their eyes were always on the screen. They weren't talking and seemed to be paying attention. Of course Baroque and Marlboro never did talk a lot anyway, not to Denton, or even much to Susie. They just sat next to each other, in the exact same posture, like twins. Part of that was surely their being less than a year apart in age, and also because Baroque and Marlboro did look like twins, at least in the face and especially their eyes, which changed when they shifted them in a different direction—less green to more brown or vice versa. It reminded Denton of his twelfth-grade biology project. The teacher had given every student in the class a jar of fruit flies, and after a while the fruit flies' eyes were supposed to change, and everybody else's fruit flies had changed eye color except Denton's. His just crawled around on the glass for an hour and then died.

He got a D– on a major nine-week project, which was totally unfair. Denton hadn't picked out the flies or put them in the jar. He hadn't asked for them. They were just there on his desk one morning. He got no college-scholarship offers like Susie, and instead had to work his way through. The damn fruit flies had made sure of that. Susie saw Baroque and Marlboro's interest in the medical shows as a step forward. Still, neither of them had actually left the house to apply for a med tech program or orderly job, and though Susie hadn't actually said it, Denton suspected even she was tired of her brothers being around.

It had pretty much shut down their sex life, because their house was a fine house but a small one. Baroque was in the spare room with just three inches of drywall between him and their bedroom. Marlboro was on the couch, and if Denton and Susie could hear the springs squeak whenever Baroque or Marlboro turned over, then they sure as hell could hear what he and Susie were up to. After the nightmare sex of their first marriages, there had been issues to work out, which they had. Until the brothers-in-law showed up, Susie tended to moan some and rock the bed a good bit, but there wasn't much of that anymore, and now Denton was starting to have some problems, and Denton had never had problems, at least with Susie.

He stopped to rest a moment, checked to make sure the double-ply plastic bag was still in his coat pocket. Paws and gallbladder—that was all he needed. Denton had to hand it to the Chinese. They were smart, and had been smart a long time. They'd invented gunpowder and a lot of other things, even spaghetti. The Chinese also knew how to cure certain male problems without having to explain them to a doctor and then after that having to take the prescription to a pharmacy where some eighteen-year-old cashier would stop chewing her bubble gum just long enough to do something stupid like say your name and the name of what you were picking up out loud, maybe even say it over a speaker like it was a frigging pep rally. No, the Chinese understood better how to do things than Americans. They explained what cured a problem and explained where to get the cure and even how to prepare it. It was the right way of doing things, which was why they pretty much owned the United States now. The way he'd been feeling the last few months, Denton wasn't sure he'd mind the Chinese taking over America completely, because everybody over there worked. If they didn't they starved. Sure, times were hard here. Denton understood that as well as anyone. He'd barely survived a layoff himself. But unlike his brothers-in-law, he'd have found something to do if he'd been laid off, even if it was picking up cans and bottles out of ditches.

Denton moved on up the trail, wondering if a caught bear would stay quiet or make a ruckus. The only sound was the water, and not even that except where a waterfall or rapid was, all the stream's slow parts covered with ice. No other sounds like a chain saw or car or dog, because this was real wilderness he was in now, and it was so cold the birds and squirrels were using their energy just to hunker down and survive. Denton felt cold even with his thermal underwear, gloves, and wool coat, and it would only get colder, because though it was midafternoon, the sun would soon start to fade behind the mountains. At least the cold would be good for preserving the bear paws and gallbladder. Denton wouldn't even have to stop and get ice for the cooler, which meant five minutes less time before he could get some distance between him and his brothers-in-law.

Denton looked down through the trees to see if he could glimpse the truck but didn't see it. All Baroque and Marlboro had to do was sit and wait, that and lean on the horn if a ranger appeared. Even they would have trouble screwing up those directions. Then again, Denton wouldn't put it past them to drive over to Bryson City for something to eat or a six-pack of beer, then forget where the hell they'd been parked. That was the worst of it.

Most people were smart at something. There were guys Denton had known in high school who weren't able to spell cat, but at least they could change their spark plugs or replace a blown fuse. Baroque and Marlboro didn't even possess smarts like that. Having clogged up the commode three times, Marlboro, it was clear, couldn't even figure out how to properly wipe his ass, and Baroque had driven the truck like a drunk ten-year-old the one time Denton allowed him to take it to town. Denton thought about calling them, just to be sure they hadn't driven off, but then he remembered they would actually need money to buy a hot dog or six-pack. Still, Denton was beginning to feel uneasy about bringing them along.

He went on, breathing hard because he was climbing steep ground, and having to be more careful too, since ice was on the trail this far up. That was something else. He'd figured, wrongly, that the cold weather would drive Baroque and Marlboro back to Florida. *Florida.* Denton said the word out loud. What kind of name for a state was that?

It wasn't a word with any backbone to it, like the hard C in the first syllable of Carolina. You could look at Florida on a map and see that it drooped down from the rest of America like a limp peter.

It was a wonder the Founding Fathers hadn't just sawed the damn state off and let it drift away. A state where the most famous person went around pretending to be an eight-foot-tall mouse. Every kid in the state had probably been to see that thing, walked up to it, and shaken its hand or paw or whatever believing it was a real mouse. Growing up to think a big animal like that wouldn't be dangerous. No surprise, then, that when the kids grew up they'd think piranhas and pythons and walking catfish were a good idea for pets, then go dump them in some nearby swamp or river, thinking that was another good idea.

And now it was as if the whole state was like those catfish, crawling up the Eastern Seaboard into North Carolina and taking over, because here in this very park there were people—people who were supposed to be in charge—who acted like bears were pets. Letting them wander along the roads so dumb-asses could throw marshmallows and french fries at them, like it was trick or treat and the bears weren't real bears but idiots in costumes. Doing it even after some fool had nearly had his arm torn off by a bear he was feeding from a car window, and probably would have had his arm torn off if someone in the car behind hadn't tossed out a bag of Cheetos. Denton had seen the whole bear spectacle firsthand just a month ago when he'd driven to Cherokee to see a client. The bears were actually lined up on the shoulder waiting for handouts. One had gotten out on the road in front of Denton's truck and stayed there with its big red tongue slobbering, like it was owed a meal. That was another thing the Chinese had going for them. They weren't big on pets. Hell, they ate their pets, or what passed for pets over here.

Denton finally saw his marker and left the trail. He paused but didn't hear anything so, if the trap had worked, maybe the creature was already dead. Denton had to admit he was relieved. If he'd caught one and it was dead, all he'd have to do was cut off the paws and do a little surgery to find the gallbladder, which shouldn't be that hard, since he'd seen the photos—greenish, shaped like a fig. If the bear hadn't died, he'd have to shoot it. He'd grown up in a place where you were supposed to enjoy being out in the woods shooting things, but he had never enjoyed being outdoors.

Denton liked being able to decide how warm or cold he was going to be, and having a toilet, and knowing exactly where everything was and knowing it was close by. But here he was, way up in the woods with a pistol and knife and trap like he was Daniel frigging Boone. And what if he got caught? Having Baroque and Marlboro as look-outs probably increased the chances about a thousand percent. He'd lose a good job at the least. Maybe end up in jail, because having the gun with him meant two federal crimes.

But there was no bear. The store-bought ham he'd hung from the limb was gone, the trap sprung. Denton looked closer, saw two silvery-brown nails and a few hairs. The bear had leaned over the trap as if reaching over a counter. Dumb luck on the bear's part, Denton knew, but at least the damn thing might be scared enough now to think twice before going after human food again. Screw it, Denton thought, bear, medicine, and, most of all, the brothers-in-law.

Denton had eighty bucks and a credit card in his billfold. He'd take Baroque and Marlboro to the bus station in Asheville. And buy two one-way tickets to Florida. They might eventually wander back, but it'd take those two screwups months or even years to get enough money to return. Susie had sent them money to come the first time, but there was no way in hell that Denton would let that happen again. As he began the walk back, Denton suddenly felt better than he had in a while. Everything was going to be all right.

Even freezing his tail off on this mountain had been worthwhile. That was another thing the Chinese believed, or at least the Buddhists among them, that you went up a mountain to gain wisdom. And he damn sure had, finally realizing what to do about the brothers-in-law.

Denton made his way back down the trail, going slow because the afternoon light was waning. He started thinking about how he'd deal with Baroque and Marlboro if they didn't want to go. Just as he decided if it came down to the pistol he wasn't above that, Denton tripped on a root and his ankle veered in one direction and the rest of his body in another. He didn't stop tumbling until he was off the trail and into the stream, ice shattering around him as he entered the tailwater of a wide, long pool face-first.

Soaked from his head all the way to his waist, Denton crawled up on the bank. His teeth chattered and he could feel his hair turning into icicles. He knew that whatever else bad had happened in his life—embalmed wife, deadbeat bears, brothers-in-law—this was worse. A whole lot worse.

He took off his gloves and pulled out the cell phone, praying it would still work. The cell phone, unlike him, had been totally immersed, but by some kind of miracle it wasn't dead. Denton's fingers were numb but he was finally able to press the right numbers and the call went through. On the eighth ring Baroque picked up and Denton explained what had happened, or at least as best he could, because his brain was clouding with every passing second, and his words didn't match up with his thoughts the way he wanted them to. It felt like years passed before Baroque understood.

"We're coming," Baroque said. "How far from the truck are you, time-wise?"

Denton didn't speak for what felt like a full minute. The connections of time and space were not so clear anymore.

"Maybe thirty minutes," he finally answered.

Denton heard Baroque speak to Marlboro, then the sound of truck doors slamming shut.

"We're on our way," Baroque said. "But we need to know if you feel cold or hot."

Denton realized that though his teeth chattered and icicles had formed in his hair he actually was, if not hot, at least warm.

"Hot," he said.

"You got to get back in the water, then," Baroque said. "You've got hypothermia. A boy on one of the shows fell in a pond and being under that cold water was all that kept him from freezing to death."

Denton tried hard to figure out if Baroque knew what he was talking about. It seemed Denton had heard of such a thing, maybe on the news, and the fact that Baroque had learned a word as long as *hypothermia*, even pronounced it correctly, struck him dimly as some kind of progress. Besides, the water would cool him off.

"You can't wait any longer," Baroque said. "In a couple of minutes you won't be able to move. We're on our way."

Denton looked at the pool, covered in ice except around the falls. Somewhere deep inside him an alarm bell went off, but it was so soft Denton couldn't figure out quite what the warning was. Baroque was still talking, telling Denton he had to do it now. Denton set the cell phone on the bank. Baroque's words were blurring. It seemed Baroque was talking real fast, though maybe that was because Denton was starting to think real slow. Breaking the ice to enter the pool seemed too much work, so Denton crawled onto the rocks above the waterfall and slid feetfirst into the pool, going in smooth as an otter.

At first they didn't see him, just the cell phone's blue-tinged screen.

"If he crawled up in the woods, he's a goner for sure," Baroque said.

Then they saw Denton hovering in the pool's center. The ice was so clear it looked like Denton was part of a magic trick.

"His eyes are open," Marlboro said.

"Of course they are," Baroque said, "and he can probably see us and hear us."

"He's not blinking."

"That's because it's like a coma, everything's shut down but his brain. His heart, I bet it's less than one beat a minute by now."

"I didn't think he'd be that blue," Marlboro said.

Baroque took a football-sized rock and threw it into the pool above Denton's head. The ice shattered, but Denton's body drifted only a few feet before it snagged on more ice.

"We'll have to go in and get him," Baroque said. Marlboro looked at the water reluctantly.

"I guess so."

"Let me get his cell phone first," Baroque said. "He'd be mad at us if we left it. Anyway, we'd better get him to the hospital. I've been thinking more about that show. The announcer might have said fifteen minutes, not fifty. I don't guess you remember?"

Marlboro shook his head.

Baroque picked up the phone and put it in his pocket and they waded in, the water over their ankles as Baroque set his hands beneath Denton's shoulders and Marlboro lifted his feet. Once on the bank, they set Denton down. Marlboro parted his legs and positioned himself between them as if hauling a stretcher.

"His being stiff does make it easier," Marlboro said.

They made their way down the trail and arrived at the parking lot. As the day's last light fell behind the mountains, they leaned Denton against the truck.

"Should we put him in the middle?" Marlboro asked.

"We can't do that," Baroque said, "not unless you want to drive all the way to town without heat. A human can't be thawed out but once."

Baroque opened the tailgate and they slid Denton in feetfirst, placing two cinder blocks, one on each side, so he wouldn't shift as much. Marlboro took the lid off the Styrofoam cooler and wedged it gently, almost tenderly, under Denton's head.

"And he can still see and hear us?" Marlboro asked when they'd finished.

"Sure." Marlboro stared at Denton.

"I can't think of anything to say to him."

They got into the cab and after a couple of tries Baroque found first gear and they made their way down the dirt road.

"He's been pretty good to us," Marlboro said. "He can be grouchy but he has let us stay with him."

"I've been thinking maybe we haven't really held up our end as much as we should have," Baroque said. "Next week I'm going over to the community college to see about that med tech degree. What we're doing helping Denton makes me feel useful."

Marlboro nodded.

"If you do that, I'll go see about an orderly job."

The road went downhill and the woods thickened. Everything was shadowy now and at the bottom of the hill was a bridge. Baroque knew from movies this was not the kind of place where anything good ever happened. A maniac or a man with a steel hook for a hand or a mutant could be hiding under the bridge. He risked shifting into second gear and found it and the truck sped up and rattled on across. Baroque let out a grateful sigh as the road rose again and the woods opened up.

"If Denton is okay, do you think they'll put us on one of the medical shows?" Marlboro asked.

"Probably," Baroque said.

"And they'll give us medals?"

"I don't know about that," Baroque said, "but if they do they should give Denton one too. The way he got himself under the ice—that was real smart."

"What do they need to get him going again?" Marlboro asked. "It doesn't have to be a special kind of hospital?"

"No, they've all been trained to do it."

"That's good," Marlboro said, as the dirt road ended at an asphalt two-lane.

The truck stalled when Baroque shifted into reverse instead of neutral. He didn't try to turn the engine back on but simply stared out the windshield, unsure which way to go. Baroque looked in one direction, then the other, but he couldn't see much because it was real dark now. The headlights would have helped, but he didn't know how to turn them on.

The CORPSE BIRD

Perhaps if work had been less stressful, Boyd Candler would not have heard the owl, but he hadn't slept well for a month. Too often he found himself awake at three or four in the morning, his mind troubled by engineering projects weeks behind schedule, possible layoffs at year's end. So now, for the second night in a row, Boyd listened to the bird's low plaintive call. After a few more minutes he left the bed, walked out of the house where his wife and daughter slept to stand in the side yard that bordered the Colemans' property. The cool late-October dew dampened his bare feet. Jim Coleman had unplugged his spotlight, and the other houses on the street were unlit except for a couple of porch lights. The subdivision was quiet and still as Boyd waited like a man in a doctor's office expecting a dreaded diagnosis. In a few minutes it came. The owl called again from the scarlet oak behind the Colemans' house, and Boyd knew with utter certainty that if the bird stayed in the tree another night someone would die.

Boyd Candler had grown up among people who believed the world could reveal all manner of things if you paid attention. As a child he'd watched his grandfather, the man he and his parents lived with, find a new well for a neighbor with nothing more than a branch from an ash tree. He'd been in the neighbor's pasture as his grandfather walked slowly from one fence to the other, the branch's two forks gripped like reins, not stopping until the tip wavered and then dipped toward the ground as if yanked by an invisible hand. He'd watched the old man live his life "by the signs." Whether a moon waxed or waned decided when the crops were planted and harvested, the hogs slaughtered and the timber cut, even when a hole was best dug. A red sunrise meant coming rain, as did the call of a raincrow. Other signs that were harbingers of a new life, or a life about to end.

Boyd was fourteen when he heard the corpse bird in the woods behind the barn. His grandfather had been sick for months but recently rallied, gaining enough strength to leave his bed and take short walks around the farm. The old man had heard the owl as well, and it was a sound of reckoning to him as final as the thump of dirt clods on his coffin.

It's come to fetch me, the old man had said, and Boyd hadn't the slightest doubt it was true. Three nights the bird called from the woods behind the barn. Boyd had been in his grandfather's room those nights, had been there when his grandfather let go of his life and followed the corpse bird into the darkness.

The next morning at breakfast Boyd didn't mention the owl to his wife or daughter. What had seemed a certainty last night was more tenuous in daylight. His mind drifted toward a project due by the week's end. Boyd finished his second cup of coffee and checked his watch.

"Where's Jennifer?" he asked his wife. "It's our week to carpool."

"No pickup today," Laura said. "Janice called while you were in the shower. Jennifer ran a temperature over a hundred all weekend. It hasn't broken so Janice is staying home with her."

Boyd felt a cold dark wave of disquiet pass through him.

"Have they been to the doctor?"

"Of course," Laura said.

"What did the doctor say was wrong with Jennifer?"

"Just a virus, something going around," Laura said, her back to him as she packed Allison's lunch.

"Did the doctor tell Janice anything else to watch out for?" Boyd asked.

Laura turned to him. The expression on her face wavered between puzzlement and irritation.

"It's a virus, Boyd. That's all it is."

"I'll be outside when you're ready," Boyd told his daughter, and walked out into the yard.

The neighborhood seemed less familiar, as though many months had passed since he'd seen it. The subdivision had been built over a cotton field. A few fledgling dogwoods and maples had been planted in some yards, but the only big tree was the scarlet oak that grew on an undeveloped lot behind the Colemans' house. Boyd assumed it was once a shade tree, a place for cotton field workers to escape the sun a few minutes at lunch and water breaks.

The owl was still in the oak. Boyd knew this because growing up he'd heard the older folks say a corpse bird always had to perch in a big tree. It was one way you could tell it from a regular barn or screech owl. Another way was that the bird returned to the same tree, the same branch, each of the three nights.

His family had moved to Asheville soon after his grandfather's death. Boyd had been an indifferent student in Madison County, assuming he'd become a farmer, but the farm had been sold, the money divided among his father and aunts. At Asheville High Boyd mastered a new kind of knowledge, one of theorems and formulas, a knowledge where everything could be explained down to the last decimal point. His teachers told him he should be an engineer and helped Boyd get loans and scholarships so he could be the first in his family to attend college. His teachers urged him into a world where the sky did not matter, where land did not blacken your nails, cling to your boots or callus your hands but was seen, if at all, through the glass windows of buildings and cars and planes. His teachers had believed he could leave the world he had grown up in, and perhaps he had believed it as well.

Boyd remembered the morning his college sociology class watched a film about the folklore of Hmong tribesmen in Laos. After the film the professor asked if similar beliefs could be found in other cultures, Boyd raised his hand. When he'd finished speaking, the professor and the other students stared at Boyd as if a bone pierced his nostrils and human teeth dangled from his neck.

"So you've actually witnessed such things?" the professor asked.

"Yes sir," he replied, knowing his face had turned a deep crimson.

A student sitting behind him snickered.

"And this folklore, you believe in it?" the professor asked.

"I'm just saying I once knew people who did," Boyd said. "I wasn't talking about myself."

"Superstition is nothing more than ignorance of cause and effect," the student behind him said.

Rational. Educated. Enlightened. Boyd knew the same words he'd heard years ago in college, the same sensibility that came with those words, prevailed in the subdivision. Most of his neighbors were transplants from the Northeast or Midwest, all white-collar professionals like himself. His neighbors would assume that since it was October the owl was migrating. Like the occasional possum or raccoon, the owl would be nothing more to them than a bit of nature that had managed to stray into the city and would soon return to its proper environment.

But Boyd did worry, off and on all morning and afternoon. He couldn't remember Allison ever having a fever that lasted three days. He thought about calling the Colemans' house to check on Jennifer, but Boyd knew how strange that would seem. Despite the carpool and their daughters' friendship, the parents' interactions were mostly hand waves and brief exchanges about pickup times. In their six years as neighbors, the two families had never shared a meal.

Though Boyd had work that he'd normally stay late to finish, at five sharp he logged off his computer and drove home. Halloween was five nights away, and as he turned into the subdivision he saw hollow-eyed pumpkins on porches and steps. A cardboard witch on a broomstick dangled from a tree limb, turning with the wind like a weathervane. At another house a skeleton shuddered above a carport, one bony finger extended as if beckoning. A neighborhood contest of sorts, and one that Jim Coleman particularly enjoyed. Each year Jim glued a white bed sheet over a small parade balloon. He tethered its nylon cord to a concrete block so that his makeshift ghost hovered over the Coleman house.

There had been no such displays when Boyd was a child, no dressing up to trick or treat. Perhaps because the farm was so isolated, but Boyd now suspected it had been more an understanding that certain things shouldn't be mocked, that to do so might bring retribution. As Boyd passed another house, this one adorned with black cats, he wondered if that retribution had already come, was perched in the scarlet oak.

It was almost dark when he pulled into the driveway behind his wife's Camry. Through the front window, Boyd saw Allison sprawled in front of the fire, Laura sitting on the couch. The first frost of the year had been predicted for tonight and from the chill in the air Boyd knew it would be so.

He stepped into the side yard and studied the Colemans' house. Lights were on in two rooms upstairs as well as in the kitchen and dining room. Both vehicles were in the carport. Jim Coleman had turned on a spotlight he'd set on the roof, and it illuminated the ghost looming overhead.

Boyd walked into the backyard. The scarlet oak's leaves caught the day's last light. *Lambent*, that was the word for it, Boyd thought, like red wine raised to candlelight. He slowly raised his gaze but did not see the bird. He clapped his hands together, so hard his palms burned. Something dark lifted out of the tallest limb, hung above the tree a moment, then resettled.

In the living room, Allison and her schoolbooks lay sprawled in front of the hearth. When Boyd leaned to kiss her he felt the fire's warmth on her face. Laura sat on the couch, writing month-end checks.

"How is Jennifer?" he asked when he came into the kitchen.

Laura set the checkbook aside.

"No better. Janice called and said she was going to keep her home again tomorrow."

"Did she take her back to the doctor?"

"Yes. The doctor gave her some antibiotics and took a strep culture."

Allison twisted her body and turned to Boyd.

"You need to cut us some more wood this weekend, Daddy. There are only a few big logs left."

Boyd nodded and let his eyes settle on the fire. Laura had wanted to switch to gas logs. Just like turning a TV on and off, that easy, his wife had said, and a lot less messy. Boyd had argued the expense, especially since the wood he cut was free, but it was more than that. Cutting the wood, stacking, and finally burning it gave him pleasure, work that, unlike so much of what he did at his job, was tactile, somehow more real.

Boyd was staring at the hearth when he spoke.

"I think Jennifer needs to see somebody else, somebody besides a family doctor."

"Why do you think that, Daddy?" Allison asked.

"Because I think she's real sick."

"But she can't miss Halloween," Allison said. "We're both going to be ghosts."

"How can you know that?" Laura asked. "You haven't even seen her."

"I just know."

Laura was about to say something else, then hesitated.

"We'll talk about this later," Laura said.

He waited until after supper to knock on the Colemans' door. Laura had told him not to go, but Boyd went anyway. Jim Coleman opened the door. Boyd stood before a man he suddenly realized he knew hardly anything about. He didn't know how many siblings Jim Coleman had or what kind of neighborhood in Chicago he'd grown up in or if he'd ever held a shotgun or hoe in his hand. He did not know if Jim Coleman had once been a churchgoer or had always spent his Sunday mornings working in his garage or yard.

"I've come to check on Jennifer," Boyd said.

"She's sleeping," Jim answered.

"I'd still like to see her, if you don't mind," Boyd said, and showed Jim a sheet of paper. "I had Allison write down what they did in class today. She'd be disappointed if I didn't deliver this."

For a moment Boyd thought he would say no, but Jim Coleman stepped aside.

"Come in then."

He followed Jim down the hallway and up the stairs to Jennifer's bedroom. The girl lay in her bed, the sheets pulled up to her neck. Sweat had matted the child's hair, made her face a shiny paleness, like porcelain. In a few moments Janice joined them. She pressed her palm against Jennifer's forehead and let it linger as though bestowing a blessing.

"What was her temperature the last time you checked?" Boyd asked.

"One hundred and two. It goes up in the evening."

"And it's been four days now?"

"Yes," Janice said. "Four days and four nights. I let her go to school Friday. I probably shouldn't have."

Boyd looked at Jennifer. He tried to put himself in her parents' situation. He tried to imagine what words could connect what he'd witnessed in Madison County to some part of their experience in Chicago or Raleigh. But there were no such words. What he had learned in the North Carolina mountains was untranslatable to the Colemans.

"I think you need to get her to the hospital," Boyd said.

"But the doctor says as soon as the antibiotics kick in she'll be fine," Janice said.

"You need to get her to the hospital," Boyd said again.

"How can you know that?" Janice asked. "You're not a doctor."

"When I was a boy, I saw someone sick like this." Boyd hesitated. "That person died."

"Doctor Underwood said she'd be fine," Jim said, "that plenty of kids have had this. He's seen her twice."

"You're scaring me," Janice said.

"I'm not trying to scare you," Boyd said. "Please take Jennifer to the hospital. Will you do that?"

Janice turned to her husband.

"Why is he saying these things?"

"You need to leave," Jim Coleman said.

"Please," Boyd said. "I know what I'm talking about."

"Leave. Leave now," Jim Coleman said.

Boyd walked back into his own yard. For a few minutes he stood there. The owl did not call but he knew it roosted in the scarlet oak, waiting.

"Janice just called and she's royally pissed off." Laura told him when he entered the house. "I told you not to go over there. They think you're mentally disturbed, maybe even dangerous."

Laura sat on the couch, and she motioned for Boyd to sit down also.

"Where's Allison?" Boyd asked.

"I put her to bed," Laura said. "You know, you're upsetting Allison as well as the Colemans. You're upsetting me too. Tell me what this is about, Boyd."

For half an hour he tried to explain. When Boyd finished his wife placed one of her hands over his.

"I know where you grew up that people, uneducated people, believed such things," Laura said. "But you don't live in Madison County anymore, and you are educated. Maybe there is an owl out back. I haven't heard it, but I'll concede it could be out there. But even so it's an *owl*, nothing more."

Laura squeezed his hand.

"I'm getting you an appointment with Doctor Harmon. He'll prescribe some Ambien so you can get some rest, maybe something else for the anxiety."

Later that night Boyd lay in bed, waiting for the owl to call. An hour passed on the red digits of the alarm clock and he tried to muster hope that the bird had left. He finally fell asleep for a few minutes, long enough to dream about his grandfather. They were in Madison

County, in the farmhouse. Boyd was in the front room by himself, waiting though he didn't know what for. Finally, the old man came out of his bedroom, dressed in his brogans and overalls, a sweat rag in his back pocket.

The corpse bird's call roused him from the dream. Boyd put on pants and shoes and a sweatshirt. He took a flashlight from the kitchen drawer and went into the basement to get the chain saw. The machine was almost forty years old, a relic, heavy and cumbersome, its teeth dulled by decades of use. But it still ran well enough to keep them in firewood.

Boyd filled the gas tank and checked the spark plug and chain lube. The chain saw had belonged to his grandfather, had been used by the old man to cull trees from his farm for firewood. Boyd had often gone into the woods with him, helped load the logs and kindling into his grandfather's battered pickup. After the old man's health had not allowed him to use it anymore, he'd given it to Boyd. Two decades had passed before he found a use for it. A coworker owned some thirty acres near Cary and offered Boyd all the free wood he wanted as long as the trees were dead and Boyd cut them himself.

Outside, the air was sharp and clear. The stars seemed more defined, closer. A bright-orange harvest moon rose in the west. He clicked on the flashlight and let its beam trace the upper limbs until he saw it. Despite being bathed in light, the corpse bird did not stir. Rigid as a gravestone, Boyd thought. The unblinking yellow eyes stared toward the Colemans' house, and Boyd knew these were the same eyes that had fixed themselves on his grandfather.

Boyd laid the flashlight on the grass, its beam aimed at the scarlet oak's trunk. He pulled the cord and the machine trembled to life. Its vibration shook his whole upper body. Boyd stepped close to the tree, extending his arms, the machine's weight tensing his biceps and forearms.

The scrub trees on his co-worker's land had come down quickly and easily. But he'd never cut a tree the size of the scarlet oak. A few bark shards flew out as the blade hit the tree, then the blade skittered down the trunk until Boyd pulled it away and tried again.

It took eight attempts before he made the beginnings of a wedge in the tree. He was breathing hard, the weight of the saw straining his arms, back, and even his legs as he steadied not only himself but the machine. He angled the blade as best he could to widen the wedge. By the time he finished the first side, sawdust and sweat stung his eyes. His heart banged against his ribs as if caged.

Boyd thought about resting a minute but when he looked back at his house and the Colemans', he saw lights on. He carried the saw to the other side of the trunk. Three times the blade hit the bark before finally making a cut. Boyd glanced behind him again and saw Jim Coleman coming across the yard, his mouth open and arms gesturing.

Boyd eased the throttle and let the chain saw idle.

"What in God's name are you doing?" Jim shouted.

"What's got to be done," Boyd said.

"I've got a sick daughter."

"I know that," Boyd said.

Jim Coleman reached a hand out as though to wrest the chain saw from Boyd's hand. Boyd shoved the throttle and waved the blade between him and Jim Coleman.

"I'm calling the police," Jim Coleman shouted.

Laura was outside now as well. She and Jim Coleman spoke to one another a few moments before Jim went into his house. When Laura approached Boyd screamed at her to stay away. Boyd made a final thrust deep into the tree's heart. He dropped the saw and stepped back. The oak wavered a moment, then came crashing down. As it fell, something beaked and winged passed near Boyd's face. He picked up the flashlight and shone it on the bird as it flew away. The corpse bird crossed over the vacant lot and disappeared into the darkness it had been summoned from. Boyd sat down on the scarlet oak's stump, clicked off the flashlight.

His wife and neighbor stood beside each other in the Colemans' backyard. They spoke softly, as though Boyd were a wild animal they didn't want to reveal their presence to.

Soon blue lights splashed against the sides of the two houses. Other neighbors joined Jim Coleman and Laura in the backyard. The policeman talked to Laura a few moments. She nodded once and turned in Boyd's direction, her face wet with tears. The policeman spoke into a walky-talky and then started walking toward Boyd, handcuffs clinking in the policeman's hands. Boyd stood up and held his arms out before him, both palms upturned, like a man who's just set something free.

DEAD CONFEDERATES

I never cared for Wesley Davidson when he was alive and seeing him beside me laid out dead didn't much change that. Knowing a man for years and feeling hardly anything in his passing might make you think poorly of me, but the hard truth of it is had you known Wesley you'd probably feel the same. You might do what I done—shovel dirt on him with not so much as a mumble of a prayer. Bury him under a tombstone with another man's name on it, another man's birth and dying day chipped in the marble, me and an old man all of the living ever to know that was where Wesley Davidson laid in the ground.

"I've a notion you're needing some extra money," Wesley says two weeks earlier at work, which isn't a big secret since the whole road crew's in the DOT parking lot that afternoon when the bank man comes by to chat about my overdrawn account, saying he's sorry my momma's in the hospital with no insurance but if I don't get him some money soon he'll be taking my truck. Soon as the bank man leaves Wesley saunters up to me.

I act like I haven't heard him, because like I said I never cared much for Wesley. He's a big talker but little else, always shucking his work off on the rest of us. A stout man, six foot tall and three hundred easy, a big old sow belly that sways side to side when he takes a notion to work. But that's a sight you seldom see, because he mainly leans on a shovel or lays in the shade asleep. His uncle's the road crew boss, and he lets Wesley do about what he wants, including come in late, the rest of us all clocked in and ready to pull out while Wesley's Ford Ranger is pulling in, a big rebel flag decal covering the back window. Wesley's always been big into that Confederate stuff, wearing a CSA belt buckle, rebel flag tattoo on his arm. He wears a gray CSA cap too, wears it on the job. There's no black guys on our crew, only a handful in the whole county, but you're still not supposed to wear that kind of thing. But with his uncle running the show Wesley gets away with it.

"You want to make some easy money or not?" he says to me later at our lunch break.

He grunts and sits down in the shade beside me while I get my sandwich and apple from my lunch box. Wesley's got three Hardee's sausage biscuits in a bag and scarfs them down in about thirty seconds, then lights a cigarette. I don't smoke myself and don't cotton much to the smelling of it when I'm eating. I could tell him so, could tell him I like eating my lunch alone if he'd not noticed, but getting on Wesley's bad side would just get me on my boss's bad side as well. It's more than just that, though. I'm willing to listen to anyone who could help me get some money.

"What you got in mind?" I say.

He points to his CSA belt buckle.

"You know what one of them's worth, a real one?"

"No," I say, though I figure maybe fifty or a hundred dollars.

Wesley pulls out two wadded-up catalog pages from his back pocket.

"Look here," he says and points at a picture of a belt buckle and the number below it. "Eighteen hundred dollars," he says and moves his finger down the paper. "Twenty-four hundred. Twelve hundred. Four thousand." He holds his finger there for a few seconds. "Four thousand," saying it again. He shoves the other page in my face. It's filled with buttons that fetch two hundred to a thousand dollars apiece.

"I'd of not thought they'd bring that much," I say.

"I'll not even tell you what a sword brings. You'd piss your pants if I did."

"So what's that have to do with me getting some money?"

"Cause I know where we can find such things as this," Wesley says, shaking the paper at me. "Find them where they ain't been all rusted up so's they'll be all the more pricey. You help and you get twenty-five percent."

And what I figure is some DOT bulldozer has rooted something up. Maybe some place where soldiers camped or done some fighting. I'm figuring it's some kind of flim-flam, like he wants me to help buy a metal detector or something with what little money I got left. He must take me for one dumb hillbilly to go along with such a scheme and I tell him as much.

He just grins at me, the kind of grin that argues I don't know very much.

"You got a shovel and pickax?" he asks. "Or did the bank repo them as well?"

"I got a shovel and a pickax," I say. "I know how to do more than lean on them too."

He knows my meaning but just laughs, tells me what he's got his mind scheming over. I start to say there's no way in hell I'm doing such a thing but he puts his hand out like stopping traffic, tells me not to yes or no him until I've had time to sift it over good in my mind.

"I ain't hearing a word till tomorrow," he says. "Think about how a thousand dollars, maybe more, could put some padding in that wallet. Think about what that money can do for your momma."

He says the words about Momma last for he knows that notion will hang heavy on me if nothing else does.

I go by the hospital on the way home. They let me see her for a few minutes, and afterward the nurse says she'll be able to go home in three days.

"She's got a lot of life in her yet," the nurse tells me in the hallway.

That's good news, better than I expected. I go down to the billing office and the news there isn't so good. Though I've already paid three thousand I'll be owing another four by the time she gets out. I go back to my trailer and there's no way I can't help pondering about that money Wesley's big-talking about. I think about how Daddy worked himself to death before he was sixty and Momma hanging on long enough to be taught that fifty years of working first light to bedtime can't get you enough ahead to afford an operation and a two-week stay in a hospital. I'm pondering where's the fair in that when there's men who do no more than hit a ball good or throw one through a hoop and they live in mansions and could *buy* themselves a hospital if they was to need one. I think of the big houses built up at Wolf Laurel by doctors and bankers from Charlotte and Raleigh. Second homes, they call them, though some cost a million dollars. You could argue they worked hard for those homes, but no harder than Momma and Daddy worked.

By dawn I know certain I'm going to do it. When I say as much to Wesley at our morning break he smiles.

"Figured you would," he says.

"When?" I ask.

"Night, of course," he says, "a clear night when the moon is waxed up full. That way we'll not give ourselves away with a flashlight."

Him thinking it out enough to use moonlight gives me some confidence in him, makes me think it could work. Because that's the other thing bothering me besides the right and the wrong of it. If we get caught we'd be for sure doing some jailhouse time.

"I done thought this thing out from ever which angle," Wesley says. "I been scouting the cemeteries here to Flag Pond, looking for the right sort of graves, them that belongs to officers. I'm figuring the higher the rank the likelier to be booty there, maybe even a sword. Finally found me a couple of lieutenants. Never reckoned to find a general. From what I read most all them that did the generaling was Virginians. Found Yankee soldiers in them graveyards as well, including a captain."

"A captain outranks a lieutenant, don't he?" I ask.

"Yeah, but them that buys this stuff pay double if it's Confederate."

"And you can sell it easy?" I say. "I mean you don't have to fence it or anything like that?"

"Hell, no. They got these big sellings and swappings all over the place. Got one in Asheville next month. You show them what you got and they'll open their billfolds and fling that money at you."

He shuts up for a moment then, because he's starting to realize how easy it all sounds, and how much money I might start figuring to be my share. He lays his big yellow front teeth out on his lower lip, worrying his mind to figure a way to take back some of what he just said.

"Course they ain't going to pay near the price I showed you on them sheets. We'll be lucky to get half that."

I know that for a lie before it's left Wesley's lips, but I don't say anything, just know that I'll damn well be there with him when he sells what we find.

"What do we do next?" I say.

"Just wait for a clear night and a big old moon," Wesley says, look-

ing up at the sky like he might be expecting one to show up any minute. "That and keep your mouth shut about it. I've not told another
person about this and I want it to stay that way."

Wait is what we do for two weeks, because that first night I look up
from my yard the moon's all skinny and looks to be no more than
something you might hang a coat on. Every night I watch the moon
filling itself up like a big bowl, scooting the shadows out in the field
back closer to the trees. Momma's back home and doing good, back
to where she's looking more to be her ownself again. The folks at
the hospital say she'll be eligible for the Medicaid come January and
that's all for the good. That means I can go with Wesley just this one
time, pay off that hospital bill, and be done with it.

Finally the right night comes, the moon full and leaning down
close to the world. A hunter's moon, my Daddy used to call it, and
easy enough to see why, for such a moon makes tramping through
woods a lot easier.

Tramping through a graveyard as well, for come ten o'clock that's
what we're doing. We've hid his truck down past the entrance, a few
yards back in a turnaround where, at least at night, no one would
likely see it. We don't walk through the gate because that's where
the caretaker's shack is. Instead we follow the fence up a hill through
some trees, a pickax and shovel in my hands and nothing in Wesley's
but a pillow sheet. It's late October and the air has that rinsed-clean
feel. There's leaves that have fallen and acorns and they crackle under
my feet, each one sounding loud as a .22 to me. I catch a whiff of a
wood stove and find the glow of the porch light.

"You ain't worried none about that caretaker?" I say.

"Hell no. He's near eighty years old. He's probably been asleep
since seven o'clock."

"He'd not have a fire going if he was asleep."

"That old man ain't going to bother us none," Wesley says, saying it like just his saying so makes it final.

We're soon moving among the stones, the moon brighter now that we're in the open. Its light lays down all silvery on the granite and marble, on the ground itself. It's quieter here, no more acorns and leaves, just cushiony grass like on a golf course. But it's too quiet, in a spooky kind of way. Because you know folks are here, hundreds of them, and not a one will say ever a word more on this earth. The only sound is Wesley's breathing and grunting. We've walked no more than a half mile and he's already laboring. A car comes up the road, headlights sweeping over a few tombstones as it takes the curve. It doesn't slow down but heads on toward Marshall.

"I got to catch my breath," Wesley says, and we stop a minute.

We're on a ridge now, and I can see a whole passel of stars spilled out over the sky. As clear a night as you can get, and I reckon it's easy enough for God to see me from up there. That thought bothers me some, but it's a lot easier to have a conscience about something if you figure it all the way right or all the way wrong. Doing what we're doing is a sin for sure, but not taking care of the woman who birthed and raised you is a worse one. That's what I tell myself anyway.

"It's not much farther," Wesley says, saying it more for his own benefit than for me.

He shakes his shoulders like a plow horse getting the trace chains more comfortable and walks down the yonder side of the hill until he comes to where a little Confederate flag is planted by a marble tombstone.

"Kind of them Daughters of the Confederacy biddies to sight-map the spot for us," Wesley says.

He pulls up the flag and throws it behind the stone like it was no more than a weed. He flicks his cigarette lighter and says the words out loud like I can't read them for myself.

"Lieutenant Gerald Ross Witherspoon. North Carolina Twenty-Fifth. Born November 12, 1820. Died January 20, 1890."

"Dug up October 23, 2007," Wesley adds, and gives a good snort. He lights a cigarette and sets himself down by the grave. "You best get to it. We got all night but not an hour more."

"What about you?" I say. "I ain't doing all this digging alone."

"We'd just get in the other's way doing it as a team," Wesley says, then takes a big suck on his cigarette. "Don't fret, son. I'll spell you directly."

I lift my pickax and go to it. Yesterday's rain had left some sog and squish in the ground so the first dirt breaks easy as wet sawdust. I get the shovel and scoop what I've loosed on the grass.

"People will know it's been dug," I say, pausing to gain back my breath.

And that's a new thought for me, because somehow up to now I'd had it figured if they didn't catch us in the graveyard we'd be home free. But two big holes are bound to have the law looking for those that dug them.

"And we'll be long gone when they do," Wesley says,

"You're not worried about it?" I say, because all of a sudden I am. Somebody could see the truck coming or going. We could drop something and in the dark not even know we'd left it behind.

"No," Wesley says. "The law will figure it for some of them voodoo devil worshippers. They'll not think to trouble upstanding citizens like us."

Wesley flares his lighter and lights another cigarette.

"We best get back to it," he says, nodding at the pickax in my hand.

"Don't seem to be no we to it," I say.

"Like I said, I'll spell you directly."

But directly turns out to be a long time. When I'm up to my chest I know I'm a good four feet down and he still hasn't got off his ass. I'm pouring sweat and raising crop rows of blisters on my palms. I'm about to tell Wesley that I've dug four feet and he can at least dig two when the pickax strikes wood. A big splinter of it comes up, and it's cedar, which I always heard was the least likely wood to rot. I ponder a few moments why that grave's not a full six foot deep and then remember the date on the stone. Late January the ground would have been hard as iron. It would have been easy to figure four foot would do the job well enough.

"Hit it," I say.

Wesley gets up then.

"Dig some around it so we got room to get it open."

I do what he tells me, clearing a good foot to one side.

"I'll take over for you," he says, and crawls into the hole with me. "Probably be easier if you was to get out," he adds, picking up the shovel, but I ain't about to because I wouldn't put it past him to slip whatever he finds into his pocket.

"I wouldn't be one to try and hide something from you," Wesley says, which only tells me that's exactly what he was pondering.

We wedge ourselves sideways like we're on a cliff edge to get off the coffin. Then Wesley takes the shovel and pries open the lid.

The moon can't settle its light into the hole as easy as on level ground so it's hard to see clear at first. There's a silk shirt you can tell even now was white and a belt and its buckle and some moldy old shoes, but what once filled the shoes and shirt looks to be little more than the wind that blusters a shirt on a clothesline. Wesley lifts the garment with his shovel tip and some dust and bones the color of dried bamboo spill out. He throws his shovel out of the hole and flicks his lighter. Wesley holds the lighter close to the belt buckle. There's rust is on it but you can make out C S stamped on the metal, not CSA. Wesley lifts the buckle and pulls off what little is left of the belt.

"It's a good one," he says, "but not near the best."

"How much you reckon it's worth?"

"A thousand at most," Wesley says after giving it a good eyeballing.

I figure the real price to be double that, but I'll be there when the bartering gets done so there's no need to argue now. Wesley grunts and gets on his knees to sift through the shirt, even checking inside what's left of the shoes.

"Ain't nothing else," he says, and stands up.

I lift myself from the hole but it's not as easy for Wesley. Though the hole's only four foot he's not able to haul himself out. He gets halfway then slides back, panting like a hound.

"I'll need your hand," he says. "I ain't no string bean like you."

I give him a tug and Wesley wallows out, dirt crumbs all over his shirt and pants. He puts the buckle in the pillow sheet and knots it.

"The other one's down that way," Wesley says, and nods toward the caretaker's shack. He slides up his sleeve and checks his watch. "One fifteen. We making good time," he says.

We start down the hill, weaving our way through the stones laid out like a maze. Then a cloud smudges the moon and there's not enough light from the stars to see our own feet. We stop and I have a worrisome thought of something holding that cloud there the rest of the night, me and Wesley bumping into stones and losing all direction, trapped in that graveyard till the dawn when anyone on the road could see us and the truck too.

But the moon soon enough wipes clear the cloud and we walk on, not more than fifty yards from the caretaker's place when we stop.

We're close enough to see the light that's been glowing is his back porch light. Wesley flares his lighter at the grave to check it's the right one and I see the stone is for both Lieutenant Hutchinson and his wife. His name is on the left so it's easy enough to figure that's the side he's laying on.

"Eighteen and sixty-four," says Wesley, moving the lighter closer to the stone. "I figure a officer killed during the war would for sure be buried in his uniform."

I get the shovel and pickax in my right hand and lean them toward Wesley.

"Your turn," I say.

"I was thinking you could get it started good and then I'd take over," he says.

"I'll do most of it," I say, "but I ain't doing it all."

Wesley sees I aim not to budge and reaches for the pickax. He does it in a careless kind of way and the pickax's spike end clangs against the shovel blade. A dog starts barking down at the caretaker's place and I'm ready to make a run for the truck but Wesley shushes me.

"Give it a minute," he says.

We stand there still as the stones around us. No light inside the shack comes on, and the dog shuts up directly.

"We're okay," Wesley says, and he starts breaking ground with the pickax. He's working in fourth gear and I know he's wanting this done quick as I do.

"I'll loosen the dirt and you shovel it away," Wesley gasps, veins sticking out on his neck like there's a noose around it. "We can get it out faster that way."

Funny you didn't think of that till it was your turn to dig, I'm thinking, but that dog has set loose the fear in me more than any time since we drove up. I take the shovel and we're making the dirt fly, Wesley doing more work in fifteen minutes than he's done in twelve years on the road crew. And me staying right with him, both of us going so hard it's not till we hear a growl that we turn around and see we're not alone.

"What are you boys up to?" the old man asks, waggling his shotgun at us. The dog is haunched up beside him, big and bristly and looking like it's just waiting for the word to pour his teeth into us.

"I said, what are you boys up to?" the old man asks us again.

What kind of answer to give that question is as far beyond me as the moon up above. For a few moments it's beyond Wesley as well but soon enough he opens his mouth, working up some words like you'd work up a good spit of tobacco.

"We didn't know there to be a law against it," Wesley says, which is about the stupidest thing he could have come up with.

The old man chuckles.

"They's several, and you're going to be learning all of them soon as I get the sheriff up here."

I'm thinking to make a run for it before that, take my chances with the dog and the old man's aim if he decides to shoot, because to my way of thinking time in the jailhouse would be worse than anything that dog or old man could do to me.

"You ain't needing to call the sheriff," Wesley says.

Wesley steps out of the two-foot hole we've dug, gets up closer to the old man. The dog growls deep down in its throat, a sound that says don't wander no closer unless you want to limp out of this graveyard. Wesley pays the dog some mind and doesn't go any nearer.

"Why is that?" the old man says. "What you offering to make me think I don't need to call the law?"

"I got a ten-dollar bill in my wallet that has your name on it," Wesley says, and I almost laugh at the sass of him. We have a shotgun leveled at us and Wesley's trying to lowball the fellow.

"You got to do better than that," the old man says.

"Twenty then," Wesley says. "God's truth that's all the money I got on me."

The old man ponders the offer a moment.

"Give me the money," he says.

Wesley gets his billfold out, tilts it so the old man can't see nothing but the twenty he pulls out. He reaches the bill to the old man.

"You can't tell nobody about this," Wesley says. "None but us three knows a thing of it."

"Who am I going to spread it to," the old man says. "In case you'd not noticed, my neighbors ain't much for conversing."

The old man looks the twenty over careful, like he's figuring it to be counterfeit. Then he folds the bill and puts it in his front pocket.

"Course you could double that easy enough," Wesley says, "not do a thing more than let us dig here a while longer."

The old man takes in Wesley's offer but doesn't commit either way.

"What are you all grubbing for anyways," he says, "buried treasure?"

"Just Civil War things, buckles and such," Wesley says. "No money in it, just kind of a sentimental thing. My great-great-granddaddy fought Confederate. I've always been one to honor them that come before me."

"By robbing their graves," the old man says. "That's some real honoring you're doing."

"I'm wearing what they can't no longer wear, bringing it out of the ground to the here and now. Look here," Wesley says.

He unknots the pillow sheet and hands the buckle to the old man. "I'll polish it up real good and wear it proud, wear it not just for my great-great granddaddy but all them that fought for a noble cause."

I've never even seen a politician lie better, because Wesley lays all of that out there slick, figuring the old man has no knowing of the buckle's worth. And that seemed a likely enough thing since I hadn't the least notion myself till Wesley showed me the prices.

The old man fetches a flashlight from his coveralls. He lays its light out on the stone. "North Carolina Sixty-Fourth" he reads off the stone. "My folks sided Union," the old man says, "in this very county. Lot's of people don't bother to know that anymore, but there was as many in these mountains fought Union as Confederate. The Sixty-Fourth done a lot of meanness in this county back then. They'd shoot a unarmed man and wasn't above whipping women. My grandma told me all about it. One of them women they whipped was her own momma. I read up on it some later. That's how come me to know it was the Sixty-Fourth."

The old man clicks off his flashlight and stuffs it in his pocket and pulls out an old-timey watch, the kind with a chain on it. He pops it open and reads the hands by moonlight.

"Two-thirty," he says. "You fellows go ahead and dig him up. The way I figure it, his soul's a lot deeper, all the way down in hell."

"You pay him this time," Wesley says to me.

I only have sixteen and am about to say so when the old man tells me he don't want my money.

"I'll take enough pleasure just in watching you dig this Hutchinson fellow up. He might have been the one that stropped my great-grandma."

The old man steps back a few feet and perches his backside on a flat-topped stone next to where we're digging. The shotgun's settled in the crook of his arm.

"You ain't needing for that shotgun to be nosed in our direction," Wesley says. "Them things can go off by accident sometimes."

The old man keeps the gun barrel where it is.

"I don't think I've heard the truth walk your lips yet," he tells Wesley. "I'll trust you better with it pointed your way."

We start digging again, getting more crowded up to each other as the hole deepens, but leastways we don't have to worry about noise any more. We're a good four foot in when Wesley stops and leans his back against the side of the hole.

"Can't do no more," he says, and it takes him three breaths to get just the four words out. "Done something to my arm."

Sure you did, I'm thinking, but when I look at him I can see he's hurting. He's heaving hard and shedding sweat like it's a July noon.

The old man gets off his perch to check out at Wesley as well.

"You look to have had the starch took out of you," the old man says, but Wesley makes no bother to answer him, just closes his eyes and leans harder against the grave's side.

"You want to get out," I say to him. "It might help to breathe some fresher air."

"No," he says, opening his eyes some, and I know the why of that answer. He's not getting out until he's looked inside the coffin we're rooting up.

Maybe it's because Lieutenant Hutchinson was buried in May instead of January, but for whatever reason he looks to have got the full six feet. The hole's up to my neck and I still haven't touched wood.

The old man's still there above me, craning his own wrinkly face over the hole like he's peering down a well.

"You ain't much of a talker, are you?" he says to me. "Or is it just your buddy don't give you a word edgewise."

"No," I say, throwing a shovelful of dirt out of the hole.

It's getting harder now after five hours of digging and shucking it out. My back's hurting and my arms feel made of syrup.

"Which 'no' you siding with," the old man says.

"No, I don't talk much."

"You wanting one of them buckles to wear or you just along for the pleasure of flinging dirt all night?"

"Just here to dig," I answer, glad when he don't say nothing more. I got little enough get-go left to spend it gabbing.

I lift the pickax again and I hit something so solid it almost jars the handle from my hands. That jarring goes up my arms and back down my spine bones like I touched an electric fence. I'm figuring it to be a big rock I'll have to dig out before I can get to the coffin. The thought of tussling with a rock makes me so tired I just want to lay down and quit.

"What is it?" the old man says, and Wesley opens his eyes, watches me take the shovel and scrape dirt to get a better look.

But it's no rock. It's a coffin, a coffin made of cast iron. Wesley crunches up nearer the wall so I can get more dirt out, and what I'm thinking is whoever had to tote that coffin had a time of it, because Momma's cast-iron cooking stove wouldn't lift lighter, and it took four grown men to move that stove from one side of the kitchen to the other.

"I'd always heard they was a few of them planted in this cemetery," the old man says, "but I never figured to see one."

The coffin spries Wesley up some. I dig enough room to the side to set my feet so they're not on the lid. Rust has sealed it, so I take the flat end of the pickax and crack the lid open like you'd crowbar a stuck window. I about break my pickax handle but it finally gives. I get down low but I can't lift the lid off by myself.

"You got to help me," I tell Wesley and he gets down beside me.

It's no easy thing to do and we both have to step lively in hardly no room to keep the lid from sliding off and landing on our feet. Soon as we get it off, Wesley puts his left hand on his right shoulder, and I'm thinking it's some kind of salute or something, but then he starts rubbing his arm and shoulder like it's gone numb on him.

"The Lord Almighty," the old man says, and Wesley and me step some to the side to get where we can see good too.

Unlike the other one, you can tell this was a man. The bones are most together and there's even a hank of red hair on his skull. You can tell he's in a uniform too, raggedy but what's left of the pants and coat is butternut. I look over at Wesley and he's seeing nothing but what's made of metal.

There's plenty to fill up his eyeballs that way. A belt buckle is there with no more than a skiffing of rust on it. Buttons too, looking to be a half-dozen. But that's not the best thing. What's best is laying there next to the skeleton, a big old sword and scabbard. Wesley reaches for it. The sword's rusted in but after a couple of tugs it starts to give. Wesley finally grunts it out. He holds the sword out before him and I can see he's figuring what it'll fetch and the grin on his face and the way his eyes light up argue a high price indeed. Then all of a sudden he's seeing something else, and whatever it is he sees isn't giving him the notion to smile any more. He lets the sword slide out his hand and leans back against the wall, his feet still in the coffin. He slides down then, his back against the wall but his bottom half in the coffin, just sitting there like a man in a jon boat. His eyes are still open but there's no more light in them than the bottom of a coal shaft.

"See if they's a pulse on him," the old man says.

I step closer to Wesley, footlogging the coffin so I won't step on the skeleton. I lay hold of Wesley's wrist but there's no more alive in it than in his eyes.

I just stand there a minute. All the bad fixes I've been in are like being in high cotton compared to where I am now. I can't even begin to figure what to do. I'm about to tell the old man to level that shotgun on me and pull the trigger for my brain's not bringing up a better solution.

"I don't reckon he'll be strutting around and playing Johnny Reb with his sword and belt buckle," the old man says. He looks at me and it's easy enough for him to guess what I'm feeling. "You shouldn't get the fantods over this," he says. "His dying on you could be all for the better."

"How do you reckon that?" I ask, because I sure can't figure it that way.

"What if he was speaking the truth when he said we're the only three that knows about this," the old man says.

"I never said a word."

"I got no doubting about that," the old man says. "Far as I can tell you don't say nothing unless it's yanked out of you like a tooth."

"I don't think he'd have spoke about this," I say. "There's not many that would think good of him if he did, and some might even tell the law. I don't figure him to risk that."

"Then I'd say he's helped dig his own grave," the old man says. "Stout as he is, I don't notion you could get him out of there alone and I'm way too old to help you."

"We might could use a rope," I say. "Pull him out that way."

"And what if you did," the old man says. "You think you can drag that hunk of lard behind you like a little red wagon. Even if you can where you headed with him?"

That's a pretty good question, because here to the truck is a good half mile. I'd have a better chance of toting a tombstone that far.

"It doesn't seem the right sort of thing to do," I say. "I mean for his kin and such not to never know where he's buried."

"Those that wears the badges ain't always the brightest bulbs," the old man says, "but they won't need the brains of a stump to figure what he and you was up to if they find him here." The old man pauses. "Is that truck his or yours?"

"His."

"You leave that truck by the river and the worst gossip on your buddy there is he was fool enough to get drunk and fall in. You bring the law here they'll know him for a grave robber. Which way you notion his kin would rather recollect him?"

The old man's whittling it down to but one path to follow. I try to find a good argument against him, but I'm too wore down to come up with anything. The old man takes out his watch.

"It's nigh on four o'clock. You get to filling in and you could get that grave leveled by the shank of morning."

"It's two graves to fill," I say. "We dug another one up the hill a ways."

"Well, get as much dirt in them as you can. Even full up they'll be queer looking with all that fresh dirt on them. I'll have to figure some kind of tall tale for folks that might take notice, but I been listening to your buddy all night so I've picked up some good pointers on how to lie."

I look at the sword and think how the blade maybe killed somebody during the Civil War and in its way killed another tonight, at least the wanting of it did.

"He was lying about this stuff not being worth much," I say. "I need the money so I'm going to sell it, but I'll go halves with you."

"You keep it," the old man says. "But I'll take what's in your partner's wallet. He'll need it no more than the lieutenant there needs that sword."

I pull the wallet from Wesley's back pocket, give it to the old man. He pulls out a ten and two twenties.

"I knew that son-of-a-bitch was lying about having no more money," he says, then throws the wallet back in the hole.

I reach the sword and scabbard up to the old man and then the buckle and buttons. I think how easy it would be for him to rooster that trigger and shotgun me. He leans closer to the hole and I see he's still got that shotgun in his hand and I wonder if he's figuring the same thing, because it'd be easy as shooting a rat in a washtub. He gets down on his creaky old knees, and I guess my fearing is clear to him for he lays down the shotgun and gives me a smile.

"I was just allowing I'd give you some help out of there," he says and offers his hand. "Just don't jerk me in there with you."

I take his hand, a strong grip for all his years, and reach my other hand over the lip. It's one good heave and I'm out.

I fetch the shovel and set to the covering up, dead tired but making good time because I'm figuring if it doesn't get done I'll have some serious jailhouse time to wish I had. Plus it's always easier to fling dirt down than up. I get the hole filled and walk up to the other grave, the shovel and pickax in one hand and the sword and pillow sheet in the other. The old man and his dog follow me. I get it half-full before the pink of morning skims Bluff Mountain.

"I got to go now," I say. "It's getting near dawn."

"Leave the shovel then," the old man says. "I can fill in the rest. Then I'm going to plant chrysanthemums on the graves, let that be the why of the dirt being rooted up."

I have no plans to find out if that's what he does do. My plan is not to be back here again unless someone's hauling me in a box. I walk on down the hill. It's Sunday so I don't see another soul on the road. I park the truck down by the river, no more than a mile from Marshall. I get my handkerchief out and wipe the steering wheel good and the door handle. Then I high-step it, staying in the woods till I'm to the edge of town. I hunker down there till full light, figuring it's all worked good as I could have hoped. They'll soon find the truck, but no one spotted me near it. Wesley and me never were buddies, never went out to bars together or anything, so there's none likely to figure me in his truck last night. I hide the sword and pillow sheet under some leaves to get later. When I cross the road in front of Jackson's Café, I figure I'm home free.

But I'm still careful. I don't go inside, just wait by some trees until

I see Timmy Shackleford come out. He doesn't live far from me and I step into the parking lot and ask if he'd mind giving me a ride to my trailer.

"You look like the night rode you hard," Timmy says.

I look in the side mirror and I do look rough.

"Got knee-walking drunk," I say. "Last thing I remember I was with a bunch of fellows in a car and said I needed to piss. They set me by the side of the road and took off laughing. Next thing I know, I'm waking up in a ditch"

That's a better lie than I'd have reckoned to spin and I figure I have picked up some pointers from Wesley. Timmy grins but doesn't say anything else. He lets me out at my trailer and goes on his way. I'm starved and have got enough dirt on me to plant a garden, but I just fall in the bed and don't open my eyes till it's full dark outside. When I come awake it's with the deepest kind of fearing, and for a few moments I'm more scared than anytime before in my life. Then my mind settles and I see I'm in the trailer, not still in that graveyard.

Come Monday at work I hear how they found Wesley's truck by the river, and most figure him down there fishing or drinking or both and he fell in and drowned. They drag the river for days but of course nothing comes up.

I wait a month before I try to sell the Civil War stuff, driving all the way to Montgomery, Alabama, to a big CSA convention where a whole auditorium is full of buyers and sellers. Some want certificates of authenticity and such, but I finally find a buyer I can do some business with. A lady at the library has pulled up some prices on the internet and I've got a good figuring of what my stash is worth. The buyer's only offering half what the value is but he's also not asking for certificates or even my name. I tell him I'll take what he's offering but only if it's cash money. He grumbles a bit about that, then finally says "stay here" and goes off and comes back with fifty-two hundred dollar bills, new bills so crisp and smooth they look starched and ironed.

It's more money than the hospital bill and I give what's left to Momma. That makes what I've done feel less worrisome. I think about something else too, how both them graves had big fancy tombstones of cut marble, meaning those dead Confederates hadn't known much wanting of money in their lives. Now that they was dead there was some fairness in letting Momma have something of what they'd left behind.

The only bad thing is I keep having a dream where that old man has shot me and I'm buried in the hole with Wesley. I'm shot bad but still alive and dirt's piled on me and somewhere up above I hear that old man laughing like he was the devil himself. Every time I dream it, I rear up in bed and don't stop gasping for nearly a whole minute. I've dreamed that same exact dream at least once a month for a year now, and I guess it's likely I'll keep doing so for the rest of my life. There's always a price to be paid for anything you get. I wish it weren't so, for it's a fearsome dream, but if it's the worst to come of all that happened I can live with it.

The WOMAN *at the* POND

Water has its own archaeology, not a layering but a leveling, and thus is truer to our sense of the past, because what is memory but near and far events spread and smoothed beneath the present's surface. A green birthday candle that didn't expire with a wish lies next to a green Coleman lantern lit twelve years later. Chalky sun motes in a sixth-grade classroom harbor close to a university library's high window, a song on a staticky radio shoals against the same song at a hastily arranged wedding reception. This is what I think of when James Murray's daughter decides to drain the pond. A fear of lawsuits, she claims, something her late father considered himself exonerated from by posting a sign: FISH AND SWIM AT YOUR OWN RISK.

She hired Wallace Rudisell for the job, a task that requires opening the release valve on the standpipe, keeping it clear until what once was a creek will be a creek once more. I grew up with Wallace, and, unlike so many of our classmates, he and I still live in Lattimore. Wallace inherited our town's hardware store, one of the few remaining businesses.

"Bet you're wanting to get some of those lures back you lost in high school," Wallace says when I ask when he'll drain the pond. "There must be a lot of them. For a while you were out there most every evening."

Which is true. I was seventeen and in a town of three hundred, my days spent bagging groceries. Back then there was no internet, no cable TV or VCR, at least in our house. Some evenings that summer I'd listen to the radio or watch television with my parents, or look over college brochures and financial-aid forms the guidance counselor had given me, but I'd usually go down to the pond. Come fall of my senior year, though, Angie and I began dating. We found other things to do in the dark.

A few times Wallace or another friend joined me, but I usually fished alone. After a day at the grocery store, I didn't mind being away from people awhile, and the pond at twilight was a good place. The swimmers and other fishermen were gone, leaving behind beer and cola bottles, tangles of fishing line, gray cinder blocks used for seats. Later in the night, couples came to the pond, their leavings on the bank as well—rubbers and blankets, once a pair of panties hung on the white oak's limb. But that hour when day and night made their slow exchange, I had the pond to myself.

Over the years James Murray's jon-boat had become communal property. Having wearied of swimming out to retrieve the boat, I'd bought twenty feet of blue nylon rope to keep it moored. I'd unknot the rope from the white oak, set my fishing gear and Coleman lantern in the bow, and paddle out to the pond's center. I'd fish until it was neither day nor night, but balanced between. There never seemed to be a breeze, pond and shore equally smoothed. Just stillness, as though the world had taken a soft breath, and was holding it in, and even time had leveled out, moving neither forward nor back. Then the frogs and crickets waiting for full dark announced themselves, or a breeze came up and I again heard the slosh of water against land. Or, one night near the end of that summer, a truck rumbling toward the pond.

On Saturday I leave at two o'clock when the other shift manager comes in. I no longer live near the pond, but my mother does, so I pull out of the grocery store's parking lot and turn right, passing under Lattimore's one stoplight. On the left are four boarded-up stores, behind them like an anchored cloud, the mill's water tower, blue paint chipping off the tank. I drive by Glenn's Café where Angie works, soon after that the small clapboard house where she and our daughter, Rose, live. Angie's Ford Escort isn't there, but the truck belonging to Rose's boyfriend is. I don't turn in. It's not my weekend to be in charge, and at least I know Rose is on the pill, because I took her to the clinic myself.

Soon there are only farmhouses, most in disrepair—slumping barns and woodsheds, rusty tractors snared by kudzu and trumpet vines. I make a final right turn and park in front of my mother's house. She comes onto the porch and I know from her disappointed expression that she's gotten the week confused and expects to see Rose. We talk a minute and she goes back inside. I walk down the sloping land, straddle the sagging barbed wire, and make my way through brambles and broom sedge, what was once a pasture.

The night the truck came to the pond, an afternoon thunderstorm had rinsed the humidity from the air. The evening felt more like late September than mid-August. After rowing out, I had cast toward the willows on the far bank, where I'd caught bass in the past. The lure I used was a Rapala, my favorite because I could fish it on the surface or submerged. After a dozen tries nothing struck, so I paddled closer to the willows and cast into the cove where the creek ended. A small bass hit and I reeled it in, its red gills flaring as I freed the treble hook and lowered the fish back into the water.

A few minutes later the truck bumped down the dirt road to the water's edge. The headlights slashed across the pond before the vehicle jerked right and halted beside the white oak as the headlights dimmed.

Music came from the truck's open windows and carried over the water with such clarity I recognized the song. The cab light came on and the music stopped. Minutes passed, and stars began filling the sky. As a thick-shouldered moon rimmed up over a ridge, a man and woman got out of the truck. The jon-boat drifted toward the willows and I let it, afraid any movement would give away my presence. The man and woman's voices rose, became angry, then a sound sharp as a rifle shot. The woman fell and the man got back in the cab. The headlights flared and the truck turned around, slinging mud before the tires gained traction. The truck swerved up the dirt road and out of sight.

The woman slowly lifted herself from the ground. She moved closer to the bank and sat on a cinder block. As more stars pierced the sky, and the moon lifted itself above the willow trees, I waited for the truck to return or the woman to leave, though I had no idea where she might go. The jon-boat drifted deeper into the willows, the drooping branches raking at my face. I didn't want to move, but the willows had entangled the boat. The graying wood creaked as it bumped against the bank. I lifted the paddle and pushed away as quietly as possible. As I did, the boat rocked and the metal tackle box banged against its side.

"Who's out there?" the woman asked. "I can see you, I can."

I lit the lantern and paddled to the pond's center.

"I'm fishing," I said, and lifted the rod and reel to prove it.

The woman didn't respond.

"Are you okay?"

"My face will be bruised," she said after a few moments. "But no teeth knocked out. Bruises fade. I'll be better off tomorrow than he will."

I set the paddle on my knees. In the quiet, it seemed the pond too was listening.

"You mean the man that hit you?"

"Yeah, him."

"Is he coming back?"

"Yeah, he's coming back. The bastard needs me to drive to Charlotte. Another DUI and he'll be pedaling to work on a bicycle. He won't get too drunk to remember that. Anyway, he didn't go far." The woman pointed up the dirt road where a faint square of light hovered like foxfire. "He's drinking the rest of his whiskey while some hillbilly whines on the radio about how hard life is. When the bottle's empty, he'll be back."

As the jon-boat drifted closer to the bank, the woman stood and I dug the paddle's wooden blade into the silt to keep some distance between us. The lantern's glow fell on both of us now. She was younger than I'd thought, maybe no more than thirty. A large woman, wide hipped and tall, at least five eight. Her long blond hair was clearly dyed. A red welt covered the left side of her face. She wore a man's leather jacket over her yellow blouse and black skirt. Mud grimed the yellow blouse. She raised her hand and fanned at the haze of insects.

"I hope there are fewer gnats and mosquitoes out there," she said. "The damn things are eating me alive."

"Only if I stay in the middle," I answered.

I glanced up at the truck.

"I guess I'll go back out." I lifted the paddle, thinking if the man didn't come get her in a few minutes I'd beach the boat in the creek cove, work my way through the brush, and head home.

"Can I get in the boat with you?" the woman asked.

"I'm just going to make a couple of more casts," I answered. "I need to get back home."

"Just a few minutes," she said, and gave me a small smile, the hardness in her face and voice lessening. "I'm not going to hurt you. Just a few minutes. To get away from the bugs."

"Can you swim?"

"Yes," she said.

"What about that man that hit you?"

"He'll be there awhile yet. He drinks his whiskey slow."

The woman brushed some of the drying mud from her skirt, as if to make herself more presentable.

"Just a few minutes."

"Okay," I said, and rowed to the bank.

I steadied the jon-boat while she got in the front, the lantern at her feet. The woman talked while I paddled, not turning her head, as if addressing the pond.

"I finally get away from this county and that son of a bitch drags me back to visit his sister. She's not home so instead he buys a bottle of Wild Turkey and we end up here, with him wanting to lay down on the bank with just a horse blanket beneath us and the mud. When I tell him no way, he gets this jacket from the truck. For your head, he tells me, like that would change my mind. What a prince."

She shifted her body to face me.

"Nothing like coming back home, right?"

"You're from Lattimore?" I asked.

"No, but this county. Lawndale. You know where that is?"

"Yes."

"But our buddy in the truck used to live in Lattimore, so we're having a Cleveland County reunion tonight, assuming you aren't just visiting."

"I live here."

"Still in high school?"

I nodded.

"I'll be a senior."

"We used to kick your asses in football," she said. "That was supposed to be a big deal."

I pulled in the paddle when we reached the pond's center. The rod lay beside me, but I didn't pick it up. The lantern was still on, but we didn't really need it. The moon laid a silvery skim of light on the water.

"When you get back to Charlotte, will you call the police?"

"No, they wouldn't do anything. The bastard will pay though. He left more than his damn jacket on that blanket."

The woman took a wallet from the jacket, opened it to show no bills were inside.

"He got paid today so what he didn't spend on that whiskey is in my pocket now. He'll wake up tomorrow thinking a hangover is the worst thing he'll have to deal with, but he will soon learn different."

"What if he believes you took it?"

"I'll make myself scarce awhile. That's easy to do in a town big as Charlotte. Anyway, he'll be back living here before long."

"He tell you that?"

The woman smiled.

"He doesn't need to. Haven't you heard of women's intuition? Plus, he's always talking about this place. Badmouthing it a lot, but it's got its hooks in him. No, he'll move back, probably work at the mill, and he'll still be here when they pack the dirt over his coffin."

She'd paused and looked at me.

"What about you? Already got your job lined up after high school?"

"I'm going to college."

"College," she said, studying me closely. "I'd not have thought that. You've got the look of someone who'd stick around here."

Wallace waves from the opposite bank and makes his way around the pond. His pants and tennis shoes are daubed with mud. Wallace works mostly indoors, so the July sun has reddened his face and unsleeved arms. He nods at the valve.

"Damn thing's clogged up twice, but it's getting there."

The pond is a red-clay bowl, one-third full. In what was once the shallows, rusty beer cans and Styrofoam bait containers have emerged along with a ball cap and a flip-flop. Farther in, Christmas trees submerged for years are now visible, the black branches threaded with red-and-white bobbers and bream hooks, plastic worms and bass plugs, including a six-inch Rapala that I risk the slick mud to pull free. Its hooks are so rusty one breaks off.

"Let me see," Wallace says, and examines the lure.

"I used to fish with one like this," I tell him, "same size and model."

"Probably one of yours then," Wallace says, and offers the lure as if to confirm my ownership. "You want any of these others?"

"No, I don't even want that one."

"I'll take them then," Wallace says, lifting a yellow Jitterbug from a limb. "I hear people collect old plugs nowadays. They might be worth a few dollars, add to the hundred I'm getting to do this. These days I need every bit of money I can get."

We move under the big white oak and sit in its shade, watch the pond's slow contraction. More things emerge—a rod and reel, a metal bait bucket, more lures and hooks and bobbers. There are swirls in the water now, fish vainly searching for the upper levels of their world. A large bass leaps near the valve.

Wallace nods at a burlap sack.

"The bluegill will flush down that drain, but it looks like I'll get some good-sized fish to fry up."

We watch the water, soon a steady dimpling on the surface. Another bass flails upward, shimmers green and silver in the afternoon sun.

"Angie said Rose is trying to get loans so she can go to your alma mater next year," Wallace says.

"It's an alma mater only if you graduate," I reply.

Wallace picks up a stick, scrapes some mud off his shoes. He starts to speak, then hesitates, finally does speak.

"I always admired your taking responsibility like that. Coming back here, I mean." Wallace shakes his head. "We sure live in a different time. Hell, nowadays there's women who don't know or care who their baby's father is, much less expect him to marry her. And the men, they're worse. They act like it's nothing to them, don't even want to be a part of their own child's life."

When I don't reply, Wallace checks his watch.

"This is taking longer than I figured. I'm going to the café. I haven't had lunch. Want me to bring you back something?"

"A Coke would be nice," I say.

As Wallace drives away, I think of the woman letting her right hand brush the water as I rowed the jon-boat toward shore.

"It feels warm," she said, "warmer than the air. I bet you could slip in and sink and it would feel cozy as a warm blanket."

"The bottom's cold," I answered.

"If you got that deep," she said, "it wouldn't matter anyway, would it?"

After we got out, the woman asked whose boat it was. I told her I didn't know and started to knot the rope to the white oak.

"Leave it untied then," she said. "I may take it back out."

"I don't think you should do that," I told her. "The boat could overturn or something."

"I won't overturn the boat," the woman said, and pulled a ten-dollar bill from her skirt pocket. "Here's something for taking me out. This too," she said, taking the jacket off. "It's a nice one and he's not getting it back. It looks like a good fit."

"I'd better not," I said, and picked up my fishing equipment and the lantern. I looked at her. "When he comes back, you're not afraid he'll do something else? I mean, I can call the police."

She shook her head.

"Don't do that. Like I said, he needs a driver, so he'll make nice. You go on home."

And so I did, and once there, did not call the police or tell my parents. I had trouble sleeping that night, but the next day at work, as the hours passed, I assured myself that if anything really bad had happened everyone in Lattimore would have known.

I went back to the pond, for the last time, that evening after work. The nylon rope was missing but the paddle lay under the front seat. As I got in, I lifted the paddle and found a ten-dollar bill beneath it. I rowed out to the center and tied on the Rapala and threw it at the pond's far bank.

As darkness descended, what had seemed certain earlier seemed less so. When a cast landed in some brush, I cranked the reel fast, hoping to avoid snagging the Rapala, but that also caused the lure to go deeper. The rod bowed and I was hung. Any other time, I'd have rowed to the snag and leaned over the gunwale, let my hand follow the line into the water to find the lure and free the hook. Instead, I tightened the line and gave a hard jerk. The lure stayed where it was.

For a minute I sat there. Something thrashed in the reeds, probably a bass or muskrat. Then the water was still. Moonlight brightened, as if trying to probe the dark water. I took out my pocketknife, cut the line, then rowed to shore and beached the boat. That night

I dreamed that I'd let my hand follow the line until my fingers were tangled in hair.

Wallace's truck comes back down the dirt road. He hands me my Coke and opens a white bag containing his drink and hamburger. We sit under the tree.

"It's draining good now," he says.

The fish not inhaled by the drain are more visible, fins sharking the surface. A catfish that easily weighs five pounds wallows onto the bank as if hoping for some sudden evolution. Wallace quickly finishes his hamburger. He takes the burlap sack and walks into what's left of the pond. He hooks a finger through the catfish's gills and drops it into the sack.

In another half hour what thinning water remains boils with bass and catfish. More fish beach themselves and Wallace gathers them like fallen fruit, the sack punching and writhing in his grasp.

"You come over tonight," he says to me. "There'll be plenty."

As evening comes, more snags emerge, fewer lures. A whiskey bottle and another bait bucket, some cans that probably rolled and drifted into the pond's deep center. Then I see the cinder block, with what looks like a withered arm draped over it. Wallace continues to gather more fish, including a blue cat that will go ten pounds, its whiskers long as nightcrawlers. I walk onto the red slanting mud, moving slowly so I won't slip. I stop when I stand only a fishing rod's length from the cinder block.

"What do you see?" Walter asks.

I wait for the water to give me an answer, and before long it does. Not an arm but a leather jacket sleeve, tied to the block by a fray of blue nylon. I step into the water and loosen the jacket from the concrete, and as I do I remember the ten-dollar bill left in the boat, her assumption that I'd be the one to find it.

I feel something in the jacket's right pocket and pull out a withered billfold. Inside are two silted shreds of thin plastic, a driver's license, some other card now indiscernible. No bills.

I stand in the pond's center and toss the billfold's remnants into the drain. I drop the jacket and step back as Wallace gills the last fish abandoned by the water. Wallace knots the sack and lifts it. The veins in his bicep and forearm ridge up as he does so.

"That's at least fifty pounds' worth," he says, and sets the sack down. "Let me clear this drain one more time. Then I'm going home to cook these up."

Wallace leans over the drain and claws away the clumps of mud and wood. The remaining water gurgles down the pipe.

"I hate to see this pond go," he says. "I guess the older you get, the less you like any kind of change."

Wallace lifts the sack of fish and pulls it over his shoulder. We walk out of the pond as dusk comes on.

"You going to come over later?" he asks.

"Not tonight."

"Another time then," Wallace says. "Need a ride up to your mom's house?"

"No," I answer. "I'll walk it."

After Wallace drives off, I sit on the bank. Shadows deepen where the water was, making it appear that the pond has refilled. After a while I get up. By the time I'm over the barbed-wire fence, I can look back and no longer tell what was and what is.

A SERVANT *of* HISTORY

A servant of history. Since accepting his employ with the English Folk Dance and Ballad Society, that was how Wilson thought of himself and, in truth, a rather daring servant. He was no university don mumbling Gradgrindian facts facts facts in a lecture hall's chalky air, but a man venturing among the New World's Calibans. On the ship that brought him from London, Wilson explained to fellow passengers how ballads lost to time in Britain might yet survive in America's Appalachian Mountains. Several young ladies were suitably impressed and expressed concern for his safety. One male passenger, an uncouth Georgian, had acted more amused than impressed, noting that Wilson's "duds" befit a dancing master more than an adventurer.

After departing the train station and securing his belongings at the Blue Ridge Inn, Wilson walked Sylva's main thoroughfare. The promise of the village's bucolic name was not immediately evident. Cabins and tepees, cattle drives and saloons, were notably absent. Instead, actual houses, most prosperous looking, lined the village's periphery. On the square itself, a marble statue commemorated the

Great War. Shingles advertised a dentist, a doctor, and a lawyer, even a confectioner. The men he passed wore no holsters filled with "shooting irons," the women no boots and breeches. Automobiles outnumbered horses. It had all been immensely disappointing. Until now.

The old man was hitching his horse and wagon to a post as Wilson approached. He did not wear buckskin, but his long gray beard and tattered overalls, hobnailed boots, and straw hat bespoke a true rustic. The old man spurted a stream of tobacco juice as an initial greeting, then spoke in a brogue so thick Wilson asked twice for the words to be repeated. Wilson haltingly conveyed his employer's purpose.

"England," the rustic said. "It's war you hell from?"

"Pardon?" Wilson asked, and the old man repeated himself.

"Ah," Wilson said. "Where do I hail from?"

The rustic nodded.

"Indeed, sir, I do come from England. As I say, I am in search of British ballads. Many of the old songs that have vanished in my country may yet be found here. But as a visitor to your region, I have little inkling who might possess them. The innkeeper suggested an older resident, such as yourself, might aid me."

Wilson paused, searching the hirsute face for a sign of interest, or even comprehension. He had been warned at the interview that the expedition would be challenging, especially for a young gentleman fresh out of university, one, though this was only implied, whose transcript reflected few scholarly aspirations. In truth, Wilson had been the Society's third choice, employed only when the first decided to make his fortune in India and the second staggered out of a pub and into the path of a trolley.

"Of course, aside from my gratitude, I have leave to pay a fair wage for assistance in locating such ballads."

The old man spat again.

"How much?"

"Three dollars a day."

"I'll scratch you up some tunes for that," the rustic answered, and nodded at the wagon, "but not cheer. We'll have to hove it a ways."

"And when might we set out?" Wilson asked.

"Come noon tomorrow. You baddin at the inn?"

"Badding?"

"Yes, baddin," the old man said. "Sleepin."

"I am."

"I'll pick you up thar then," the rustic said, and resumed hitching his horse.

"May I ask your name, sir," Wilson said. "Mine is James Wilson."

"I a go ba rafe," the old man answered.

They left Sylva at twelve the next day, Wilson's valise settled in the wagon bed, he himself on the buckboard beside Iago Barafe. They passed handsome farms with fine houses, but as they ventured farther into the mountains, the dwellings became smaller, sometimes aslant and often unpainted. To Wilson's delight, he saw his first cabin, then several more. They turned off the "pike," as Barafe called it, and onto a wayfare of trampled weeds and dirt. As the elevation rose, the October air cooled. The mountains leaned closer and granite outcrops broke through stands of trees.

The remoteness evoked an older era, and Wilson supposed that it was as much the landscape as the inhabitants that allowed Albion's music to survive here. He thought again of his university dons, each monotoned lecture like a Lethean submerging from which he retained just enough to earn his degree. Now, however, he, James Wilson, would show them that history was more than their ossified blather. It was outside libraries and lecture halls and alive in the world, passed down one tongue to another by the humble folk. Why even his guide, obviously illiterate, had a name retained from Elizabethan drama.

A red-and-black serpent slithered across the path, disappeared into a rocky crevice.

"Poisonous, I assume," Wilson said.

"Naw," Barafe answered, "nothin but a meek snake."

Soon after, they splashed across a brook.

"We're on McDawnell land now," the older man said.

"McDowell?" Wilson asked.

"I reckon you kin say it that way," Barafe answered.

"The family is from Scotland, I presume," Wilson said, "but long ago."

"They been up here many a yar," the old man said, "and it's a passel of them. The ones we're going to see, they got their great-granny yet alive. She's nigh a century old but got a mind sharp as a new-hone axe. She'll know yer tunes and anything else you want. But they can be a techy lot, if they taken a dislikin to you."

"If my being from England makes them uncomfortable," Wilson proclaimed, "that is easily rectified. My father is indeed English and I have lived in England all my life, but my mother was born in Scotland."

Barafe nodded and shook the reins.

"It ain't far to the glen now," he said.

The wagon crested a last hill and Wilson saw not a dilapidated cabin but a white farmhouse with glass windows and a roof shiny as fresh-minted sterling. Yet within the seemingly modern dwelling, he reminded himself, a near centenarian awaited. A fallow field lay to the left of the house, and a barn on the right. Deeper in the glen, cattle and horses wandered an open pasture, their sides branded with an M. A man who looked to be in his fifties came out on the porch and watched them approach. He wore overalls and a chambray shirt but no sidearm.

"That's Luther," Barafe said.

"I presumed we might be greeted with a show of weaponry."

"They'd not do that less you given them particular cause," Barafe answered. "They keep the old ways and we're their guests."

When they were in the yard, Barafe secured the brake and they climbed off the buckboard and ascended the steps. The two rustics greeted each other familiarly, though their host addressed his elder as "Rafe." Wilson stepped forward.

"James Wilson," he said, extending his hand.

"Good to meet you, James," the other replied. "Call me Luther."

Their host took Wilson's valise and opened the door, then stood back so the guests might enter first and warm themselves in front of the corbelled hearth. The parlor slowly revealed itself. A carriage clock was on the mantel, beside it a row of books that included the expected family bible but also a thick tome entitled *Clans of Scotland.*

More of the room emerged. A framed daguerreotype of a white-bearded patriarch dominated one wall, on the opposite, a red-and-black tartan, its bottom edge singed. Two ladder-back chairs were on one side of the hearth and on the other a large Windsor chair plushly lined in red velvet.

"Please sit down," their host said. "I saw you coming from a ways off so stoked the fire for you."

A middle-aged woman entered the parlor with a silver platter. On it were bread and jelly and coffee, silverware and saucers, two cloth napkins. Luther placed a footstool between his guests, and the woman set the platter down.

"This is Molly," their host said, "my wife."

The woman blushed slightly.

"We just finished our noon dinner," she said. "If we'd known you were coming, we'd have waited."

Like Barafe, Luther and his wife had prominent accents, yet both spoke with a formality that acknowledged "d's" and "g's" on word endings. Barafe sat down and tucked his napkin under his chin with an almost comic flair. Wilson sat as well, only then saw that the Windsor chair was occupied.

The beldame's face possessed the color and creases of a walnut hull. A black shawl draped over her shoulders, obscuring a body shrunken to a child's stature. The old woman appeared more engulfed than seated, head and body pressed into the soft padding, shoe tips not touching the floor. And yet, the effect was not so much of a small woman as of a large chair, which, like the velvet lining, gave an appearance of regal authority.

"Granny," Molly said. "We have guests."

Wilson stood.

"I am pleased to make your acquaintance, madam," he said, and gave a slight bow.

"This here is James Wilson," Barafe said, suddenly impelled to use surnames. "He come all the way from England to learn old tunes."

The matriarch blinked twice and then stared fixedly at Wilson. Her eyes were of the lightest blue, as if time had rinsed away most of the color, but there was liveliness inside them. Wilson sat back down.

"He's gonna learn 'em and haul 'em back to England," Barafe added, all but waving a Union Jack over Wilson's head.

"I do indeed come from England, madam," Wilson said, "but my mother is a proud Scot and I too proudly claim the heritage of thistle and bagpipe."

The proclamation was a bit disingenuous. Wilson's mother, though born in Scotland, had moved to London at sixteen and rarely spoken of her Scots roots. Nor had she encouraged her son to think of himself as anything but English. The sole acknowledgment was a blue-and-black tartan that hung, rather forlornly, on an attic wall. The old woman made no reply, and Wilson, wondering if he should summon forth other lore worthy of a loyal scion of Scotland, decided on a more direct tack.

"And of course I will gladly pay you for your trouble," Wilson added.

"If Granny learns you some songs, you'll pay no money for them," Luther said, "but it's her notion to do or not do."

At first it appeared that the matriarch might not deign to respond. Then the sunken mouth slowly unsealed, revealing a single nubbed tooth.

"I can sing a one," the old woman said, "but I'll need a sup of water first."

Wilson opened his valise and took out the fountain pen and ink-bottle, a calfskin ledger. He set the ink bottle by his chair, opened the ledger, and wrote Jackson County, North Carolina, United States, October 1922.

"If you could give me the title of the ballad first, that would be helpful," Wilson said with proper deference.

"It's called 'The Betrothed Knight,'" the old woman answered.

Her voice was low but surprisingly melodic. Wilson wrote rapidly as the matriarch sang of a deceived maiden. Several words were pleasingly archaic, but even better for his purposes, the mention of a knight supported England as the ballad's place of origin. Dipping the pen into the ink during the refrain, Wilson set down all the words in one listening.

"That's a bully one," Barafe said.

"Yes," Wilson agreed. "Most excellent indeed. Do you know more, madam?" The old woman appeared reluctant, so Wilson tried another approach. "Your name will appear on the page with the bal-lad," he noted, "so you will be properly honored."

The appeal to vanity had the opposite effect intended. The old woman asked why she should get "notioned" for something that wasn't hers. She pulled the shawl tight around her neck and chin as if to muffle any further word or song. Luther went to the hearth and picked up the poker, stabbed at the fire until the slumbering flame sparked back to life. As their host leaned the poker by the hearth, Wilson saw that, by accident or design, the poker's prod was shaped like an M. Wilson nodded toward the bookshelf and its tome.

"Of course sharing your ballads does Scotland a great service as well," Wilson noted. "You are preserving a vital part of your ances-tors' and descendants' history."

The old woman did not speak but her eyes were now attentive.

"And part of mine as well," Wilson reminded her.

He racked his brain for something beyond the Merry Olde Eng-land perspective of Scotland as a mere barnacle on England's ship of empire. Macbeth and a joke about bagpipes and testicles emerged first, then, wedged between William the Bruce and Bonnie Prince Charlie, a muddle of dates-feuds-clans and, finally, tam-o-shanters and tartans. Tartans. Wilson left the chair and walked over to the red-and-black tartan, let a thumb and finger rub the cloth. He nodded favorably, hop-ing to impart a Scotsman's familiarity with weave and wool.

"Our tartan hangs on a wall as well, blue and black it is, the proud tartan of Clan Campbell, and no doubt ancient as yours, though bet-ter preserved, which is to be expected, since ours has not traveled such distances."

"And not burned," the old woman said grimly.

Luther and Molly glared at Wilson, and despite the fire, a gust of cold air seemed to fill the room.

"Your tartan," Luther asked, "an azure blue?"

"Well, yes," Wilson answered.

"Argyle," the beldame hissed.

Wilson removed his finger and thumb from the tartan.

"Pardon me," he said. "I'm certain the tartan has been as well cared for as possible. It has just endured a longer journey than ours, across an ocean. And my touching it, I meant no disrespect."

Barafe looked up from his plate, finally aware that some drama was unfolding around him.

"What did you say to vex Granny McDonald?" Barafe asked.

For a few moments the only sound was the ticking of the clock. A disquieting thought nudged Wilson, some connection between English Kings and Argyle Campbells and, thanks to Iago Barafe's sudden gift of enunciation, Clan McDonald.

"Perhaps we should go," Wilson said, stepping over to pack up his valise. "I'm sure we have taken up enough of your time."

"Not till I sing one more song," Granny McDonald said.

Luther latched the front door before crossing the room to the fireplace. He lifted the poker but, instead of poking the fire, nested the prod in the flames.

"You go on out and get your horse some water from the spring, Rafe," Luther McDonald said.

Wilson watched as Barafe hesitated, then gave his erstwhile charge a shrug and stood. Molly unlatched the door, locking it back after the old man passed through.

"This song," the old woman said, "it's called 'The Snows of Glencoe.' Be it one you know?"

"I do not, madam," Wilson stammered.

Wilson did, however, know about the Glencoe massacre. He had been roused from his usual classroom stupor when his don mentioned Clan Campbell's involvement. That had sparked enough interest in Wilson to ask his mother about the event. It's all in the past, his mother had told him, and refused to say more.

"The previous ballad really will suffice," Wilson said. "I have another appointment and must be going."

"Sit down and listen," Luther McDonald said.

Wilson did as he was told and the beldame began to sing.

They came in a blizzard and we offered them heat
A roof o'er their heads and dry shoes for their feet

We wined them and dined them they ate of our meat
And slept in the house of McDonald.

Some died in their beds in the grasp of their foe
Some fled in the night and were lost in the snow
Some lived to accuse them who struck the first blow
That slaughtered the house of McDonald.

They came from Fort Henry with murder in mind.
The Campbells had orders Prince William had signed
Put all to the swords these words were underlined
And leave none alive named McDonald.

The old woman's lips tightened into a mirthless smile. For a few moments no one moved. Then Luther retrieved the poker from the fire, placed his free hand close enough to gauge the heat. Wilson withdrew a wallet from his back pocket.

"I wish to make payment for the songs as well as your hospitality," he said, and rapidly began pulling out bills.

"We'll take no money," his host answered. "No man, not even a king, can buy off a McDonald."

When his ship docked in London harbor six weeks later, Wilson's tongue had not fully healed. Months passed before he was able to convey his thoughts aloud, and during those mute months he showed little desire to do so with pen and paper. Nevertheless, the previously unknown ballad Wilson brought back caused a sensation, in part because its purveyor had placed himself in such peril to acquire it. One London newspaper proclaimed James Wilson worthy of mention with Sir Walter Raleigh and Captain John Smith, those earlier adventurers who also left their civilized isle to venture among the New World's Calibans.

TWENTY-SIX DAYS

It's almost twelve thirty when I'm done sweeping the front steps, so I go inside to stash the broom and dustpan and lock the closet. In the foyer, there's a crisis hotline flyer and a sign-up sheet beneath. Professor Wardlaw has volunteered for Friday, her usual night. I walk out of Cromer Hall and into a November day warmer and sunnier than you usually get in these mountains. The clock tower bell rings. In my mind I move the heavy metal hands ahead ten and a half hours. Kerrie is already in bed. Over at the ATM, students pull out bank cards like winning lottery tickets. Probably not one of them ever thinks that while they're sitting in a classroom or watching a basketball game kids their own age are getting blown up by IEDs. I think again about how we wouldn't be in Afghanistan if there was still a draft. You can bet it'd be a lot different if everyone's kids could end up over there. Just a bunch of stupid hillbillies fighting a stupid war, that's what some jerk on TV said, like Kerrie and the rest don't matter. There's times I want to grab a student by the collar and say you don't know how good you got it, or I tell myself I've given my daughter more than my parents gave me. That's easier than thinking how if I'd had more ambition years back and gotten a welding certificate or degree at Blue Ridge Tech, made more money, Kerrie wouldn't be over there.

I cross the street separating the campus from town and go into Crawford's Diner. Professor Wardlaw's in a booth with Professor Maher and Professor Lucas, who also have offices in Cromer Hall. Ellen brings my plate quick as I sit down at the counter. She has it ready, since I get just thirty minutes for lunch. I eat free, a perk, like Dr. Blanton letting us use his computer. Ellen pours my ice tea and gives me a fork and knife and napkin.

"Not a good morning?" I ask, because Ellen's waitress smile looks frayed.

"It's been okay," she answers, speaking softer as she nods at the professors. "That one with the black hair is who said it, ain't she?"

"Yeah," I say, "but she didn't mean nothing by it, not really."

"When they came in, I had a notion not to serve them at all," Ellen says.

"You know she does a lot of good," I say.

"That still don't excuse her saying such a thing though," Ellen answers, and takes the water and tea pitchers off the counter.

I watch in the mirror as Ellen fills glasses and makes small talk, except at Professor Wardlaw's booth. Ellen lifts her eyes as she passes so that even if they do want something she'll not notice. I shouldn't have told her what Professor Wardlaw said, or made it worse by pointing her out in the parking lot. Ellen's as good a wife as a man could ask for, but she'll hold a grudge.

I check the wall clock. It's 12:50 so I finish and take the plate to the kitchen. Ellen's there changing an order and we talk a minute about Kerrie's application. I come back and the professors are going out the door, backpacks hanging from their shoulders. A five-dollar bill is on the table. I follow them back to Cromer Hall. Someone's spilled a drink near the entrance, ice cubes scattered like dice across the floor. There's a folding yellow caution sign by the entrance, so I set it up. I'm walking down the hallway to get my mop and bucket when I hear my name. Professor Korovich is standing by her office door, a stack of books in her hands.

"I have these for Kerrie," she says.

I thank her and put them on the closet shelf beside the paper towels and disinfectants. I lift the mop bucket to the sink and fill it, pour in the Lysol and head down the hall. Professor Wardlaw's office door is open but she's alone. I think about last month when Professor Korovich gave me other books for Kerrie. When I came back up the hall, Professor Wardlaw was in her office talking to Professor Maher. Nadia doesn't realize that he'll just turn around and sell them, but better the flea market than toilet paper for an outhouse, Professor Wardlaw told her.

I mop the foyer and put the caution sign back up. I get my broom and dustpan and sweep the stairwells, then empty the bathroom trash cans and clean the toilets and sinks. When the 3:30 bell rings, the last classrooms empty so I sweep them. Since tomorrow's a holiday, most of the faculty's gone home. I get out my master key and empty their trash cans. When I get to Professor Korovich's office, the light's still on. She's been at the college only since August and all her family is in Ukraine. Sometimes we talk about how hard it can be when you're separated from your loved ones.

I knock and she tells me to come in.

"How is Kerrie?" she asks, saying the name so the first part's longer than the last.

"She's doing fine," I tell her.

"Less than a month now?"

I nod as I empty her garbage can.

"Not so long," Professor Korovich says, and smiles.

I ask about her family. She tells me her mother's home from the hospital and I tell her I'm glad to hear that. I thank her again for the books and close the door. By the time I've done all the offices, the hall clock says 4:20. I check the bathrooms a last time and punch out.

There's a note tucked under my windshield wiper from Ellen saying she's working till five. I think about going over to the café and having a cup of coffee but decide to wait in the truck. Sometimes I'll find a magazine in a trash can to bring home, but I don't have anything like that so I look over the books Professor Korovich gave me. Three are about teaching but one is called *Selected Stories of Anton Chekhov.* I open it and start reading a story about a man whose child has died. He tries to tell other folks what's happened but no one wants to hear it so he finally tells his horse. You'd think a story like that would be hokey, and maybe it is to some people, but when Ellen gets in the truck she asks if I'm okay. She says I look like I've been crying.

Before I can answer, Ellen raises her hands to her mouth.

"Kerrie's fine," I say quickly. "It's allergies or something."

Ellen's hands settle back in her lap but now they're woven together like she's saying a prayer. Maybe she is saying one.

"Kerrie's fine," I say again.

"You'd figure it would be soothing that she's made it this long," Ellen says as I pull out of the lot, "but the closer we get to her coming home, the scareder I am."

I put my hand on her shoulder and tell her everything's going to be fine. When we pass in front of the quad, we both check the clock.

"A bunch of folks came in for early supper and Alex asked me to stay," Ellen says.

"We'll be on time," I say.

"I did make an extra nine dollars just on the tips."

"That's good," I say, and smile. "You must have given them better service than I saw some folks get at lunch."

I stop at a crosswalk and a group of college students pass in front of us.

"They don't deserve good service," Ellen says.

"They complain?"

"No, but Alex don't miss much." Ellen nods at the books between us. "Professor Korovich gave us some more?"

"Yes," I say. "Remind me to tell Kerrie."

We get lucky on the lights, three greens and one red, but once we pass the city limits sign a car is piddling along and I'm stuck behind it. The road's curvy and the driver's going thirty in a fifty-five zone. It's two miles before the road straightens and I can pass. By the time we pull into the lot that says patient parking, we're running late but Dr. Blanton's car is still outside. We hurry in and I tell him we're sorry to be late.

"Don't worry about that," he says. "I'm just glad you won't miss your call."

He nods at the waiting room floor. There's a red stain wide as a tractor tire.

"A logger nearly cut his arm off this morning. Tonya and I got a lot of it up but the floor needs a good scouring."

"Yes sir," I say, and check the clock.

"I left five more dollars, for the extra work on the floor," Dr. Blanton says, and takes out his keys. "Tell Kerrie the man that brought her into this world says to be careful, doctor's orders."

"We'll tell her," Ellen says.

Dr. Blanton leaves and Ellen goes in to make sure the Skype camera works and that the chat is set up. I go to the storeroom and fill up the mop bucket, then add the bleach and set it in the lobby. It's time for Kerrie to call so I go into Dr. Blanton's office. Ellen's in the chair and I stand behind her. When the box comes up, Ellen clicks "answer." Kerrie appears on the screen and it's like every other time, because a part of Ellen and me that's been knotted up inside all day can finally let go.

Since it's already Thanksgiving over there, Ellen asks if they'll have turkey and dressing for lunch and Kerrie says yes but it won't taste nearly as good as what Ellen makes. When I ask how things are going, Kerrie says fine, like she always does, and tells us she has two more days before she has to go back out. Ellen asks about a boy in her unit who got hurt by an IED and Kerrie says he lost his leg but the doctors saved the sight in one eye.

For a few moments, nobody says anything, because we all know it could have been Kerrie in that Humvee one day earlier. Ellen asks about school. And Kerrie says the head of the education department at N.C. State is matching up the tuition costs with the army's college fund. They've been really helpful, she says. I tell her about the books and Kerrie says to be sure and thank Professor Korovich.

Maybe it's because the picture's a little blurry, but one second I see something in Kerrie's face that reminds me of when she was a baby, then something else reminds me of her in first grade and after that high school. It's like the slightest flicker or shift makes one show more than the others. But that's not it, I realize. All those different faces are inside me, not on the screen, and I can't help thinking that if I remember every one, enough of Kerrie's alive inside me to keep safe the part that isn't.

We stay on awhile longer, not saying anything important, but what we talk about doesn't matter as much as seeing Kerrie and hearing her voice, knowing that she's made it safe through one more day and night. Afterward, we clean up the office, mopping the waiting room last. The bloodstain's a chore. We get on our hands and knees, rubbing the linoleum so hard it's like we're trying to take it off too. We finally get done and Ellen picks up the two twenties and the five on the receptionist's desk. The money we get from Dr. Blanton goes into an envelope we're giving Kerrie the day she gets home. It'll be nearly two thousand dollars, enough to help her some at college. On the way home I turn on the radio. It's a station Ellen and me like because it plays lots of songs we heard while dating, songs we listened to when we were no older than Kerrie.

Several stores already have their Christmas decorations up, and they brighten the town as we drive through. As I wait for a light to turn, I think about Ellen being more scared the closer we get to Kerrie coming home. It's like Kerrie's been lucky so long that the luck's due to run out. I can't help thinking that we can still get a phone call saying Kerrie's been hurt. Or even worse, a soldier showing up with his cap in his hands.

The light turns green and I pass the clock tower, behind it Cromer Hall. The office windows are all dark, but there are lights on at the student center. Some students won't be going home for the holidays, and because of that someone in town has a phone close by, ready if it rings. I think about a young woman who's hurt and scared making that call, and how someone will be there to listen.

LAST RITE

When the sheriff stepped onto her porch, he carried his hat in his hands, so she knew Elijah was dead. The sheriff told how drovers had found her son's body beside a spring just off the trail between Boone and Mountain City, a bullet hole in the back of his head, his pockets turned inside out. He told her of the charred piece of fatback in the skillet, the warm ashes underneath, the empty haversack with the name Elijah Hampton stitched into it. The drovers had nailed the skillet in a big beech tree as a marker and then buried him beside it.

"Murdered," Sarah said, speaking the word the sheriff had avoided. "For a few pieces of silver in his pocket."

It wasn't a question but the sheriff answered as it were.

"That's what I reckon."

"And you don't know who done it."

"No, ma'am," the sheriff said. "And I'll not lie to you. We'll likely never know."

The sheriff held the haversack out to her.

"Your daughter-in law didn't want this. She said she couldn't bear the sight of his blood on it. You may not want it either."

Sarah took the haversack and laid it beside the door.

"So you've already been to see Laura," she said.

"Yes, ma'am. I thought it best, her being the wife."

The sheriff reached into his shirt pocket.

"Here's the death certificate. I thought you might want to see it."

"Just a minute," Sarah said.

She stepped into the front room and took the bible and pen from the mantle. She sat in her porch chair, the bible open on her lap, the piece of paper in her hand.

"It don't say where he died," Sarah said.

"No, ma'am. That gap where they found him, it's the back of beyond. Nobody lives down there, ever has far as I know."

The sheriff looked down at her, his pale-blue eyes shadowed by the hat he now wore.

"Mrs. Hampton," he said, "they don't even know what state that place is in, much less what county."

Sarah closed the bible, the last line unfilled.

Eight months later the dew darkened the hem of her gingham dress as Sarah walked out of the yard, the cool slickness of the grass brushing her bare feet and ankles. Sarah followed Aho Creek down the mountain to where it entered the middle fork of the New River. She stepped onto the wagon road and followed the river north toward Boone, the sun rising over her right shoulder. Soon the river's white rush plunged away from the road. Her shoulder began aching, and she shifted the haversack to her other side.

Sarah stopped at a creek on the outskirts of town. She drank from the creek and unwrapped the sandwich she'd brought with her, but the first mouthful stuck in her throat like sawdust. She tore the bread and ham into pieces and left it for the birds before opening the haversack. Sarah knew she looked a sight but could do nothing about it except take out the lye soap and face cloth and wash the sweat from her face and neck, the dust from her feet and ankles. She took out her shoes and put them on and then walked into Boone, the main street crowded with farmers and their families come to spend Saturday in town. Sarah searched the storefronts until she found the sign that said BENEDICT ASH-SURVEYOR.

His age surprised her, the smooth brow, the full set of teeth. Like the unweathered sign outside his door, the surveyor's youth made Sarah wonder how experienced he was. The surveyor must have realized clients would wish him older, for he wore a mangy red beard and a pair of wire-rimmed glasses he did not put on until Sarah appeared at his door. Sarah told him what she wanted and he listened, first with incredulity and then resignation. He'd been in Boone less than a month and needed any client he could get.

When Sarah finished, the surveyor spread a map across his desk. He took off the glasses and studied the map intently before he spoke.

"My fee will be six dollars. It'll be a full day to get there, do the surveying, and get back. I don't work Sundays, so I'll go first thing Monday morning."

Sarah took a leather purse from the haversack, unsnapped it and removed two silver dollars and four quarters.

"Here. I'll pay you the rest when you're done." She poured the silver into his hand. "What time do we leave on Monday, Mr. Ash?"

"We?" he asked.

Sunday night Sarah had trouble falling asleep. She lay in bed thinking about how Laura had come to church that morning dressed in a blue cotton dress, her dark widow's weeds now packed away.

"You'd think she'd have worn them a year," Anna Miller whispered as they watched Laura enter the church with Clay Triplett.

"She has to get on with her life," Sarah replied without conviction.

She watched Laura lean close to Clay Triplett as the singing began, their hands touching beneath the shared hymnal. Sarah tried to be charitable toward her daughter-in-law, reminding herself that Laura was barely eighteen, that she had been married to Elijah less than a year. The young could believe bad times would be balanced out by good. They could believe the past was something you could box up and forget.

After the service Sarah asked Laura if she wanted to make the journey with the surveyor and her. Sarah wasn't sure if it pleased or disappointed her when Laura said yes. Sarah asked to borrow one of the horses, offered to pay.

"You know I wouldn't charge you, Mrs. Hampton," Laura said. "I'll bring the horse over this afternoon on my way to Boone. I'll spend the night with my aunt in town."

Then Laura had walked over to where Clay Triplett waited in the shade of a live oak tree. He'd tipped his hat to Sarah, then helped Laura into his wagon to take her home.

It had been almost suppertime when Laura brought the horse.

"I reckoned you'd want Sapphire," Laura said. "Elijah always said she was your favorite."

Laura opened her grip and removed a photograph of Elijah taken when he was twelve years old. She handed the photograph to Sarah.

"I think it best if you keep this now. Something else to remember him by."

"Why are you giving me this?" Sarah asked, and Laura blushed.

"Me and Clay, we're going to get married."

"I figured as much," Sarah said, her voice colder than she intended.

"I'd hoped you'd understand, Mrs. Hampton," Laura said.

Sarah looked at the photograph, Elijah dressed in his Sunday church clothes though it had been a Saturday morning in a photographer's studio in Boone. Elijah stared at her from a decade away, his eyes dark and serious.

"You keep it," Sarah finally said, handing the photograph back. "I won't forget what he looked like. You probably will."

Laura let the photograph lay on her open palms. She gazed intently, as though seeing something in it she had not noticed before.

"I loved Elijah," Laura said, not looking up.

"I still do," Sarah had replied.

Sapphire whinnied out in the barn, the same barn she had been foaled in seven springs ago. Will had died the previous winter, Sarah and Elijah had delivered the colt. Sarah wondered if Sapphire remembered the barn, remembered she had been born there.

In the darkness Sarah finally fell asleep and dreamed that Elijah was calling her. He was not the man he'd grown up to be. It was a child's voice Sarah heard in the laurel slick she stumbled and shoved through, branches welting her face and arms and legs as she thrashed deeper into the slick, her legs growing wearier with each blind step, the voice that called her never closer or farther away. Sarah woke with the quilt thrown off the bed, her brow damp as if fevered. She lay in the dark and waited for first light, remembering what was not dream but memory.

It had been August and Elijah was five. She and Will were hoeing the cornfield by the creek. She left Elijah at the end of a row, the whirligig Will had carved for him clasped in his hand. When she reached the end of the row Elijah was gone. They searched all afternoon, working their way back to the farmhouse and then above the pasture where the woods thickened, the same woods where they had heard a panther that spring. She shouted his name until her throat was raw and her voice no more than a harsh whisper.

As night came on Will took the horse to get more help. Sarah lit the lantern and followed the creek, calling his name with what voice she had left. A half mile downstream he answered, his trembling voice rising out of a laurel slick that bordered the creek. She pushed and tripped through the laurel, making wrong guesses, losing her sense of direction in the tangle of leaves and branches. She found him lying on a matting of laurel leaves, the whirligig still clutched in his hand. That was just like him, Sarah thought. Even as a child he'd been careful not to lose things. Careful in other ways too, so that even at eight or nine he could be trusted with an axe or rifle.

Sarah and Laura met the surveyor Monday morning in front of his office. He had not bothered to wear the glasses, but an owlshead pistol bulged from the holster on his hip.

"That three dollars," he said to Sarah. "I can take it now and lock it in my office."

"I'd just as lief wait till you earned it," Sarah replied.

They rode west out of Boone, she on Sapphire, Laura on the gray stallion Will had named Traveler, the surveyor on his roan. The land soon became steeper, rockier. Sarvis and beard-tongue bloomed on the road's edge while dogwoods brightened the woods. The horses breathed harder as the air thinned. Sarah felt lightheaded, but it was more than the altitude. She had been unable to eat any supper or breakfast.

They passed Oak Grove and Villas, then turned north, through Silverstone. Sarah wondered what people thought of this strange procession, of the armed young man wearing denim pants and a long-sleeved cotton shirt, the clanking surveying equipment draped on the roan's flanks like armor, the nineteen-year-old girl dressed in widow's weeds behind him, and Sarah last, also in black, holding the reins and a family bible, forty-two but already an old woman. Sarah stared down at her hands and noted how coarse and wrinkled they were, how the purple veins stretched across their backs as if worms had burrowed under her skin.

Outside of Silverstone the wagon road narrowed until it was no longer a road but a trail. The Stone Mountains loomed like thunderheads. The surveyor carefully scanned the woods that pressed close to the trail and the stone outcrops they passed under, his free hand resting on his holster. Sarah felt Sapphire strain as the grade steepened and the thin air grew even thinner. A rattlesnake slithered across the path and she patted the Sapphire's flank and spoke gently until the animal calmed. Sapphire remembered her, though the horse had been gone from the farm for nineteen months.

She had given Sapphire and the other two horses to Elijah the last morning he awoke under her roof. Sarah had fixed him breakfast but he was too excited to do anything but push the eggs and grits around his plate. Elijah talked of the house he was building at the foot of Dismal Mountain, the house where he and Laura would spend their first night together under an unshingled roof. Sarah called the horses a wedding gift though to her way of thinking they were already more his than hers. He had been the one who looked after them after Will died. Elijah had been only fourteen, but there had not been a morning or evening he forgot to feed or groom the horses. He'd treated the animals with care, like everything else in his life. Which was why he'd not ridden Sapphire to Mountain City. Elijah feared the mare might break a leg on the rocky backslope of the mountain. Always careful, Sarah thought, but somehow not careful enough with what was most precious of all.

They traveled another hour before entering the gap, the mountains and woods closing around them, sunlight mere glances in the treetops. No birds sang and no deer or rabbit bolted into the undergrowth at their approach. The trees leaned over the trail as if listening.

"I didn't know it to be this far," the surveyor grumbled. "To be honest, Mrs. Hampton, I don't believe six dollars is enough."

"My son lost his life for less money," Sarah said.

They came to the spring first, the bare, packed ground of a campsite beside it. They dismounted and let the horses drink. The skillet rusted on the big beech a few yards down the trail and in the woods behind it they found the swelling in the ground. Like it's pregnant, Sarah thought. The drovers had done as much as could be expected. A flat creek rock no bigger than her bible leaned at the head of the grave. No markings were on it. A few broomsedge sprigs poked through the brown leaves that covered the grave. Another winter and Sarah knew the rock would fall, the grave settle, and no one would know a man was buried here.

She wondered if she'd be alive by then. Her stomach had troubled her for months. Ginseng and yellowroot, the draught the doctor had given her, did not help. She had no appetite, and last week she'd coughed up a bright gout of blood.

The surveyor spoke first. "I'm going to get my equipment and go a ways up that ridge." He pointed west where a granite-faced mountain cut the sky in half. "It's too steep for the horses so you all stay here. It shouldn't take me more than an hour," he said, and walked away.

Laura kneeled beside the grave and cleared the leaves from the mound. She took a handkerchief from her dress pocket and unknotted it.

"I brung some wildflower seeds to put on his grave," Laura said. "You want to help plant them, Mrs. Hampton?"

Sarah looked at Laura and realized why Elijah had been so smitten with her. Laura's eyes were dark as July blackberries, her hair yellow as corn silk. But pretty didn't last long in these mountains. Too soon, Sarah knew Laura would stand before a looking-glass and find an old woman staring back .

"I'll help," Sarah said, and kneeled beside her daughter-in-law.

The ground was loose so the planting didn't take very long. When they finished, Sarah stood, her hands stained by the dark loamy earth. "I'll be at the spring with the horses," Sarah said.

She was tired from the journey, the night without sleep. She took the blanket off Sapphire and spread it on the ground where Elijah had died. She lay down and closed her eyes, the bible laid beside her.

She slept and soon Elijah called her again. It was dark and she could see nothing, but he was close this time, just a few yards deeper into the laurel slick. Branches slashed at her face but she kept stumbling forward. She was close now, close enough to reach out her hand and touch his face.

"Mrs. Hampton."

The surveyor stood above her, the equipment burdening his shoulder, his face scratched and sweaty, one of his shirtsleeves torn.

"Where's Laura?" he asked.

"At the grave," Sarah said. Her right arm stretched out before her, open palm pressed to the rocky dirt. She raised that hand to shield her eyes, for it was now midday and sunlight fell through the trees straight as a waterfall.

"North Carolina, Watauga County," the surveyor said as he took a handkerchief from his pocket and wiped his brow. "Granite, yellow-jackets, snakes, and briars, that's all that mountain is. I really think it only fair that you pay me two dollars extra. Why just look at my shirt, Mrs. Hampton."

Sarah did not look up. She took the pen and bottle of ink from the haversack and opened the bible. She found Elijah's name, his dates, and place of birth. Sarah clutched the pen and wrote each letter in slow, even strokes, her hand casting a shadow over the drying ink.

BLACKBERRIES *in* JUNE

On those August nights when no late-afternoon thunder-storm rinsed the heat and humidity from the air, no breeze stirred the cattails and willow oak leaves, Jamie and Matt sometimes made love surrounded by water. Tonight might be such a night, Jamie thought. She rolled down the window and let air blast away some of the cigarette smoke that clung to her uniform and hair. She was exhausted from eight hours of navigating tables with hardly a pause to stand still much less sit down, from the effort it took to lift the sides of her mouth into an unwavering smile. Exhausted too from the work she'd done at the house before her shift at the restaurant. The radio in the decade-old Ford Escort didn't work, so she hummed a Dixie Chicks song about chains being loosened. That's what she wanted, to be unchained in the weightlessness of water. She wanted to feel Matt lift and hold her so close their hearts were only inches apart.

In a few minutes the road fell sharply. At the bottom of the hill she turned off the blacktop onto what was, at least for now, more red-clay washout than road. The Escort bumped and jarred as it made its way down to the lake house. *Their* house, hers and Matt's. Barely a year married, hardly out of their teens, and they had a place they owned, not rented. It was a miracle Jamie still had trouble believing. And this night, like every night as she turned into the drive, a part of her felt surprise the house was really there.

But it was, and already looking so much better than in June when she and Matt signed the papers at the bank. What had been a tangle of kudzu and briars was a yard and garden. Broken windows, rotten boards and rust-rotten screens replaced. Now Jamie spent her mornings washing years of grime off walls and shelves. When that was done she could start caulking the cracks and gashes on the walls and ceilings. Matt reshingled the roof evenings after he got off, working until he could no longer see to nail. As he must have this night, because the ladder lay against the side of the house. In another month, when the shingles had been paid for, they would drive down to Seneca and buy paint. If things went well, in a year they'd have enough saved to replace the plumbing and wiring.

Matt waited on the screened-in porch. The light wasn't on but Jamie knew he was there. As she came up the steps his form emerged from the dark like something summoned out of air. He sat in the porch swing, stripped to his jeans. His work boots, shirt and socks lay in a heap near the door. The swing creaked and swayed as she curled into his lap, her head against his chest. Her lips tasted the salty sweat on his skin as his arms pulled her closer. She felt the hardness of Matt's arms, muscled by two months of ten- to twelve-hour days cutting pulpwood. She wished of those hard muscles a kind of armor to protect him while he logged with her brother Charlton on the ridges where the Chauga River ran through Big Laurel Valley.

You best get a good look at your husband's pretty face right now, Charlton had said the first morning he came to pick up Matt. Feel the smooth of his skin too, little sister, because a man who cuts pulpwood don't stay pretty long.

Charlton had spoken in a joking manner, but she'd seen the certain truth of it in her brother's face, the broken nose and gapped smile, the raised, purple ridges on his arms and legs where flesh had been knitted back together. Jamie had watched Charlton as he and Matt walked to the log truck with its busted headlights and crumpled fender and cracked windshield. A truck no more beat-up and battered than its owner, Jamie had realized in that moment. Charlton was thirty years old, but he moved with the stiffness of an old man. Doctor Wesley in Seneca said he needed back surgery, but Charlton would hear nothing of it. Her sister-in-law, Linda, had told Jamie of nights Charlton drank half a bottle of whiskey to kill the pain. And sometimes, as Matt had witnessed, Charlton didn't wait until night.

The porch swing creaked as Jamie pressed her head closer to Matt's chest, close enough so she could not just hear but feel the strong, sure beat of his heart. First get the house fixed up, Jamie thought. Then when that's done she and Matt would start taking night classes again at the technical college. In a year they'd have their degrees. Then good jobs and children. It was a mantra she recited every night before falling asleep.

"Want to get in the lake?" Matt asked, softly kissing the top of her head.

"Yes," Jamie said, though she felt, to use her mother's words, tired as a rag, but in some ways that was what made their lovemaking so good, especially on Saturday nights—finding in each other's bodies that last ounce of strength left from their long day, their long week, and sharing it with each other.

They walked down the grassy slope to where a half-sunk pier leaned into the lake. On the bank they took off their clothes and stepped onto the pier, the boards trembling beneath them. At the pier's end the boards became slick with algae and water rose to their ankles. They felt for the drop-off with their feet, entered the water with a splash.

Then Jamie was weightless, the water up to her breasts, her feet lifting from the silt as she wrapped her arms around Matt. The sway of water eased away the weariness of eight hours of standing, eased as well the dim ache behind her eyes caused by hurry and noise and cigarette smoke. Water sloshed softly against the pier legs. The moon mirrowed itself in the water, and Matt's head and shoulders shimmered in a yellow glow as Jamie raised her mouth to his.

They slept late the next morning, then worked on the house two hours before driving up the mountain to her grandmother's for Sunday lunch. Behind the farmhouse, a barn Jamie's grandfather had built in the 1950s crumbled into a rotting pile of tin and wood. In a white oak out by the boarded-up well, a cicada called for rain.

"Let's not stay more than an hour," Matt said as they stepped onto the front porch. "That's as long as I can stand Linda."

Inside, Jamie's parents, Charlton, Linda and their children already sat at the table. Food was in serving bowls and the drinks poured.

"About to start without you," Linda said sharply as they sat down. "When young ones get hungry they get contrary. If you had kids you'd know that."

"Them kids don't seem to be acting contrary to me," Matt said, nodding at the three children. "The only person acting contrary is their momma."

"I'm sorry," Jamie said. "We were working on the house and lost track of time."

"I know you all are trying to save money, but I still wish you had a phone," her mother said.

Grandma Chastain came in from the kitchen with a basket of rolls. She sat down at the table beside the youngest child.

"Say us a prayer, Luther," she said to her son.

For a few minutes they ate in silence. Then Charlton turned to his father.

"You ought to have seen the satinback me and Matt killed Wednesday morning. Eight rattles and long as my leg," Charlton said. "Them chain saws have made me so deaf I didn't even hear it. I'm just glad Matt did or I'd of sure stepped right on it."

"Don't tell such a thing, Charlton" Grandma Chastain said. "I worry enough about you out in them woods all day as it is."

"How's your back, son?" Jamie's mother asked.

It was Linda who answered.

"Bothers him all the time. He turns all night in bed trying to get comfortable. Ain't neither of us had a good night's sleep in months."

"You don't think the surgery would do you good?" Grandma Chastain asked.

Charlton shook his head.

"It didn't help Bobby Hemphill's back none. Just cost him a bunch of money and a month not being able to work."

When they'd finished dessert, Jamie's mother turned to her.

"You want to go with me and Linda to that flower show in Seneca?"

"I better not," Jamie said. "I need to work on the house."

"You and Matt are going to work yourselves clear to the bone fixing that house if you're not careful," her mother said.

Jamie's father winked at Jamie.

"Your momma's always looking for the dark cloud in a blue sky."

"I do no such thing, Luther Alexander," her mother said. "It's just the most wonderful kind of thing that Jamie and Matt have that place young as they are. It's like getting blackberries in June. I just don't want them wearing themselves out."

"They're young and healthy, Momma. They can handle it," Charlton said. "Just be happy for them."

Linda sighed loudly and Charlton's lips tightened. The smile vanished from his face. He stared at Linda but did not speak. Instead, it was Grandma Chastain who spoke.

"You two need to be in church on Sunday morning," she said to Jamie, "not working on that house. You've been blessed, and you best let the Lord know you appreciate it."

"Look at you," Linda said angrily to Christy, the youngest child. "You got that pudding all over your Sunday dress." Linda yanked the child from her chair. "Come on, we're going to the bathroom and clean that stain, for what little good it'll do."

Linda walked a few steps, then turned back to the table, her hand gripping Christy's arm so hard the child whimpered.

"I reckon we all don't get lucky with lake houses and such," Linda said, looking not at Matt but Jamie, "but that don't mean we don't deserve just as much. You just make sure your husband saves enough of his strength to do the job Charlton's overpaying him to do."

"I reckon if Charlton's got any complaints about me earning my pay he can tell me himself," Matt said.

Linda swatted Christy's backside with her free hand.

"You hush now," she said to the child, and dragged her into the bathroom.

For a few moments the only sound was the ticking of the mantle clock.

"You don't pay Linda no mind," Charlton said to Matt. "The smartest thing I done in a long while is let go that no-account Talley boy and hire you. You never slack up and you don't call in sick on Mondays. You ain't got a dime from me you ain't earned."

"And I wouldn't expect otherwise," Matt said.

"Still, it's a good thing Charlton's done," Jamie's mother said as she got up, "especially letting you work percentage." She laid her hand on her son's shoulder as she reached around him to pick up his plate.

"You've always been good to look after your sister, and I know she'll always be grateful, won't you, girl?"

"Yes, ma'am," Jamie said.

The bathroom door opened and Christy came out trailing her mother, her eyes swollen from crying.

"We ought to be going," Matt said, pushing back his chair. "I need to get some more shingles on that roof."

"You shouldn't to be in such a rush," Grandma Chastain said, but Matt was already walking toward the door.

Jamie pushed back her chair.

"We do need to be going."

"At least let me wrap you up something for supper," Grandma Chastain said.

Jamie thought about how much work they had to do and how good it would be not to have to cook.

"OK, Grandma," she said.

Matt was in the car when she came out, the engine running and his hands gripping the steering wheel. Jamie placed the leftovers in the back seat and got in beside Matt.

"You could have waited for me," she said.

"If I'd stayed any longer I'd of said some things you wouldn't want me to," Matt said, "and not just to Linda. Your mother and grandma need to keep their advice to themselves."

"They just care about me," Jamie said, "about us."

They drove back to the house in silence and worked until dusk. As Jamie cleaned the blinds she heard Matt's hammer tapping above like he was nailing her shut inside the house. She thought about the rattlesnake, how it could have easily bitten Matt, and remembered twelve years earlier when her mother and Mr. Jenkins, the elementary-school principal, appeared at the classroom door.

"Your daddy's been hurt," her mother had said. Charlton was outside waiting in the logging truck, and they drove the fifteen miles to the county hospital. Her father had been driving a skid loader that morning. It had rained the night before and the machine had turned over on a ridge. His hand was shattered in two places, and there was nerve damage as well. Jamie remembered stepping into the white room with her mother and seeing her father in the bed, a morphine drip jabbed into his arm like a fang. If that skidder had turned over one more time you'd be looking at a dead man, her father had told them. Charlton had quit high school and worked full-time cutting pulpwood to make sure food was on the table that winter. Her father eventually got a job as a night watchman, a job, unlike cutting pulpwood, a man needed only one good hand to do.

"I get scared for you, for us," Jamie said that night as they lay in bed. "Sometimes I wish we'd never had the chance to buy this place."

"You don't mean that," Matt said. "This place is the best thing that might ever happen to us. How many chances do folks our age get to own a house on a lake? If we hadn't seen Old Man Watson's sign before the realtors did, they'd have razed the house and sold the lot alone to some Atlanta retiree at twice what we paid."

"I know that," Jamie said, "but I can't help being scared for you. It's just like things have been too easy for us. Look at Charlton. Him and Linda have been married ten years and they're still in a trailer. Linda says that good luck follows us around like a dog that needs petting all the time. She thinks you and me getting this house is just one more piece of luck."

"Well, the next time she says that you tell her anybody with no better sense than to have three kids the first six years she's married can't expect to have much money left for a down payment on a house, especially with a skidder to pay off as well."

Matt turned his head toward her. She could feel the stir of his breath.

"Linda's just jealous," he said, "that and she's still pissed off Charlton's paying me percentage. Linda best be worrying about her own self. She's got troubles enough at home without stirring up troubles for other people."

"You mean Charlton's drinking?"

"Yeah. Every morning this week he's reeked of alcohol, and it ain't his after-shave. The money they waste on whiskey and her on make-up and fancy hair-dos could make a down-payment, not to mention that Bronco when they already had a perfectly good car. Damn, Jamie, they got three vehicles and only two people to drive them."

Matt placed his hand on the back of Jamie's head, letting his hand run through her cropped hair, hair shorter than his. His voice softened.

"You make your own luck," Matt said. "Some will say we're lucky when you're working in a dentist's office and I'm a shift supervisor in a plant, like we hadn't been planning that very life since we were juniors in high school. They'll forget they stayed at home nights and watched TV instead of taking classes at Tech. They'll forget how we worked near full-time jobs in high school and saved that money when they wasted theirs on new trucks and fancy clothes."

"I know that," Jamie said. "But I get so tired of people acting resentful because we're doing well. It even happens at the café. Why can't they all be like Charlton, just happy for us?"

"Because it reminds them they're too lazy and undisciplined to do it themselves," Matt said. "People like that will pull you down with them if you give them the chance, but we're not going to let them do that to us."

Matt moved his hand slowly down her spine, letting it rest in the small of the back.

"It's time to sleep, baby," he said.

Soon Matt's breathing became slow and regular. He shifted in the bed and his hand slipped free from her back. First, get the house fixed up, she told herself as she let her weariness and the sound of tree frogs and crickets carry her toward sleep.

Two more weeks passed, and it was almost time for Jamie to turn the calendar nailed by the kitchen door. Jamie knew soon the leaves would soon start to turn. Frost would whiten the grass and she and Matt would sleep under piles of quilts Grandma Alexander had sewn. They'd sleep under a roof that no longer leaked. After Charlton picked up Matt, Jamie caulked the back room, the room that would someday be a nursery. As she filled in cracks she envisioned the lake house when it was completely renovated—the walls bright with fresh paint, all the leaks plugged, a porcelain tub and toilet, master bedroom built onto the back. Jamie imagined summer nights when children slept as she and Matt walked hand in hand down to the pier, undressing each other to share again the unburdening of water.

Everything but the back room's ceiling had been caulked when she stopped at one-thirty to eat lunch and change into her waitress's uniform. She was closing the front door when she heard a vehicle bumping down through the woods to the lake house. In a few moments she saw her father's truck, behind the windshield her father's distraught face. At that moment something gave inside her, as if her bones had succumbed to the weight of the flesh they carried. The sky and woods and lake seemed suddenly farther away, as if a space had been cleared that held only her. She closed her hand around the key in her palm and held it so tight her knuckles whitened. Her father kicked the cab door open with his boot.

"It's bad," he said, "real bad." He didn't cut off the engine or get out from behind the wheel. "Linda and Matt and your momma are already at the hospital."

She didn't understand, not at first. She tried to picture a situation where her mother and Linda and Matt could have been hurt together—a car wreck, or fire—something she could frame and make sense of.

"Momma and Linda are hurt too?" Jamie finally asked.

"No," her father said, "just Charlton." Her father's voice cracked. "They're going to have to take your brother's leg off, baby."

Jamie understood then, and at that moment she felt many things, including relief that it wasn't Matt.

When they entered the waiting room, her mother and Linda sat on a long green couch. Matt sat opposite them in a blue plastic chair. Dried blood stained his work shirt and jeans. He stood up, came and embraced her. Jamie smelled the blood as she rested her head against his chest.

"We were cleaning limbs," Matt said, "and the saw jumped back and dug into his leg till it got to bone. I made a tourniquet with my belt, but he still almost bled to death." Matt paused. "Charlton shouldn't have been running that saw. He'd been drinking."

Matt held her close a few more moments, then stepped back. He nodded toward the corner where Linda and her mother sat.

"You better say something to your momma and Linda," Matt said, and released her arms. Jamie let go too. It was only then that she realized the key was still in her closed right hand. She slipped it into her uniform pocket.

Her mother stood when Jamie approached, but Linda stayed on the couch, her head bowed.

"Pray hard, girl," her mother said as she embraced Jamie. "Your brother is going to need every prayer he can get."

"You seen him yet, Momma?" she asked. Jamie smelled the Camay lotion her mother rubbed on every night. She breathed deep, let the smell of the lotion replace the smell of blood.

"No, he's still in surgery, will be for at least another hour."

Her mother released her and stepped back.

"I can't stand myself just sitting her," her mother said, and nodded at Jamie's father standing beside the door marked SURGERY. "Come on, Luther. I'm going to get us all some doughnuts and coffee and I need you to help carry it." She turned to Jamie. "You stay here and look after Linda."

Jamie sat in the place her mother had left. Linda's head remained bowed, but her eyes were open. Jamie looked up the wall clock. Two-twenty three. The red minute hand went around seven more times before Jamie spoke.

"It's going to be all right, Linda," she said. It was the only thing she could think to say.

Linda lifted her head, looked right at Jamie. "You sound pretty sure of that. Maybe if it was your husband getting his leg took off you'd think different."

Linda wasn't thirty yet, but Jamie saw something she recognized in every older woman in her family. It was how they looked out at the world, their eyes resigned to bad times and trouble. I don't ever remember being young, Grandma Alexander had once told her. All I remember is something always needing to be done, whether it was hoeing a field or washing or feeding children or tending cows and chickens.

The elevator door opened and Jamie's parents stepped out, their hands filled with paper bags.

"You think this couldn't have happened to Matt," Linda said, raising her voice enough that Jamie's parents came no closer. "You think it happened because Charlton had been drinking."

"I don't think any such thing," Jamie said.

Linda looked at her in-laws.

"I got three young ones to feed and buy school clothes for, and a disability check ain't going to be enough to do that."

"We'll do everything we can to help you," Jamie's father said, and offered Linda a styrofoam cup of coffee. "Here. This will give you some strength."

"I don't need strength," Linda said, her voice wild and angry. "I need the money Charlton overpaid Matt. Money that should be ours. Money we need worse than they do."

Linda looked at her father-in-law.

"You know Charlton paid hourly pages to everybody else who worked for him."

"I earned every cent he paid me," Matt said. He had left his seat and stepped closer, standing next to Jamie now. "I been there every day and I've cut plenty of days dawn to dark. It's bad what's happened to Charlton, and I'm sorry it happened. But me and Jamie don't owe you anything." Jamie placed her hand on Matt's arm, but he jerked it away. "I ain't listening to this anymore."

"You owe us everything," Linda shouted as Matt walked toward the elevator. "If Charlton hadn't taken you on you'd never have been able to make a down-payment on that lake house." Linda looked at Jamie's parents now, tears streaming down her face. "A lake house, and the five of us in a beat-up doublewide."

The surgery room door opened, and a nurse glared at them all briefly before the door closed again.

Jamie's mother sat down on the couch and pressed Linda's head to her bosom.

"We're all going to do everything possible to get you all through this, Linda, and that includes Matt and Jamie."

Linda sobbed now, her face smeared with mascara. Minutes

passed before she lifted her head. She tried to smile as she brushed tears from her cheek and slowly lifted herself from the couch. Jamie's father gripped Linda's upper arm when her knees buckled.

"I know I look a sight," Linda said. "I best go to the bathroom and tidy up so Charlton won't see me like this." Linda looked at Jamie. "I'm sorry," she said.

Jamie's father walked Linda to the restroom and waited by the door.

"Come here, girl," her mother said to Jamie.

Jamie did not move. She was afraid, almost as afraid as when she'd seen her father's face through the windshield.

"I need to call the restaurant, let them know what's going on."

"That can wait a few minutes," her mother said. "We need to talk, and right now."

Jamie remained where she was.

"I know you're put out with Linda," her mother said, "and I don't blame you. Grieving don't give her no excuse to talk that way to you and Matt." She paused, waited for Jamie to meet her eyes. "But you know you got to help them."

Jamie turned and stared at the wall clock. She thought how only two hours earlier she had been caulking the back room of the lake house.

"Me and your daddy will do what we can, but that won't be near enough. Your daddy says even if the skidder's sold it'll bring no more than two thousand dollars. We're not talking about just Linda here. We're talking about your niece and nephews."

"Why are you saying this to me, Momma?" Jamie said. "Matt's going to have to find another job now, and there's no way he'll make the kind of money Charlton paid him. We need all the money we got just to make the payments on the lake house, much less fix it up. We'll have tuition to pay as well come spring."

The elevator door opened. Jamie hoped it was Matt, but a chaplain got off and walked past them toward the intensive care unit.

"You've been blessed, Jamie," her mother said. "Linda's right. Charlton never let anyone but Matt work percentage. You could give Charlton the difference between what Matt got paid and the six dollars an hour anybody else would have got."

"But we'd have to sell the lake house," Jamie said. "How can you ask me and Matt to do that?"

"The same way I'd have asked your brother to quit high school. Only I never had to ask. He knew what had to be done and did it without me saying a word to him. Seventeen years old and he knew what had to be done." Her mother laid her hand on Jamie's. "That lake house, you had no right to expect to such a place so young. You know it was a miracle you got it in the first place. You can't expect miracles in this life, girl."

The bathroom door opened and Linda came out. She and Jamie's father walked toward them

"Maybe not, Momma," Jamie said, her voice low but sharp, "but when they come a person's got a right to take them."

"You got to do what's best for the whole family," her mother said, speaking quietly as well. "You got to accept that life is full of disappointments. That's something you learn as you grow older."

There had been complications during the surgery, and Jamie was unable to see Charlton until after seven-thirty. His eyes opened when she placed her hand on his, but he was too drugged to say anything coherent. Jamie wondered if he even understood what had happened to him.

When Jamie and Matt got back to the lake house it was dark, and by then things had been decided, but not before harsh words had been exchanged.

"Come on," Matt said, reaching his hand out to hers after they got out of the Escort. "Let's go down to the lake, baby. I need one good thing to happen in my life today."

"Not tonight," Jamie said. "I'm going on in."

She changed into her nightgown. Matt came in soon afterward naked and dripping, work clothes and boots cradled in his arms. Jamie stepped out of the bathroom, a toothbrush in her hand.

"Put those clothes out on the porch," she said. "I don't want to smell that blood anymore."

Jamie was in bed when he came back, and soon Matt cut out the light and joined her. For a minute the only sound was the crickets and tree frogs. The mattress' worn-out bedsprings creaked as Matt turned to face her.

"I'll go see Harold Wilkinson in the morning," Matt said. "He knows I did good work for Charlton. I figure I can get eight dollars an hour to work on his crew, especially since I know how to run a skidder."

Matt reached out and laid his arm on Jamie's shoulder.

"Come here," he said, pulling her closer.

She smelled the thick, fishy odor of the lake, felt the lake's coldness on his skin.

"They'll be needing help a long time," Matt said. "In two, three years at most we'll have jobs that pay three times what we're making now. Keeping this house is going to save us a lot of money, money we can help them with later."

Matt paused.

"You listening to me."

"Yes," Jamie said.

"Linda's parents can help too. I didn't hear your momma say a word about them helping out." Matt kissed her softly on the cheek.

"They'll be all right. We'll all be all right. Go to sleep, babe. You got another long day coming."

But she did not fall asleep, not for a while, and she woke at first light. She left the bed and went to the bathroom. Jamie turned on the faucet and soaked a washcloth, wrung it out and pressed it to her face. She set it on the basin and looked at the mirror. A crack jagged across the mirror like a lightning bolt. Something else to be replaced, she thought.

CHEMISTRY

The spring my father spent three weeks at Broughton Hospital, he came back to my mother and me pale and disoriented, two pill bottles clutched in his right hand as we made our awkward reunion in the hospital lobby. A portly, gray-haired man wearing a tie and tweed jacket soon joined us. Dr. Morris pronounced my father "greatly improved, well on his way to recovery," but even in those first few minutes my mother and I were less sure. My father seemed to be in a holding pattern, not the humorous, confident man he had been before his life swerved to some bleak reckoning, but also not the man who'd lain in bed those April mornings when my mother called the high school to arrange a substitute. He now seemed like a shipwreck survivor, treading water but unable to swim.

"All he needs is a hobby," Doctor Morris said, patting my father's back as if they were old friends, "to keep his mind off his mind." The doctor laughed and straightened his tie, added as if an afterthought, "and the medicine, of course." Dr. Morris patted my father's back again. "A chemistry teacher knows how important that is."

My father took half of Dr. Morris's advice. As soon as we got home, he brought the steel oxygen tank clanging down from the attic and gathered the wet suit, mask and flippers he hadn't worn since his navy days. He put it all on to check for leaks and rips, his webbed feet flapping as he moved around the living room like some half-evolved creature.

"I'm not sure this was the kind of hobby Dr. Morris had in mind," my mother said, trying to catch the eyes behind the mask. "It seems dangerous."

My father did not reply. He was testing the mouthpiece while adjusting the straps that held the air tanks. That done, he made swimming motions with his arms as he raised his knees toward his chest like a drum major.

"I've got some repairs to make," he said, and flapped on out to the garage. While my mother cooked a homecoming supper of pork chops and rice, he prepared himself to enter the deep gloaming of channels and drop offs with thirty minutes of breath strapped to his back.

My father still wore his wet suit and fins when he sat down at the supper table that evening. He ate everything on his plate, which heartened my mother and me, and drank glass after glass of iced tea as if possessed by an unquenchable thirst. But when he lay his napkin on the table, he did not refill his glass with more tea and reach for the pill bottles my mother had placed beside his plate.

"You've got to take the medicine," my mother urged. "It's going to heal you."

"Heal me," my father mused. "You sound like Dr. Morris. He said the same thing right before they did the shock treatments."

My mother looked at her plate.

"Can't you see that's exactly why you need to take the pills? So you won't ever have to do that again." She raised her napkin to soak a tear from her cheek, her voice a mere whisper now. "This is not something to be ashamed of, Paul. It's no different from taking penicillin for an infection."

But my father was adamant. He pushed the tinted bottles to the center of the table one at a time as if they were chess pieces.

"How can I teach chemistry if I'm so muddled I can't find the classroom?" he said.

That spring my allegiances were with my mother, who anchored our family in ways I had not appreciated until my father had been hospitalized. The following Monday my father resumed teaching, and I was her confederate at school. Between bells I peeked into a classroom filled with periodic charts, styrofoam carbons, and atoms wired together like fragile solar systems. In March Mr. Keller, the vice-principal, had found my father crouched and sobbing in the chemical storage room, a molecular model of oxygen clutched in his hands, so it was with relief in those last weeks of my junior year that I found my father manning his desk between breaks, braced and ready for the next wave of students.

One morning he was looking up when my halved face appeared at his door. He saluted me sharply.

"Petty Officer Hampton reports no men overboard, sir," he said to me.

"Well, at least he's got his sense of humor back," my mother said when I reported the incident.

In mid-June my father announced at Sunday breakfast he was no longer a Presbyterian. Instead of sitting with us on the polished-oak pews of Cliffside Presbyterian, he would be driving up to Cleveland County's mountainous northern corner to attend a Pentecostal church.

"It's something I've got to do," my father said.

My mother laid her napkin on the table, looked at my father as if he'd just informed us he was defecting to Cuba.

"We need to talk, Paul," she said. "Alone."

My parents disappeared behind a closed bedroom door. I could hear my father's voice, moderate and reassuring, or at least attempting to be. My mother's voice, in contrast, was tense and troubled. They talked an hour, then dressed for church. I was unsure who'd prevailed until my father came out of the bedroom wearing not a suit but a shirt and tie. He cranked our decade-old Ford Fairlane and headed north into the mountains, as he would Sunday mornings and Wednesday nights for the rest of his life. Meanwhile, my mother and I drove our newer Buick LeSabre in the opposite direction, down toward Broad River to Cliffside Presbyterian.

I was not made privy to what kind of understanding, if any, my parents had reached about his change in church affiliation, but it was obvious as well as inevitable that my mother found this religious transmutation troubling. A lifelong Presbyterian, she distrusted religious fervor, especially for a man in such a tenuous mental state, but I suspect she also felt something akin to betrayal—a rejection of much of the life his marriage to her had made possible.

My mother had been baptized in Cliffside's Presbyterian church, but my father, who'd grown up in the high mountains of Watauga County, had been Pentecostal before their marriage. His conversion signaled a social as well as religious transformation, a sign of upward mobility from hardscrabble Appalachian beginnings, for in this Scots-Irish community where Episcopalians were rare as Eskimos, he worshipped with the Brahmins of the county's Protestant hierarchy.

My father had appeared a dutiful convert, teaching Sunday school, helping prepare the men's breakfasts, even serving a term as an elder, but he'd been a subversive convert as well. On Sunday mornings he entertained me with caustic remarks about the propriety of the services and Presbyterians' inability to sing anything remotely resembling a "joyful noise." When the choir rose to sing, my father winked at me, pretended to stuff plugs in his ears. My mother looked straight ahead at such times, trying to ignore my father's shenanigans, but her lips always tightened.

"That wafer might as well be a burnt marshmallow for all the passion it evokes in that crowd," my father said one Sunday as we drove home. "If Jesus Christ and his disciples marched in during a service, the ushers would tell them to have a seat, that the congregation would be glad to hear what they had to say as soon as the monthly business meeting was over."

My mother glared at my father but addressed her words to the backseat where I sat.

"Just because a service is orderly and dignified doesn't mean it isn't heartfelt," she said. "Don't trust people who make a spectacle of what that believe, Joel. Too often it's just a show, a way of drawing attention to themselves."

As we entered summer, our lives took on a guarded normality. My father taught a six-week summer school session. My mother resumed, after a two-month absence, her part-time job as a bookkeeper for my Uncle Brad's construction firm. I worked for my uncle as well, driving nails and pouring concrete. My uncle also gave us free reign of the lake house he'd bought years earlier when he'd had the time to use it, so on Saturday mornings we drove up Highway Ten to spend the day at South Mountain Reservoir, where cool mountain breezes and teeth-chattering water might revive us after a week of wilting piedmont humidity. No doubt my mother packed up food and swim suits each Saturday in hopes the lake might be beneficial for my father after a week of remedial teaching in an unairconditioned classroom.

My father was eager that I share his new hobby. He gave me demonstrations on how to use the scuba apparatus. At supper he spoke excitedly of water's other side. He often wore his diving equipment around the house, once opening the door to a startled paperboy while wearing a mask and fins. My mother was reluctant to let me participate, but she acquiesced when I promised not to go into the reservoir's deep heart, where a diver had drowned the previous summer. So on Saturday afternoons she read paperbacks on the screened porch and cast nervous glances toward the lake as my father and I shared the diving equipment. When my turn came, I fell backwards off the dock and into the lake, watching a rushing away sky as I hit the water and sank, air bubbles rising above my head like thoughts in a comic strip.

I could never see more than a few yards, but that was enough. Arm-long catfish swam into view sudden as a nightmare, their blunt, whiskered faces rooting the bottom. Snapping turtles big as hub-caps walked the lake floor, their hand-grenade heads ready to bite off a careless finger. I found what no longer lived down there as well: fish suspended like kites, monofilament trailing from their mouths to line-wrapped snags below; drowned litters of kittens and pup-pies; once an out-of-season deer, a gash on its head where the antlers had been. On the reservoir's floor even the familiar startled. Gaudy bass plugs hung on limbs and stumps like Christmas ornaments; branches snapped off like black icicles; a refrigerator yawned open like an unsprung trap.

Each time I entered the water my foreboding increased, not chest-tightening panic but a growing certainty that many things in the world were better left hidden. By August I'd joined my mother on the porch, playing board games and drinking iced tea as my father disappeared off the dock towards mysteries I no longer wished to fathom.

On one of these August afternoons after he'd finished diving, my father decided to drive out to the highway and buy ice so we could churn ice cream. "Come with me, Joel," he said. "I might need some help."

Once we turned onto the blacktop my father passed two convenience stores before pulling in to what had once been a gas station. Now only a weedy cement island remained, the pumps long uprooted. HOLCOMBE'S STORE, nothing more, appeared on a rusting black-and-white sign above the door. REDWORMS AND MINNERS FOR SALE was scrawled eye level on a second sign made of cardboard.

We stepped inside, adjusting our eyes to what little light filtered through the dusty windows. A radio played gospel music. Canned goods and paper plates, toilet paper and boxes of cereal lined the shelves. A man about my father's age sat behind the counter, black hair combed slick across his scalp, a mole above his right eyebrow the size and color of a tarnished penny. The man stood up from his chair and smiled, his two front teeth chipped and discolored.

"Why hi, Brother Hampton," he said warmly in a thick mountain accent. "What brings you up this way?"

"Spending Saturday on the lake," my father said, then nodded toward me. "This is my son, Joel."

"Carl Holcombe," the man said, extending his hand. I felt the calluses on his palm, the wedding ring worn on his right hand.

"We're going to make ice cream," my father said. "I was hoping you had some ice."

"Wish I could help you but I weren't selling enough to keep the truck coming by," Mr. Holcombe said.

"How about some worms then?"

"That I can help you with." Mr. Holcombe came around the counter, walking with a slight limp as he made his way to the back of the store.

"How many boxes?" he asked, opening a refrigerator.

"Four," my father said.

My father laid a five-dollar bill on the counter. Mr. Holcombe rang up the sale.

"See you at church tomorrow?" Mr. Holcombe asked, dropping coins into my father's hand. My father nodded.

I tried not to stare at the mole as Mr. Holcombe filled my hands with the cardboard containers.

"Your daddy," he said to me, "is a godly man, but I suspect you already know that."

He closed the cash register and walked with us to the entrance.

"I hope you all catch something," he said, holding the tattered screen door open.

"Why did you buy the worms?" I asked my father as we drove off.

"Because he needs the money," my father said. "We'll let them go in the garden."

"Mr. Holcombe's a friend of yours?" I asked, wondering if my father would note the surprise in my voice.

"Yes," my father said. "He's also my pastor."

The following Wednesday my father left to attend his midweek church service. I'd already asked my mother if I could borrow the Buick that evening, so when he departed so did I, following the Fairlane through town. At the stoplight I too turned right onto Highway Ten. Since the previous Saturday I'd been perplexed as to what could compel my father, a man with a university education, to drive a good half-hour to hear a preacher who, if his spelling and grammar were any indication, probably hadn't finished high school.

Outside of town it began to rain. I turned on the Buick's windshield wipers and headlights. Soon hills became mountains, red clay darkened to black dirt. I swallowed to relieve the ear pressure from the change in altitude as the last ranch-style brick house, the last broad, manicured lawn, vanished from my rear-view mirror.

Stands of oaks and dogwoods crowded the roadsides. Gaps in the woods revealed the green rise of corn and tobacco, pastures framed by rusty barbed wire fences. Occasionally I passed a prosperous looking two-story farmhouse, but most homes were trailers or four-room A frames, often with pickups, cars, and appliances rusting in the side yards, scrawny beagles and blue-ticks chained under trees.

The rain quit so I cut off the windshield wipers, let the Fairlane get farther ahead of me. I came over a rise and the Fairlane had already disappeared around a curve. I sped up, afraid I'd lost my father, but coming out of the curve I saw his car stopped in the road a hundred yards ahead, the turn signal on though our Buick was the closest car behind him. My father turned onto a dirt road and I followed, still keeping my distance though I wondered if it were really necessary. He slowed in front of a cinder-block building no bigger than a woodshed, pulling into a makeshift parking lot where our ancient Fairlane looked no older than the dozen other cars and trucks. I eased off the road on a rise above the church and watched my father walk hurriedly toward the building. A white cross was nailed above the door he entered.

I could hear an out-of-tune piano, a chorus of voices rising from the open door and windows into the August evening, merging with the songs of crickets and cicadas. I waited half an hour before I got out of the Buick and walked down the road to the church. At the front door I paused, then stepped into a foyer small and dark as a closet. A half-open door led to the main room. The singing stopped, replaced by a single voice.

I peered into a thick-shadowed room whose only light came from a single bare bulb dangling from the ceiling. Mr. Holcombe stood in front of three rows of metal chairs where the congregation sat. At his feet lay a wooden box that looked like an infant's coffin. Holes had been bored in its lid. Mr. Holcombe wore no coat or tie, just a white, short-sleeved shirt, brown slacks, and scuffed black loafers. His arm oustretched, he waved a bible as if fanning an invisible flame.

"The word of the Lord," he said, then opened the bible to a page marked by a paper scrap. "'And they cast out many devils, and anointed with oil many that were sick, and healed them,'" Mr. Holcombe read. He closed the bible and went down on one knee in front of the wooden box, his head bowed, like an athlete resting on the sidelines. "Whoever is afflicted, come forward," he said. "Lord, if it is your will, let us be the instrument of thy healing grace."

"Amen," the congregation said as my father left the last row and kneeled beside Mr. Holcombe. Without a word the congregation rose and gathered around my father. An old woman, gray hair reaching her hips, opened a bottle and dabbed a thick, clear liquid on my father's brow. The other members laid their hands on his head and shoulders.

"Oh, Lord," shouted Mr. Holcombe, raising the bible in his hand. "Grant this child of God continued victories over his affliction. Let not his heart be troubled. Let him know your abiding presence."

The old woman with the long hair began speaking feverishly in a language I couldn't understand, her hands straining upward as if she were attempting to haul heaven down into their midst.

"Praise God, praise God," a man in a plaid shirt shouted as he did a spastic dance around the others.

My father began speaking the strange, fervent language of the old woman. The congregation removed their hands as my father rocked his torso back and forth, sounds I could not translate pouring from his mouth.

Mr. Holcombe, still kneeling beside my father, unclasped the wooden box. The room suddenly became silent, then a whirring sound like a dry gourd being shaken. At first I did not realize where the noise came from, but when Mr. Holcombe dipped his hand and forearm into the box the sound increased. Something was in there, something alive and, I knew even before seeing it, dangerous.

Mr. Holcombe's forearm rose out of the box, a timber rattlesnake coiled around his wrist like a thick, black vine. The reptile's head rose inches above Mr. Holcombe's open palm, its split tongue probing the air like a sensor.

I turned away, stepped out of the foyer and into the parking lot. My eyes slowly adjusted to being outside of the church's dense shadows. I stood there until the scraping of chairs signaled the congregation's return to their seats. They sang a hymn, and then Mr. Holcombe slowly read a long passage from the book of Mark.

I walked back to the Buick. Halfway there, I saw the headlights were on. I tried the battery five times and gave up, dragging the jumper cables from the trunk and opening the hood in hopes someone might stop and help me. No cars or trucks passed, however, and in a few minutes people came out of the church, some pausing to speak but most going straight to their vehicles. I sat in the car and waited as I saw our Fairlane leave the parking lot.

My father pulled off the road in front of the Buick, hood to hood as though he already knew the problem. I stepped out of the car.

"What happened?" he asked.

I wasn't sure how to answer his question, but I gave the simplest answer.

"The battery's dead," I said, holding up the jumper cables as if to validate my words.

He opened the Fairlane's hood. We clamped the cables to the batteries, then got back in and cranked the engines. My father unhooked the cables and came around to the Buick's passenger side. He dropped the jumper cables on the floorboard and sat down beside me. Both engines were running, the cars aimed at each other like a wreck about to happen.

"Why did you follow me?" my father asked, looking out the window. There was no anger in his voice, just curiosity.

"To find out why you come here."

"Do you know now?"

"No."

The last two cars left the church. The drivers slowed as they passed, but my father waved them on.

"Dr. Morris says I've got too much salt in my brain, a chemical imbalance," my father said. "It's an easy problem for him with an easy solution, so many milligrams of Elavil, so many volts of electricity. But I can't believe it's that simple."

Perhaps it was the hum of the engines, my father looking out the window as he spoke, but I felt as though we were traveling although the landscape did not change. It was like I could feel the earth's slow revolution as August's strange, pink glow tinted the evening's last light.

My father shut his eyes for a moment. He'd aged in the last year, his hair gray at the edges, his brow lined.

"Your mother believes the holy rollers got me too young, that they raised me to see the world only the way they see it. But she's wrong about that. There was a time I could understand everything from a single atom to the whole universe with a blackboard and piece of chalk, and it was as beautiful as any hymn the way it all came together."

My father nodded toward the church, barely visible now in the gloaming.

"You met Carl Holcombe. His wife and five-year-old daughter got killed eleven years ago in a car wreck, a wreck that was Carl's fault because he was driving too fast. Carl says there are whole weeks he can't remember he was so drunk, nights he put a gun barrel under his chin and held it there an hour. There was nothing in this world to sustain him, so he had to look somewhere else. I've had to do the same."

Though the cars still idled, we sat there in silence a few more minutes, long enough to see the night's first fireflies sparking like matches in the woods. My father's face was submerged in shadows when he spoke again.

"What I'm trying to say is that some solutions aren't crystal-clear. Sometimes you have to search for them in places where only the heart can go."

"I still don't think I understand," I said.

"I hope you never do," my father said softly, "but from what the doctors at Broughton told me there's a chance you will."

My father leaned over, switched on the Buick's headlights.

"We need to get home," he said. "Your mother will be worried about us."

The pill bottles remained unopened the rest of the summer, and there were no more attempts to cauterize my father's despair with electricity. Which is not to say my father was a happy man. His was not a religion of bliss but one that allowed him to rise from his bed on each of those summer mornings and face two classes of hormone-ravaged adolescents, to lead those students toward solutions he himself no longer found adequate. I did not tell my mother what I had seen that Wednesday evening, or what I refused to see. I have never told her.

My father died that September, on an afternoon when the first reds and yellows flared in the maples and poplars. We'd driven up to the lake house that morning. My father graded tests until early afternoon. When he'd finished he went inside and put on his diving gear, then crossed the brief swath of grass to the water—moving slow and deliberate on the land, like an aquatic creature returning to its natural element. Once on the dock he turned toward the lake house, raised a palm, and fell forever from us.

My mother and I sat on the porch playing Risk and drinking tea. When my father hadn't resurfaced after a reasonable time, my mother cast frequent glances toward the water.

"It hasn't been thirty minutes yet," I said more than once. But in a few more minutes half an hour had passed, and my father still had not risen.

I ran down to the lake while my mother dialed the county's EMS unit. I dove into the murky water around the dock, finding nothing on the bottom but silt. I dove until the rescue squad arrived, though I dove without hope. I was seventeen years old. I didn't know what else to do.

The rest of the afternoon was a loud confusion of divers and boats, rescue squad members and gawkers. The sheriff showed up and, almost at dusk, the coroner, a young man dressed in khakis and a blue cotton shirt.

"Nitrogen narcosis, sometimes called rapture of the deep," the coroner said, conversant in the language of death despite his youth. "A lot of people wouldn't think a reservoir would be deep enough to cause that, but this one is." He and the sheriff stood with my mother and me on the screened porch, cups of coffee in their hands. "If you go down too far you can take in too much nitrogen. It causes a chemical imbalance, an intoxicating effect." The coroner looked out toward the reservoir. "It can happen to the most experienced diver."

The coroner talked to us a few more minutes before he and the sheriff stepped off the screened porch, leaving behind empty coffee cups, no doubt hoping what inevitable calamity would reunite them might wait until after a night's sleep.

Once he had no further say in the matter, my father was again a Presbyterian. His funeral service was held at Cliffside Presbyterian, his burial in the church's cemetery. Mr. Holcombe and several of his congregation attended. They sat in the back, the men wearing short-sleeve shirts and ties, the women cotton dresses that reached their ankles. After the burial they awkwardly shook my hand and my mother's before departing. I've never seen any of them since.

In my less generous moments I perceive my mother's insistence on Presbyterian last rites as mean-spirited, a last rebuke to my father's Pentecostal reconversion. But who can really know another's heart? Perhaps it was merely her Scots-Irish practicality, less trouble for everyone to hold the rites in Cliffside instead of twenty miles away in the mountains.

After my father's death my mother refused to go back to the lake house, but I did and occasionally still do. I sit out on the screened porch as the night starts its slow glide across the lake. It's a quiet time, the skiers and most of the fishermen gone home, the echoing trombone of frogs not yet in full volume. I listen to sounds unheard any other time—the soft slap of water against the dock, a muskrat in the cattails.

I sometimes think of my father down in that murky water as his lungs surrendered. I think of what the coroner told me that night on the porch, that the divers found the mask in the silt beside him. "Probably didn't even know he was doing it," the coroner said matter-of-factly. "People do strange things like that all the time when they're dying."

The coroner is probably right. But sometimes as I sit on the porch with darkness settling around me, it is easy to imagine that my father pulling off the mask was something more—a gesture of astonishment at what he drifted toward.

The NIGHT the NEW JESUS
FELL to EARTH

The day after it happened, and Cliffside's new Jesus and my old husband was in the county hospital in fair but stable condition, Preacher Thompson, claiming it was all his fault, offered his resignation to the board of deacons. But he wasn't to blame. He'd only been here a couple of months, fresh out of preacher's college, and had probably never had to deal with a snake like Larry Rudisell before. A man or a woman, as I've found out the hard way, usually has to get bit by a snake before they start watching out for them.

What I mean is, Preacher Thompson's intentions were good. At his very first interview the pulpit committee had told him what a sorry turn our church had taken in the last few years, and they hadn't left out much either. They told him about Len Deaton, our former choir director, who left his choir, wife, and eight children to run off to Florida with a singer at Harley's Lounge who wasn't even a Baptist. And they told about Preacher Crowe, who had gotten so senile he had preached the same sermon four weeks in a row, though they didn't mention that a lot of the congregation hadn't even noticed. The committee told him about how membership had been slipping for several years, how the church was in a rut, and how when Preacher Crowe had finally retired in November, it had been clear that some major changes had to be made if the church was going to survive. And this was exactly why they wanted him to be the new minister, they told him. He was young and energetic and could bring some fresh blood into the church and help get it going in the right direction. Which was exactly what he tried to do, and exactly why Larry was able to talk his way onto that cross.

It did take a few weeks, though. At first Preacher Thompson was so nervous when he preached that I expected him to bolt for the sanctuary door at any moment. He wouldn't even look up from his notes, and when he performed his first baptism he almost drowned poor little Eddie Gregory by holding him under the water too long. Still, each week you could see him get a little more comfortable and confident, and by the last Sunday in February, about two months ago, he gave the sermon everybody had been waiting for.

It was all about commitment and the need for new ideas, about how a church was like a car, and our church was in reverse and we had to get it back in forward. You could tell he was really working himself up because he wasn't looking at his notes or his watch. It was 12:15, the first time he'd ever kept us up after twelve, when he closed, telling us that Easter, a month away, was a time of rebirth, and he wanted us all to go home and think of some way our church could be reborn too, something that would get Cliffside Baptist Church back in the right gear.

Later I wondered if maybe all the car talk had something to do with what happened, because the next Sunday Preacher Thompson announced he'd gotten many good suggestions, but there was one in particular that was truly inspired, one that could truly put the church back on the right road, and he wanted the man who had come up with the idea, Larry Rudisell, to stand and tell the rest of the congregation about it.

Like I said earlier, once you've been bitten by a snake you start looking out for them, but there's something else too. You start to know their ways. So I knew right off that whatever Larry was about to unfold, he was expecting to get something out of it, because having been married to this snake for almost three years, I knew him better than he knew himself. Larry's a hustler. Always has been. It was as if he came out of his momma talking out of both sides of his mouth, trying to hustle her, the nurse, the doctor, whichever one he saw first.

Larry stood up, wearing a sport coat he couldn't button because of his beer gut, no tie, and enough gold around his neck to fill every tooth in Cleveland County. He was also wearing his sincere "I'd swear on my dead momma's grave I didn't know that odometer had been turned back" look, which was as phony as the curls in his brillo-pad hairdo, which he'd done that way to cover up his bald spot.

Then Larry started telling about what he was calling his "vision," claiming that late Friday night he'd woke up, half blinded by bright flashing lights and hearing a voice coming out of the ceiling, telling him to recreate the crucifixion on the front lawn of Cliffside Baptist Church, at night, with lights shining on the three men on the crosses. The whole thing sounded more like one of those UFO stories in *The National Examiner* than a religious experience, and about as believable.

Larry looked around and started telling how he just knew people would come from miles away to see it, just like they went to McAdenville every December to see the Christmas lights, and then he said he believed in his vision enough to pay for it himself.

Then Larry stopped to see if his sales pitch was working. He was selling his crucifixion idea the same way he would an '84 Buick in his car lot. And it was working. Larry has always been a smooth talker. He talked me into the back seat of his daddy's car when I was seventeen, talked me into marrying him when I was eighteen, and talked me out of divorcing him on the grounds of adultery a half dozen times. I finally got smart and plugged up my ears with cotton so I couldn't hear him while I packed my belongings.

Larry started talking again, telling the congregation he didn't want to take any credit for the idea, that he was just a messenger and that the last thing God had told him was that he wanted Larry to play Jesus, and his mechanic, Terry Wooten, to play one of the thieves, a role, as far as I was concerned, Terry had been playing as long as he'd worked for Larry. When I looked over at Terry, the expression on his face made it quite clear that God hadn't bothered to contact him about all of this. Then I looked up at the ceiling to see if it was about to collapse and bury us all. Everybody was quiet for about five seconds. Then the whole congregation started talking at once, and it sounded more like a tobacco auction than a church service.

After a couple of minutes people remembered where they were, and it got a little more civilized. At least they were raising their hands and getting acknowledged before they started shouting. The first to speak was Jimmy Wells, who had once bought an Olds '88 from Larry and had the transmission fall out not a half-mile from where he had driven it off Larry's lot. Jimmy was still bitter about that, so I wasn't too surprised when he nominated his brother-in-law Harry Bayne to play Jesus.

As soon as Jimmy sat down, Larry popped up like a jack-in-the-box, claiming Harry couldn't play Jesus because Harry had a hearing aid. When Jimmy asked why that mattered, Larry said they didn't have hearing aids back in olden times and Jimmy said nobody would care and Larry said yes they would care and it'd ruin the whole production. Jimmy and Larry kept arguing. Harry finally got up and said if it meant that much to Larry to let him do it, that he was too hungry to care anymore.

Preacher Thompson had pretty much stayed out of all this till Harry said that, but then he suggested that Harry play the thief who gets saved, leaving Terry as the other one. The Splawn brothers, Donnie and Robbie, were nominated to be the Roman soldiers. To the credit of the church, when Preacher Thompson asked for a show of hands as to whether we should let this be our Easter project, it was close. My hand wasn't the only one that went up against it, and I still believe it was empty stomachs as much as belief in Larry and his scheme that got it passed.

But it did pass, and a few days later Preacher Thompson called me up and asked, since I was on the church's building and grounds committee, if I would help build the crosses. You see, I'm a carpenter, the only full-time one, male or female, in the church, so whenever the church's softball field needs a new backstop or the parsonage needs some repair work, I'm the one who usually does it. And I do it right. Carpentry is in my blood. People around here say my father was the best carpenter to ever drive a nail in western North Carolina, and after my mother died when I was nine, he would take me with him every day I wasn't in school. By the time I was fourteen, I was working fulltime with him in the summers. I quit school when I was sixteen. I knew how I wanted to make my living. I've been a carpenter for the last fifteen years.

It was hard at first. Since I was a woman, a lot of men didn't think I could do as good a job as they could. But one good thing about being a carpenter is someone can look at your work and know right away if you know what you're doing. Nowadays, my reputation as a carpenter is as good as any man's in the county.

Still, I was a little surprised that Preacher Thompson asked me to work on a project my ex-husband was so involved in. But, being

new, he might not have known we had once been married. I do go
by my family's name now. Or maybe he did know, figuring since the
divorce was over five years ago we had forgiven each other like Chris-
tians should. Despite its being Larry's idea, I did feel obligated since
I was on the building and grounds committee, so I said I would help.
Preacher Thompson thanked me and said we would meet in front of
the church at ten on Saturday morning.

On Saturday, me, Preacher Thompson, Larry, and Ed Watt, who's
an electrician, met on the front lawn. From the very start, it was obvious Larry was going to run the show, telling us the way everything
should be, pointing and waving his arms like he was a Hollywood
director. He had on a white, ruffled shirt that was open to his gut, his
half-ton of gold necklaces, and a pair of sunglasses. Larry was not just
trying to act like but look like he was from California, which meant,
as far as I was concerned, that, unlike Jesus, he actually deserved to
be nailed to a cross.

Larry showed me where he wanted the three crosses, and he gave
me the length he wanted them. His was supposed to be three feet
taller than the other two. Preacher Thompson was close by, so we
acted civil to one another till I walked over to my truck to go get the
wood I'd need. Larry followed me, and as soon as I got in the truck
and cranked it, he asked me how it felt to have only a pillow to hold
every night. "Lot of advantages to it," I said as I slowly drove away.
"A pillow don't snore and it don't have inch-long toenails and it don't
smell like a brewery." I was already out of shouting distance before he
could think of anything to say to that.

I was back an hour later with three eight-inch-thick poles, just
like the ones I used to build the backstop for the softball field, and
a railroad crosstie I'd sawed into three lengthwise pieces for the part
the arms would be stretched out on. I'd also gotten three blocks of

wood I was going to put where their feet would be to take the strain off their arms.

As I turned into the church parking lot, I saw that Wanda Wilson's LTD was parked in the back of the church. She was out by the car with Larry, wearing a pink sweatshirt and a pair of blue running shorts, even though it was barely 60 degrees, just to show off her legs. When they saw me they started kissing and putting their hands all over each other. They kept that up for a good five minutes, in clear view of not just me but Ed Watt and Preacher Thompson too, and I thought we were going to have to get a water hose and spray them, the same way you would two dogs, to get them apart.

Finally, Wanda got into her LTD and left, maybe to get a cold shower, and Larry came over to the truck. As soon as he saw the poles in the back of the truck he got all worked up, saying they were too big around, that they looked like telephone poles, that he was supposed to be Jesus, not the Wichita Lineman. That was enough for me. I put my toolbox back in the cab and told Preacher Thompson Benny Brown was coming over with his post-hole digger around noon. I pointed at Larry. "I forgot all about Jesus being a carpenter," I said. "I'm taking all of this back over to Hamrick's Lumberyard." Then I drove off and didn't look back.

Why is it that some men always have to act like they know more than another human being just because that other human being happens to be a woman? Larry's never driven a nail in his life, but he couldn't admit that I would know what would make the best and safest cross. I guess some people never change. Ever since the divorce was made final, Larry has gone out of his way to be as ugly as possible to me. The worst thing about being divorced in a small town is that you're always running into your ex. Sometimes it seems I see him more now than I did when I was married to him. I can live with that.

But it's been a lot harder to live with the lies he's been spreading around town, claiming things about me that involved whips and dog collars and Black Sabbath albums. You'd think nobody would believe such things, but like the bible says, it's a fallen world. A lot of people want to believe the worst, so a lot of them believed Larry when he started spreading his lies. I couldn't get a date for almost two years, and I lost several girlfriends too. Like the song says, "Her hands are callused but her heart is tender." That rumor caused me more heartache than you could believe.

I have no idea what they did after I drove off that Saturday, but the Sunday before Easter the crosses were up, so after church let out just about everybody in the congregation went out on the front lawn to get a better look.

I've always said you can tell a lot about a person by how carefully they build something or put something together, but looking at Larry's crosses didn't tell me a thing I didn't already know. Instead of using a pole for the main section, he had gotten four-by-eight boards made out of cedar, which anybody who knows anything about wood can tell you is the weakest wood you can buy. The crossties and footrests were the same. I'm not even going to mention how sorry the nailing was.

I walked over to the middle cross, gave it a push, and felt it give like a popsicle stick in sand. I kneeled beside it and dug up enough dirt to see they hadn't put any cement in the hole Benny Brown had dug for them but had just packed dirt in it. I got up and walked over to the nearest spigot and washed the red dirt off my hands while everybody watched me, waiting for me to pass judgment on Larry's crosses.

"All I'm going to say is this," I said as I finished drying my hands. "Anybody who gets up on one of those things had better have a whole lot of faith." Of course Larry wasn't going to let me have the last word. He started saying I was just jealous that he'd done such a good job, that I didn't know the difference between a telephone pole and a cross. I didn't say another word, but as I was walking to my truck I heard Harry Bayne tell Larry he was going to have to find somebody else to play his role, that he'd rather find a safer way to prove his faith, like maybe handling a rattlesnake or drinking strychnine. I went back that night to look at the crosses a last time. I left convinced more than ever that the crosses, especially the taller middle one, wouldn't support the weight of a full-grown man.

On Good Friday I went on over to the church about an hour before they were scheduled to start, mainly because I didn't believe they would be able to get up there without at least one of the crosses snapping like a piece of dry kindling. There were already a good number of people there, including Larry's cousin Kevin, who wasn't a member of our church or anybody else's, but who worked part-time for Larry and was enough like Larry to be a good salesman and a pitiful excuse for a human being. Kevin was spitting tobacco juice into a paper cup while Mrs. Murrel, who used to teach drama over at the high school, dabbed red paint on his face and hands and feet, trying to make him look like the crucified thief Larry had talked, paid, or threatened him into playing. Besides the paint, the only thing he was wearing was a sweatshirt with a picture of Elvis on it and what looked like a giant diaper, though I'd already heard the preacher explain to several people it was supposed to be what the bible called a loincloth. Terry Wooten was standing over by the crosses, dressed up the same way, looking like he was about to vomit as he stared up at where he would be hanging in only a few more minutes.

Then I saw the sign and suddenly everything that had been going on for the last month made sense. It was one of those portable electric ones with about a hundred colored light bulbs bordering it.

"The Crucifixion Of JESUS CHRIST Is Paid For and Presented By LARRY RUDISELL'S Used Cars Of Cliffside, North Carolina" was spelled out in red plastic letters at the top of the message board. Near the bottom in green letters it said, "If JESUS Had Driven A Car, He Would Have Bought It At LARRY'S." It was the tackiest, most sacrilegious thing I'd ever seen in my life.

Finally, the new Jesus himself appeared, coming out of the church with what looked like a brown, rotting halo on his head—it was his crown of thorns—fifty yards of extension cord covering his shoulder, and a cigarette hanging out of his mouth. He unrolled the cord as he came across the lawn, dressed like Kevin and Terry except he didn't have any red paint on his face. Larry didn't have a fake beard either. He wanted everyone to know it was Larry Rudisell up on that cross. He walked over to the sign and plugged the extension cord into it.

You know what it's like when the flashbulb goes off when you're getting a picture taken and you stagger around half blind for a while? Well, that's about the effect Larry's sign had when it came on. The colored lights were flashing on and off, and you could have seen it from a mile away. Larry watched for a minute to make sure it was working right and then announced it was twenty minutes to show time so they needed to go ahead and get up on the crosses. Preacher Thompson and the Splawn brothers went and got the stepladders and brought them over to where the crosses were. Terry and Kevin slinked over behind the sign, trying to hide. It was obvious Larry was going to have to get up there first.

Larry took off his sweatshirt, and I realized for the first time they were going to go up there with nothing except the bedsheets wrapped around them. It wasn't that cold right then, but like it always is in March, it was windy. I knew that in a few minutes, when the sun went down, the temperature would really fall fast.

While Donnie and Robbie Splawn steadied the cross, Larry

crawled up the ladder. With only the loincloth wrapped around him, he looked more like a Japanese Sumo wrestler on *Wide World of Sports* than Jesus. When he got far enough up, Larry reached over, grabbed the crosstie, and put his feet on the board he was going to stand on. He turned himself around until he faced us. I'll never know how the cross held, but it did.

It was completely dark, except of course for Larry's sign, by the time Terry and Kevin had been placed on their crosses. As I watched I couldn't help thinking that if they ever did want to bring back crucifixion, the three hanging up there in the dark would be as good a bunch to start with as any. I looked over my shoulder and saw the traffic was already piled up, and the whole front lawn was filled with people. There was even a TV crew from WSOC in Charlotte.

At 6:30 the music began, and the spotlights Ed Watt had rigged up came on. I had to admit it was impressive, especially if you were far enough away so you didn't see Larry's stomach or Terry's chattering teeth. The WSOC cameras were rolling, and more and more people were crowding onto the lawn and even spilling out into the road, making the first traffic jam in Cliffside's history even worse.

The crucifixion was supposed to last an hour, but after twenty minutes the wind started to pick up, and the crosses began making creaking noises, moving back and forth a little more with each gust of wind. It wasn't long before Terry began to make some noises too, screaming over the music for someone to get a ladder and get him down. I didn't blame him. The crosses were really starting to sway, and Terry, Kevin, and Larry looked like acrobats in some circus high-wire act. But there wasn't a net for them to land in if they fell.

Preacher Thompson and Ed Watt were running to get the ladders, but at least for Larry, it was too late. His cross swung forward one last time, and then I heard the sound of wood cracking. Donnie Splawn heard it too, and he tripped on his Roman Soldier's robe as he ran to get out of the way. Larry screamed out "God help me," probably the sincerest prayer of his life. But it went unanswered. The crosses began to fall forward, and Larry, with his arms outstretched, looked like a man doing a swan dive. I closed my eyes at the last second but heard him hit.

Then everything was chaos. People were screaming and shouting and running around in all directions. Janice Hamrick, who's a registered nurse, came out of the crowd to tend to Larry till the rescue squad could get there and take him to the county hospital. Several other people ran over to stabilize the other two crosses. When Terry saw what happened to his boss, he stained his loincloth. His eyes were closed, and he was praying so fast only God could understand what he was saying. Kevin wasn't saying or doing anything because he had fainted dead away the second his cousin hit the ground.

It's been three weeks now since all this happened. Larry got to leave the county hospital, miraculously, alive, on Easter morning, but his jaw is still wired shut, and it's going to stay that way for at least another month. But despite the broken jaw and broken nose, he still goes out to his car lot every day. Since people over half the state saw him hit the ground, in slow motion, on WSOC's six o'clock news, Larry's become western North Carolina's leading tourist attraction. They come from more miles away than you would believe just to see him, and then he gets his pad and pencil out and tries to sell them a car. Quite a few times he does. As a matter of fact, I hear he's sold more cars in the last two weeks than any two-week period in his life, which is further proof that, as the bible tells us, we live in a fallen world.

Still, some good things have happened. When Preacher Thompson offered to resign, the congregation made it clear they wanted him to stay, and he has. But he's toned down his sermons a good bit, and last Sunday, when Larry handed him a proposal for an outdoor manger scene with you know who playing Joseph, Preacher Thompson just crumpled it up and threw it in the trashcan.

As for me, a lot of people remember that I was the one who said the crosses were unsafe in the first place, especially one person, Harry Bayne. Two weeks ago Harry took me out to eat as a way of saying thank you. We hit it off and have spent a lot of time together lately. We're going dancing over at Harley's Lounge tonight. I'm still a little scared, almost afraid to hope for too much, but I'm beginning to believe than even in a fallen world things can sometimes look up.

The HARVEST

"It's a drearysome day," Uncle Earl said, hunching his jean jacket tighter around his shoulders, "but maybe it'll clear up before the service tomorrow."

I looked out the windshield and figured otherwise. Fog could stay in our valley for days. It was like the mountains circling us poured the fog in and set a kettle lid on top. That grayness came seeping through the walls and into the house too. Bright things like a quilt or button jar lost color and footsteps sounded lonesome.

The road curved and the Tilsons' farmhouse appeared. A car was parked beside Mr. Tilson's blue pickup.

"That's Preacher Winn's car," Daddy said. "Probably best just to go on to the field."

Daddy eased the truck onto the far side of the road and we got out. Uncle Earl took the butcher knives and sacks from the truck bed and we walked down the slope and through a harvested cornfield, damp stalks and shucks slippery under our feet. The cabbage patch was beside the creek. Two of the rows had been cut but four hadn't.

Uncle Earl nodded towards the field across the road. The fog was thicker here in the bottomland and it took a few seconds to see the tractor. It lay on its side, one big black wheel raised up, the harrow's tines like long fingers.

"He shouldn't have been on a hill that steep," Uncle Earl said.

"No," Daddy said. "But I've known many a man who at least had a chance to learn from that same mistake."

They set down the sacks and kneeled at two row ends.

"Stay between us," Daddy said to me. "We'll cut and you sack."

They began cutting, left hand on the cabbage head while the butcher knife chopped underneath.

"We'll be filthy as hogs by the time we finish," Uncle Earl said, brushing wet dirt off his overalls.

"Try to keep your clothes clean, son," Daddy said. "I got need for you to do something else when we finish."

"At least as clean as a ten-year-old-boy can stay," Uncle Earl said.

I dragged the sack behind me up the row, feeling it stick harder to the ground each time I put another cabbage inside. Daddy and Uncle Earl stopped every few minutes to help catch me up. I followed Uncle Earl and Daddy as they carried six full sacks to the row ends.

"Let's ease up a minute," Daddy said.

"Fine by me," Uncle Earl said.

Daddy put his hands flat above his tailbone and leaned backwards. Uncle Earl sat down cross-legged and took out a pack of rolling papers and a tobacco tin from his bib pocket.

"A day like this you feel your aches more," Daddy said.

Uncle Earl nodded as he sifted tobacco onto the paper, twisted the ends and lit one end. A car engine started up at the farmhouse. In a few moments the car drove away, quickly invisible except for its yellow headlights.

"We best get back to it," Uncle Earl said, and picked up the last four sacks we had. "I can cut and smoke both."

"We'll need two more sacks, three to be safe," Daddy said to me. "You willing to go get a couple?"

"I guess so," I said. "Should I ask first?"

"No," Daddy said. "There's no cause to do that. Just go to that shed by the barn. They'll be some in there."

"Three?"

"Yes," Daddy said. "Three's plenty."

I left them and made my way through the cornfield and up to the road. The fog thinned as the ground slanted upward. I fixed my eyes on the shed and kept them there so I wouldn't see the tractor. I had to use both hands to swing the shed door open, then wait for the dark to be less dark. In a back corner, burlap sacks hung above a mound of potatoes. I smelled them as I lifted the sacks off the nail. It was a dusty, moldy smell, but a green alive smell dabbed in it too. I stepped out and shouldered the door closed. Across the road, the bottomland had disappeared. It was like the fog had opened its mouth and swallowed the cabbage patch whole.

The sacks were in my right hand. I squeezed them tighter as I made my way across the road and through the cornfield. Soon after, Daddy and Uncle Earl came out solid from the gray. The last cabbages were cut and gathered and Daddy and Uncle Earl hefted a sack over each shoulder and walked to the truck. Three trips and it was done.

"Twelve full sacks," Uncle Earl said when he and Daddy had loaded the last one in the truck bed.

"You still of a mind to take it to Lenior today?"

"Yes," Daddy said, "but I need to ask her if she wants some for canning."

"Then we better go see," Uncle Earl said. "The preacher's gone so it's likely as good a time as there'll be."

We walked across the road and into the yard, where Daddy and Uncle Earl stopped.

"Take your shoes and socks off, son," Daddy told me. "Then go up there and knock."

I did what he said and went up on the porch.

Mrs. Tilson opened the door. She wore a black dress and I could tell she'd been crying. She looked at me like she didn't know who I was, then fixed her eyes on Daddy and Uncle Earl, who stood in the yard with their hands in their front pockets.

"We cut the rest of the cabbage, Faye," Daddy said. "We didn't know if you wanted to keep any for canning. If you do, we'll put it in the root cellar for you."

Mrs. Tilson put her hands over her eyes. Then, real slow, she let her hands rub hard against her skin, like she was pulling off a mask to see better.

"Sell it," she said. "That's what Alec always does. Done."

"We'll do that then," Daddy said. "We'll see you at the funeral tomorrow but if there's anything you need done before that, let us know."

Mrs. Tilson didn't say anything or even nod. She just stepped back inside and shut the door.

"Mrs. Tilson, she's grateful to you for helping out," Daddy said when we got back in the truck. "She may never say that though. It's a hard time for her and she'll likely not want to ponder anything about these days."

"Anyway," Daddy said as he cranked the engine, "you done good."

BADEYE

I remember Badeye Carter. I remember his clear eye, the patch, the serpent tattooed on his shoulder, the long, black finger-nails. I remember his black '49 Ford pickup, the rusty cowbell dangling from the sideview mirror, the metal soft drink chest in the back filled with shaved ice, the three gallon jars of flavoring—cherry, lemon, and licorice, the Hav-a-Tampa cigar box he kept his money in. I remember how he always came that summer at bullbat time, those last moments of daylight when the streetlight in our neigh-borhood came on and the bats began to swoop, preying on moths attracted to the glow.

That summer was the longest of my life. Time seemed to sleep that summer. Sometimes a single afternoon seemed a week. June was an eternity. It must have seemed just as endless for my mother, for this was the summer when my obsession with snakes reached its zenith, and our house seemed more a serpentarian than a home. And then there was Badeye, to my mother just as slippery, and as dangerous.

I was eight years old. Every evening when I heard the clanging of the cowbell, I ran to the edge of the street, clutching the nickel I had begged from my father earlier that day. I never asked my mother. To her Badeye was an intruder, a bringer of tooth decay, bad eating habits, and other things.

Every other mother in Cliffside felt the same way, would refuse to acknowledge Badeye's hat-tipping "how you doing, ma'ams" as he stopped his truck in front of their houses. They would either stare right at him with a look colder than anything he ever put in his paper cones, as my mother did, or, like our next door neighbor Betty Splawn, turn her back to him and walk into the house.

Their reasons for disliking Badeye went beyond his selling snow-cones to their children. They knew, as everyone in Cliffside knew, that while Badeye was new to the snowcone business, he had been the town's bootlegger for over a decade. Being hard-shell Southern Baptists, these women held him responsible for endangering their husbands' eternal souls with his moonshine brought up from Scotland County.

There was also the matter of his right eye, which had been blinded ten years earlier when Badeye's wife stabbed him with an ice pick as he slept. Badeye had not pursued charges, and the ex–Mrs. Carter had not explained her motivation before heading to Alabama to live with a sister, leaving the women of Cliffside to wonder what he must have done to deserve such an awakening.

Cliffside's fathers viewed Badeye more sympathetically. They tended to believe his snowcones would cause no lasting harm to their children, sometimes even eating one themselves. As for the bootlegging, some of these men were Badeye's customers, but even those who did not drink, such as my father, felt Badeye was a necessary evil in a town where the nearest legal alcohol was fifteen miles away. These men also realized that each of them had probably done something during their years that warranted an icepick in the eye. Badeye's right eye had died for all their sins.

So it was our fathers we went to, waiting until our mothers were washing the supper dishes or otherwise occupied. Our fathers would fish out nickels from the pants pockets, trying not to jingle the change too loudly, listening, like us, for the sound of our mothers' approaching footsteps.

Badeye always stopped between our house and the Splawns'. Donnie Splawn, who was my age, his younger brother, Robbie, and I would gather around the tailgate of Badeye's truck, our bare feet burning on the still-hot pavement. Sometimes we would be joined by another child, one who had gotten his nickel only after Badeye had passed by his house, forced to chase the truck through the darkening streets, finally catching up with him in front of our houses. It was worth it—that long, breathless run we had all made at some time when our mothers had not washed the dishes right away or when we had been playing and did not hear the cowbell until too late— because Badeye's snowcones tasted better than anything we'd ever sunk our teeth into.

Donnie and I were partial to cherry, while Robbie liked lemon best. Donnie and Robbie tended to suck the syrup out of their snowcones, while I let the syrup in mine pool in the bottom of the paper cone, a last, condensed gulp so flavorful that it brought tears to my eyes.

Our mothers tried to fight back. They first used time-honored scare tactics, handed down from mother to daughter for generations. My mother's version of the "trip to the dentist with snowcone-rotted teeth" horror story was vividly rendered, but while it did cause me to brush my teeth more frequently for a while, it did not slow my snowcone consumption. The story's only lasting impact on me was a lifelong fear of dentists.

When my mother realized this conventional story had failed, she assumed the cause was overexposure, that stories, like antibiotics, tended to become less effective on children the more they were used, so she came up with a new story, one unlike any heard in the collective memory of Cliffside's children. The story concerned an eight-year old boy in the adjoining county who had contracted a rare disease carried specifically by flies that lit on snowcones. The affliction reduced the boy's backbone to jelly in a matter of days. He now spent all of his time in a wheelchair, looking mournfully out of his bedroom window at all the non-snowcone-eating children who played happily in the park across the street from his house. The setting of the story in Rutherford County was a stroke of genius on my mother's part, for it helped create a feeling of "if it could happen there, it could happen here" while at the same time being far enough away from Cliffside so as not to be easily discredited. The park across the street was also a nice touch. But even at eight I realized the story was too vivid, the details too fully realized (my mother even knew the victim's middle name) to be anything other than fiction.

My mother, along with other mothers, realized another strategy was needed, so in an informal meeting after Sunday School in late June, Hazel Wasson, Dr. Wasson's wife, was appointed to find out if the law could accomplish what the horror stories had failed to do. Mrs. Wasson spent the following Monday morning in the county courthouse in Shelby. To her amazement as well as everyone else's, Badeye had all the necessary licenses to sell his snowcones. Mrs. Wasson's next stop, this time accompanied by Clytemnestra Ely, was to call on the country sheriff, who appeased the women by promising to conduct an illegal-liquor search on Badeye's premises the following afternoon, and, according to my mother, about thirty minutes after calling to let Badeye know they were coming. The sheriff and two of his deputies conducted their raid and claimed to have found nothing.

"I don't know why we even bothered to try," I heard my mother tell Betty Splawn the following morning, "what with Cleveland County politicians being his most loyal customers."

In the first week of July my mother spearheaded a last, concerted effort against Badeye. She found a recipe for freezing Kool-Aid in ice-cube trays. The cubes were then broken up in a blender or placed inside a plastic bag and crushed with a hammer. According to the final sentence of the recipe, which my mother chanted again and again, trying to convince not only me but herself as well, the result was "an inexpensive taste treat every bit as good as the commercial snowcone all children love." As the Kool-Aid hardened in the freezer, my mother called other mothers. By late afternoon every child in Cliffside had been served a dixie cup filled with my mother's recipe, but while we condescendingly ate these feeble imitations, they only served to whet our appetite for the real thing. My mother threw away the recipe and dumped the remaining trays of Kool-Aid cubes into the kitchen sink.

After this fiasco, Badeye seemed invincible. There were occasional minor victories: a husband might be coaxed or bullied into not giving his children nickels for a few days, or a son or daughter might wake up in the middle of the night with a toothache, which the mother could blame on Badeye's snowcones. The child would promise to repent, to never eat another one. But he or she always did, just as the fathers, after a day or two of ignoring their children's pleas, began to slip nickels to their offspring.

At my house, my mother had simply given up her battle against Badeye. This change was in part a matter of the weather. Our house, like almost all in Cliffside, was unairconditioned. The energy that had fueled my mother's horror stories and her recipe search was being steadily sapped away by the heat of the North Carolina summer.

But, most of all, my mother had another problem that made Bad-eye seem little more than a nuisance—my growing snake collection. The previous summer I had caught a green snake in our backyard and brought it into our kitchen. My mother had screamed, dropped the plate she had been drying, and run out the front door. She did not stop running until she reached the Splawns' house, where she called my father at the junior college where he taught. My father rushed home and ran inside, my mother watching from the Splawns' front yard. When my father and I had come out a few minutes later, the snake was, to my mother's horror, still very much alive, although safely contained in a mason jar.

That snake was the first of a dozen garter and green snakes I would catch in our back and side yards that summer. Despite my mother's pleas, my father refused to kill them. Instead, he punched holes in the jar lids and encouraged me to keep them a couple of days before turning them loose again. My father tried to assure my mother, lectured her on the value of snakes, how most were nonpoisonous, were friends of mankind who helped control mice and rats. He had even brought a book on reptiles home from the college library to support his views. But my mother had her own book to refer to—the bible, and in its first chapters found enough evidence to convince her that snakes had been, since the Garden of Eden, mankind's worst enemy. Now, with the aid of her husband, her son was making "pets" out of them, further proof to her of man's fallen nature.

My mother had hoped that my fascination with reptiles was, like the hula hoop, a passing fad that would be forgotten once the snakes went underground for the winter. This might have happened except for my father.

Up to this point in my life, my father and I had been rather distant. Part of the problem was that, possessing an artistic temperament, he was distant towards everyone, his mind fixed on some personal vision of truth and beauty. But even the times he had tried to establish some kind of rapport had been unsuccessful, since these attempts consisted of Saturday morning trips to the basement of the college's fine arts building. Once there my father sat me on a stool and placed a football-sized lump of clay in front of me, assuming that a five- or six-year-old boy would find a morning spent making pottery as enjoyable as he did.

He was wrong, of course. I quickly became bored and wished I were home watching cartoons. I watched the clock hands crawl towards lunchtime, daydreaming of fathers such as Mr. Splawn, who had taught Donnie how to throw a curveball and took him bass fishing at Washburn's pond.

It was the snakes that brought us together. To my amazement my father shared my interest in reptiles and even spoke of having caught snakes when he was a child. And it was he who, during that long, snakeless winter of my seventh year, kindled my interest with books checked out of the college's library.

By March I rivaled Dr. Brown, the college's biology teacher, as Cliffside's leading herpetologist. With my father's assistance, I had read every book on reptiles in Cliffside Junior College Library. I also owned a book on snakes better than any found there, a massive tome big as our family bible, a Christmas present from my father titled *Snakes of the World*.

It was this book, more than anything else, that turned my hobby into an obsession. Unlike most of the books from the college's library which had small, black-and-white photographs, *Snakes of the World* had 14 x 18 inch color plates. Opening the dull reddish-brown cover of that book was the visual equivalent of biting into one of Badeye's snowcones, for though my mother could never have comprehended it, I found these creatures indescribably beautiful. Not all of them, of course. Some, like the water moccasins or timber rattlesnakes, had thick, bloated bodies and flattened heads and were colored black or dull brown. There were others, however, that were stunning in their beauty: the bright-green tree boa, for instance, found in the Amazon; or the gaboon viper, an Asian snake, its dark-blue color prettier than the stained glass windows of our church.

The most beautiful one of all, however, the coral snake, was found not in Australia, or Asia, or Africa, but in the American South. A picture of a coral snake appeared on page 137 of my book, and in the right-hand corner of that page was a paragraph that I quickly memorized:

> Because of its alternating bands of black, red, and yellow, the North American Coral Snake (Micrirus fulvius) is one of the most brilliantly colored snakes in the World. A secretive, nocturnal creature found in the Southern United States, it is rarely encountered by humans. The North American Coral Snake is a member of the cobra family, and thus, despite its small size (rarely exceeding three feet in length), is the most venomous reptile in the Northern Hemisphere.

I celebrated my eighth birthday in late March. As the fried chicken cooled and the candles started to droop on top of the cake, my mother and I assumed my father was in the basement of the fine arts building throwing pots, having forgotten it was his only child's birthday. But we were wrong. Just as we started to go ahead and eat, my father came in the back door, grinning, a wire mesh cage in his right hand. He placed it on the dining room table between the green beans and my cake.

"Happy Birthday, son," he said.

It took me a few seconds to identify the creature coiled in the bottom of the cage as a hog-nosed snake, but it only took my mother about half a second to drop her fork, shove back her chair, and make a frantic exit into the kitchen. After taking a moment to compose herself, she appeared at the doorway separating the kitchen from the dining room.

"I will not have a live snake inside my house, James," she said. "Either me or that snake is leaving right now."

It was clear my mother was not bluffing, so my father carried the cage out to the carport, moving some stacks of old art magazines to clear a space in the corner farther from the door. When I asked where the snake had come from, he told me he had driven to Charlotte that afternoon and had visited three pet shops before finally finding what he wanted.

As March turned into April, the temperatures began to rise. The dogwood tree in our side yard blossomed, and snakes began to crawl out of their burrows. Because my father had absolutely no interest in keeping up his property, our back and side yards were a kudzu-filled jungle, a reptile heaven. It was here that I spent most of my spring afternoons. My reading had made me a much more success-ful snake hunter than I had been the previous summer. Instead of wandering around hoping to get lucky and spot a sunning snake, my method became much more sophisticated. I covered the back and side yards with large pieces of tin and wood as well as anything else that might provide a snake shelter. Each piece was placed carefully so that a snake could crawl under it with little difficulty. My efforts paid almost immediate dividends, for I now not only caught green snakes and garter snakes but also other species, including several small king snakes, and in late May, a five-foot-long black snake.

My father had borrowed a dozen wire cages from Dr. Brown, so I was able to keep the snakes I caught for several weeks at a time, longer if they ate well in captivity. I cleared out more space on the carport as I filled cage after cage. When school let out the first week of June, my snake-hunting range extended beyond my own yard. I caught thick-bodied water snakes in Sandy Run Creek, red-tongued green snakes in the vacant lot next to my grandmother's mill house in Shelby, orange and white corn snakes in my Uncle Earl's barn, tiny ring-necked snakes in the dense woods behind Laura Bryant's house. My father borrowed more cages from the junior college.

By this time the hot weather had brought out Badeye as well, and for a while my mother fought a renewed battle against both, using similar tactics. Having grown up in the rural South, she had a rich repository of snake stories to draw on, so every night before I went to sleep, my mother would pull a chair beside my bed and try to frighten me out of my hobby. She told of timber rattlesnakes dropping out of trees, strangling children by wrapping around their necks, of copperheads lying camouflaged in leafpiles, waiting for someone to step close enough so they could inject their always-fatal poison, of blue racers, almost as poisonous as copperheads, so swift they could chase down the fastest man, and hoop snakes, capable of rolling up in a hoop, their tails poison-filled stingers.

My mother's bedtime stories were graphic, and there is little doubt they would have cured most children of not only snake collecting but sleep as well. But I found them humorous, even less convincing than her snowcone horror stories because I knew her tales had absolutely no basis in fact. Timber rattlesnakes did not climb trees, and they were vipers, not constrictors. Blue racers were nonpoisonous, incapable of speeds greater than five miles an hour, even in short bursts. Hoop snakes were nonpoisonous also, and unable to roll into a hoop, though as made clear, "Reports to the contrary continue to persist in primitive, superstitious regions of the United States."

My mother bought baseball cards and a half-dozen Indianhead pennies, trying to get me interested in collecting something besides snakes. She purchased a chemistry set, believing the possibility of my blowing myself up a lesser danger than my snake collecting. Her efforts were futile. I traded the baseball cards to Jimbo Miller for a half-dozen rat snake eggs he found in a sawdust pile and bought bubblegum with the pennies. The chemistry set gathered dust in the basement.

By this time my mother was having nightmares about snakes several times a week. Dark circles began to appear under her eyes. For the first time in my life, I watched her refuse to defer to my father, the biblical view of serpents in Genesis evidently balancing out the command that wives should obey their husbands, the danger to her son tipping the scales. Every evening at supper she would lecture my father on the catastrophe that was about to occur.

Sometimes she even succeeded in breaking through the trance-like state he spent most of his waking hours in. At these times my father related the information gleaned from the books he had read to me the past winter. He tried to convince my mother that her fears were groundless, that the truly dangerous snakes—water moccasins, rattlesnakes, and coral snakes—were at least two counties away. He assured my mother that she didn't have to worry about the copperheads because I had promised him that if I did come across one I would not try and catch it, would keep my distance.

My mother's sense of impending doom was not assuaged. Her fear of snakes was more than cultural and religious; it was instinctual as well, too deeply embedded in her psyche to be dealt with on a rational level. Facts and statistics were useless. She threatened to get rid of the snakes, gather up the cages and take them away herself, but I knew she wouldn't do it, couldn't do it. Her fear of snakes was so great she had not even set foot in the carport since the arrival of the hog-nosed snake in March.

By the dog days of August I had thirty cages in the carport, and every one had a snake in it. The feeding of the snakes and the cleaning of the cages left me little time for snake-collecting field trips, but by this time the snakes were coming to me.

Not by themselves, of course, slithering by the hundreds toward our house. That occurred only in my mother's dreams. In late July Frank Moore, who owned, published, and wrote the *Cleveland County Messenger*, had done an article about me and my hobby, making me a county-wide celebrity and bringing a steady stream of visitors to our carport. Most came emptyhanded, just wanting to see my collection, but others brought milk pails and wash buckets, mason jars and once even a cookie tin. Inside were snakes, some alive, some dead. The live ones I put into cages; the dead ones that were not too badly mangled by hoe, buckshot, or tire I placed, depending on their size, in quart or gallon jars filled with alcohol. Though months earlier my mother had told my father and me that she would not allow a "live" snake in her house, she had said nothing about dead ones, so I kept these snakes in my room where, almost every night, they crawled out of their jars and into my mother's dreams.

Badeye came too. One night after completing his rounds, he drove back by the house and, seeing me alone in the carport, parked his truck across the street. The carport lightbulb was burned out, the only light coming from the streetlamp across the road, so I took each snake out of its cage so Badeye could see them better. Unlike the other people who visited the carport that summer, Badeye did not keep his distance from the snakes once I took them into my hands. He moved closer, his blue eye only inches away as he studied each one intently.

When I had put the last snake back in its cage, Badeye rolled up one of the sleeves of his soiled, white t-shirt.

"Look here," he said, pointing to a king cobra, hood flared, tattooed on his upper arm. I moved closer and saw, incredibly, the cobra uncoil slightly, its great head sway back and forth. Badeye grinned as I stepped back, stumbled over a stack of newspapers.

"I've got to go," he said. "I've got a long drive downstate to make tonight." I watched him slowly walk back to the truck, slide behind the steering wheel, then disappear into the darkness. As I walked back to the carport, I saw my mother watching from the living room window. Tears flowed down her cheeks.

I did not sleep much that night. Part of the reason was the heat. The temperature had been over ninety-five every day for three weeks. Rain was only a memory. The night brought no cool breezes, only more hot, stagnant air. But it was more than the heat. It was the cobra on Badeye's arm and my mother's tears. I sweated through the night as if I had a fever, listening to the window fan beat futilely against the darkness.

The following evening Badeye gave Donnie and Robbie their snowcones first, even though I had beaten them to his truck. After they left, Badeye jumped out of the truckbed and opened the door on the passenger side.

"I've got something for you," he said. "Saw it on the road last night when I was driving back from Laurinburg."

Badeye held an uncapped quart whiskey bottle up to my face.

"It's the prettiest snake I ever saw," he said.

And so it was, for a small coral snake lay in the bottom of the bottle.

"Is it alive?" I asked, hoping for a second miracle. Badeye shook the bottle. The snake pushed its black head against the glass, tried to climb upward before collapsing on itself.

"Here," he said, placing the bottle in my hand, though still gripping it with his own. "It's yours if you will do one thing for me."

"Anything," I said, meaning it.

"You know Bub Ely, don't you, and where he lives, that white house next to Marshall Hamrick's?"

I nodded. It was only a half mile away.

"Well, I need to get something to him, but I can't take it by right now." Badeye grinned. "His wife don't approve of me. Tonight, say about eleven, after everyone goes to sleep, could you take it over to his house? Just put it in the garage. Bub will find it in the morning."

I said I would. Badeye ungripped the whiskey bottle, opened the glove compartment.

"Here," he said, handing me a mason jar filled with a clear liquid that looked like water.

"You know what it is?" Badeye asked.

I nodded.

"Good," he said, sliding behind the steering wheel. "You'll know to be careful with it." Badeye's voice suddenly sounded menacing. "Don't get careless and drop it."

After checking to make sure my parents were not watching out the window, I carried the moonshine and placed it in the high grass beside the dogwood tree in the side yard. Then I carried the whiskey bottle into the carport. I opened a cage with a king snake in it, let it crawl out and disappear into the nearby stacks of books and newspapers. I tipped the bottle, watched the coral snake slither out of the bottle's neck into the cage. I carried the cage to the edge of the carport so that more of the glow from the streetlight would fall on the snake.

The coral snake was everything I had dreamed it would be, and much, much more. As beautiful as it had appeared in the photographs. I saw now how the camera had failed. The black, red, and yellow bands were a denser hue than any camera could capture. The small, delicate body gave the snake a grace of movement lacking in larger, bulkier snakes.

I lost all track of time and did not hear my father open and close the carport door. I was unaware of his presence until he crouched beside me and peered into the cage.

"That looks like a coral snake," he said in an alarmed voice as he picked up the cage for a better look.

"It's a scarlet king snake," I quickly lied.

"Are you sure?" my father said, still looking intently at the snake.

"I'm sure, Dad. Positive."

"But the bands are black, red, and yellow. I thought only coral snakes had those."

"Look," I said, trying to sound as convincing as possible, "scarlet king snakes have the same colors. Besides, coral snakes don't live this far west. You know that."

"That's true," my father said, putting the cage down. "Come on in," he said, standing up. "It's already past your bedtime."

I followed my father inside and waited in my darkened room three hours until my parents finally went to sleep. Then I sneaked into the kitchen, took the flashlight from the cupboard, and eased out the back door. I found the moonshine and walked up the street towards Bub Ely's. It was 11:30 according to my Mickey Mouse watch.

The lights were off at the Ely house, but there was enough of a moon that I did not need the flashlight to make my way to the garage. Once there, however, I did not lay the jar down in the corner. Instead, I unscrewed it. Everything that Badeye had put in my hands before had been magical. I wanted to know what magic the jar held. I pressed it to my lips, poured a mouthful. I held it there for a moment, and despite the kerosene taste, made a split-second decision to swallow instead of spit it out. When I did, I gagged, almost dropped the jar. My eyes teared. My throat and stomach burned. When the burning finally stopped, I placed the jar in a corner, walked slowly home.

I will never know for sure if what I did next would have happened had I not sampled Badeye's moonshine, but I did not go inside when I got home. Instead, I went to the carport to look at the coral snake, placing the flashlight against the cage for a better view. Finally, just looking wasn't good enough. I opened the cage and gently placed my right thumb and index finger behind the snake's head, but my hold was too far behind the head. The coral snake's mouth gripped my index finger.

I snatched my hand out of the cage, slung the snake from my finger, and screamed loud enough to be heard over the window fan in my parent's room. I knew the small, barely bleeding mark would not cause the agonizing swelling of a copperhead or rattlesnake bite. The coral snake's poison affected the nervous system, the heart. I also knew that several people recently bitten by coral snakes in the Southeast had died. It was this knowledge that paralyzed me, made me unable to move, for my books had assured me the chances of a child's dying from a coral snake's bite were even greater.

And I very well might have died, if my father had not been able to act in a focused manner. He ran out into the carport in his underwear, took my trembling hands and asked what had happened. I pointed to the snake coiled on the concrete floor.

"It's a coral," I whimpered, and showed him the bite mark.

My mother was at the doorway in her nightgown, asking my father in a frantic voice what was the matter, though a part of her already knew.

"He's been bitten," my father said, walking rapidly towards my mother.

"I've got to call the hospital, tell them they need to get antivenom rushed here from Charlotte."

My father was now on the carport steps. He turned to my mother.

"Get him to the hospital. Quick. I'll get over there fast as I can."

My father brushed by my mother, who had not moved, only stood there looking at me. He brought her the car keys. "Go," he shouted, urging her out the door.

My mother saw the coral snake coiled on the concrete between us, but she did not hesitate. She stepped right over it and caught me as I collapsed in her arms.

The sound of rain pelting the windows woke me. I opened my eyes to whiteness, the unadorned walls of Cleveland County Hospital. My father and mother were sitting in metal chairs placed beside my bed. Their heads were bowed, and at first I thought they were asleep, but when I stirred they looked up, offered weary smiles.

Three days later I was released, and in a week I was feeling healthy enough to help my father fill my Uncle Earl's pickup truck with my snake collection. We first drove down to Broad River, taking the bumpy dirt road that followed the river until we were several miles from the nearest house. We opened the cages, watched the contents slither away.

Then we drove back towards home, stopping a mile from Cliffside at the town dump. My father backed the truck up to the edge of the landfill and we lowered the tailgate. We threw the snake-and-alcohol-filled jars out of the truck, watched them shatter against the ground, and knew they would soon be buried forever under tons of other things people no longer wanted.

As for Badeye, I ignored his offers of free snowcones. My parents ignored his apologies. After several attempts at reconciliation failed, Badeye stopped slowing down as he approached our house, even sped up a little as his truck glided past into the twilight.

That October Badeye left Cliffside. When he pulled into Heddon's Gulf station, his possessions piled into the back of his truck, and Charlie Heddon asked him where he was moving to Badeye only shrugged his shoulders and muttered, "Somewhere different." No one ever saw him again.

I remember my mother staring out the kitchen window that autumn as the dogwood tree began to shed its leaves. It would not be until years later that I would understand how wonderful those falling leaves made her feel, for they signaled summer's end and the coming of cold weather, the first frost that would banish snakes (including the coral snake that we never found), as well as Badeye and his snow-cones. But I also remember the first bite of my first snowcone that June evening when Badeye suddenly appeared on our street. Nothing else has ever tasted so good.

LOVE *and* PAIN
in the NEW SOUTH

Darlene walks through the open sliding door dragging two trees' worth of divorce papers. Lord, she is beautiful, even as she harps on me about keeping the door open while the air conditioner is running in the other room. Darlene and her lawyer are setting me up where I won't have an extra dime for the next five hundred years, and she's telling me I need to watch my power bill. I follow her into the den, wishing I had a pair of blinders like they put on mules. Seeing her again after two months is killing me. It's like trying to give up smoking and someone putting a lighted cigarette in your hand.

I look out the window and see Carl Blowmeyer in his backyard, barbecuing what looks like a large dog and staring this way. Blowmeyer is one of many northern retirees who have moved down here to live cheaper and to educate southerners about how to drive on snow. The one or two times each year the white stuff falls, Blowmeyer stands on main street with a Mr. Microphone and tells drivers what they're doing wrong.

Spring and summer mornings he's out in the yard with his lawnmower, Weed Eater, and electric hedge clippers.

Blowmeyer's grass is cut shorter than most golf course greens. He crawls around his yard on hands and knees to find wild onions and crabgrass. Now Blowmeyer is stretching his neck to see over the hedge, wanting to watch every minute of the soap opera next door. His shorter, grub-white wife stands on a lawn chair. They love my pain.

Darlene pushes empty Dos Equis bottles to the edge of the coffee table so she can spread out the divorce papers. She looks at the bottles and shakes her head. Darlene's never had a drink in her life, and she used to punish me for my weakness by buying the cheapest beer she could find.

"That beer is six dollars a six pack," she says.

"I bought it to help out the Mexicans," I say. "They're in bad shape down there."

"Read and sign," she says. "Stanley's expecting me back at nine."

I read. She will get the house, the car, and most of the five thousand in the bank. As far as I can tell, I get the pickup and all the food in the refrigerator.

I finish reading but I don't look up. I'm thinking about the day we got married and how she looked right into my eyes and swore all that stuff about for better or for worse and for richer or for poorer. And now all those words, all those promises, have come to this.

"I loved you," I say. "I think I might still. I didn't mean to kill the monkey. I'd swear on a bible I didn't." Once I start talking I can't stop. I sound like the worst drunk you ever sat next to in a bar.

I am a little drunk. If I'd been sober as a cow I'd have said the same thing—except I wouldn't have said it.

"I wanted a child," Darlene says. "You wouldn't give me a child. You gave me a monkey and then you killed it."

"Couldn't," I say. "Couldn't. The doctors said it happens sometimes. It's nothing a man can help."

"Stanley says you could help it. He says you didn't want a child, so your mind told your body to kill all those sperm. It's psychological, something you wouldn't understand. And then you killed Little Napoleon. Stanley says Little Napoleon was our symbolic child, and you killed him because you hated him. Stanley knows what he's talking about. His minor at Auburn was psychology."

I pick up the pen and begin to sign. I'm too much of a Baptist not to believe I'm guilty, even when I'm not exactly sure what I'm guilty of. Darlene is at least partly right. I had hated the monkey. Buying it had been a big mistake, but things had gotten so tense by then I felt I had nothing to lose. She had said she needed something else to love, something more than me. I couldn't give her a child, so I drove to Asheville. A spider monkey was the closest thing I could find.

She had loved the monkey, and at first even loved me again. It was the Indian summer of our marriage. We were like a family. Every Friday after supper we would go to Greene's Cafe and eat banana splits, then drive over to Shelby and play putt-putt, just like any other family. I tried my best. I even went with Darlene and Little Napoleon to Stanley's office for his shots and checkups. But the monkey hated me from the very beginning. At night if I got up to go to the bathroom, it would wait till I started making water, then come flying out of the darkness, grab a calf, and draw blood. It got so bad I just stayed in bed and held it. Now I have chronic bladder problems.

Yes, I hated the little bastard, but I didn't kill it on purpose. How could I know it had crawled into the washing machine when I went to the pantry to get the Tide. It was probably hiding in the bottom, waiting for me to stick my hand in so it could bite me again.

The marriage was as good as over by the rinse cycle. Darlene took the corpse to Stanley's office. He is part owner of the pet cemetery, so he arranged the funeral service and the burial. I wasn't allowed to attend. Then Darlene started what she called "grief therapy" with Stanley, the only veterinarian/psychologist in western North Carolina. After the first week Darlene became a vegetarian. "Animals have souls," she had said. "To eat one is a barbaric act."

"What about plants?" I had asked. "If animals have souls, why not plants? Where do you draw the line?"

"That's exactly the kind of thing Stanley told me you'd say," she had said.

Three weeks later she moved in with Stanley.

I finish signing the papers. "As soon as this divorce is final," Darlene says, "Stanley and I are getting married." She gathers the papers together.

"It's not too late to give us another try," I say.

"Yes, it is," she says, already bored with the conversation.

"I tried to make you happy. I gave up the farm. I wore a tie and worked with jerks so we could afford this house."

"The farm was going broke," Darlene says. "You would have been bankrupt in another two years. You'll have to do better than that."

"I quit chewing tobacco and started listening to public radio. I increased my vocabulary. I tried not to act like a redneck."

"And failed," she says.

"I tried to give you a baby. I suffered indignities. I filled Dixie cups with semen in strange doctors' offices."

"I suffered indignities too," Darlene says. "And it wasn't even my problem."

"I loved you," I say and there's enough truth in that to make her look away, at least for a moment.

"I'll prove it," I say. "I'll change. I'll quit drinking, become a vegetarian."

"You can't change enough," she says, taking the documents off the coffee table.

"I'll be friendly to the neighbors. Invite them over to eat salads. I'll make the salads myself."

"Not enough," Darlene says, standing up.

"I'll buy you a new monkey and I will love it."

"Not enough," she says, walking out of the den. "No other monkey could ever replace Little Napoleon."

"I'll walk over hot coals. I'll watch whales."

"Not enough," she says from the kitchen.

I hear her car engine and remember one other thing. I hurry through the kitchen. I'm almost outside when I smash against nothing. Then the whole world shatters around me. I fall out on the pavement. Pieces of glass cover my body. I'm bleeding in a hundred places.

Darlene's headlights are shining on me. I slowly stand up, pulling glass from my skin. Darlene rolls down her window and shouts over the engine. "Not enough," she says, and drives off.

Blowmeyer runs over with a barbecue fork in his hand, the albino gasping to keep up.

"She shot him," he tells his wife. "Five or six times." Blowmeyer is so excited he has spilled barbecue sauce on his pants.

"Go get the movie camera, Lorraine," he tells his wife. "And call the rescue squad."

The albino disappears. I ignore Blowmeyer. I lie down on the grass, close my eyes and feel pain cut through the alcohol and the nest of spiders scrambling around inside my head, that other kind of pain, the worst kind.

I don't open my eyes until I hear the rescue squad wail into the driveway, almost hitting Blowmeyer, who is filming it all.

"Save me a copy," I tell Blowmeyer as the attendants take my arms and walk me to the back of the ambulance. "I'm OK," I keep telling them, wanting to believe it. "I'm fine."

SHILOH

Benjamin Miller awoke beneath a shroud of white petals, several of which lay like soft coins over his eyes. The ground trembled vaguely now, the cannon and mortars wheeled elsewhere. He did not hear the explosions, only felt them. All he heard was a ringing in his left ear. Benjamin rested with his eyes closed a while longer, made slight movements to assay what had struck him to the ground, how bad it was. He turned his right boot in and out and then his left, felt no pain or absence of foot or leg, arms and hands the same. He moved a hand over his groin and stomach and chest, felt no spill of intestines or stoved-in ribs. Only his head was injured, the hair on one side matted with blood. He touched the wound, gauged its width. In one place the skin unpursed and his finger slid slickly over smooth bone. Smooth, not cracked. He patted the rest of his head, then nose, jaw, and teeth and found all where they should be.

Benjamin brushed the petals from his eyes and found himself staring into a jaybird-blue sky. He knew where he was, remembered thinking how pert the peach trees looked as his regiment approached the orchard. He'd even notioned to take some seeds back with him to Watauga County. No farmer he knew had grown peaches there, probably too cold, but if anyone could, it would be Emma. Lilies and roses, cherry and apple trees, raspberry bushes—everything Emma put into the earth found life at its appointed time, as if even plants responded to her gentleness. Old Jacob Story, their one near neighbor, listened when Emma said the moon's horns were turned wrong to seed a corn field, or not to plant peas before daffodils bloomed. I've farmed near sixty year, Jacob said, but I'll cover nary an acorn until Emma allows it's the time.

Benjamin raised himself to one knee, then stood. More petals fell, puddled the ground white around him. The ringing in his ear increased and the world leaned left. On the edge of his vision a gold tinge. Benjamin blinked, hoping the world might realign, but the tilt and gold tinge remained. Because my head's been knocked off plumb, he told himself, and there ain't no tonic but to lean with it. He looked around, shifted his eyes to bead the world before moving his head. He found himself standing alone amid the fallen, friend and foe entangled like logs in a splash dam. A few yet moved but most did not. Some surely made sounds—death rattles, moans, prayers, curses, or pleas. His deafness was a blessing. Two faces Benjamin knew well, recognized three others by hair and girth. All dead. His musket and cap lay side by side as if posed for a tintype. He left them where they lay. The canteen was still strapped to his shoulder and the haversack tied to his back.

He staggered from the orchard, passing trees stripped of every blossom, others branchless, some mere stumps. If an enemy soldier yet lingered, Benjamin was an easy target. But no shot came. He made his way into a small wood and came to a creek, the banks narrow and the current quick. He remembered the old belief and pondered his waking in the orchard, the pall of white petals. The throbbing in his head increased. He took a deep breath and felt it lift his lungs. No dead man need do that, he told himself, but waited a few moments before swinging his boot forward. The water let him cross over. Benjamin took off the haversack and sat with his back against an oak tree. He laid an open palm on the ground. Only the slightest vibration, like thunder murmuring after a storm.

His throat was raw from smoke and thirst so he drank what water the canteen held. Benjamin probed the wound again, tried to recall a raised musket butt, a Minie ball glancing his skull. Nothing came. What he remembered was charging into the orchard with Dobbins and Wray beside him. Keep your lines, a lieutenant shouted but amid the like trees and smoke all direction was lost. Men blundered into each other, shooting and stabbing all who came near. Lead filled the air like slant hail. One man climbed into a peach tree's highest branches, hunched there crying with hands over ears. Benjamin's last memory was of Wray clutching his arm for a moment, then letting Benjamin go and falling.

I give both sides their best chance to kill me, Benjamin told himself. They'll not portion another. He went to the creek and used his handkerchief and water to clean the wound as best he could. He refilled the canteen and went back to the oak. Corn dodgers and jerky were in the haversack but instead of eating he took the letter from his shirt pocket, unfolded it.

My dearest husband,

I rite you this mourning from the home that I pray soon you return to. I have sown the fields for our crops, wich you say I am good at. Now I must pray the signs hold true. May your hands and mine together reap what Ive sown. What news I have of others you may wish to here. The youngest Watson boy run off to fight with his brothers. Widow Canipe died of the flux and Jess Albrights baby died last week of putrid fever. Theys a red cross

*on his cabin door so even the others are sore afflicted. Joe Vickers
was killed in Virginia. But that is more than plenty sad tidings.
Your Father has been a heep of good to me, helping plow the fields
and fixing fences. Folks say in town that this war will last not a
year. I pray so if not sooner. For I feel all ways night and day the
lonely in my heart and will ever so until you are with me again. I
go now to town to mail this letter, dearest husband, nowing that
this paper I hold you will hold to.*

    Your loving wife always
    Emma

Benjamin refolded the letter but kept it in his hand as his eyes
closed. He and Emma had grown up on adjoining farms, like
brother and sister, playing leap frog and red rover together, walking to the school and church, sharing chores. He'd been a feisty boy
and one day when he was twelve, he found a corn snake in the barn.
Something wrong inside him wanted to scare Emma with it. She'd
fallen while running away, scraping her knees and elbow. He had
flung the snake into the weeds and gone to her, shut-mouth with
shame. As Emma wiped tears off her face, he'd offered his hand to
help her up, not expecting her to take it. But she did. He had helped
her to the creek, taken his handkerchief, and gingerly wiped the
dirt from the knees and elbow. They did not speak the whole time,
nor mention it afterward, but that night by his bed Benjamin had
prayed that God would seine all meanness forever out of him so he
might be worthy of her.

He must have passed out, because when he awoke the ground no longer trembled. The ringing in his ears had lessened, as had the world's
slant. The letter still lay in his hand. He placed it in the pocket closest to his heart and then shed coat and belt and all other allegiance

to anyone but himself. He listened for a few moments, heard nothing but a redbird, then rose and walked through the shallow wood and into a pasture, below it a farmhouse and a wagon road. The dwelling appeared deserted, its occupants fled or hidden. When Benjamin got to the road, he looked up to gauge direction. An orange sun burned low on the tree line. Buzzards circled the battlefield. Some appeared to enter the sun, then spiral down blackly as if turned to ash. He followed the road east, not knowing where he headed, only what he left behind.

The next day he saw an old man alone in his field. I've not come to rob or harm you, Benjamin said as he approached. The farmer looked doubtful until Benjamin flattened the back of Emma's letter on a well guard, took a pencil from the haversack and asked the way to Knoxville. So you had plenty enough of that tussling, the farmer asked afterward. Benjamin answered that he had. Even with that busted head you got more sense than them still at it, the farmer said, and told Benjamin to wait a minute, came back from his root cellar with salt meat and potatoes. The old man would not have it otherwise, so Benjamin had stuffed the victuals in the haversack and gone on.

He traveled for two weeks, first north to Nashville and then following the Cumberland Turnpike east. Several times he'd hidden as Union and Confederate soldiers passed, once a whole regiment. Another time, at night, the clatter of cavalry. He'd been spotted only once. Two soldiers on horseback fired their muskets but did not leave the pike to pursue him.

One night a few miles from Knoxville, Benjamin felt Emma's presence. Despite the afternoon heat, he'd made good time, so near dusk bedded in a meadow. When he awoke, a wet moon had peeled away the ground dark and replaced it with a silvery sheen. No breeze rustled or night bird called. No sound of water, or distant train. A stiller moment he had never known. Benjamin stepped onto the road and whispered her name. Though Emma did not answer, he knew she was very near. Then she wasn't, and he felt a distance between them that was more than the miles yet to walk. The next morning Benjamin believed all of it, the silver light, her presence, part of a dream, until he saw his fresh boot prints in the dust.

He followed a drover's trace into the mountains and the air quickly cooled. It was as dangerous a place as he had been. Not just soldiers traversed here but also outliers who, with no cause other than profit, took no prisoners. But the few people he met, including a pair of drovers, passed with eyes lowered. They feature me the dangerous one, Benjamin told himself. As he went higher into the mountains, dogwoods that in the lowlands had shed their white yet clutched flowers, as if time was spooling backward. The fancy pleased him.

The land leveled and somewhere unmarked he passed from Tennessee into North Carolina. Not just Carolina but Watauga County, he reminded himself. Emma was probably in the field hoeing or planting. He imagined her looking up as she wiped her brow or rubbed dirt from her hands—gazing toward the gap at this very moment, already sensing his return. Sounds eight months unheard—the chatter of boomers, a raven's caw—he heard now. Yellow ladyslippers Emma used for tonics flowered on the trace edge. A chestnut three men couldn't link arms around curved the path. Everything heard and everything seen was a piece of himself restored. He thought of the soldier in the peach tree. It had been as if the man was trying to climb out of hell itself. And now I have, Benjamin thought. A whole mountain range stood between him and the horror and meanness.

Late the next afternoon he spotted a church spire, soon after the backs of store fronts. Boone, the county seat where he'd been conscripted. He could be easily recognized here, so waited in the woods as the last farm wagons left town, shopkeepers locked or barred their doors. Night settled in and with it a breeze that smelled of coming rain. Only now, for the first time since he'd left them in the orchard, Benjamin pondered Dobbins and Wray. They too had been conscripted farm boys, Kentucky born. The three of them had been of like nature, quiet men who didn't dice or drink. At night they kept their own campfire, where they spoke of their farms in such detail that the three homesteads merged into one shared memory. There were friendly disputes over the merits of brightleaf versus burley tobacco, the best way to cure a ham. On the night before the battle, they spoke quietly of crops being tended by wife and kin. I'd nary have figured to miss staring at a mule's ass dawn to dusk, Wray said, but I surely do.

They knew from the massing of troops this was to be a battle, not a skirmish. That last morning their regiment had passed a Dunker church, beyond it a plowed field tended only by scarecrows. The braggarts and raw cobs spoke little now as the battle's racket encircled them like a noose. Officers rode back and forth on skittish horses. Those who'd gone before them littered the ground, so many Benjamin wondered if a single man yet survived. Soon they smelled gunpowder, watched its smoke drift toward them. More bodies appeared. Dobbins picked up a dirt clod, squeezed it. Habit, Benjamin thought, as Dobbins let the grains sift through his fingers. Good soil, Wray had asked. Not the best, Dobbins had answered, but I reckon it to cover our bodies well enough.

The courthouse clock chimed nine, and he stepped from the woods. As he walked a deserted side street, Benjamin thought of the peach seeds he might have placed in his haversack. He'd eaten the fruit once here in Boone, sold off a wagon up from South Carolina, the peach purpled just past ripeness, fuzzy and soft in the hand. It had been like eating pulpy honey. Better not to have brought them, he decided, for if they did grow, they might barb his memory come spring.

Once he was outside of Boone, a soft rain began to fall. Benjamin lay down in a laurel slick beside Middlefork Creek, the stream he would follow eight miles until it led him into the pasture below the cabin. Tired as he was, he could not sleep, and would have gone on had the moon and stars offered the way. The laurel leaves caught the rain, let it pool into thick drops that soaked his clothes. For the first time since leaving the battle, Benjamin wished for his field coat. A bone-deep cold entered his body. He clasped his arms over his chest, tucked his knees close. After a while his feet grew numb. Teeth clicked like struck marbles. Just the wet and cold, he told himself, but thought of last winter in camp. Putrid fever had caused the same symptoms. Eight men had died. Those not yet afflicted had filled their mouths with garlic and pinches of gunpowder. A sergeant marked red crosses on dead men's haversacks. Some had believed that, like consumption, the contagion could drowse in a body for weeks, maybe months, waiting for rain or cold to awaken it.

The rain had thinned to mist by first light. Benjamin did not eat, simply got to his feet and started walking. Fog narrowed the world as he followed Middlefork Creek up the mountain. The few farmhouses loomed briefly out of the white, sank back. A dog barked once and he heard an axe cleaving wood, but that was all. Soon the fog thinned, just wisps sliding over low ground.

Until the war, there'd not been a night he and Emma were more than a furlong apart. Trips to Boone or visits to kin might last all day, but come eventide the families returned. From age twelve until they'd married, Benjamin listened for the Watsons' wagon to clatter past. Once it did, he'd watch from a porch or window as the lantern floated from barn to cabin, disappearing when the Watson's front door closed. In those few moments of darkness, Benjamin teased himself into believing Emma and her family had vanished forever. He would hold his breath, feel his heart gallop until, slowly, light began to glow inside the cabin, sifting through chinks, the one glass window. As it did, he felt a happiness almost painful.

As he approached Jacob Story's farm, Benjamin saw that the corn stood dark and high. No hard frost or gullywasher had come. The signs held true, not only for the corn but also the beans and tobacco. Smoke rose from Jacob's chimney. Noon-dinner time already, he thought. Benjamin followed the trailway through a stand of silver birch, straddled a split-rail fence, placed one foot on his land and then the other. He had hoped Emma would be in the cabin. That way he could step onto the porch, open the door, and stroll in no different than he would coming from field or barn. Benjamin wanted their separation to seem that way, to never speak of the war or their months apart. He wanted it to become nothing more than a few dark moments, like a lantern carried through a cabin's low door.

Emma was not inside, though, but kneeling on the creek bank, next to the cattle guard where the water quickened. He could not see her face because she was looking down, her left arm and hand in the water. She was wearing her Sunday dress, the dress she'd worn on their wedding day. When Benjamin called her name, she did not look up. He walked faster, shouted her name. Emma's eyes remained on the water and now he saw that her right hand hovered above the creek like a dragonfly. The fingers and palm descended and touched the surface, then lifted, did the same thing again and then again.

He crossed into the cornfield, not stumbling over hoe furrows because there were none. Then he was on the bank opposite Emma, the creek so narrow that he could almost jump it. *Emma*, he said, almost a whisper. She lifted her head but offered no smile or words or tears. She looked past him, as if he wasn't even there.

Benjamin tried to remember the streams he'd crossed, which ones flowed fast and which ones did not. He had stepped over the creek near the peach orchard, after that crossed smidgen branches and wide rivers, sloshing through some, walking bridges over others. But what of today, recalling last night's shivering cold. He'd not eaten or drunk, and from Boone to here not once crossed the creek. He looked past Emma, searching for a mound of dirt, a wooden cross or flat stone. He looked for his own grave.

His gaze moved across pasture and wood, corn crib and barn, seeing no sign of such until his eyes settled on the cabin. A red cross was painted on the door. For a few moments, his eyes remained there. Then he looked at Emma. Her head was down and her hand touched the water, this time entered the creek's flow a moment. When she withdrew the hand, something about her had lightened, wisped away like dandelion seeds. *Emma*, he said. She raised her hand and pointed to Benjamin's and then to the water. He lowered his hand into the current and she did the same. The water pressed against his palm. Just for a moment, Benjamin felt another hand touch his. When he looked up, Emma was gone.

Since her grave wasn't on the farm, it would be behind the church. Benjamin could walk the two miles, but that would delay his going back west into Tennessee. He turned and began the trek back to Boone. In a week he would be on the Cumberland Turnpike.

He'd walk the Pike in daylight and soon enough men wearing butternut or men wearing blue would meet him. Whichever side appeared first Benjamin would join. A month or two might pass but there'd be another battle. The armies would finish their business with him. He would hold out his hand again and this time Emma would take it.

OUTLAWS

When I was sixteen, my summer job was robbing trains. I'd mask my lower face with a black bandana, then, six-shooter in hand, board the train with two older bandits and demand "loot." Fourteen times a day I'd get shot by Sheriff Masterson, stagger off the metal steps, and fall into the drainage ditch beside the tracks. Afterwards, we'd wait thirty minutes for the next train, which was the same train, to come hooting up the tracks. Years later I would publish a short story about that summer, and one of my fellow bandits would read it. But that was later.

My aunt, who worked as a cashier at Frontier Village, had gotten me the job. Despite my being sixteen, she'd cajoled Mr. Watkins, who preferred college students, into hiring me. He can play Billy the Kid, she'd told him. Anyway, with a mask on who can tell how old he is? So it was that on a Saturday morning in June I changed into my all-black outlaw duds in the Stagecoach Saloon's basement. The Levis and cowboy shirt hung loose on my hips and shoulders, and I had to gouge another notch in my gun belt. My hat sank so low my neck looked like a pale stalk on a black mushroom.

I found one a smaller size in the gift shop. The boots were my own.

My fellow outlaws, both from Charlotte, were Matt, a junior pre-med major at UNC-A, and Jason, who'd just graduated from there. His major was theatre arts, which should have been a tipoff for his performance on the last day we worked together. After stashing our clothes in the lockers, we walked over to the depot where Donald, a paunchy, silver-haired man who claimed he'd been John Wayne's stunt double in *Rio Bravo*, went over the whats and whens a last time. He sent us on our way with advice gleaned from eight summers' experience: there will always be smart alecs onboard and any acknowledgment just egged them on, and be prepared for anything—kids jabbing at your eyes with gift shop spears, teenagers kicking your shins, adults setting you on fire with cigarettes. They even do that to me, Donald said, and I'm the guy wearing the white hat.

So nine to five, five days a week with Mondays and Tuesdays off, the three of us waited for the train whistle to signal it was time for our hold-up. We had no horses, so ran out of the woods firing pistols at the sky until the locomotive and its three passenger cars halted. We entered separate compartments and Sheriff Masterson took us on one at a time. Clutching our gut-shot bellies, we'd stagger to the metal steps, roll into the ditch, and lie there until the train crossed the trestle and curved back toward the depot.

Getting shot and dying was the easy part. By July, all of us had plenty of wounds besides scrapes and bruises from falling. We'd been burned, poked, tripped, and pierced by weaponry that ranged from knitting needles to sling-shot marbles. After each failed robbery, we'd retreat to a hideout with its cache of extra blanks and pistols, three lawn chairs, toilet paper, and a Styrofoam cooler filled with sandwiches and soft drinks. Stretched out above it all, a green camouflage tarp kept everything, most of all us, dry when it rained. Our contributions to the hideout were some paperbacks and Jason's transistor radio, which was always tuned to the college station.

One morning in mid-July Jason nodded toward the radio.

"You don't even know what they're saying, do you kid?" Jason asked as he rolled a joint.

"Everybody look what's going down," I said, after a few moments.

"But what's it *about*?" Jason asked.

"I don't know," I answered.

"It's about not wanting to get your ass shot off in Vietnam," Jason said.

Matt looked up from a copy of *Stranger in a Strange Land*.

"I didn't hear anything about Vietnam."

"When you graduate and your deferment's up you'll hear it," Jason said, "especially when they send you one of these."

He took a letter from his pocket and gave it to Matt.

"You gonna to try to get out of going?" Matt asked as he handed it back.

"I have gotten out, for four years, but yeah, I plan on keeping an ocean between me and that war." Jason grimaced. "I never got picked for anything good in my life, varsity baseball, homecoming king, class president. Hell, I didn't even get picked for glee club, but I fucking get picked for this."

"So what will you do?" Matt asked.

"I'll convince them I'm nuts. Acting's what I'm trained for, man. I'll speak in tongues while I do handstands if I have to. Maybe shit my britches right before I go in. I've heard that works. They'll 4F me in a heartbeat."

"Don't bet on it," Matt said. "The army's on to that dirty diaper scam. A buddy of mine tried it. He walked in with shit gluing his pants to his bare ass. The army doc told him not to worry, that he'd probably shit himself even worse when the VC started shooting at him."

"I'll come up with something else then," Jason said. "Like I said, I'm an actor."

"Oh yeah," Matt said. "Sure you will."

"So you don't think I can pull it off?"

"Well, it's not like you've been giving Academy Award performances this summer," Matt said. "The kid here does a better death scene than you do."

"Maybe I'm saving up for a more challenging audience than those dipshits on the train," Jason said.

"You better be saving up for a bus ticket to Toronto," Matt said.

Jason lit the joint and inhaled deeply, offered it to me as he always did before passing it to Matt.

"Bob Dylan's right, kid," Jason said. "Don't trust anybody over thirty about anything, but especially Vietnam. There's nothing good about being over there."

"I heard they got great dope," Matt said as he passed back the joint.

"Yeah, it's called morphine," Jason answered. "Medics give it to you while they're trying to stitch you back together."

"Some cool animals, too," Matt deadpanned. "Cobras and pythons. Leeches, tigers, and bears, oh my."

"Fuck you," Jason said.

"Just trying a little levity," Matt said.

"We'll see how funny you think it is when you get your letter."

"If I get in med school they can't touch my ass."

"If," Jason said. "From what you said about your GPA that's a big if."

"I've got a year to pull it up," Matt said.

Jason turned to me.

"Growing up around here, you probably believe all that shit about the evil commies, right?"

"I don't know," I said.

"What about your parents?"

"My cousin's over there and Daddy says he ought not be, him or any other American."

"Might be some hope for you hicks after all," Jason said, and held out what was left of the joint to me. "Don't you want to try it just once?"

I shook my head and he threw the remnants down, ground them into the dirt with his boot toe. The train whistle blew.

"Time to get shot," Matt grinned. "In honor of that letter, the kid and I will let you lead us into battle."

"Keep joking about it, asshole," Jason said. "They may get you yet. But me, I'll figure a way out. You'll see."

Frontier Village didn't shut down until after Labor Day, but Matt and I went back to school the last Monday in August. After that Jason would work solo. All through August, Jason talked about ways of getting a deferment, but it wasn't until our last weekend together that he'd figured out what to do.

That Saturday I'd never seen him so animated. He paced manically in front of us, grinning.

"It's radical, boys," he said, "but one hundred percent foolproof."

"Enlighten us," Matt said.

"One of my buddies in Charlotte called last night. He ran into a guy we went to high school with, a real dumbass who sawed off his fingers in shop class. Not all of each finger, just the top joints. The thing is, it wasn't that big a deal. You hardly noticed after a while. I mean, it wasn't like girls wanted to throw up when they looked at his hand. Hell, I think it made him *more* popular with girls. They felt sorry for him so voted the fucker homecoming king. He even played on the baseball team. Here's the kicker, though. He's so dumb he *volunteers* to go, but they don't let him because he won't be able to handle a rifle well enough. All I've got to do is slice off some finger joints and I'm 4F the rest of my life."

"Don't even talk this bullshit," Matt said, and nodded at me. "Look at the kid here, he's already about to faint."

"If you want something to faint about, kid," Jason said, "let me tell you about my cousin who got killed in Nam last winter, though killed is putting it nicely. He took a direct mortar hit. All the king's horses and all the king's men couldn't put him back together again, so they kept the casket closed at the viewing. Anyway, the next morning before the funeral, my uncle gets it into his head he has to see the body and my father goes to the funeral home to stop him. He takes me with him, maybe figures he'll need me to help wrestle my uncle out of there. When we get there the undertaker comes jabbering that he couldn't stop him, that my uncle has jimmied the coffin open. So we go in the back room where the coffin is and my uncle is holding something up, or I guess I should say part of something . . ."

"Don't tell anymore," Matt said. "The kid's got his own cousin over there."

"You don't want to hear it," Jason asked me.

I shook my head.

"Still think I'm bullshitting about doing it?" Jason asked, "or having cause to?"

"No, man," Matt said. "I've joked with you some. You know, it's a way of dealing with bad shit like this. You're right, they may come after my ass in a year, but fucking maiming yourself, that's not acting crazy, it is crazy. Even if you could actually do it, what if they found out it was on purpose? Hell, they might take you anyway, or put you in Leavenworth."

"You think I'm going to chop them off in front of those assholes?" Jason said. "It will look like an accident, but I may need you to help me, Mr. Pre-Med."

"Sure thing," Matt said. "I can see it on my application. Medical Experience: Chopped off fingers for draft dodger. Yeah, that'll get me into Bowman Gray."

"I'm just talking about afterward, so I won't bleed to death," Jason said. "The whole point of not serving is so I *won't* die."

"Stop talking this bullshit," Matt said.

"I'm going to do it tomorrow," Jason said. "You boys just wait and see."

I didn't sleep well that night, waking before dawn. In the dark, even the worst things seemed possible. I thought of what I'd seen on TV, soldiers and civilians on stretchers, some missing limbs, some blind, some dead, worst of all the monks who sat perfectly still as they transformed into pyramids of fire. I could report Jason to Mr. Watkins, or even ask my parents what to do, but this seemed something they had no part in. Or just stay home. Yet that seemed wrong as well. But then the morning sun revealed the same window that had always been there, the same bureau and mirror. Revealed my world and what was possible in it. He won't do it, I told myself, it's just talk. When my aunt came by at 8:15, I was ready.

I went down the Stagecoach Saloon steps, Jason and Matt already undressing. As we changed into our outfits, I noticed a blue backpack beside Jason's locker.

"What's in there?" I asked.

"What would you do if I said a hatchet?" Jason asked.

When I didn't respond he grinned.

"Courage is what's in there," he answered. "At least half a bottle of it still is."

We walked down the tracks to our hideout, the backpack dangling from Jason's shoulder. Things I'd paid no mind to other mornings, the smell of creosote on the wooden cross-ties, how sun and dew created bright shivers on the steel rails, I noticed now. I was lagging behind. Matt waited for me while Jason walked on.

"Don't worry, kid," Matt said softly. "Even if he was serious, he'll chicken out."

"You sure?" I asked.

"He's just trying to mess with our heads."

Once we were in the woods, Jason opened the backpack and took out the half-filled bottle, *Beefeater* on the label.

"We'll have one successful robbery this summer," Jason said, "rob Uncle Sam of a soldier to zip up in a body bag."

He unscrewed the cap and lifted two white pills from his front pocket. He shoved them in his mouth and drank until bubbles rose inside the glass. Jason shuddered and lowered the bottle. For a few minutes he just stood there. Then he set the bottle down, took out a pocketknife, and cut the rawhide strips tethering the holsters to his legs.

"Keep them in your pocket for tourniquets," he said, offering the strips to Matt. "Once the wheel rim takes the fingers off, I'll need them on my wrists."

"No way," Matt said.

"What about you, kid?" Jason asked, his voice slurring. "You too chickenshit to help me?"

I nodded and looked at Matt's watch. Five minutes until the train would be here. Jason lifted the bottle and didn't stop drinking until it was empty. He held his stomach a few moments like he might throw up but didn't. He raked his right index finger across the left palm.

"That quick and it's done," Jason said, and pulled his pistols from their holsters, flung them to the ground. "Won't be using my trigger fingers anymore, here or anywhere else."

"You're drunk and crazy," Matt said.

"Yea, I guess I am drunk and that acid, man, it just detonated. ''Scuse me while I kiss the sky.'"

Jason looked upward, then twirled around and lost his balance. He tumbled onto the ground, rose to his knees and saluted us, before keeling back over.

"What are we going to do?" I asked.

"I'll stay with him," Matt said. "I don't think he'll be moving for a while, but just in case you'd better stop the train before it gets near here."

I left the woods and stepped onto the track. As the train came into view, wood and steel vibrated under my feet. The whistle blew. I jogged up the track waving for the train to stop, but I was just an outlaw taking his cue too soon. Mack, the engineer, blew the whistle again. I was close enough to see his face leaning out the cab window. He looked pissed-off and he wasn't slowing down. I jumped into the ditch and the engine rumbled past.

I looked ahead and saw Jason running out of the woods, Matt trailing. Jason lay down by the tracks and stretched his arms, clamping both hands on the rail. Mack grabbed the handbrake but it was too late.

Jason's hands clung to the rail when the left front wheel rolled over them.

That's how I wrote the scene's conclusion years later, then added a couple of paragraphs about an older narrator recalling the event. A standard initiation story, nothing especially new but done well enough for *Esquire* to publish.

What actually occurred was that I didn't see Jason's hands, just that his arms stretched toward the track. Then he was rolling into the ditch, forearms tucked inside the curl of his body. Matt and I scrambled into the ditch beside him. Jason screamed for a few moments, fetuslike until he slowly uncoiled and began laughing hysterically.

"You dumb fuckers thought I'd really do it," he gasped.

"Asshole," Matt said, and walked back into the woods.

Jason turned toward the train and raised his hands.

"Don't shoot, I'm unarmed," he shouted, and started laughing again.

Mack shouted back that Jason was good as fired. Passengers gawked out windows as the train wheels began turning again. Donald stood sad-faced on a top step, white hat held against his chest as though mourning our perfidy.

Back at the hideout, Matt lifted the empty bottle.

"Water?"

"Yep," Jason answered.

"And the acid?"

"Two aspirin," Jason said. "Water and two aspirin, boys. That's all the props I needed. Now what do you say about my acting ability?"

"The stuff about your cousin and uncle," Matt said. "That part of the performance too?"

"Of course," Jason nodded. "You have to create a believable scenario."

"The draft notice?" I asked.

"No, kid, that's all too real, but I figure if I can convince you two that I'm crazy I can convince them. This was my rehearsal."

"You're an asshole," Matt said again. "One of us could have gotten hurt because of your prank. We could lose a day's pay too."

"Don't worry," Jason said. "I'm going to turn myself in right now, tell them all of it was my doing. They won't do anything to you when they know that."

Jason stuffed the pistols back in his holsters and picked up his backpack.

"Hey, I was just having a little fun," he said.

"I hope I never see that son-of-a-bitch again," Matt said when Jason had left. "How about you?"

"That would suit me fine."

But four decades later in Denver I did see Jason again, the cowboy hat replaced with a VFW ball cap.

"Remember me?" he asked. "We used to be outlaws together."

I didn't at first, but as he continued to talk a younger, recognizable face emerged from the folds and creases.

"It's a good story," Jason said, nodding at the *Esquire* he clutched. "You got the details right."

"Thanks," I said. "You exaggerate, of course, make characters better or worse than in real life."

"Don't worry," he said. "I know I was an asshole."

I pointed at the hat. "You end up over there?"

"Yeah, you guys were easier to fool than the army," Jason said. "Of course, the induction center didn't provide me a train to freak them out with."

"Well, at least you came back."

"I did that," Jason said.

"My cousin, he didn't."

"I'm sorry to hear that, I truly am," Jason said, and after a few moments. "What about Matt? You ever see him after that summer?"

"No."

"I always wondered if he got sent over there. I looked for him on the wall. His name wasn't on there so maybe he got into med school. I guess I could find out on the internet. When you were writing that story, did you ever do a search on us?"

"I couldn't remember your last names," I answered. "But I don't think I would have anyway. Like I said, it's fiction."

Jason had rolled up the magazine. It resembled a runner's baton as he tapped it against his leg. The bookstore was almost empty now, just the owner and two teenagers browsing the sci-fi section.

"When I dream it isn't fiction," Jason said, "for me or for them."

"Them?"

"Yeah, them," Jason said, stashing the magazine in his back pocket. "You remember who Lieutenant Calley was?"

"I remember."

"Come with me," he said. "There's something I want to show you."

From a shelf marked MILITARY, Jason took down a book and opened it to a page of black-and-white photographs. The top two photos were of Calley, but below was one of eight nameless soldiers, helmets off, arms draped around each other.

Jason pointed at the second soldier to the left.

"Recognize me?"

Except for shorter hair, he looked the same as at Frontier Village. Jason stared at the photograph a few more moments.

"Three of these guys were dead within a month," he said. "The Vietnamese say the ghosts of American soldiers who got killed are still over there. They hear them at night entering their villages, even villages that were Viet Cong during the war. They leave food and water out for them." Jason looked up from the page. "Their doing that, I think it matters."

Jason leafed farther into the book, stopped on a page with no photographs. His index finger slid down a few lines and stopped. I read the paragraph.

"You know my last name now," Jason said, reshelving the book.

The teenagers walked toward checkout, a graphic novel in hand as the owner placed a CLOSED sign on the door.

"After I came back to the states," Jason said. "I told myself that if the people around me had been through what I'd been through—three of your buddies killed and scared shitless you're next, then being in a village where any woman or child could have a grenade and all the while your superior ordering you to do it—they would have acted no differently. To see it that way allows you to move on. You got unlucky in a lottery and put in some shit most people are spared. You just followed the script you'd been given."

"Here's the thing," Jason said after a pause. "It's always been okay when I am awake. I've held down a good job at a radio station almost forty years, and though my wife and I got divorced a while back, we raised two great kids. Both college grads, employed, responsible, I'm blessed that way, even have a grandchild coming. So I handle the daylight fine. But night, it used to be different, because in my dreams I'd be back there. Everything was the same, the same villagers in the same places they'd been before. In the dreams I'd already know what was going to happen, not just that day, but what would happen afterwards—the accounts and testimonies, the hearings, Calley's court martial, the newspaper articles and TV reports. But even knowing all that, when the order was given, *I would do it again*. I didn't have one dream where I didn't.

Until one day I was in the vet affairs office and I read your story. That night, I dreamed I was there again, but I had no hands, which meant I couldn't hold a rifle. I walked among them, even into their huts, and they weren't afraid, and I wasn't afraid either because I knew I had no hands to hurt them. And then, as the months passed, I'd dream that though I had no hands, I balanced a bowl of rice between my wrists. I'd go into the huts and crouch, set the bowl carefully on the floor and after they'd each taken a handful of rice, I'd lift it back up and go to the next hut."

Jason paused and took the rolled-up magazine from his pocket, held it out between us.

"I went to the newsstand and bought this copy. I read the story every night for a while, then just a few pages, and then only a few paragraphs. It wasn't long until I had those paragraphs memorized. I'd lie there in the dark and speak them out loud. Now, two, three nights a week I'm back there, but always without my hands."

Jason nodded at the magazine.

"You can have this if you want."

"No," I said. "You keep it."

"Afraid I might forget?"

His smile did not conceal the challenge in his eyes.

"No," I answered.

"Okay. I'll keep it then," Jason said. "Thank you for writing the story the way you did. That's why I came, to thank you, to tell you it's helped. I want to believe it's helped more than just me. I mean, if ghosts enter villages, maybe they enter dreams too."

He held out his hand and we shook.

"If Matt ever shows up at one your signings, wish him well for me."

After Jason left, I talked to the bookstore owner a few minutes, then walked back to my hotel. It was only five blocks but I wasn't used to Denver's altitude, so I was out of breath when I got there. I had a couple of drinks at the bar, then took the elevator up to my room. The curtains were pulled back and Denver sparkled below. Jason's home was down there and I wondered if he was already asleep. In the darkness beyond the city, jagged mountains rose. On the flight back to Carolina the next morning, I saw them from the passenger window. They were different from the mountains back home. Young, treeless, no hollowed out coves. Snow lay on summits, yet to be softened by time.

"The Dowry"—first published in *The Southern Review*, reprinted in *Nothing Gold Can Stay*

"A Sort of Miracle"—first published in *Nothing Gold Can Stay*

"The Corpse Bird"—first published in *The South Carolina Review*, reprinted in *Burning Bright*

"Dead Confederates"—first published in *Shenandoah*, reprinted in *Burning Bright*

"The Woman at the Pond"—first published in *The Southern Review*, reprinted in *Nothing Gold Can Stay*

"A Servant of History"—first published in *Nothing Gold Can Stay*

"Twenty-Six Days"—first published in *The Washington Post*, reprinted in *Nothing Gold Can Stay*

"Last Rite"—first published in the *Greensboro Review*, reprinted in *This Is Where We Live: New North Carolina Short Stories, Casualties*, and *Chemistry and Other Stories*

"Blackberries in June"—first published in *Chemistry and Other Stories*

"Chemistry"—first published in *Casualties*, reprinted in *Chemistry and Other Stories*

"The Night the New Jesus Fell to Earth"—first published in *A Carolina Literary Companion*, reprinted in *The Night the New Jesus Fell to Earth and Other Stories from Cliffside, North Carolina*

"The Harvest"—first published in *The Book of Men Anthology*, edited by Colum McCann

"Badeye"—first published in *The Night the New Jesus Fell to Earth and Other Stories from Cliffside, North Carolina*

"Love and Pain in the New South"—first published in *Charleston Magazine*, reprinted in *The Night the New Jesus Fell to Earth and Other Stories from Cliffside, North Carolina*

"Shiloh," previously entitled "The Return"—first published in *TriQuarterly*

"Outlaws"—first published in *Oxford American*